I0630621

Praise For

SEEDS OF THE POMEGRANATE

"...A riveting and intelligent novel with a powerful message."

—*Kirkus Reviews*

* * *

"In Samuels' impressive debut, an artist reckons with illness and loss while pursuing her career in early 1900s Sicily and New York City....Readers will be satisfied by this nuanced character portrait."

—*Publishers Weekly*

* * *

"The diverse company of characters, with all their fears and foibles, are brilliantly rendered. Samuels has created a thoroughly engrossing historical novel from aspects of her own family heritage, weaving complications and danger into the narrative with admirable skill and effective writing. A gripping story, from the first page to the last, and very highly recommended."

—Margaret Porter, award-winning, best-selling author of *Sequins and Starlight, The Myrtle Wand,* and *The Limits of Limelight*

* * *

"...utterly compelling and immersive. Tremendous!"

—Désirée Zamorano, author of *Dispossessed* and *The Amado Women*

* * *

"Suzanne Samuels' *Seeds of the Pomegranate* shows the unpaid labor and lost opportunities for women in a brutal immigrant Italian family, and one woman's determination to create art and a life for herself against all the rules and conventions. In luminous prose, Samuels weaves the myth of Persephone in the Underworld through this tale of art and love surviving repression and familial obligations. A remarkable debut."

—Julia Park Tracey, author of *Silence* and *The Bereaved*

"Samuels' writing brings these characters to life so vividly that we recognize their dual natures; the good as well as the flaws, even allowing us to conjure a bit of sympathy for the scoundrels....*Seeds of the Pomegranate* keeps us on the edge of our seats with fast-paced action, clever dialogue, plot twists, and a satisfying ending for Mimi Inglese, at long last."

—Lora Chilton, author of *1666: A Novel*

* * *

"Not since Helen Barolini's *Umbertina* have we seen a novel by an Italian American woman that so richly explores the immigrant experience from a woman's point of view ... Suzanne Uttaro Samuels, like her protagonist, writes with the heart—bringing Mimi's story vividly, and powerfully, to life."

—Dr. Stacey Lee Donohue, Professor of English, Central Oregon Community College

* * *

"...A rich debut about immigration, the intersection of art and commerce, and what we are willing to sacrifice for family."

—Laura Spence-Ash, author of *Beyond That, the Sea*

* * *

"Samuels' taut story of a young woman's struggle to outwit the relentless darkness of New York's gangster underworld is terrifyingly captivating."

—Joan Fernandez, Author of *Saving Vincent, A Novel of Jo van Gogh*

* * *

"Historical fiction as it is meant to be enjoyed: richly detailed, immersive, and compelling."

—N.J. Mastro, author, *Solitary Walker: A Novel of Mary Wollstonecraft*

* * *

"...[Samuels'] vivid prose and meticulous research bring alive the precarious life of an unusual woman whose family allegiances entangle her in organized crime."

—Carolyn Korsmeyer, author, *Riddle of Spirit and Bone*

* * *

"A beautifully written novel of historical fiction with characters who jump off the page..."

—Lisa Montanaro, author of the award-winning *Everything We Thought Was True*

* * *

"...Mimi Inglese gives new meaning to boldness. A good story that champions courage."

—Elaine Stock, author of *The Last Secret Kept* and the *Resilient Women of WWII Trilogy*

SEEDS

of the

POMEGRANATE

A Novel

SUZANNE UTTARO SAMUELS

Sibylline
PRESS

AN IMPRINT OF ALL THINGS BOOK

Sibylline Press
Copyright © 2025 by Suzanne Uttaro Samuels
All Rights Reserved.

Published in the United States by Sibylline Press,
an imprint of All Things Book LLC, California.
Sibylline Press is dedicated to publishing the brilliant work of women
authors ages 50 and older.
www.sibyllinepress.com

Distributed to the trade by Publishers Group West

Trade ISBN: 9781960573445
eBook ISBN: 9781960573506
Library of Congress Control Number: 2025933346

Book and Cover Design: Alicia Feltman

This is a work of fiction. Names, characters, places, brands, media,
and incidents are either the product of the author's imagination or
are used fictitiously. Any resemblance to similarly named places or to
persons living or deceased is unintentional.

HUMAN AUTHORED: Any use of this publication to train artificial intel-
ligence (AI) technologies to generate text is expressly prohibited.

SEEDS

of the

POMEGRANATE

A Novel

SUZANNE UTTARO SAMUELS

To My Great-Grandaunt
Mattia "Mimi" Inglese

CHAPTER 1

Palermo, Sicily

1905

WHEN I ENTERED THE STUDIO that morning, there was no model posed on the marble pedestal. No vase overflowing with flowers; no bowl of fruit. Tomorrow, the Academy closed for the summer so that our teacher, Monsieur Laurent, could join the other painters in the south of France. The other students worked busily at their easels, the only sounds the whisper of brushstrokes on canvas and the occasional scraping of the stools against the wood floor. The air was dense with turpentine and sweat.

I wound my way through the crowded room to my easel, where my latest work stood drying. *Binvinutu*. My family's manor house, nestled amidst the fields high in the Trapani Mountains of western Sicily. I'd finished late last night and left the studio unsure about the changes I'd made. In the light of day, though, I could see the painting was good.

All year, I'd been preparing for admission to the Palermo Academy of Fine Arts. My portfolio was stuffed with copies of the Old Masters. Botticelli and da Vinci. Michelangelo and Raphael. Proof that I was a competent artist, prepared to enter the two-year course of study.

But this painting—*Binvinutu*—showed I was more than just capable. Mamma would say I was conceited. I didn't care. Monsieur said I had talent. I could be the first woman admitted to the Academy.

I watched as my teacher made his way around the other students' stools and easels, quietly pointing out where a perspective could be sharpened, or a hue deepened. By the time he reached me, my heart was pounding. Dark spots flashed in front of my eyes. I tried to take a few deep breaths. There was a tightness there I hadn't felt before. Nerves. Nonna always said I let my emotions get the better of me.

Monsieur pointed to the three figures I'd painted last night. "You've added these."

I nodded. Rosalia, Caterina and I, garbed in purple and yellow, magenta and green, garish colors Mamma never would have permitted. In the painting, we moved easily through a field of flowers, something that would have been impossible with the headscarves and head-to-toe mantles we were actually forced to wear outside the house.

On my canvas, though, we were young women, our lives just beginning. Not crones, hidden from the world. Monsieur studied the composition for a long time. So long, in fact, that I began to worry that I'd taken things too far.

"Your sisters?" he asked, finally.

I pointed to the figure in the middle. "Rosalia." Then the smaller one at the end. "Caterina."

Monsieur narrowed his eyes. "You decided on the composition weeks ago. I'm wondering: why add these now?"

My stomach dropped. Next, Monsieur would tell me to paint over the figures with a pergola or a copse of trees.

"It wasn't finished," I mumbled.

"And it's complete, now?"

Not trusting my voice, I nodded.

"How do you know this, Mademoiselle?"

I hesitated before saying the only thing I could think of: It felt right.

Monsieur smiled broadly. "Yes, Mademoiselle. You painted with your heart, not your brain. This is what an artist does."

But when Monsieur called my classmates to attention, telling them to *regardez* my painting, I heard what they said under their breath. My work was superficial. Dripping with sentimentality. And worst of all, *feminine*.

My cheeks burned. I tried not to cry. That's what these men wanted. Nonna said it was because they were jealous. But it went far beyond that: my classmates hated me. Since I'd arrived in September, they'd splattered my stool with red paint and left sanitary towels in my art box. To my face, they called me a dried-up spinster and hissed that I'd stolen the spot of a more deserving man.

If it hadn't been for Teo, they probably would have forced me out. Teo. The best student at the *atelier*. He said I had talent. He'd been my friend. My lover. I glanced over at his stool and easel, abandoned in the corner. In the loft above the classroom, where Teo and I had made love, his paintings were crated and stacked. He'd left no forwarding address.

The afternoon shadows grew long. Finally, the church bell chimed five. My classmates began to pack up. Over the din, Monsieur reminded us to sign our paintings. "The Admissions Committee will be here July first. Leave your portfolios under your easels so they can review all your work."

Just one or two of us would gain admission. Every man thought it would be he.

When the studio was mostly empty, Monsieur returned to my easel. I was tucking my brushes and tubes of paint into their box. Nonna said we'd leave at first light. I was still trying to figure out how to leave word for Teo.

Monsieur looked at the painting. "Remarkable, Mademoiselle. Really."

Whether he meant my painting or the actual estate, I wasn't sure. *Binvinutu* was one of the largest *latifundia* in western Sicily, bequeathed to some distant Inglese ancestor in exchange for fealty to the British crown.

"I've asked the Committee to review your portfolio first," Monsieur continued. "I have no doubt that they'll offer you admission."

Since I was a little girl, scrawling in the dirt with a stick, I'd been working toward this. I should be proud. Instead, my eyes began to well with tears.

My teacher pressed his handkerchief into my hands. "Don't listen to your classmates," he whispered. "Have faith. Your work is good." His kindness only made the tears fall faster. "Come to my studio. Later today. There's something I want you to see."

When I didn't respond, he added that I should bring my Nonna. That hardly needed saying. Nonna was my chaperone. Other than the time I spent at Monsieur Laurent's, we were never apart.

Nonna, who'd left her newborn in an orphans' wheel to save his life, then served on the battlefields as a nurse during the Italian Wars of Independence. She never would have let a bunch of stupid men make her feel bad, or cry in front of her teacher.

I swept away the tears and told Monsieur that Nonna and I would be there.

CHAPTER 2

I WALKED QUICKLY TO THE HOTEL. It was just two blocks away, but by the time I got there, I was struggling to catch my breath. Like Teo on that last day, the small voice inside whispered, gasping for air at the top of the loft ladder.

In the apartment, Nonna was packing, a handwritten list on the bed beside her valise. She'd brought only a few things to Palermo—a blouse, a pair of bloomers and stockings, her prayer book and rosary. Too few items, I thought, to warrant a list. I told her Monsieur wanted to speak with us. She looked at me grimly. Nonna didn't like surprises.

"Has there been trouble?" she asked gravely.

I told her I didn't think so. Nonna went down on her knees and prayed, for what, I didn't know. When she stood, she pulled on her black woolen shawl. Together, we made our way toward Monsieur's private studio. Monsieur's assistant ushered us into the room. My teacher was standing at the center, next to a large canvas covered with sheeting.

Out of respect for Nonna's title, Monsieur bowed deeply to her. He ushered her to a chair near the window then motioned for me to join him at the canvas.

"I've asked you here to show you this." He drew off the sheeting. "It's Henri Matisse's latest. *The Joy of Life.*"

There is a saying in Sicilian: *Colpo di Fulmine.* To be struck by the thunderbolt. Looking at that painting, that's how I felt.

Heavy brushstrokes of bold, contrasting colors. In the background, some figures danced in a circle; others played flutes or gathered flowers. In the front, several figures reclined. Two of these lay together on the indigo and aqua grass, their limbs entwined.

"What do you think?" Monsieur asked.

I didn't know what to say.

Monsieur laughed. "I was speechless, too."

"It's like *Seascape*," I said finally, thinking of the Matisse painting that Monsieur had displayed when we'd begun to study modern art. A cliff. The sea. A simple composition, but the majesty and power of the ocean were unmistakable.

"Do you remember what the critics said when they saw that painting?"

I nodded. How could I forget? One said that the work was like "a pot of paint flung in the face of the public." Another said that it was the work of a "wild beast," heedless of color theory or even simple aesthetics. At the time, I felt sorry for Matisse.

Monsieur stood close to me. "An artist who is trying to do something new will always face criticism," he said.

I looked at the composition before me. *The Joy of Life*. A riot of clashing colors: blues against oranges, greens alongside purples. The lovers in the foreground: the woman, with her enormous red and peach breasts; her much smaller partner behind. All around, figures moved joyously or made music or planted seeds. This was the joy of living. I'd felt it when I was with Teo, our limbs entwined, breathing together, our inhales and exhales perfectly in sync.

Dear Teo. I'd assumed we'd attend the Academy together. We wouldn't marry: serious artists—especially women—didn't marry. But we could work alongside each other. Like Mary Cassatt and Edgar Degas, or Rosa Bonheur and Anna Klumpke. Maybe eventually, we'd share a home. My godfather, Zio Vito, promised he'd be my patron, like a modern-day Medici. He'd been the one to convince Mamma to let me study in Monsieur's *atelier*. She'd worried that I'd be molested, or worse, seduced.

But there had been no molestation. When Teo laid down the oil-cloth, I went to him willingly. No seduction, either. Unless it was that Teo had introduced me to a pleasure so profound that when he left, it was like a part of me died. In the months since he'd been gone, I woke in the night, my fingers probing those forbidden places, desperate to experience again what I'd felt with him.

Monsieur's voice brought me back to the present. "What do you think Matisse wants us to see here?"

I took in the painting, my eyes moving from one figure to the next. The dancers. The gardeners. The musicians. The reclining couple. "It's a circle," I said, finally.

Smiling, Monsieur nodded. "Why do you think Matisse composed the piece this way?"

Suddenly I saw. "It's the seasons. The cycle of life."

Monsieur gently touched his fingertips to the lovers in front. "Winter." He moved onto the other figures. "Spring. Summer. Fall."

I motioned toward the large reclining woman. "She's like Persephone."

For the first time, Nonna turned her head toward us. All those statues she'd shown me and my sisters, tucked into alcoves and ancient temples in Girgenti and the hill towns. The goddess Persephone. Worshipped long before the Greeks or Romans had taken Sicily. Her red and blush pomegranate, its seeds ensuring her return to the Underworld each fall. Her emergence above ground in the spring, bringing new life.

"Yes," Monsieur said. "Persephone's a popular subject for artists. Though this depiction is unusual. Isn't it?"

I nodded. In every Renaissance or Baroque painting or sculpture, the goddess was a victim. Abducted by Hades. Forced down to the Underworld. Tricked to eat those seeds. But the ancient Persephone was no victim: she enjoyed being queen of the Underworld. Not willing to fully relinquish her power and return to earth as Demeter's dutiful daughter, she ate those seeds.

This was the real story of Persephone. One of power. Choice.

This was Matisse's Persephone, too—at the center of human existence, of life and death, joy, and love.

"Artists must be brave," Monsieur continued. "To challenge what is known. Accepted. To strive to see things in a new way. Artists must tell the truth. Even if that makes them unpopular. I know you understand this, mademoiselle."

He smiled so gently that for a moment, I forgot about the taunting and the jeering, all the times I'd been told I could never be an artist.

Nonna appeared at my side. "Mimi will be a great artist," she said, solemnly.

A wave of gratitude washed over me. It was Nonna who'd convinced Pappa I shouldn't marry. It was she who'd approached my zio and asked if he could make arrangements for me to study with Monsieur Laurent. If not for Nonna, I'd be married to some duke or earl, locked away in some estate, my only aspiration to birth the next generation of mealy-mouthed nobles.

"Go home," Monsieur said. "Wait for your letter from the Admissions Committee." He smiled. "I'll see you at the Academy in the fall."

As I turned to follow Nonna from the room, I felt light-headed. Darkness encroached on my field of vision. This had happened more and more lately. Nonna said I was run-down. I'd feel better after I had a good rest. Now, though, I took some deep breaths and willed myself not to pass out.

CHAPTER 3

THE NEXT DAY, NONNA and I set off for home with our bags, my paint box, and a new sketch pad I'd bought the week before at the art store on the *Via Roma*. Our carriage left Palermo and turned west, toward the coast. Past fishing villages and marshlands swarming with mosquitoes. Along rows of prickly pears, their spiny pads crowned with magenta blooms. By the mud huts of the *contadini*, clustered together like ant hills.

Just outside the city center, women shuffled along, shrouded head to toe in black mantles, their trains dragging in the dirt. Every woman, whether peasant or noble, wore the heavy tunic and confining headscarf. At Monsieur's Academy, I'd been free of the garb. Now, though, I could feel its suffocating weight and the way it limited my field of vision, like blinders on a horse. The tight collar and shoulders. The sleeves, reaching past my wrists. Impossible to draw or paint in. Thankfully, Nonna decreed that in the alcove studio off my bedroom at *Binvinutu*, I could wear a simple shift. At all other times, I'd be forced to wear that terrible outfit.

We turned away from the ocean, up into the mountains. Past the temples of Segesta. The woods of Zingaro. Still, we climbed upwards, pebbles skittering under the carriage wheels. Into the town of Partanna, and a few minutes later, off the main road onto the lane that led to our manor house. *Binvinutu*. Limestone, glowing gold in the setting sun.

We pulled up to the entryway. Our butler, Federico, rushed to our carriage.

"The Don and Donna Inglese are in the parlor, along with Signorinas Rosalia and Caterina." Federico blinked a few times. "Monsieur Cascioferro is there, too." I was excited. Zio would be so happy when I told him that Monsieur said I'd be admitted to the Academy.

As we got closer, I heard the music. Chopin's *Preludes*. My sister Rosalia's favorite music. I think she liked Chopin because, like her, he had a weak constitution. The croup. The grippe. Fevers and ague. Rosalia seemed to catch every illness that passed through *Binvinutu*.

Federico opened the door. The playing stopped. A moment later, Rosalia bounded into view.

"Mimi!" she cried, throwing her arms around my neck.

I breathed in her sweet smell, as familiar as my own. I'd missed her. Waking in the morning, our arms around each other in the bed we shared, or whispering late into the night about the future. I would be a great artist; she, a musician.

But only I would get to pursue my dream. Rosalia would marry in the fall.

Pappa embraced me. He smelled of cigars and brandy. "Say hello to your mother," he murmured. "She's been awaiting your return."

We both knew that wasn't true. For some reason, I annoyed my mother. Even when I did what she wanted—dressing in the crinoline she laid out for me, the fabric scratching against my legs, or trying to take an interest in the endless gossip Mamma and her friends cultivated—always, there was that whiff of disapproval.

"Hello, Mamma." I bowed low to my mother, as I'd been doing since she and Pappa became noble, ten years ago. It was strange. One day, we were living in some cramped rooms above my mother's father's butcher shop; the next, we were the daughters of the baron, Don Inglese. All because Nonna claimed Pappa as her son—*il properio figlio*, according to the alterations made to the birth registry. I'd never gotten used to it.

Mamma turned her cheek to me. I rose and kissed her, then my youngest sister, ten-year-old Caterina, who clung to Mamma's skirts like she was still a little girl.

"You're too thin," Mamma said, looking down her nose at me. "Your hair is a mess."

I passed a gloved hand over my hair, trying to tuck in the strands that had come undone on the long carriage ride from Palermo.

Zio Vito came toward me, his arms wide. "My dear goddaughter! You've returned."

My cheeks felt hot. Doing my best to sound modest—because Mamma was still staring at me—I mumbled something about my portfolio.

Zio smiled broadly. "It will go well. My investments always pay out." *Investment.*

I tried not to look at Pappa. He'd wanted to pay the tuition. But with the new mineshaft and the compensation he still owed to the families of the nine *carusi* boys, child laborers who'd died in his sulfur mine explosion, there hadn't been money. He'd promised to repay Zio once the work was done and he'd sold another load of sulfur to the British. But here was Zio, acting like there was no debt.

Zio embraced me. He and Pappa were the same age, but Zio's arms were muscular. He held me so tightly that I started to cough. Mamma sneered at me. If we were alone, she'd tell me to cut it out. Like I was trying to embarrass her. But I couldn't stop.

The roads were dusty," Nonna said, putting her hand on her own chest. "Not good for breathing. Mimi should rest."

I went upstairs with Nonna, to the room I shared with Rosalia. The walls were covered with my artwork. My first painting: a still life of the poppies that grew in the field off the kitchen. Another of our dog, Wolfie, curled around the brazier on a cold winter morning. And my favorite: the portrait I'd done of Rosalia when she was ten or eleven. The way she tilted up her chin. The ferocity in her expression. It was hard to believe that she'd soon be someone's wife.

Nonna arranged to have a bath drawn for me, with water so hot that my first instinct was to jump out, like a frog lowered into a pot of boiling water. She kept her hand on my shoulder. I slowly lowered myself down. Even before the bath started to cool, I began hacking, water sloshing all over the floor. A look of concern flashed across Nonna's face. I knew it wasn't about the mess I'd made. She and the maid helped me out of the tub.

They settled me into bed. The room started to spin. I kept my eyes on my painting of Rosalia. It was hard to breathe, every inhale and exhale an ordeal, like someone was sitting on my chest.

Nonna pulled the coverlet over me. There was a rap on the door. It was Pappa. He asked how I was.

"Like all artists, her health is delicate." Nonna spoke so quietly that I had to strain to hear.

I wanted to remind Nonna: Mamma liked to say I came from peasant stock. It was an insult. Not a compliment.

"Yes," Pappa said. "She is an artist." He spoke quietly. Reverently. He'd been the first to believe in me. Maybe it was because he was an orphan, left in the wheel when he was just a baby. Saddled with the name *Camastrino*, which marked him as a bastard. My Pappa knew what it was like to want more.

Later, after Nonna had plastered my chest with a mustard poultice, I told myself I'd soon be well. Still, I couldn't help but think of Persephone, the taste of pomegranate on her tongue, wanting, more than anything, to be the master of her fate.

CHAPTER 4

I WOKE EARLY THE NEXT MORNING. Gingerly, I touched the skin on my chest. The mustard poultice was gone. Where it had been, the skin was puckered and raw. Rosalia lay next to me in her usual place. We'd been up for hours, whispering about Palermo and Teo. Art school. The duke.

I took a tentative breath, bracing myself for a coughing fit. But my chest was lighter. Looser. Nonna had been right. It had been the dust from the road. But as I pulled my nightgown over my head, I started to shiver. I thought of Teo. The last time we'd lain together, he'd shivered like this, though the brazier in the studio was blazing.

I told myself it was the mountain air. The way the temperature dropped at night. The cool breezes that swept in from the peaks. I'd get used to it again. My teeth chattering, I managed to slip on a dress from my closet. Then I took a heavy shawl from my closet and wrapped it around my shoulders.

As I started downstairs, my legs and arms felt clumsy, like they belonged to someone else. I gripped the banister, trying not to tumble forward. I made my way to the kitchen. Nonna was there. She was reading her Bible.

She raised her eyes to me. "What's wrong?" she said.

"I'm fine," I said, moving to fill the tea kettle with water.

"Come here," Nonna ordered. When I did, she put her hand on my brow. "You're burning up."

"It was cold in my room," I stammered. "It's the shawl," I said, shrugging it off one shoulder.

But Nonna was a nurse. She always knew when someone was sick.

"Back to bed, Mimi." Nonna pulled the tails of the shawl more tightly around me. "Cook will make some broth for you."

I tried to remind her what she had said the night before. The road had been dusty. I was tired. Nonna ignored me.

"Upstairs," she ordered.

She followed me. When we got to the bedroom, she put her hand on Rosalia's shoulder. When my sister didn't rouse, Nonna began to shake her.

"We were up late last night," I explained. "Talking."

Nonna shook Rosalia harder. Finally, she opened her eyes.

"Is it time for Mass?" Rosalia asked, groggily.

Nonna pulled off her sheet. "Go to the guest room," she ordered. "You'll be sleeping there from now on."

I tried to tell Nonna we wouldn't do it again. We'd been apart for almost a year. My voice was gravelly. Like Teo's, I thought, for the second time that morning. Before he disappeared.

"It's safer this way," Nonna said.

"You said it was just the dust."

There was a flash of anger before Nonna regained her usual composure. "You'll sleep in separate rooms," she repeated.

Something kept me from asking how long we'd have to sleep apart. I think I knew what Nonna would say: We should get used to it. Soon, Rosalia would be in the duke's bed, and I'd be back in Palermo. Our days of childhood were drawing to a close.

But we still had this summer.

So began the pattern that would continue through that fateful month. I was confined to my bed. But after everyone had gone to sleep, Rosalia would slip back into our room. We'd pull the covers over our heads and laugh, and whisper, and talk. Near dawn, my sister would slip out of bed and return to the guest room.

After about a week, my fever broke and Nonna let me start sketching. I wanted to go outside, but the weather was too unpredictable. Anyway, I wasn't an Impressionist. I didn't need to be outside for inspiration. The scene for a new painting—maybe the first I'd do as a student at the Palermo Academy —had been taking shape in my mind. The countryside I'd passed through on my way home from Palermo, with those fishing villages and marshlands. The prickly pears and waist-high grasses. Summer in Sicily.

That morning, I opened my new sketchpad. I sketched quickly. There was the craggy mountainside. The marshes and grasslands. A wheat field in the foreground, the conical seed pods swaying in the breeze. Without thinking, I added one lone figure, at the center of the canvas.

"Persephone," I whispered, though this figure wasn't reclining, as Matisse's had been. My Persephone's arms were outstretched, like a conductor directing a great orchestra. At her feet was a pomegranate, cut open to reveal the pearly seeds.

Lying in bed that night, I told Rosalia about what I'd drawn. "I'll give it to you," I said. "It'll be a wedding present."

"You'll show me tomorrow?" she asked excitedly.

Teo always said an artist should guard against showing their work too soon. "It's like a clay sculpture," he'd once explained. "Soft. Pliable. Too easily altered by other people's ideas of what it should be."

"Soon," I promised my sister.

Rosalia put her arms around my neck and drew me close. I had a terrible premonition that she'd never see my Persephone. It was silly. The painting would be done long before she married the duke or I left for Palermo.

I woke up the next morning feeling unsettled. I went to the window and looked out over the Madonies. My eyes found the place where the mountains met the plains. Just beyond was the entrance to Pappa's sulfur mines. A labyrinth snaked below. This is where Persephone's power lay. In the Underworld.

I returned to my sketch. Placing my pencil on its side, I shaded in that place where the mountain met the valley. A smudge to mark the place the grass had burned after last year's mine explosion. The entrance to Hades. On the field in front of it, Persephone. Not dancing or making love. But reigning supreme. Hades' Queen.

I drew Persephone's arms open wider, welcoming everyone to the Underworld. Just out of sight were the Fields of Asphodel, with their ghostly gray-white flowers. People who'd lived ordinary lives would spend eternity there, the scent making them forget the lives they'd lived. People who'd done extraordinary things went to Elysium, where the wind softly blew and honey-sweet fruit grew in fragrant meadows. Beneath it all lay Tartarus, where the truly evil were sent and the fires burned continually.

I ran my pencil over Persephone again, making her even bigger, more prominent. Before she'd become Queen of the Underworld, there'd been no Tartarus. No Asphodel. No Elysium. There was only chaos, where the bad preyed on the good with impunity, as they had in life. But Persephone and her seeds had changed all that.

I put down my pencil. The sketch was just an outline—pencil marks on linen—but already, there was Persephone, as she should be. There was no Hades, cajoling her to stay, or Mother Demeter, trying to pull her back to Olympus. Persephone might return to the surface of the Earth. After all, there could be no spring without her. But this was her choice, too. Though I could see her above ground, her eyes were on the horizon, already counting the days until she could return to the place she'd chosen.

I went to my bed, so exhausted that I slept through the lunch bell. When Nonna came in and placed her hand on my brow, I was far away. But when she returned a few minutes later, and laid that terrible poultice on my skin, I knew I was sick again. I tried to open my eyes, but they were too heavy. Around me, there were voices. Nonna. Pappa. Mamma. Loud. Insistent. Fearful. Saying something about a doctor.

I tried to ask about Rosalia, but the coughing was so bad that I couldn't get the words out. Nonna called for more pillows. That helped, until it didn't. I started gasping for air. Nonna loosened my chemise and pulled off the now-cold, stiff poultice. I cried out in pain as the air hit my poor, burned skin. Then the maid was there with a small bottle and a cloth. She gave these to Nonna, who tipped the bottle over onto that cloth. Without any warning, Nonna placed the cloth on my face. I tried to push her away—with that cloth over my nose and mouth, it was even harder to breathe. But the more I struggled, the more I breathed through that sweet-smelling cloth. And as I faded away, I thought of those fields of asphodel—the flowers of forgetfulness, and how relieving it would be to forget everything and just rest.

CHAPTER 5

I LAY THERE AS LIGHT GAVE WAY to shadow, and light again. There was murmuring, like thunder on the horizon. Too far off to care about.

One morning—and it must have been morning because it was so bright—I heard someone praying the Requiem. Maybe I was in my coffin. Laid out like my two-year-old brother, Antonino, had been, so long ago.

When I woke again, I smelled smoke. In the summer, wind from the Sahara fanned the flames of wildfires that erupted in the forests and plains of western Sicily. A few years ago, one particularly devastating blaze had destroyed all the chestnut trees in the Madonie Forest.

I didn't think to cover my mouth. When I began to cough again, I knew I wasn't dead. I felt a cool hand on my arm.

"Relax, Signorina Mimi." A white-coated man was standing there. "I'm Dr. Florio. I've been taking care of you."

I struggled to make out what he was saying. Then I remembered. I'd been sick. Nonna had called for a doctor.

I tried to lift my head to look for her. It was too heavy. "Nonna?" My voice was gravelly.

There was a swish of movement. The smell of sandalwood. Nonna.

"My sweet Mimi." She pressed her lips against my forehead, like she had when I was small. When she pulled away, she made the sign of the cross. "The fever has broken. Thank you, blessed Madonna."

I tried to focus on Nonna's face, translucent as an alabaster statue, though the skin around her eyes was swollen and red.

"Where have I been?" I whispered, like I was returning from a voyage to a faraway place.

"Ill." Nonna turned to look out the window. Someone had taken down the damask curtains. Silvery tendrils danced just outside, spiraling into the azure sky. The smoke curled in on itself, like the spirals of a girl's hair. The memory came to me. Lying with Rosalia in bed, her wavy hair spilling over the pillow.

"Rosalia?" I asked.

Nonna's bottom lip began to quiver. She pulled her wrinkled handkerchief from her dress pocket and turned away. Her shoulders were shaking.

I looked past her, through the window. The smoke had begun to change. Steel gray, tinged with charcoal. I was thinking about how I'd have to use a tiny brush to work the darker hue into the composition when I started to cough again. A deep, exquisitely painful hacking that left me gasping for air, wheezing and clawing at the neck of my nightgown. Darkness descended, threatening to drag me under.

Then there were hands everywhere. Pulling off my sheets. Grabbing me under the arms and forcing me upright. Someone slapped me hard on the back. A pea-sized, mucousy thing was on my tongue.

"Spit it out," Nonna ordered. I did, the plug slithering past my lips. For a moment, I could breathe. Then I began to wheeze again. Another slap on the back.

"Breathe, Mimi."

Nonna had said the same thing when little Antonino was born. We'd just moved to *Binvinutu*. The birth of a boy after we three girls seemed to portend good fortune. But after Nonna helped birth him, he lay limply in her arms, slick with blood.

"Breathe, Antonino," she whispered, before hitting him between his tiny shoulder blades. When he cried in protest, Nonna smiled. "Sometimes babies need to be encouraged to breathe."

At the time, it struck me as strange. Breathing was something I'd never thought about. Now, struggling to manage even a short inhale, I understood.

"Small breaths in and out," Nonna said. "Sip the air."

I was so focused on breathing that at first, I didn't notice how the smoke had changed. Thick and charcoal-colored, it billowed outside the window. Advancing and retreating, leaving behind a shimmering curtain of iron-gray flecks.

Controlled fire was a fact of life at *Binvinutu*. After every harvest, the overseer set the wheat fields ablaze. But those fires burned white, preparing the soil for the next planting. The smoke outside my window, though, was more like soot. Darker even than the plumes that spiraled up from the sulfur mine the day it exploded last year. Pappa said the new shaft would be safer. Sunk deeper, there'd be less wind-blown dust and less chance of fire.

Thinking of that smudge on my sketch, I remembered how far away the mines were. No. This smoke seemed to be coming from much closer. Maybe the courtyard, just underneath my window. We kept pots of calla lilies on the flagstones. I can't remember the scullery man ever setting a fire there.

I tried to sit up. But there was a pain in my side so terrible that I fell back on my pillow. My fingers found the place. A swath of bandages, so thick I couldn't even feel it when I pressed down. I struggled to remember what had happened.

I'd been working on a sketch. Persephone. I was going to give it to Rosalia when she wed the duke. I looked around our room. My sister wasn't there.

"Where is Rosalia?" I asked again. Nonna turned away. When she turned to face me again, she was holding a gauze square. She placed it over my nose and mouth, firmly, so that even if I wanted to object, I couldn't.

When I woke up again, the sun was low in the sky. Somewhere behind me, people were talking. Mamma and Pappa.

"It was bound to happen," Mamma said. "With her in Palermo, doing whatever she was doing."

"She was taking art lessons." Pappa's voice was flat. He sounded tired.

"So much for that. All that money, wasted."

Mamma always said things like that. But the money hadn't been wasted. I was going to the Academy. Monsieur Laurent said I'd be a great artist.

Pappa stood up. "We'll talk about this when she's better."

Mamma snorted. "Better? She's not going to be better. Tuberculosis. It's a life sentence."

The images came to me at once: Claude Monet's wife, enshrouded in gauze, her jaw stiffening in rigor mortis. Edvard Munch's sister, wan and wasted, looking into the light. The painter Marie Bashkirtseff, her works characterized by *chiaroscuro*—the contrast of dark and light.

"Shhh!" Nonna said. "She's awake."

Pappa came to my side. I longed for him to say that everything would be all right, as he always did. He asked how I was feeling. Blithely, like it was an afterthought. Surely, he wouldn't be this calm if I had tuberculosis. Mamma was exaggerating. It wouldn't be the first time.

Before I could answer, Pappa motioned to the doctor I'd seen earlier. "Dr. Florio says you're doing well."

The doctor nodded. It couldn't be the consumption. I asked again about Rosalia. Pappa bit his lip and looked away.

I felt a gnawing, deep in my gut. Something was wrong. Nonna came to me. She laid her hands on mine. There was sadness in her eyes. I didn't want to ask. I couldn't help it.

"Where is my sister?" My voice was panicky.

"Caterina is in the parlor."

"And Rosalia?"

Again, Nonna ignored the question.

"What happened?" I asked.

"You had an operation."

"So I'm better?"

Nonna's lips were turned down. Now I saw how sunken her cheeks were. She squeezed my hand. The gnawing in my belly was worse.

"Am I better?" My voice sounded brittle.

"You're out of danger."

"I don't understand—."

"You almost died."

"It was just the dust from the road." My voice broke. "A summer cold."

"No."

At that moment, I knew the truth.

"Tuberculosis," I whispered.

Nonna nodded.

"Have you been sick?" I asked.

She shook her head. She'd once told me that she'd been a nurse for so long that she didn't get sick anymore.

"Rosalia?"

Nonna swallowed hard. Then she nodded. "She was sick, too."

I touched the bandage. "Did she have an operation?"

Nonna glanced at the doctor. He turned toward the window. Tiny white embers were falling amidst an ebony backdrop, like the Milky Way on a moonless night.

But it was daytime.

"She needs to stay calm," Dr. Florio said, quietly. "If she reopens those stitches, I'll have to go in again."

Nonna said nothing.

"She should have another dose of chloroform," he added.

Nonna took my hand. "That won't be necessary." She was holding her rosary. The beads were still warm. "You have to be strong, Mimi. Do you understand?"

I nodded, though I desperately wanted Nonna to stop talking.

She held me fast, the crucifix at the end of her beads digging into my skin. "Rosalia is gone," she whispered.

I shook my head. "She's across the hall. In the guest room. I'll get her." I started to pull off the sheet. There was a searing pain in my side.

"No, Mimi. She's not in the guest room."

"You made her sleep there. We wanted to be together, but you made her leave." I sounded like a petulant child.

I kicked away the blanket and started to get up. Nonna gently pushed me back down. Out the window, I could see the smoke. Dark as pitch. But I remembered what my first art tutor had said: Black wasn't a color. It was the absence of color. Did that mean the smoke didn't exist?

Nonna and the doctor were arguing now. The doctor, insisting on the chloroform. Nonna saying I should be told the "truth"—whatever that was—and the sooner, the better. Pappa was mumbling that I should be allowed to rest.

"We'll tell her afterwards," Pappa said.

But I didn't want to rest. What I wanted was my sketchpad. Nothing made sense—not that bandage, or the stitches, or what Nonna had said about Rosalia not being in the guest room. Drawing would help me figure things out.

I tried to get up again. This time, Nonna stood back, holding her hands up like she was giving up.

I pulled on my shawl. "I'm going across the hall. To see Rosalia."

When I couldn't get my legs to hold me, Nonna signaled for the maid to bring a chair on wheels. Nonna helped me into the chair and then wheeled me to the guest room. The bed had been stripped to the blue and white ticking mattress. Rosalia was gone.

Something inside me started to give way. Nonna wheeled me back to my bedroom.

The smoke outside the window was jet black. Ominous. Nonna came around to face me. "You've been sick."

"You said that."

Nonna drew back. I'd never spoken to her like that before.

She straightened her shoulders, as if something had been decided. "You almost died."

I shrugged. "I was sick. Now I'm better."

"Mimi, you have tuberculosis. Do you understand what this means?"

Camille Monet. Sophie Munch. Marie Bashkirtseff. "But I had an operation."

"That was to save your life. Not to cure you. Without that operation, you would have died. You still might die. You have to take care of yourself."

All those times Nonna had chided me for staying up late or missing a meal. "I'll do better. I promise."

"That's not enough, Mimi," Nonna said. "You can't paint anymore."

"But I can. The Admissions Committee is reviewing my portfolio. Monsieur Laurent says I'll be admitted—."

Nonna shook her head. "You misunderstand me. I'm not saying you aren't able to paint. You're a gifted artist. I'm saying you will no longer be permitted to paint. The paint and solvents are bad for the lungs."

I shook my head. "No! I'm going to be the first woman admitted to the Academy. They're reviewing my portfolio," I repeated.

Nonna laid her hand on me. "There is no more portfolio. Do you understand, Mimi? It was destroyed to prevent contagion."

"You're wrong. It's at the studio, with *Binvinutu*!"

She shook her head. "Everything's gone. You must accept this, Mimi."

I screamed that Nonna was an old woman. She couldn't stop me from painting.

Nonna wheeled my chair closer to the window. The smoke was billowing, blacker than any paint I'd ever seen. She pointed down, toward the courtyard. "Look."

I followed the smoke down. The maid's copper wash tub was on the flagstones. A fire raged inside. It licked at the sides of the tub and the air above it. Someone approached. It was our butler, Federico.

He was holding my paint box and sketchpad. I watched as he unlatched the lid of the box and flipped it open. In slow motion, I saw the flash of metal and glass—the tubes of paint, the brushes, the tiny glass water jars—dumped into the raging fire.

"No!" I screamed, trying to rise from the chair. But Nonna held me there. She made me watch as the fire hissed, then roared, devouring the box and everything inside. Just as it began to die down, Federico placed my sketchpad on top. At first, it looked like the weight of it would smother the fire. Then it was aflame.

Something heavy was being dragged across the flagstones. I didn't want to look. Nonna wheeled me closer.

My paintings — the ones that had hung on my wall. The poppies. Wolfie. Rosalia. The field hands picked one up and laid it on the fire. Then the next and the next, until they made a mighty bonfire.

I turned to Nonna. "Why?" I cried. "Why would you let them do this?"

"I keep telling you, Mimi. Things have changed. You must accept this." Nonna spoke calmly, like she was talking to a child on the verge of a tantrum.

There were no curtains on the windows. No way to look away. Like those poor doomed souls trapped in Tartarus, I was made to watch as that fire raged, consuming everything I'd made. Watching it all burn, I should have felt something. Pain. Fury. Desolation. But I was numb. I pressed down hard on that gauze bandage. The pain was excruciating, but there was also relief. The blood soaked through the fabric, warm against my fingers.

Nonna pulled my hand away from my wound. She stayed there, her fingers encircling my wrists, as we watched the smoke turn from black to steel gray to silver. Mamma left. Then Pappa and Dr. Florio.

When the fire had died out, Nonna spoke again, calmly. "You will find a new purpose, Mimi. You have your whole life ahead of you."

But what was life without my art?

"There's always something else you can do," Nonna continued. "You'll see."

"I don't want to marry."

"You won't marry."

"Mamma will insist, now that I'm not going to be an artist."

Nonna shook her head. "Listen to me, Mimi. You're not going to marry. Dr. Florio says the strain of childbirth would kill you."

"So what will I do?" I asked.

"You'll stay here. At *Binvinutu*. You'll be a help to your family."

"Like playing nursemaid to my sisters' children?"

"Perhaps. Caterina will marry well. She'll have many children. But she's a nervous girl. She'll need your help."

"And Rosalia?"

For a moment, the question hung in the air.

When I saw the tears on Nonna's cheeks, I finally understood. Rosalia was gone. I began to scream, the sound seeming to come from someplace outside myself. A moment later, I smelled the chloroform and then felt the gauze pressing against my nose and mouth. And I slipped away.

CHAPTER 6

I WAS SITTING ON THE BENCH in the courtyard, fallen leaves swirling in tiny cyclones around my feet, when I heard the horses. I stood and tucked the pencil into my bag. Tea with Zio Vito at four. This passed for excitement in the dreary life I'd been living for the last two years. Anyway, I shouldn't be late. Looking at my sketch, I saw there wasn't much more I could do with this drawing. A nest nestled in an oak branch. Tiny birds tucked beneath their mamma's shimmering breast.

Pappa would say I should sign the drawing, *M Inglese* in the corner, like I had with my paintings. A careful signature that identified the piece as mine without drawing attention to the fact that I wasn't a man. *M Inglese*. Not Claude Monet or Henri Matisse, and certainly not VINCENT. But this was just a pencil drawing. A study, Monsieur Laurent would have called it. Proof that I'd mastered some technical skill. Or worked out some problem, like the columns of numbers Pappa was always adding up on the scratch pad he kept next to the ledger. But I couldn't feel that bird in my heart. It might as well have been a rock or a bunch of twigs.

I slipped inside the kitchen. Already I could hear Zio in Pappa's study, his voice echoing across the entry hall. At tea in the sunroom, the men would talk of banal things—Zio's hound's latest litter of puppies, or the pedigree of a horse recently acquired. But Zio's voice now was angry. I ducked into an alcove in the hallway so I could hear.

"It better not be like that shitty wheat harvest," Zio hissed.

Like Pappa was responsible for the stalks withering and turning black.

"It'll be a good harvest," Pappa promised, his voice strained. "Those olive trees have been producing for generations."

Cook would say that Pappa was tempting the fates. He should touch iron or rub his lucky coin. But they say bad things come in threes. Counting on my fingers, I made a tally. First, the fire in the sulfur mine; second, the tuberculosis; third, the wheat rust.

"Explain something to me, Nino." There was the scratch of a match, then the smell of Zio Vito's cigar—leather and toasted almonds. "*Binvinutu* is the biggest estate in Partanna. When my father worked for your grandfather, there were no explosions. No blights. But since you've taken over, it's been one catastrophe after another."

Pappa mumbled something I couldn't hear.

Zio's voice was clear. "You keep saying that. And I keep pouring money into this place. But it can't go on forever. I have other obligations." It was quiet for a moment. The cigar smoke wafting through the window was so heavy I had to put my sleeve over my face to keep from coughing.

"I'll increase your share to fifty percent," Pappa said. "We'll be partners." But *Binvinutu* was Pappa's birthright. He couldn't just give half of it away.

Zio laughed. "What would I want with a place like this? My business is in Palermo. And America."

If Pappa was unlucky in business, Zio was the opposite. He'd spent most of the last year in the United States, opening stores in New York and New Orleans. Soon, he'd return to America. Pappa said he'd be gone at least a year.

Pappa stammered something about bankers and a loan and foreclosure. "They'll take everything. Please, Vito. This is our family's home. Yours and mine."

Zio snorted. "Your home. Not mine. The future is in America. Not here."

Pappa repeated himself, saying they'd get by after the harvest. "I don't need another barrel of olive oil. What I need is an engraver." Cook said that Zio had a finger in every pie. But why would Zio need an engraver?

From behind me, I heard someone clear his throat. I turned. Federico was there.

"May I help you, Signorina Mimi?" He said it in a way that left no doubt that he knew I'd been eavesdropping.

"I was just—resting."

"Tea is in an hour." Federico offered his arm. "I'll help you to your room."

I had no choice. I took Federico's arm.

Once in my room, I pulled open the window. It was across the courtyard from Pappa's office, close enough to hear the low rumble of Pappa's and Zio's voices, but too far to make out what they were saying. If I had Nonna's faith, I would have begged the Madonna to soften Zio's heart. If I had Mamma's short temper, I'd have cursed Zio for being a bad *compare* to Pappa.

If I were Pappa's son, though, I could reason with Zio. Figure out a way that he wouldn't be so angry, so Pappa could keep *Binvinutu*. But I was only an invalid girl.

Maybe I should go downstairs and help Caterina with the table. She'd be wed next year. Mamma said it was high time she understood the basics of entertaining. I should find a way to be kind to Caterina. But there was a burning in my gut. My sister was healthy. Nothing had changed for her.

I went to my table and opened my sketchpad to the bird I'd been drawing that morning. When I'd first seen it outside my window, its tiny feet clutching the olive tree branch and rejoicing that winter had passed, I thought of Rosalia. That happened all the time. As I was drawing, waking from sleep, or walking in the garden, she'd come to me. If I had a paintbrush, I'd have painted that blue bird in pinks and golds. Persephone's hues. The colors of rebirth.

But that little bird wasn't Rosalia. I picked up my pencil. I drew each barb and quill exactly as it was. No emotion—joy or pain, hope or despair. Just a tiny bird with wings and a tail. I'd always looked down on artists whose work depicted "real life." They were only copying someone else's creation. Looking at that stilted drawing, though, I realized even this was beyond me. I should give up. Accept my fate. But that pencil always found its way back into my grasp.

Just before three, the door to Pappa's study opened. Teatime. I went downstairs to the sunroom. Zio was at the head of the wicker table. When he saw me, he stood and opened his arms wide.

"Mimi." He pulled me into a tight embrace. When he released me, he put his hand on his chest. "How are you feeling?" he asked. "Are you better?"

"Yes, thank you, Zio," I lied. He must know I'd never be better.

Zio motioned to the chair next to his. "Sit, my dear. There is something I want to talk with you about."

I looked at Pappa to see if this was all right with him. He was staring out the window. Zio pulled out the chair next to him. I sat.

"Your father tells me you've been doing art again," Zio began. Pappa winced. He knew those drawings weren't art.

Zio took my hands in his. "Let me see what you've been working on."

I felt a flicker of excitement, but I reminded myself that Zio was just humoring me. I went to my room to retrieve the sketchbook. When I returned, Pappa was still at the table, his shoulders curled forward. Zio stood over him, his hands on his hips, his jaw clenched. The moment he saw me, though, Zio's expression softened.

"Ah, Mimi. Come." Zio held out his hands. "Let's see your latest masterpiece."

I hated when people treated me like a simpleton, like the consumption had laid waste to my brain and not my lungs. But I flipped open to the nest.

Zio raised his eyebrows. "This is wonderful. So realistic! And look at all that detail—the twigs and moss, the bird's beak, her eyes. And those feathers!" Zio slid the pad to Pappa. "Look at this, Nino! See what your daughter can do!"

For a moment, I felt proud, the way I had once when people had praised my paintings. But that pencil sketch wasn't art.

Still, Zio carried on about how amazing that bird was. How it should be in a museum, where people could admire it. "You know," he said, leaning in. "I'd pay good money for this."

Did Pappa hear this? Maybe I could help with *Binvinutu* after all.

"How much?" I blurted out.

Zio laughed. "An artist and a businesswoman, eh?" He reached into his silk waistcoat and drew out his money clip. "Here," he said, extracting a five lire note.

The paper was stiff. The ink felt tacky, like it was newly printed. Other than the few *centesimi* Pappa gave me for the convent bakery or the alms box, money was unfamiliar to me.

I tried to catch Pappa's eye. I wanted to signal to him that this note would help pay for whatever trouble he was in. But Pappa didn't look at me. I pocketed the bill anyway.

I began to tear the drawing from the pad. Zio stopped me. "You keep the sketch for now. I have a proposition for you."

I nodded, not trusting myself to speak.

"I need a logograph for my business. Do you know what that is?"

"A logograph?" The word felt strange in my mouth.

"It's like a label. A mark that tells people something is yours."

I couldn't imagine anyone not knowing that something was Zio's, but I nodded.

"It'll be like this." He took a pen from his vest and turned to a new page in my sketchpad. "It's a rectangle. With the name of my company on top." In large block letters, he wrote *Mercantini Imports and Exports*. "It will be on everything I send to America. Olive oil cans; tins of anchovies, boxes of pasta. But I need something in this space." He circled the blank space beneath the lettering. "Something that the *paesani* can look at and know: this is *Mercantini*. The best. Do you understand?"

"So you need a drawing?"

"Something that people will know is mine. Something distinctive. Sicilian."

When I didn't respond, Zio continued. "Think of it, Goddaughter. Your work will be on thousands of crates. You'll be famous!"

Like Matisse's water lilies. Or Rosa Bonheur's cows. Or Van Gogh's fantastical stars.

"What should I draw?" I asked.

Zio put out his hands, palms up. "You're the artist. Make some sketches. I'll be back next week. We'll go see the blacksmith—he'll be making the logo and he'll be able to help. For now, think about things that will remind the *paesani* of home. Familiar images. Things that will make them feel less homesick."

But I'd seen how they lived. An entire family crowded into a hovel with dirt floors and no running water. The children, clothed in only rags, their arms and legs spindly, their bellies swollen. Yet here was Zio, suggesting that, even if everything was true about America—that there were opportunities for anyone who wanted to work, that even the poor could become rich—there'd be a new kind of hunger. A yearning for home, a wistfulness for a Sicily that probably never was, at least not for the poorest—the *puviri*.

"So will you help me, Mimi?" Zio asked.

I turned toward Pappa. This was his decision. No unmarried woman did anything without her father's approval. Still, Pappa wouldn't look at me.

"Mimi?" Zio repeated.

Pappa always says, *When opportunity knocks, open the door.* Before I got sick, I assumed my life would be one door opening after another. Maybe Zio was offering me one last door, left open just a crack.

Trying to keep my voice steady, I told him I would.

CHAPTER 7

THE CONVERSATION BETWEEN MAMMA and Nonna started inno-
cently enough. The maid had just finished laying out the breakfast. She
stood before Mamma, awaiting direction. I was finishing another sketch
for Zio, the third in as many months: a palm tree like the giant one in
the village square. Caterina had just come from morning matins. She sat
across from me, eyes closed and hands clasped in prayer.

Mamma plucked three cubes from the sugar bowl. She stirred each
into her espresso, then took a sip, pinky out. "Things must be perfect
for Signora Cassata." She settled the cup back onto its saucer. "A fire in
the brazier. The best Limoges. Be quick about it. And tell the footman.
We'll be using the main entrance. Now go." With a flick of her wrist, she
dismissed the girl.

Only when the maid left did Nonna speak. "The matchmaker is
coming?" Her voice was cold.

Mamma kept stirring her espresso though the sugar must have
long since dissolved. "You must have forgotten. We talked about this.
Caterina will marry. Signora Cassata says there's interest."

When Caterina opened her eyes, they looked glassy, like a
mannequin's.

Nonna sometimes mixed up words, saying book when she meant
newspaper, and Bible when she was looking for her rosary beads. By the
way Nonna's eyes narrowed, though, I knew Mamma was lying. There

had been no talk of a matchmaker. She stared at Mamma a long time. Finally, she spoke.

"The Mother Superior at Santa Maria said they'd accept a modest convent dowry out of respect for the family."

"We've talked about this, Matri. She's not going to the convent."

Caterina clasped her hands tightly. Back in her room, she'd start to work on her cuticles. By tonight, they'd be a bloody mess.

Nonna continued. "She's a devout girl. Meant for the cloisters, not for some nobleman's bed."

"Matri! Don't be so crass." Mamma motioned in my direction. But I was no innocent.

Nonna continued. "Maria, you and I both know that Caterina is delicate. The stress of being a wife and mother will be too much."

I thought Mamma would lash out and repeat what she whispered about to her friends: Nonna knew nothing about being a wife or mother. She'd abandoned her only child to the orphans' wheel and then hidden herself away in the cloisters.

But Mamma was focused on my sister. "She'll have to adjust. Like the rest of us." I guess Mamma was remembering how Pappa had cut her monthly allowance last fall after the wheat crop failed.

Nonna shook her head. "This will go badly, Maria. The Madonna intends for Caterina to have a different path."

"The Madonna intends that?" Mamma's voice dripped with sarcasm. But I'd been wondering about the Madonna, too. Nonna said I'd been saved from the tuberculosis for some reason. But besides Zio's logo—which seemed unimportant—She'd been silent.

"Caterina has the gift of sight," Nonna continued. "You know this, Maria."

Shortly after I'd awoken from the tuberculosis, Caterina started saying that the Madonna was beckoning to her. Nonna decreed that it was a miracle. Mamma wasn't convinced.

"Enough fairy tales," Mamma said harshly. "Someone needs to think about this family's future."

By that, Mamma meant her own future. When Pappa died, *Binvinutu* would pass to some distant male relative. If Caterina were married, Mamma would live with her at her husband's estate. But if Caterina went to the nunnery, Mamma would be forced to live with one of her brothers—one, a hog farmer, the other, a fat renderer. If I was still alive, I'd go, too.

Nonna slipped her hands into her sleeves, a gesture that must have picked up from living with the nuns. Maybe she'd been a rebel as a young woman—she'd have to have been, to allow herself to be impregnated by one man and then refuse to marry another. How she'd survived thirty years in that convent—with someone telling her when to sleep, how to pray, and what to think—I'd never understand. Whatever sins she'd committed before finding her way to that dingy, cheerless place had to have been redeemed.

But Caterina had done nothing wrong. Why would she want to spend her life praying and fasting, confined to a room with scarcely enough room for a cot? She could live a good life. Married to a man who could provide for her. Mother to a brood of children who would worship her. It wasn't a life I'd ever wanted, but there was power and freedom in being the lady of a noble household.

Mamma squared her shoulders. Contests with Nonna usually ended with Mamma in tears. Maybe not this time. "Things have been settled," she repeated. "Caterina will marry."

The set of Nonna's jaw told me that this wasn't over.

But why should Caterina be allowed to shut herself away, leaving me and Mamma dependent on the charity of some distant relative? We all had to do things we didn't want to do.

I looked at my sketch of the palm tree. When Zio asked for a logo, he'd made it sound so easy. But the blacksmith, Signore Zuccheri, had rejected every one I'd brought him. The first, a traditional Sicilian cart and pony, was too complicated, with its plumed headdress and ornate wheels. The second, an olive branch heavy with fruit, wasn't distinctive enough. The olives could have come from Spain or Greece.

The blacksmith insisted the logo should be something that couldn't be found anywhere but Sicily. I wondered why, if you were leaving, you'd want to be reminded of things you couldn't get anywhere else. But when I'd asked Zuccheri, he'd brushed away my words.

Mamma downed her espresso then set the cup back on its saucer. "Anyway. Nino wants Caterina to marry."

Nonna raised her eyebrows. "Did he tell you that?"

"He didn't need to. He wants to be a grandfather. Caterina's the only one who can keep the Inglese line alive."

There was the clink of beads as Nonna released her rosary into her pocket. "Caterina's children won't be Inglese. If only you'd been able to give him one son who'd survived."

With that, Mamma crumpled in her seat, "I tried," Mamma croaked. "I tried to give Nino a son." She put her hand over her eyes and began to cry.

For now, Nonna had won.

A few hours later, there was a rapping at the front door. The matchmaker. Signora Cassata looked like a hedgehog. Round and prickly, with beady eyes and a long snout.

When Nonna rose to welcome her, grasping the woman's stubby hands in her own, I thought maybe the old woman had forgotten about the convent and Caterina's visions. But Nonna was the Donna Inglese— the Lady of *Binvunutu*. Even if she didn't want the matchmaker there, she had to maintain a sense of decorum.

After the tea had been poured and Signora partook of not one, but two lemon *cassatelle*, she wiped the powdered sugar from her mouth and turned her little hedgehog eyes to Nonna.

"There is interest from two parties. The Duke of Bevilaqua, for his third son. And Don Acamo from Girgenti, for his firstborn. Both are excellent matches. And both require substantial dowries."

Mamma nodded, like the dowries weren't an issue. But I'd overheard Pappa ask Zio to sell off another field in preparation.

"The Duchy of Bevilaqua will go to the oldest son," the matchmaker said. "The third son will occupy one of the other palazzos—all quite impressive. But Don Acamo's son is the firstborn. He'll inherit a smaller estate, but it will all be his." Signora raised one hand, then the other, as if weighing the options. It made no difference to me. A palazzo or an estate, I'd still be dependent on a stranger when Pappa died.

Without waiting to be asked, the matchmaker signaled the maid for more tea. She picked up another *cassatelle*. After some small talk with Nonna about their shared acquaintances in Girgenti, Signora stood. Again, she addressed Nonna.

"Talk to Don Inglese about it. When you decide, send word to me, and we'll arrange for the banns to be announced. Easter comes early this year. You'll need to decide right away if you want her to wed before Lent." Without even a word to Mamma, the woman left.

That night at dinner, I waited for Nonna to tell Pappa about Signora's visit. When Nonna still hadn't said anything by the cheese course, Mamma blurted out that the matchmaker had paid a call.

"Good news," Mamma added, her smile a thin, tight line.

Pappa drizzled honey on his ricotta. Only when the swirling stream of amber had finished trickling onto the white cheese did he ask Mamma about Signora.

Mamma nearly jumped from her chair. "The Duke of Bevilacqua is eager to make a match for his third son. Imagine that! The richest duchy in Girgenti." She clapped her hands. "A dream come true!"

Caterina started scratching her neck, so hard that her nails left tracks on the skin. If Pappa noticed, he ignored it. Reaching across the table, he took Mamma's hand in his. "You've worked so hard, my dear. Caterina is the perfect noblewoman."

The perfect puppet, I thought.

Pappa drew out a cigar from his vest pocket. He tapped the end against the linen tablecloth. "The wedding will be splendid. Caterina will travel by horseback to the cathedral. Villagers will hold torches. There will be a carpet of rose petals the full length of the aisle. Afterwards, a ten-course meal. The best of the best. Piedmont truffles, Beluga caviar, red prawns."

I thought of that terrible conversation I'd overheard between Zio and Pappa. Was there really money for all of that?

Maybe Mamma was thinking about it, too. "Vito will pay. He's the godfather, after all."

"I am the father. I will pay." Pappa lit his cigar. "Don't look so worried, Maria. We're going to have our best olive harvest yet."

"We can't wait until February. We need money now." Mamma motioned toward the water-stained ceiling. The buckled and splintering floors. "We can't have a wedding with the house looking like this."

"Can't the wedding wait until next fall?" Pappa asked. "Caterina's hardly an old maid."

My sister began to pull hard on a lock of hair that had come undone from her chignon. At least it was in the back. Her veil would cover whatever damage she did to herself.

"You could go to the bank," Mamma pressed. "Ask for credit for the repairs."

"Mortgage *Binvinutu* to some stranger? No. I won't do it."

"Debt is good. It's how you build a business. Remember my father."

"Yes, yes. I know." Pappa's voice was flat. "He mortgaged his butcher shop to buy that pasture in Misilmeri."

"That's how you get rich. Now all the best people buy from him. The nobility, the English, the Continentals."

Even I knew what the villagers said about Mamma's father—that the old man passed off donkey meat as veal.

Quietly, Pappa said he'd ask Zio. "A loan," he said quietly. "I'll repay him."

But the money Zio put up for my tuition had been a loan, too. I'd heard nothing about Pappa repaying that. My stomach clenched. A daughter shouldn't pity her father, but I couldn't help it.

The logograph. Zio offered to pay me for it. Probably not much, but it had to help. Maybe it would be enough for the sugared almonds for the wedding guests. Pappa wouldn't have to know. I'd slip the money into the wooden box he kept on his dresser.

I excused myself and headed to my studio. I had to finish the palm tree sketch.

CHAPTER 8

HAIL PELTED THE ROOF of the conservatory, the sound like pebbles thrown against the glass. I touched my side, feeling for the edge of the bandage beneath my clothes. Since the January winds had started to blow, Nonna had been wrapping my skin with formalin-soaked poultices.

"To keep you well," she said, each morning. But we both knew the truth: Things weren't finalized with the duke's son yet. If I got sick, the duke might reconsider. With Signore Cassata coming today, maybe that meant the banns would finally be announced, and Nonna would leave me alone. I pressed my fingers gently against the poultice. Underneath, the skin was raw. Nonna insisted it would heal, just as Dr. Florio's terrible incision had. Though when I touched that twisted splatter of skin, it was numb. Like it belonged to someone else.

The maid entered the parlor. She went to the writing desk where Mamma sat, pen in hand, bent over a piece of monogrammed stationery. All morning, Mamma had been trying to craft a letter to the duchess with some drivel Signore Cassata had recommended about how she was grateful Caterina was marrying into such an esteemed family.

The maid cleared her throat. "Signore Cascioferro has arrived."

Mamma consulted the cloisonné watch that hung at her waist. "Two hours late. If I were in my right mind, I'd turn him away."

Ungrateful. Even after Zio had provided the fat dowry and paid for the repairs.

Pappa's voice reached us, high and tight, accompanied by the low rumble of Zio's voice. A moment later, the conservatory door opened. Pappa and Zio strode in. Instead of the matchmaker, the blacksmith, Signore Zuccheri, was with them, his muddy cuffs streaking the parquet.

"What's he doing here?" Mamma demanded. I was surprised, too. Pappa and I had only ever met him in his blacksmith shop, surrounded by his apprentices.

Zio laughed. "Is that any way to treat a guest?"

Mamma got to her feet. Gathering her skirts, she announced that she had a letter to write. She left the room, leaving her stationery and pens.

Zio held out his hands to me. "Dear Mimi." He kissed one cheek, then the other. His lips were warm. I tried not to think about how cold my skin must feel to him. "Signore Zuccheri tells me you've made excellent progress on the logograph. He says one of the sketches is perfect."

After the pony cart and the olive branch, the blacksmith had rejected my palm tree and jasmine flower. When I showed him the pomegranate, I thought he'd say no to that, too. Instead, he said he thought it might work. I tried to remember exactly what the blacksmith had said. "Acceptable." Or maybe even "good." Certainly not perfect. Though men often exaggerated when they talked with Zio.

I stood. "I'll get the sketch." But Federico appeared, my pad in hand. He handed it to Zio, who paged through it, brows knitted, until he got to the pomegranate.

He ran his fingers over the drawing. "*Bene,* Mimi. This is excellent. Genius, really. Every Sicilian knows about the pomegranate. How Hades used its seeds to trap Persephone and keep her from her Mamma. So much pain. But as they say, suffering is the ancient law of love." Zio turned abruptly to the blacksmith. "What do you think?"

"It will make a good logo," the blacksmith said. "Simple. Recognizable."

"And Sicilian. That's the most important part. They'll see that

pomegranate and know right away: *Mercantini Import and Exports.*"
Zio turned to Pappa. "See? I told you she could do this."

The ground beneath me shifted. There'd been a time when Pappa
thought I'd be a great artist. Now he thought I couldn't manage even
one stupid sketch.

Zio pulled a gold coin from his pocket and pressed it into my palm.
"Twenty lire for a job well done."

I closed my fingers over it, feeling its cold, beaded edge. Twenty lire
would pay for more than just the sugared almonds.

"I have another job for you now," Zio said. "If you'd like."

I tightened my grasp on the lire coin. It was warming to my touch.
I nodded.

Zio smiled broadly. He put my sketchpad on the table, then
motioned to the blacksmith, who placed his battered satchel beside it.

"We need an engraving of the pomegranate," Zuccheri said. He
pulled out a pocket knife, then cut my sketch from the pad. It was careful, even surgical in its precision, and it made me think of how Dr. Florio
had used his knife to navigate the space between my ribs.

After he'd laid four lead discs on the corners, the blacksmith pulled
a piece of copper and a chamois from his satchel. Using the cloth, he polished the surface until it gleamed. When he was done, he looked at Zio.

Zio motioned toward me. "Give it to her," he said, with more than
a little impatience.

Again, the blacksmith reached into his satchel. This time, he drew
out a small burled-wood case. It looked like one of Mamma's jewelry
boxes, with a sterling silver clasp and a cartouche plate on top. He
placed it in front of me. On the cartouche were the initials MCI. My
initials—for Mattia Camastrino Inglese—though I went by Mimi, and
after Pappa became Inglese, Mamma had been adamant that we never
use that bastard name, Camastrino, again. The blacksmith turned the
box toward me—ceremoniously, as if he were presenting some kind
of treasure. Maybe a necklace, like Zio had given my sister Caterina
for her trousseau?

He opened the lid. Instead of jewelry, though, six slender instruments were nestled inside, each with a mushroom-shaped handle. Burins. But not like the ones my first tutor had used to teach me lithography. These were smaller, the handles slender and tapered in the middle. I started to reach for one of them, a small scythe, like the peasants used in the wheat fields. Remembering my manners, I stopped.

Zio pushed the box closer. "Go ahead."

I picked up the scythe and ran my fingers along its angled blade.

"They're yours." Zio leaned back in his chair and clasped his hands behind his neck. "I had them made for you."

That conversation I'd overheard in Pappa's study. Zio needed an engraver. Did he mean for it to be me?

Zio picked up one of the straight-edged burins. "It's smaller. More delicate. Made for a girl's hand. Your hand."

How many times had my hand cramped, grasping a paintbrush with a too-wide handle for too many hours? I hadn't complained. Pain and suffering were part of an artist's life. Like Michelango, crippled from all those years on his back, painting the Sistine Chapel. Or Rodin, his hands gnarled and twisted from wresting life from a marble block.

The blacksmith cleared his throat. "Signorina. Have you ever used one of these?"

I nodded. No need to tell him that it had been only once. Or that I'd struggled mightily to grasp what my old tutor said: I should focus on the blank space around where the pear would be and chisel out that space. I'd been skeptical: How could something come from nothing? Anyway, I didn't need burins when I had a canvas and paint. What a fool I'd been, so sure of what my life would be.

The blacksmith started to ask if I knew how to crosshatch.

Zio put up his hand. "Whatever she doesn't know, she can learn later. Now let's get started. I want that logograph for my next shipment."

Zio turned. He made his way to the window. Pappa followed. They started talking, too quietly for me to hear.

The blacksmith tapped my pomegranate with his hammer-hook finger. "You'll use the burin to trace this onto the copper. Just the pomegranate. No leaves or branches. Start with the straight edge." He held out the burin. "You'll be cutting through the paper onto the copper."

That had to be wrong. "I should trace it onto the copper," I said. "To preserve the sketch."

The blacksmith exhaled hard, annoyed. "It's a template, Signorina. Like embroidery. You do know how to do that, don't you?"

All those doilies and napkins Caterina had made for her trousseau. The daisy chains and rosettes traced on tissue paper; the needles that punctured the paper and pulled through the brightly colored thread. But I reminded myself. If Zio was right—and he was always right—my pomegranate would be everywhere. I wouldn't need my sketch.

I took the burin handle from the blacksmith's outstretched hand. As I did, Zuccheri took my pointer finger and put it on top of the blade. There was something improper about how he pressed down on my hand. I looked at Zio and Pappa—had they seen this disrespect? But they were too engrossed in conversation.

"Just an outline," the blacksmith whispered. "Not too deep." He smelled faintly of leather and manure. The blade penetrated the paper. Signore's breath was warm on my neck, like Teo's had been when we lay together on the oilcloth. "Keep an even pressure on the metal," Zuccheri added. There was a stirring in my belly that I hated myself for.

Signore stepped back abruptly. "You do it." His voice was husky.

I lifted the burin from the paper. "By myself?"

I was immediately furious with myself. I didn't need the blacksmith or anyone else to help me do my work. I tightened my grasp on the burin handle and probed the slit in the paper. I bore down, continuing along to the stem and then up the other side. Just the silhouette of the fruit, with the wedge cut out. I focused on the calyx, a crown like Persephone wore. Goddess of the Spring and then Queen of the Underworld. I kept my burin blade pressed to the copper. Each of the five points of the calyx. Then the wedge cut from the fruit. The pearly seeds, as perfectly round as the sphere. I lost track of time, like I did sometimes when I was working on something challenging. I made the final cut. The blacksmith returned. He picked up the tattered sketch, revealing the pomegranate on the gleaming surface of the copper plate. Just an outline. Fruit. Calyx. Seed. With none of the details or color that I would have added if I was painting. But it was good.

The blacksmith ran his fingers over the copper. He probed one of the points. "You went a little too deep here. But I can press it out so it sits right for Don Vito's printer."

"His printer?"

He nodded. "The guy at his factory. He makes sure the colors are right."

"But I can do the colors." Before I could tell him that Monsieur Laurent said my coloration was exceptional, he told me I'd be busy with other things.

"What things?" I asked.

He ignored me. "Just remember that an engraving must be done in reverse so that it's the same as the original. With this—." He motioned dismissively toward the pomegranate. "It doesn't matter. But in the future—."

My heart started beating faster. Before I could ask what he meant, he picked up my sketch. It hung in tatters, like the remains of a cut-out doll. He crumpled it into a ball, then tossed it into the brazier. It lay there for a moment, smoldering atop the charred almond shells. Then it burst into flames.

I tried not to think of that terrible fire. Of my paintings and sketch-pad, my paints and brushes, all consumed in the flames. I started to feel that lump in my throat I got before I started crying. If the blacksmith saw, he'd tell Zio I was too emotional to be trusted with anything important. I wanted this work—whether or not it was art, this was something I could do. I pressed my fingertips against my eyes, forcing the tears to retreat. And I waited for Zio.

CHAPTER 9

Mamma was frustrated. If she'd been born noble, she would have known the proper protocol for seating at a wedding banquet. For the last hour, though, she'd pored over the *Golden Book of the Sicilian Nobility* and was still no closer to understanding whether the Count of Sclafani should be seated closer to the bridal couple than the Count of Chiaramonte. More than three hundred wedding guests to be arranged on that immense seating chart, each one's family crest on a card piled next to Mamma, and the *Golden Book* as indecipherable as if it were in Greek.

Nonna was in her usual chair by the window, Caterina's trousseau chest open at her feet. The old woman was trying to finish the lacework on the chemise. If you looked closely, you could see the tiny crimson droplets along the seam edge. Caterina's blood. As the wedding drew nearer, my sister couldn't make even one stitch without pricking herself. Mamma chalked it up to excitement, but I'd begun to wonder if my sister meant to hurt herself. Maybe she thought the duke would call off the wedding. But the banns had been read. And Caterina would be wearing gloves.

In the hallway, there was a staccato of footsteps, each note measured and sure. Federico. Mamma thrust the card with the Sclafani crest into my hands and called for him.

The butler appeared. He gave a half-bow. "Yes, Donna Inglese?"

As usual, he seemed bored. Like he'd seen it all before. Maybe he had. His great-grandfather had come to Sicily from London with my great-great-grandfather, whose name had long been lost, having adopted *Inglese*—Englishman—soon after his arrival. Federico's grandfather and father had followed suit, spending their lives in service to the Inglese. It was understood that Federico's sons and grandsons would continue the tradition.

Mamma began to ramble. "The plasterer will finish today. Don Inglese has been called away. Again. You'll need to inspect the work. You know how peasants are. Always trying to pass off their inferior work."

"Yes, Signora." Federico's expression was unreadable.

"I don't know how it'll all get done. The wedding is in two weeks. We still need to finalize the Mass with Monsignor. Settle what's owed to Signora Cassata. Buy the Champagne. But now Vito is back, and he expects Nino to be at his beck and call. "

Nonna glared at Mamma. It was an inappropriate thing to say, especially in Federico's presence. But Mamma was right. Since Zio returned from New York, Pappa spent all his time with him. When I asked Pappa why Zio had returned so early—this trip was to have lasted a year, and it was less than six months—Pappa said Zio had his reasons.

"He's a businessman," Pappa told us, as if that was enough. But even I knew that this kind of change in plans wasn't good.

Mamma tried to wave Federico away. He didn't move. "Before he left this morning, Don Inglese informed me that Signore Cascioferro would be staying for dinner," Federico said. "The cook had planned to prepare pheasant. Should I instruct her to make the veal, instead?"

Mamma snorted. "Vito's favorite meal? No. We'll have the pheasant. Now go. Bring word when you've inspected the plastering."

Mamma thrust her hand toward me. I gave her back the Sclafani card. She pinned it to Table VI, where the Count of Lampedusa was already seated. The Lampedusas and the Sclafanis had been feuding for years. I didn't remind Mamma. Something was wrong. I think we all knew it.

When Pappa returned with Zio, it was late in the day. I was in the parlor, working on a sketch for Caterina. The drawing was of her favorite cat, Giorgio, an orange tabby who spent his days terrorizing the mice in Cook's kitchen, and the nights curled up on my sister's pillow. My sister would be gone soon, Nonna reminded me. It would be good for her to have something to call to mind home, a painting like the one of *Binvinutu* I'd begun for Rosalia, its ashes long since swept into the bin.

Zio strode into the parlor. "Mimi!" He embraced me, kissing one cheek, then the other. "I heard you were sick."

"Just a few days in February. I'm well now."

"No doubt thanks to your Nonna's care."

"Thanks to the Madonna," Nonna corrected.

But Zio was right. It was Nonna who'd sponged me down with frigid water, her fingers turning blue, and who'd cupped my chest, night and day, with such force that small, round bruises covered my skin. Whatever the Madonna had done, it was Nonna who kept the tuberculosis at bay.

After we finished dinner—veal marsala, the wine reduced to a syrup just like Zio liked it—the men remained at the table. Despite having been overruled about the pheasant (I suspected Nonna had made this decision), Mamma was in good cheer. Maybe she'd looked around at the smooth walls and restored mosaics and remembered it was because of Zio.

My godfather pushed back from the table. "I got fat in America." Zio rubbed his rounded belly. "Those Jews with their knishes. Like calzones, but with potato. Tasty. Not very healthful. But this," he gestured grandly toward the platter where the marsala sauce was congealing. "This makes a man strong. Like they say, 'meat makes meat.'"

Pappa raised his glass. "It's good to have you back, my friend." I wondered if this was true. When he'd read the telegram saying Zio was returning early from America, Pappa had cried out like he'd been struck.

Zio smiled. "It is good to be back in the bosom of friends."

Mamma raised her glass. "To friends. At least now you won't miss your goddaughter's wedding."

At the mention of her upcoming nuptials, Caterina started twisting the pinky ring Nonna had given her in hopes that she'd leave her torn-up cuticles alone.

Zio turned to Pappa. "You didn't tell them?"

"Tell us what?" Mamma's voice was shrill.

Pappa laid his hand on hers. "You need to stay calm."

People always tell you to stay calm when there's a good reason to be upset. Like the mine explosion. "Stay calm," Pappa had said, even as word arrived of the small bodies, twisted and charred beyond recognition. Or the terrible fungus that infested the wheat fields—"Stay calm," though it obliterated the harvest. Maybe Mamma was remembering, too, because she slid her hand out from under his.

Pappa downed his wine, then signaled for Federico to refill it. "There's been a change in plans. Vito has already informed the duke."

Mamma's mouth fell open. "What do you mean, 'a change in plans?' The guests have already responded. The banns have been announced. The dressmaker has done the final fitting."

Caterina stopped twisting the ring and whispered to Nonna, "I'm not getting married?" When Nonna didn't respond, my sister turned to Mamma. "Does this mean I can go to the convent?"

Mamma's mouth was opening and closing, like a fish hooked on a line.

Zio laughed. "My dear Caterina. A girl like you doesn't go to the nunnery. The young men would scream in outrage. They'd break down the convent door and steal you away. No. A girl like you becomes a bride. Not to some anemic man-boy like the duke's son. But a man who can be Romeo to your Juliet."

"She's marrying the duke's son!" Mamma banged the table. The tiny hand-cut crystals on the candelabra swung side to side like pendulums. "It's going to be the wedding of the year. All the best people are coming."

Zio snorted. "The *prominenti*. A bunch of washed up has-beens."

Mamma looked stunned, like she'd been struck. And what was it, if not a blow to everything she'd aspired to? The fancy houses. The extravagant parties. The air of superiority every noble woman wore like a sable around their shoulders.

Zio continued. "Nino has arranged a new match. More advantageous. Better for the future."

Mamma narrowed her eyes. "What do you mean, better?"

"Go ahead, my friend," Zio motioned to Pappa.

Pappa gulped down his wine. "Thank you, *compare*. The man we have in mind is smart. A hard worker. Hungry to make a name for himself."

Mamma sniffed. "The duke's son already has a name. One of the best in Sicilia. Caterina cannot marry below her station."

Zio laughed. "All this outdated thinking—about titles and stations. As if we hadn't fought a revolution to get rid of it all. If you haven't noticed, Maria, the nobility is finished. Has been since Garibaldi."

The mantle clock ticked by the minutes. Pappa broke the silence. "In time, we'll be glad it turned out this way."

"How will I ever face the Rosary Ladies?" Mamma said. "They'll assume Caterina behaved dishonorably. That's the only reason a wedding gets canceled this late."

"But we know the truth," Zio said. "Caterina is pure."

Mamma glared at Zio. Everyone knows that people prefer scandalous rumors over truth. "Even if she does marry this—Romeo, Monseigneur will never let us use the center aisle. She'll be married in the chancel, like a common servant or washerwoman."

Mamma began to weep. I can't say I blamed her. She'd spent most of the last year planning this wedding.

Zio reached across the table to take Mamma's hand. "That's the best part. Caterina won't be married here."

Mamma looked up, stunned. "But the wedding is always at the bride's church."

Zio stood and opened his arms wide. "Yes. But not when the wedding takes place in America!"

For a moment, there was silence. Then Zio continued. "Caterina's groom is already in New York. Oh, but I'm sorry. This is the job of the father. Please, Nino. Tell them what you've decided."

Pappa hesitated. This was Zio's plan, not his.

"He's from Avellino," Pappa said. "His name is Amoruso."

"That means lover," Zio interrupted, his eyes twinkling.

Pappa tried to smile. It looked more like a wince. "He went over to America three years ago. He's been working as a barber. A respectable occupation."

"And a lucrative one," Zio added.

"And his family?" Mamma asked. "Do they have properties in Palermo?" I could practically see Mamma scanning the As in the *Golden Book* for Amoruso.

Pappa answered that they were from Nicosia, near Catania.

"Tell them about how he's been supporting his family," Zio urged. "Sending money every month."

So much for the *Golden Book*. Some noble families might be struggling, but I'd never heard of a nobleman who'd gone to America to make his fortune. And Catania was on the east coast, cut off from the rest of Sicily by the Trapani Mountains. I don't think we knew a single noble family from there.

"He'll soon have enough to bring them all to America," Pappa said.

"Just in time for the wedding." Zio winked.

"Who will give Caterina away?" Mamma blurted out. "You, Vito?"

"I'll be there. But her Pappa will give her away." Zio smiled. "Her Mamma, too."

Mamma's mouth formed into a perfect O of surprise. "New York?" Mamma sputtered. "We're going to New York?"

Zio beamed. "Second Class on the *S.S. Sofia Hohenberg*. The tickets will be my wedding gift!"

Mamma's eyes bulged. She'd never traveled anywhere but Palermo. "But all that travel. I get seasick thinking about it."

Zio smoothed back his pomaded hair. "I traveled to America on the *Sofia*. Ten days. Like being rocked in a cradle."

"Ten days there and ten days back," Mamma corrected. "Almost a month of travel. I'm not sure I can—."

Pappa interrupted her. "It will only be one way, Maria. We'll be staying in New York for a little while."

Mamma turned on him. "What are you talking about?"

Zio rushed in. "You'll have a townhouse in the swankiest part of the city. Your neighbors will be doctors. Lawyers. All of them, *prominenti*. But self-made. The American way. You'll see, Maria. It'll be an adventure!"

"I don't want an adventure."

Pappa took Mamma's hand. "*Cara mia.* I know this isn't what we talked about. But it's a good thing. We can be rich in America. Richer than we could ever be here. You'll have everything you ever wanted. A house that's finer than any in Palermo. Indoor plumbing. Electric lights."

From the corner, Nonna asked what Pappa would be doing in America. I was surprised. Nonna was usually the first to know Pappa's plans. But maybe it had slipped her mind, like last month's visit from the Mother Superior of our local convent, where Nonna was chief patroness.

But when Pappa gently took the old woman's hands in his own, I understood this was news to her, too.

"I'll be working, Matri," Pappa said. "Managing Vito's new store. The biggest Sicilian market in the neighborhood."

Zio slapped Pappa's back. "Not just the neighborhood. It'll be the biggest market in all of New York City."

"This is what you want to do, Nino?" Nonna stood there, no rosary beads in hand. No appeals to the Madonna.

Pappa nodded. "It's my chance to do something and not be judged by my name, or my family's name, or the fact that I have no father."

Nonna shook her head. "I understand. Should I ask the Mother Superior to prepare a place for Mimi and me?"

Every fiber of my being screamed *No!* A cell in the convent, scarcely big enough for a narrow cot. The single, keyhole window, slender as a shard of glass.

"No nunnery, Matri," Pappa continued. "There's no money for that dowry. Anyway, you know how I feel. The family should stay together."

"But how, Nino? An old woman." She gestured toward me. "And an invalid. The Americans are strict. You need to be able to work. Provide for yourself."

I almost blurted out that I could work. I'd done the engraving of the pomegranate. I still had my burins.

Before I could say anything, Zio took Nonna's hand. "Let us worry about that, Donna Inglese."

And it was settled.

CHAPTER 10

I WAS IN THE PORTICO, doing one last sketch of the old chapel and the cemetery beyond, Rosalia's grave covered with wild irises. The carriage was already piled high—top heavy like one of those flamingos who perched on one spindly leg at the salt marsh in Marsala—when they tried to add another steamer trunk. As the trunk began to slip, the men fell over each other trying to grab hold of it. When it finally hit the ground, punctuated by the sound of crystal shattering, it felt like it had been falling a long time.

Mamma ran from the house. She fell on her knees beside the trunk. Even from where I stood, I could see the dent in the brass trim and the cracked wood panel.

The old Mamma would have fired the men on the spot, even though it was their last day here. But the new Mamma—the one who'd emerged since Zio told us we'd be moving to America—buried her head in her hands and sobbed.

Federico appeared. He set the trunk upright, the broken glass settling to the bottom. Standing beside Mamma, he asked if he should open the trunk. I was surprised when Mamma shook her head no. Then I remembered how long it had taken before I could bring myself to look out my window onto the cobblestones where that fire had been. There is a limit to what a person can bear.

The front door opened. Pappa and Nonna stepped out. Pappa was wearing a new wool traveling coat; Nonna wore her old cloak, turned gray from use. Mamma had insisted on buying us new coats from that impossibly expensive shop in Palermo that specialized in outfitting people for the colder weather on the Continent. Nonna refused, saying she was too old for new things.

Pappa must have heard the trunk crash, but he walked past Mamma. "*Amuninni*," he said, over his shoulder. "Let's go."

It was cruel, and Pappa wasn't cruel. Forgetting herself, Mamma wiped her nose on the sleeve of her velvet coat. She was once again the daughter of a hog butcher and wife of a bastard. It was as if she'd never been Inglese.

"Come on," Pappa repeated. "We need to stop at Vito's for the tickets."

I half-expected Mamma to say again that Zio should have given us the tickets yesterday. Or the day before. He'd been here almost every day for weeks, locked in the study with Pappa. But she just sat on the ground, shoulders slumped, chin on her chest.

Pappa paused to look at my sketch. He pointed to the chapel. "The old ways. It'll be good to be rid of them."

Maybe. But what about the chapel limestone, glowing in the morning light, or the irises that ran riot over the graveyard? I felt a heaviness inside. *Binvinutu* had been my prison, but already, I'd begun to miss it. Maybe that's how Persephone felt, always leaving one place or the other.

Having deposited Nonna in the carriage, Pappa returned to the house. When he came out again, Caterina was on his arm. She was tugging at the bodice of her new coat. The salesman in Palermo had insisted—coats, not cloaks, or people would know we were immigrants. *Guapparusi*, he spat out, the word itself, foul. I was glad to give away my cloak. Since I'd been sick, it hung on me like a banquet-size tablecloth on a tea table. The coat fit me better, though some fabric still puddled at my middle.

But there was no fabric pooling around Caterina's chest or belly. When she'd slipped it on in the store, the salesman had kissed his fingertips and said she was beautiful. But seeing her fuss with the collar and buttons, anyone could see she didn't feel beautiful. She'd been only four when we'd come to live at *Binvinutu* and had spent her life hidden under a veil and mantle. But this coat, with its wide lapels, nipped-in waist and flared hem, accentuated her full breasts and rounded hips. She'd have to get used to it. The trunk on the top of the carriage was filled with clothes like that.

Pappa had tried to talk Mamma out of those purchases. We'd be living amidst the *paesani*. It was better to be inconspicuous—that's how he put it. But Mamma had held up the ship's brochure and pointed to the photographs—the swanky dining room, the elegant reading room, the shuffleboard courts. They needed the proper attire, Mamma said. Who knew what *prominenti* we might be mixing with in Second Class?

I'd seen Pappa huddled over his ledger late at night, adding up endless columns of numbers. I tried not to worry about where he'd gotten the money for all those fancy clothes.

My own trunk was filled with black and gray blouses and skirts, folded neatly beside Nonna's faded gowns. One simple hat with a single ostrich feather, and a straw boater to protect against the sun—whatever sun there might be, that far north.

Pappa helped me to the carriage. Before I stepped onto the mounting block, I slipped my sketchpad into my satchel.

"Do you have your burins?" Pappa asked.

I nodded.

"Keep the box close." He must have said this to me ten times already, though Mamma's garnet necklace and bracelet were packed away in a trunk.

When we were settled into the carriage—Nonna and Mamma on the bench facing forward, Caterina and I across from them—Pappa pulled a key ring from his vest pocket.

"I'll be up front with the driver." He locked the carriage door, something I don't ever remember him doing. As we pulled away from *Binvinutu*, Mamma leaned out the carriage window, watching as the house receded. I could have reminded her of Lot's wife. Nothing good came from looking back.

Just outside Pappa's ruined sulfur mine, kudzu vines snaking up and around the trees and making it nearly impossible to see the boarded-up entrance, Nonna pulled out her rosary. Sitting across from her, Caterina followed suit, slipping her precious mother-of-pearl rosary from its pale lavender pouch. They were reverse images of each other—crone and maiden, dark and light, Demeter and Persephone—but both certain that the Madonna had a plan and that things happened for a reason. I felt a flicker of jealousy for their blind faith.

I felt for the burin box in my satchel, each instrument tucked into its place on the satin. Zio had hinted there'd be work for me in the United States. Another logograph. Maybe something more. Anything was possible. Hadn't Mary Cassatt, one of the greatest artists of our time, come from America? Elizabeth Gardner, too, though people said she was little more than Bouguereau's slut. Still, she'd lived openly with the painter. Sharing his studio and his bed. No Siciliana, peasant or noble, could do that.

Dr. Florio opposed the move, though he'd reluctantly given Nonna the name of a "lung man" in New York.

"Still, I advise against it," he'd told her at my last appointment. "Three and a half million people there. Ten times the number as in Palermo. All that garbage. The cold air. The disease passed from person to person. Signorina will have a relapse. She could die."

Nonna tucked the card into her skirt pocket, next to her rosary. "They're doing new things in America. Building hospitals. Doing research. The cure will come from there."

My heart leapt. A cure.

Dr. Florio shook his head. "Consumption has been with us for thousands of years. The best we can hope for is to make the sufferers more comfortable."

Nonna appeared to think for a moment before she continued. "When my granddaughter first got sick, you thought she wouldn't survive. Yet here she is. You have all these fancy degrees"—Nonna gestured toward the wall of baroque-framed certificates—"but you suffer from a lack of faith. I'll keep my granddaughter well in America. Until they find a cure."

Jostling along that road, I felt the same lightness I'd felt when I left Dr. Florio's office that day. Things might be different in America. I might be whole again.

CHAPTER 11

IT WAS WARM IN THE CARRIAGE. Mamma dozed, her jaw slack; Nonna snored softly. After about an hour, the driver started down the mountain. Caterina looked up from her beads, her eyes wide. We'd traveled down this road to Palermo so many times—to the opera or a society ball, or to Christmas and Easter services at Monreale. But she always seemed to forget that while the horses might momentarily lose their footing, sending pebbles skittering down the path, the harness around their rear haunches held fast.

Trying to hold my annoyance at bay, I asked if she wanted to read from the Liturgy of the Hours.

Caterina took out the small book. She'd placed scraps of ribbon between the leaves to mark her favorite saints. Gold for Santa Agata, forced into a brothel and then tortured, her breasts pulled off with a pair of pinchers. Red for Santa Lucia, who had her eyes gouged out and her skin flayed. Drab brown for Caterina's favorite, Santa Rosalia, who'd lived as a hermit, devoting herself to prayer and contemplation.

"Rosalia's cave was there." Caterina pointed toward the mountains, purple in the morning haze. "She lived alone. But the Madonna was with her." Caterina was looking in the distance, at something I couldn't see. "I know where she is. The Madonna showed me."

For a moment, I didn't know what to say. Caterina sounded crazy, like the beggar who wandered the streets of town, hitting himself in the head and chest and yelling at *streghe*—witches—that no one else could see. But I reminded myself, my sister was nervous. Things would be better once we were settled in New York City.

"Let's read another story." I opened to the gold ribbon. Agata.

"They're not stories," Caterina corrected. "They're the word of God."

"Yes, of course." But if the lives of the saints weren't stories, I don't know what was. My finger on the first line of the passage, I started reading aloud. "*With a festal spirit as though to a wedding banquet. Agata went to prison—*"

Caterina interrupted. "What's that?" She pointed out the window.

I half-expected she was imagining things again. But when I leaned out, there was a cloud of dust just behind us. The sound of horses' hooves, dull against the dirt road. As the galloping got closer, pebbles struck the undercarriage. Strange men's voices. Nonna woke, immediately alert. She touched Mamma's leg, then put her finger to her lips. It was no use.

"Bandits!" Mamma screamed. "Oh, Madonna!"

The hooves came closer, surrounding the carriage. I heard the cocking of rifles. Our driver slowed.

"Where do you think you're going?" an unfamiliar voice demanded.

Pappa answered that we were on our way to Palermo. His voice sounded strained. He was trying to stay calm.

The man didn't stand aside. "This is a private road."

I thought Pappa would say the man was mistaken. Because this was the road we'd taken every time we went to Palermo. No one had ever stopped us before.

Instead, Pappa said that it was the only way through the mountains. For a moment, it was so quiet I could hear the high-pitched whistling of the starlings hiding in the splurge beside the road.

"What's in these trunks?" the man demanded.

Too quickly, Pappa said, "Household goods. Clothes. Nothing of value."

The bandit snorted. "Who's inside the carriage?" Too late, I realized we should have closed the shades. Because there he was. In the window. He smiled, his teeth tobacco-stained.

"Ah. Here's where the valuable cargo is." His eyes passed over me and settled on Caterina. I reached into my satchel. My hand found the straight edge burin. I don't know what I was thinking—he had a shotgun slung over his shoulder and a round of ammunition around his waist.

Before I could make another move, Pappa jumped down from the coach bench and appeared at the window. He flattened his hand against the door frame so that he was between us and the bandit.

"Tell me, friend," Pappa asked, his voice stronger now. "Who owns this road?"

Caterina held her book to her breast. Her lips moved in silent prayer.

The bandit leered at her. Another man appeared behind him, cradling his shotgun.

With one arm still on the window frame, the first bandit reached for Caterina. "You're a pretty one, aren't you?" She pressed herself against the bench but still his filthy fingers brushed her cheek. I took hold of the burin handle, pressing it against my palm.

Pappa repeated his question, his voice sharp. "Did you hear what I asked you?" Pappa slipped his hand into the pocket where he kept his pistol. "Who does this road belong to?"

I held the burin even more closely, I tried to work out the logistics. But what was an old man with a pistol and an invalid with a burin against a horde of bandits with shotguns?

The bandit answered. "It's Don Vito Cascioferro's road. His private road. If you want to pass through, you'll have to pay. And it's expensive." He lunged for Caterina, catching a bit of her skirt.

Zio never would have allowed this. But Zio wasn't here. I held the burin even more closely, the blade knife-sharp against my palm.

"Good." Pappa kept one hand on his pistol. With the other, he reached into his vest.

"Careful, old man," the second bandit warned.

Pappa drew out a folded piece of paper and held it out to the first man.

"You read it," the man demanded. Of course. He was a peasant. Illiterate.

"It's a letter from Don Cascioferro." Pappa unfolded it. "Ensuring safe passage to America."

"Are you the engraver?" he asked Pappa. He must be talking about the blacksmith. There was respect in his voice.

Pappa ignored the question. "Signore and I are business partners. I'm going to America to open some stores there."

The bandit eyed Pappa suspiciously. "Don Cascioferro takes care of his own business in America. Why would he send you?"

After Pappa carefully refolded the paper and put it back in his pocket, he responded. "You'll have to ask him that yourself."

"And all of you are going? Even the girl?" He motioned toward Caterina.

Pappa didn't even look at my poor sister. "Yes. She's part of the plan." Pappa's voice was so cold that it sent shivers down my spine. "But you can check with Don Cascioferro. Send a man ahead to Palermo. Our ship leaves at five." Pappa took out his pocket watch. "There's probably still time. But the Don will be unhappy if we miss it. There isn't another boat for a week."

I'd never seen Zio angry, but from the way the bandit grimaced, he had. He stepped back from the carriage. But the others started protesting, saying they should hold us hostage or at least take the luggage. That's when the bandit pointed his shotgun into the sky and fired it. There was the flutter of wings, as all at once the starlings took flight.

After the men had gone and the sound of the horses' hooves was only a distant thrumming, Pappa unlocked the carriage door. It was a flimsy lock. It wouldn't have kept anyone out.

"Everyone all right?" Pappa asked.

"Yes, we're fine," Nonna said. At some point, she must have put her arm around Mamma, who was clinging to her like a frightened child.

"And you girls? Are you all right?"

Not trusting myself to speak, I nodded. Caterina did, too.

I thought Pappa would reassure us. Tell us that the bandits wouldn't have hurt us. Or that Zio's letter would keep us safe from whatever perils might come. But he just turned away. A moment later, he stepped up the carriage steps and settled onto the bench again.

It was then that I felt the stickiness on my palm. I pulled my hand from my satchel. I was still holding the burin. When I released it, blood seeped from a gash on my thumb where I'd been grasping the blade. Nonna gave me her handkerchief. I wrapped it around my finger. The carriage started again, my thumb throbbing as blood flowed onto that cloth.

CHAPTER 12

JUST PAST THE CITY GATE in Palermo, I half-expected the driver to turn right onto the street that led to Monsieur Laurent's *atelier*. But the driver continued. Past the Piazza Marino, with its huge strangler fig, some branches reaching greedily upward while others obeyed a more diabolical imperative, growing downward, into darkness.

Deeper into the city, past the stalls selling fried artichokes and fresh macaroni. Past the houses of the *puviri*, festooned with garlands of orange peels to mask the rank odor. Further still, past the barefoot fisherwomen hawking their wares in short sleeves, their skirts just grazing their ankles. The air was cooler here, briny with sea air.

The bell tower clock struck one, the deep reverberation echoing down the narrow streets.

"Those damn bandits are going to make us late," Pappa said from the coach bench.

"We're close to Don Cascioferro's factory," the driver replied, the first words I'd heard him say since we'd left *Binvinutu*.

At the seawall, we turned west, past the piers, with the ocean liners lined up, one dazzling ship after another. I thought I saw our ship, the *Sofia Hohenberg*, its red and green flag waving in the wind. Further out, brightly colored *barca* tossed in the waves like toy boats. Then we were at the sea fortress, moving along its crumbling yellow walls. The road rose steeply after that, the seawall the only thing that kept us from tumbling off the cliff. Near the top, the driver turned away from the waterfront and onto a side street. A few men milled about. I shuddered, seeing how much they resembled the bandits, with bullet-studded bandoliers and rifles slung over their shoulders.

We stopped in front of a warehouse that took up an entire block. Two stories, with shutters left open to let in the air. The sound of machines filled the air. *Click-a, click-caaah,* followed by the snap of release and the whirring of a wheel.

Pappa jumped down and started toward the factory.

Mamma leaned out the window. "Where are you going? Nino!"

Before he disappeared into the warehouse, he called out over his shoulder that he was just getting the tickets.

Mamma kept ranting. "You can't leave us here! It's dangerous! All these men with their guns. Oh, Madonna. I'm going to be sick. Nino. Nino!"

Nonna looked up from her beads. "Enough, Maria. This is Vito's factory. No one's going to hurt us here."

A moment later, the warehouse doors swung open. Mamma dug her fingernails into my arm.

"The bandits," Mamma hissed.

But these weren't bandits. Each was pushing a hand truck loaded high with crates. One turned to load his crates onto a lorry.

Caterina cried out. "Mimi! It's your drawing!"

There, printed in crimson on the crates, was my pomegranate, with MERCANTINI IMPORT EXPORT above it.

The warehouse doors swung open wide. Zio walked out, Pappa trailing behind. Before the doors slammed shut, I saw what looked like dozens—no, hundreds—of crates inside, all with my logograph, stacked on floor-to-ceiling shelves.

Zio walked toward our carriage. "Mimi!" he called. "Where's my artist?" He pulled open the door. After he greeted Nonna, Mamma and Caterina, he reached out to me. "Come. I want to show you the operation."

"Me?"

"Of course, you. I thought you'd like to see your engraving. The practical side of art."

My hand tucked under his arm, I went inside the factory. I glanced back toward Pappa but there was so much commotion—so many machines and boxes and carts—that I quickly lost sight of him. The smell was overpowering. The piney scent of turpentine combined with fishy linseed oil. I pulled my scarf over my nose and mouth to keep from breathing it in. Zio steered me down a hallway, toward a room at the end. Inside was a machine with a large drum and an immense wheel. A young man struggled to turn the wheel. His shirt was damp with sweat, and his turned-up sleeves revealed thickly muscled forearms.

"Luca!" Zio called.

The man looked up. "Don Cascioferro."

Zio turned to me. "Luca is our printer."

The young man nodded but his hands remained on the wheel. I watched as he rolled the canister to the end, then returned it to where he'd started. He pulled up a swath of canvas and then peeled away a piece of paper. On it was my pomegranate.

Zio asked how the printing was going.

"The label?" Luca asked, as if there was something else he was working on.

Zio nodded.

"It's going well. We should be ready to ship the crates by the end of the week."

Zio clapped Luca on the back. "Bene. Luca, I'd like to present Signorina Inglese. Our artist."

The blood rose in my cheeks. The pomegranate was hardly a masterpiece. Still, Luca was looking at me with something like admiration. Like I wasn't just a too-skinny girl with dark circles under her eyes and hollowed-out cheeks. I wasn't a curiosity, like that duck-billed creature they'd just discovered in Australia. Not bird. Or fish. Or mammal.

I guess Zio saw it, too.

"You're famous here. You and your pomegranate. Luca, why don't you show Signorina how you're using her engraving plate to make the labels?"

"Of course." Luca stood so quickly that he bumped his knee on the table leg.

I felt light—like at any moment, I might fly away. Maybe this was what beautiful women felt like all the time. It would be hard to be modest with men acting like that.

Luca lifted the cover of the printing press and picked up my plate from the printing bed. He held it gently, like it was something precious. "First, we ink the engraving." He picked up cloth stained with dark red ink, the same shade as the logo. He rubbed the cloth against the copper using a circular motion. "Then we wipe it off. See? The ink stays in the cuts you made with your burin."

Basic intaglio printing. Every artist knew the method.

"How do you use the machine?" I was surprised at the impatience in my voice. If Luca was offended, he didn't show it.

"Once the drum is inked, you put the plate here." He put the engraving back on the bed. "Then you roll the drum on top of it. Like this." He took hold of the wheel and turned it. The drum moved forward.

"So it's like a hand press."

"You know about that?" Luca was beaming like I'd given him a gift. "Yes, it's like a hand press. But bigger."

"Why does it need to be bigger?"

"To make more prints. You lay the engraving plates in here. Side by side. You can do ten, twenty prints at once." Luca rolled the cylinder all the way forward.

"But you'd need more engraving plates. More copies," I asked, thinking of how easy it would have been to copy that stupid pomegranate. I could have made fifteen or twenty plates. At twenty lire a plate, Zio would have paid me four hundred lire. With that much money, maybe we wouldn't have had to leave *Binvinutu*.

Zio waved Luca away. I was sorry to see him go.

My godfather took my hand. "I'm glad you stopped by, my dear.

Now you know both parts of the operation—the engraving and the printing. Those are useful things to know."

I thanked him, though I couldn't imagine how any of it would be helpful.

"It's good that you have those burins. There is a lot of work for engravers in America. Logographs, like the pomegranate. But other things, too. If you stay open to those opportunities, you'll do well there."

"I can help Pappa at his store," I offered.

"No, Mimi. I'm talking about real work. Your work. As an *artist*." Zio placed his hand on my shoulder. "You think that part of your life is over," he continued, his voice gentler than I'd ever heard it. "But there are great things for you in America. Do you understand what I'm telling you, goddaughter? That's where your destiny lies."

He reached into his vest for a cigar. "There's a woman in America I want you to meet. Her name is Stella Frauto." He struck a match against the bottom of his shoe.

"Is she an artist?"

Zio smiled. "She is many things. You'll see. In America, an ambitious woman can go as far as any man. Especially if she has talent."

Ambitious. I'd never heard any woman described like that.

"I want to help my family." The appropriate thing to say, though the moment the words left my mouth, I heard how insincere they sounded.

Zio exhaled, a gray ring rising toward the rafters. "You're a good girl, Mimi. An obedient daughter. But it's all right to want more."

I wanted to ask what he meant. Before I could figure out how, the clock tower struck 1:30.

Zio waved me toward the door. "Come. The ship will be boarding soon."

On the way out, we passed a table where a man was stooped over a palette. Ink, not paint, judging by its flat texture. Bluish-green. Could he be here to add color to my pomegranate? But there were no leaves or branches on my logo. He must have been doing something else for Zio. A wave of jealousy washed over me. I reminded myself: I was going to America. I was going to make real art and be independent, like that woman, Stella Frauto.

I was already back in the carriage, headed down toward the harbor, before I realized Zio hadn't told me how to find her.

CHAPTER 13

THE *S.S. SOFIA HOHENBERG* was a sturdy ship, with a black belly, a gleaming white top and portholes running from front to back. But the ship, like her namesake—the wife of Duke Ferdinand, a woman who was too low-born to be queen—was outclassed. To the one side, the sleek, modern *Oceanic*; to the other, the *Bulgaria,* half again as tall. Just the kind of thing to start Mamma complaining.

Our driver left us at the Second Class boarding ramp and headed toward Baggage to drop our luggage. We climbed the short ramp to the ship, Pappa in front, Mamma and Caterina just behind, Nonna and I in the back. A young man stood at the top, a tray of Champagne glasses in hand and a crisp linen towel slung over his arm. He was about my age. Handsome, with straw-colored hair and hazel eyes.

The man offered Pappa a glass. "Welcome aboard, Don Inglese." He turned to me. "Mademoiselle?"

I reached for a glass.

Mamma slapped down my hand. Later, I'd get an earful about how proper girls didn't drink alcohol.

"*Sono desolato.*" After bowing to Mamma in formal apology, the young man turned to Pappa. "I am Hans. Your steward. *Benvenuti a bordo.* Please, this way to your cabins." He spoke Italian, not Sicilian. Pappa followed him anyway.

On the Steerage Deck below us, the *puviri* had just begun to board. Already, it was crowded. Above us was First Class. Mamma was staring up at it, like a child with her nose pressed up against the window of a toy shop. When Zio said it would attract less attention for us to travel Second Class, Mamma had been so disappointed she didn't talk for a week. Hans led us inside the ship. An orchestra was playing. Vivaldi or Schubert. Something celebratory. Past the clusters of women in their pastel gowns and men in their morning coats, all sipping Champagne. One woman held a tiny dog with a rhinestone collar.

"Your cabins are mid-ship," Hans said. "The most comfortable in Second Class. Hardly any rolling." He held out his hands, palm-down, and moved them from side to side.

"Rolling?" I asked.

"The *mal de mer*. Seasickness. It's less bad here."

He stopped at a cabin with double doors. "Signore and Signora." He opened the door for my parents. "We set sail at six. I'll reserve a table for you on the Promenade Deck. That's up front."

"Grazie, Hans." Pappa reached into his vest pocket and pulled out a roll of crisp bills. Not violet or gray-blue, like the five or ten lire note. No, these were the same blue-green I'd seen at Zio's factory. There were 5s in the corners. He gave the bill to Hans.

Hans bowed. He closed my parents' door, then led Nonna, Caterina and me to the cabin next door. It had two beds and a small dresser. The room was so narrow that if you sat on one bed, you could easily reach the other. A cot was wedged into the corner. Hans left. Nonna slipped her rosary beads from her pocket and went down on her knees. Caterina followed. Together they knelt, eyes closed, praying for whatever it was they prayed for. I reached into my satchel, my knuckles brushing against my burin box, and pulled out my sketchpad. I sketched quickly. Hans's head. His hair, thick. Straight. The V of his torso. His narrow hips.

Before I knew it, a half-hour had passed and Pappa was at our door. "Come on deck. It's time to say our goodbyes."

Nonna begged off, saying she was tired. Caterina tried to, as well, but Mamma wouldn't hear of it.

"You need to be seen," Mamma said, smoothing out Caterina's skirts. She turned toward me. "You, too. But leave that here," she gestured toward my sketchpad. For a moment, I considered hiding it in the waistband of my skirt—I wanted to finish my sketch of Hans. But I'd be on this ship for ten days with Mamma. I didn't need to get on her bad side this early. I tucked the sketchpad under my pillow.

My sister and I followed Mamma and Pappa out to the deck. The ship was moving under our feet, making me feel unsteady. I thought about the rolling motion Hans had made with his hands.

I asked if we'd left port.

Pappa smiled. "You'll know it when we set sail, my dear." A long time ago, he'd been a soldier in the Navy, stationed in the Red Sea. He never talked about it. He was hurt over there. Sometimes, when it rained, he limped.

We found the table with the *RESERVED* card, *Inglese* written in fancy script. Pappa straightened the card. Hans appeared. He offered Pappa another glass of Champagne. "It's Monopole. Our signature Champagne. We'll be embarking at exactly six. Captain Wagner is a stickler for time."

Pappa nodded. "Ship's captains set their watches by the stars."

Hans smiled. "At sea, you can see every star God ever made." His eyes met mine. "The Milky Way. You've never seen anything so beautiful."

I looked up. The sky was cloudless. A blank canvas.

Mamma cleared her throat, impatient. Hans got the hint. He asked whether there was anything else we needed.

Mamma placed her hand to her throat. "I'm parched. Bring me something. Without spirits."

"And the young ladies?" Hans asked.

Mamma flicked her wrist. "They can have the same."

Hans returned with another glass of Monopole for Pappa and three glasses of ginger lemonade. He set the glasses before us. "The captain's about to strike the bell for embarkation."

Already, passengers had begun to gather at the railing. Beautiful women in couture gowns, their hair piled high in elaborate updos, their breasts nearly spilling out of their tight, low-cut bodices. They were Continentals, or maybe wealthy Americans, completing their Grand Tour of Europe. No Sicilian woman would wear something so immodest.

Pappa stood, his Champagne glass in hand. "Come, my dears. Let's go to the railing to bid *au revoir*." I got to my feet.

Caterina followed. But Mamma grabbed her elbow. "We'll stay here, Caterina. We don't want to be molested." Again, that reminder. Men were stirred to passion when they saw my sister. Me, they didn't even notice. But I reminded myself: there was freedom in invisibility.

I joined Pappa at the railing. He motioned to the right, beyond the small colorful boats bobbing in the waves. "That way is France and England. Straight ahead is America." He squinted as if, by doing this, he could see those countries from here.

Below us, the steerage deck was crowded with passengers grasping string bags or paper sacks. They stood shoulder to shoulder, calling to well-wishers on the dock. A sea of black, gray and brown. Some *puviri* cupped their hands around their mouths and called to others on the dock, though their words must have been lost in the crowd's roar.

Pappa gestured toward them. "They're here to say goodbye. Most will never see each other again."

Pappa promised we'd return some day. Maybe Caterina or her children would. But for Nonna, and probably me, this would be a one-way voyage.

The ship's bell sounded, a deep, sonorous tolling. Down below, the deckhands threw off the ropes tethering the ship to the dock. We eased away. A cry went up among the *puviri* and their well-wishers. Excited hollering, but gasps and cries, too.

Pappa took my hand in his. "Don't be sad, *cara*." He pressed my hand to his lips.

But I wasn't sad. I knew how it would have been if I'd stayed in Sicily. My world getting smaller, as Pappa sold off more of *Binvinutu* and the people I loved passed from my life—Nonna, Pappa, Caterina. Like a tapestry left in the sun, the colors would fade, leaving my life sun-bleached and fragile. In time, I might even forget that I'd once had ideas, and that my art had allowed me to express them.

"In New York, we'll live in a fancy house near the park," Pappa continued. "Go to the opera. To the moving picture show. There's even a circus there."

I thought of my burins, tucked into their case. Zio said I could make money with them. With that money, I could buy some paints. Maybe even oils—who would know? I could find a quiet place in that park. Paint something that I wanted to paint. Be an artist again.

"Yes, Pappa." I looked at the crowd below. Amidst the black-gray sameness of steerage, bits of color began to appear. Like flecks of paint on a blank canvas. "What is that?" I asked.

"Yarn. A farewell tradition among the *puviri*."

Holding fast to the tails, the steerage passengers began tossing balls of yarn to well-wishers on the dock. Soon the air was filled with hundreds of tendrils of yarn. Pink, red, yellow, green, blue. A rainbow connecting the ship to shore. I imagined catching one of those balls and holding it, taut as a line with a fish caught on it.

The ship's bell sounded again.

"More Champagne?"

Pappa turned toward the waiter—not Hans—and held out his glass. He launched into a series of questions: Where was the waiter from? Where had he last sailed? How long had he been with the steamship company? Between answers, the young man glanced from left to right. He was anxious to be off, refilling other glasses. Pappa didn't notice.

The ship continued to ease away from the dock. The yarn unspooled. Meters and meters of color stretched over the water. A tingle ran down my spine. The story of Noah and his ark. The rainbow, God's promise that the storms had passed, and better days were ahead. Looking at all those colors, I felt hopeful, like I imagine Noah would have been when he'd first seen all those clouds part and those colors appear.

The ship began to pull away from the dock. The passengers and well-wishers each struggled to keep hold of their ends of the yarn. The ship blew its horn again. We eased further from the dock. The yarn grew tauter. The arcs flattened. One by one, the strands broke free, billowing upward, like fantastical spirals of smoke. The next moment, they fell to the sea, where they disappeared below the surface.

CHAPTER 14

AFTER WE DEPARTED PALERMO, I stayed on deck with Pappa while Mamma and Caterina went to prepare for dinner. The other women on the Second Class deck had gone, too. The men remained, talking loudly and slapping each others' backs. Pappa raised his hand to summon the waiter. When the waiter arrived—not Hans, but another man, again—Pappa ordered a brandy. "And one for my daughter, too." His voice was slowed, his words dulled. How much Champagne had he drunk?

The waiter brought my drink. He placed it on a linen napkin. My stomach felt queasy. I forced myself to take a sip.

"Brandy is a businessman's drink." Pappa's lower lip curled in disgust. "And you're a businessman. Or at least that's what Vito thinks." Pappa gulped down the rest of his drink and threw his glass over the railing. "For *bona furtuna*." He turned toward me. "And God knows we'll need all the luck we can get over there." I expected him to slip his hand into his pocket and draw out his lucky coin. Instead, he breathed in and out slowly, the way he did when he was trying to control his anger. The bright sound of a violin floated up from Steerage.

Just beyond the waves was Monte Monaco, the northeast cliff long ago used by Arab soldiers guarding against attack. That was the story of Sicily—one invasion after another, until it was impossible to know who was the victor, and who the vanquished. But the *puviri* didn't seem to be thinking about the blood spilled by their ancestors, or their responsibility to this place. They'd abandoned the tiny plots their families had worked for generations. Having let go of Sicily, they'd turned toward the future. To want only what was before you—how freeing that would be.

The ship made its way toward the open ocean. Just above the horizon, the perfect crescent moon floated like an image painted on the backdrop for a play. My tutor said the moon is always there, even when you can't see it. I took the pencil from my clutch. Smoothing my cloth napkin, I began to sketch. Lightly at first, just a hint of the orb—even that part hidden from view. Then a sharper delineation. Dark and Light. The curved edge and tapered top and bottom. I drew by feel, my eyes never leaving that sliver.

The ship began to pitch up and down. I kept my eyes on that slipper moon. Suddenly, the ship rose sharply. When it came down, I fell into the railing. I looked down at the sea below. A wave of nausea passed over me.

Pappa took my hand. "Keep your eyes on the horizon."

Men milled around the deck. The last thing I wanted was to be sick in front of them. I tried to focus on the line where sea met sky. But I'd begun to sweat. I was salivating, the taste in my mouth bitter and metallic. I gagged, then vomited, a disgusting stream of yellowish-green liquid splashing across the deck in front of me. There was the scurrying of feet and the sound of a bucket being dragged from somewhere near. Pappa pulled me to my feet. My bodice was wet and smelled of brandy and vomit. People stared. I squeezed my eyes closed. Pappa's arm was around my shoulders. Leaning heavily on him, I staggered back to my cabin.

It was only much later that I realized I'd abandoned my sketch of the moon on the table.

By the time Pappa brought the ship's doctor, I wasn't thinking about my drawing, or the vomit on the deck, or the men staring. All I was thinking was that I wanted to die.

"It started just outside the port," Pappa told the doctor. "It's been worse since Gibraltar."

The doctor stood by my feet. He was writing in a black notebook he had propped against his round belly. Nonna was watching him.

The doctor didn't look up. "Two days. And she's taken no food or drink?" The doctor's fingers looked like sausages. I was sorry the moment I thought it. I dry-heaved into the basin.

"She's got to start eating. And drinking. That's even more important." The doctor tucked his notebook and pen into his bag. He pulled out a stethoscope and held up its bell. "I need to examine the Signorina."

Pappa stepped forward. "Is that really necessary? You said it yourself. It's seasickness."

The doctor asked Nonna to help sit me up.

They handled me like I was a rag doll. After the doctor had looked in my nose and mouth, he put the bell over my chest. His eyes narrowed, then widened, as he moved from confusion to clarity.

"Off with the nightdress. I need to get a better listen to her lungs."

Pappa put out his hand. "We should let her rest." I could hear the fear in his voice. "That's the only thing that really helps when you're seasick—."

Nonna tugged at my nightgown. I tried to push her away. The doctor held my arms. Nonna wrested the gown from me. The overhead fan was turning slowly, a slight catch with each revolution. Shivering in the breeze, I felt my nipples harden. I tried not to think about Pappa standing nearby.

The doctor placed his stethoscope on my back. Dr. Florio had always warmed the bell, that act a small mercy. This doctor didn't bother. He placed it flat on my skin. Once, twice, a dozen times. Probing, like Cook checking for rotten spots on a melon.

"Deep breath," he ordered.

I tried to do what he said but I started coughing.

The doctor put his sleeve over his mouth. That's how I knew he knew. His hand gently on my back, he eased me down on the bed. His thick fingers probed the incisions. I saw them again, the way I had the first time Dr. Florio removed the bandages.

The ship's doctor sighed heavily. "Who treated her?"

Nonna answered that it was Dr. Florio, at the *Villa Igaie.*

"I know of him. He did this?" I saw rather than felt him brush his fingers across the scars.

"Yes."

"The surgical cure. I've heard they've had good results. Did he do a total collapse of the lung?"

Nonna nodded.

"She's been well since?"

"Yes." Nonna didn't mention the cold I'd had last winter or those foul poultices.

I was grateful when the doctor pulled the sheet over me.

"Sometimes the sea air irritates the lungs. A consumptive must take care to stay inside."

No problem there, I thought. Just the thought of being back on that rolling deck made me retch again.

The doctor placed his hand on my back. "You will feel better, Signorina." He reached into his pocket and drew out a small pouch. He gave it to Nonna. "She'll need to take one of these every four hours until the vomiting passes. Signorina's health is fragile. Dehydration can be the beginning of the end for a consumptive."

That kind of thing usually made Nonna roll her eyes and mutter about how the speaker was being *melodrammaticu.* Instead, Nonna untied the pouch and emptied its contents into her hand.

"It's belladonna," the doctor explained. "To treat the vomiting."

Nonna nodded.

"Do you know about belladonna?"

Pappa interrupted. "My mother is a trained nurse."

The doctor raised his eyebrows. Respectable ladies weren't nurses. "If you're trained, Signora," he said, the emphasis on the *if,* "you know about the importance of correct dosing. One pill at a time. Never closer than four hours."

"Because of the hallucinations," Nonna said.

"Yes. She'll take the pill by rectum until the vomiting stops."

Pappa interrupted. "That's not necessary. Mimi's a good girl. She'll take the pill."

The doctor put his stethoscope back into his satchel. "She could be the Virgin Mary herself. We have to get that pill into her. If she doesn't stop vomiting, there's a good chance she'll relapse."

Pappa whispered something to the doctor.

The doctor snapped shut the satchel. "I'm sorry the rectal administration offends your sensibilities, Sir. But do you understand what will happen if she has active signs of the disease when we arrive in New York harbor?"

"We have a letter from Dr. Florio, saying she's well."

The doctor shook his head. "But she isn't well. And things will be worse—much worse—if the consumption returns. She'll be shipped back to Sicily. Or to Quarantine Island, outside New York harbor. Hundreds of sick steerage passengers are dropped there every day. A miasma of diphtheria, cholera, scarlet fever. How long do you think Signorina will last? There's a cemetery on that island. When burials get backed up, they burn the bodies. Is that what you want, Signore Inglese? Now please, wait outside. I'll come out when we're done."

Pappa left the cabin. The doctor told Nonna to help me onto my side.

"Knees to your chest," the doctor ordered.

I did as he said.

He pushed my top leg forward.

"Hold her there."

Nonna was barely a hundred pounds but I couldn't move if I tried. I wrapped my arms around my chest. My heart was pounding.

The ship's doctor spread my buttocks. I gasped when he inserted his finger inside me. He pulled it out, then put it in again, holding my rectum open as he inserted the pill. A cry escaped my lips. I made myself remember: Walking the fields before dusk, my sketchpad in hand. Rising to find my easel standing at the window, my paint palette waiting. The same places I'd retreated to whenever Nonna put those terrible poultices on my chest.

I was vaguely aware of the doctor stepping back. He was breathing heavily, like a pig left in its pen at midday. There was the sound of water being poured into the metal washbasin. Nonna released her hold on me.

The doctor opened the door. Pappa stepped back inside. His eyes on the floor, Pappa asked how long it would be before I was well.

"The seasickness usually resolves by the fourth or fifth day. By the time we reach the Sargasso Sea."

I tried to remember where that was. Before we left, Pappa had run his finger across the globe in his study. The blue expanse, stretching from Old World to New. I remembered the words: *Sargasso Sea,* in small print, somewhere on the edge of things. But I couldn't recall where.

"Two or three days from now?"

"Yes, usually by the time we're about halfway across."

"She'll be better by New York?" Pappa's voice was tight. He was nervous now. I looked at the doctor to see his response.

"Most patients are fully recovered by then."

"So the authorities don't need to know about this," Pappa asked, though it wasn't a question.

"I don't *have* to mention it, as long as the passenger is well by the time I do my medical clearance." The doctor rocked on his heels. "The authorities expect that the ship's doctor will exercise his discretion in reporting such things, especially among our more delicate First and Second Class passengers."

"I understand." Pappa put his hand in his pocket. I thought he was reaching for his lucky coin. Instead, he took out his wallet. "Thank you for your consideration." He pulled out one of those blue-green bills.

The doctor hesitated for a moment before palming the bill. "Signora has enough pills to last until the Sargasso. I'll come and see the young lady then."

When they were all gone, my fingers found those delicate folds between my legs, and my anus, puckered like a medlar fruit. The skin felt raw, like someone had passed a strip of sandpaper over it. I looked up. The sunlight through the prisms of the crystal chandelier made tiny rainbows on the ceiling. Like those strands of yarn, though now they lay, sodden, at the bottom of Palermo Harbor.

I must have slept, because when I awoke, the rainbows had faded. Someplace nearby, music was playing. Nonna was standing by my bed. She held that pouch.

"It's time for your next pill." She loosened the strings. I wanted to get up. Run away. But there was that terrible quarantine hospital. Bodies stacked up in piles. Smoke spiraling upward from the crematorium. I rolled onto my side. When Nonna had finished, I told myself it wasn't so bad.

Nonna pulled the sheet over me. "We'll try some water in a little while. If you can keep that down, you'll take the next pill by mouth."

I slept so deeply that I didn't remember Nonna returning with the water. When I awoke again, she was there with the next pill.

"Sit up."

I tried to push myself into a seated position, but my body was too heavy. Nonna pulled me up and placed a pillow on each side of me so I wouldn't roll off the bed. She'd done the same thing with Caterina when she was a baby.

I swallowed the pill easily. Things would be better now.

A few hours later, the first spider appeared. I'd been half-asleep when I felt it, crawling onto my hand and up the inside of my arm. Under my armpit and onto my torso. Just above the scar on the left side of my chest, it bit me—its tiny fangs piercing the skin. It moved onto my nipple. When it finished gnawing on the nipple, it crept over my belly to my privates. I slapped it away. Another appeared. I was dimly aware of my own voice, crying out in terror. By the time Noma returned to give me my third pill, there were dozens of spiders, crawling all over my body and biting off little bits of me.

"Sit up," Nonna directed.

I tried to, but the spiders were biting my palms and my backside. Impatient, Nonna pulled me into a seated position. Didn't she see them all, crawling on the blanket and up the walls?

"The spiders—"

She ignored me. "Take this. You'll sleep." She pushed the pill past my lips, then held the water glass to my lips. "Drink."

The pill was on my tongue, hard and round.

"Drink," she repeated, forcing the rim of the glass against my mouth. The water trickled past my lips. Nonna tipped the glass further, more water filling my mouth. Then she put the glass on the nightstand and cupped her hand over my mouth. "Swallow. Or I'll give it to you the other way."

I could already feel the spiders, swarming over my buttocks and squeezing through that puckered medlar. I swallowed. The pill stuck in my throat.

Nonna made the sign of the cross and went down on her knees. "Two more days until the Sargasso. We must pray to the Madonna to make you well."

I could feel that small, hard pill in my throat. Like a spider, making its way inside me. When it reached my stomach, there'd be more spiders. They'd eat me alive. I had to protect myself. But I had no shotgun, like the ones the bandits slung over their shoulders. There were no knives, no forks, on my bedside table. But my burins—that tiny scythe I'd cut my palm on. I could use that to cut off the spiders' legs and sever their terrible heads from their bodies. I looked around the room. No sign of my burin case. I should get out of bed. Find that case. But I couldn't get my body to move. My eyes were heavy. I couldn't keep them open.

By the time Nonna returned, I was engaged in a full-on battle with the spiders, my skin raw and bruised from trying to get them off me.

I lunged toward Nonna. "Please," I cried. "Help me. The spiders—!"

Her rosary beads were around her neck, the way the Sisters of Charity wore theirs. I could use them to hit the spiders and scare them away. But when I went to take the beads from around her neck, Nonna took hold of my wrists. She turned my right arm over, then her left. She sighed deeply. "The spiders aren't real. You're hallucinating." She went to the dresser and got out a pair of stockings. She unrolled the first stocking and secured one end to the bedpost. The other one, she tied to my right wrist. Before I could register what she was doing, she'd used the second stocking to tie my left wrist to the other post.

"I'm sorry, Mimi. It's just until we get to the Sargasso and your seasickness passes. Then you'll be able to stop taking the pills."

I pulled against my bindings, every movement drawing the knots more tightly. The spiders would come, by the hundreds. They'd feed on me until nothing was left. I was powerless to protect myself.

Nonna took the pouch from her pocket. I pressed my lips together. She pried open my mouth and placed the pill on my tongue. I spit it out. She got onto the bed and straddled me. This time, she pinched my nose so I couldn't breathe. I opened my mouth. With one hand, she shoved the pill to the back of my tongue. She forced my mouth closed. It wasn't a choice. I swallowed that pill, and the next and the next. Time passed, measured not in minutes or hours, but in the advance and retreat of the spiders.

Until that moment when Nonna said she'd given me the last pill, and I wept, grateful.

CHAPTER 15

WHEN I WAS A LITTLE GIRL—before we became Inglese and moved to *Binvinutu*—we lived on the coast of Marsala. Every Sunday, Pappa brought me and my sisters to the water and showed us how to dive down deep, like conch divers do. I wasn't a strong swimmer, so I never reached the bottom. Even a foot or two below the surface, though, the ocean changed. The water became a deep blue velvet; a low hum, the only sound. When the spiders finally left me alone, I slumbered so deeply it was like being enveloped in the ocean again. When I awoke, it was like rising to the ocean's surface. The light was brighter than I remembered, the sounds, louder, more distinct.

"The Sargasso is so pretty." Caterina's voice. "All those leaves floating on the surface."

The Sargasso Sea. Halfway to America.

Caterina prattled on. "Maybe Mimi will draw it. When she wakes up."

My eyelids were heavy, but I could make out the outline of my sister, perched on the edge of my bed, a washcloth in her hands.

Nonna sat next to her. "We've talked about this, Caterina. Mimi won't be leaving this cabin. Stop daydreaming and finish washing your sister's face."

A cool rag swept my brow. I closed my eyes again.

"A ship can get tangled up in seaweed," Caterina continued. "That happened last year. No one was on board when they found it. A ghost ship." She was speaking quickly, like a gramophone set at a too-high speed.

"Enough." I understood Nonna's impatience. When Caterina was stuck on something, it was impossible to distract her.

I felt Caterina's breath on my face. "It'll be all right, Mimi," she whispered. "If the seaweed traps us, the Madonna told me she'd rescue us. You. Me. Nonna. Mamma and Pappa. But not the rest of them. Because they're sinners."

What was she talking about? I struggled to open my eyes.

"The seaweed will pull them under." Caterina sounded satisfied. Even gleeful.

Caterina had turned toward the basin. "They made you sick." She folded the cloth and placed it on the washstand. "The *puviri*. They deserve to drown." She said it so casually that it sent chills down my spine.

She turned back towards me. "Mimi! You're awake!"

Nonna sent Caterina for Pappa. By the time he arrived, Nonna had helped me change into a clean nightgown.

Pappa kissed my hand. "The worst is behind you, my dear." He'd said something similar when I awoke from the tuberculosis, though the worst things—discovering I'd lost Rosalia and my art—hadn't happened yet. But I reminded myself: I hadn't had a relapse. I was headed toward a new life in America.

Pappa was jabbering about all the things they'd been doing since leaving port. The five-star dinner at the Captain's Table. The tug of war tournament. The archeologist who'd lectured about his fantastical Egyptian finds.

Caterina pulled at Pappa's sleeve. "And the Sargasso Sea. Don't forget to tell Mimi about that."

"I could tell Mimi about the soup, served in a turtle shell, or the dessert set afire. I could explain about old King Tutankhamun or the cow goddess." Pappa laughed. "But the seaweed—that's what you want to talk about?"

"Please, Pappa—the ocean is so beautiful, spinning around and around." Caterina made a sweeping motion with her arms.

Pappa launched into a long-winded description about how the Gulf Stream met the North Atlantic current, the waters rushing towards each other. Creating, paradoxically, a place of stillness. "Imagine that." He gazed out the porthole, a faraway look in his eyes. "Out of chaos, calm."

Pappa helped me to my knees so I could see the ocean, too, the sunlight glinting on its blue-green surface. "The Sargasso," I murmured.

Caterina climbed over me, pressing her face against the window. "You can't see it from here," she declared. "We have to go on deck."

Pappa chuckled but Caterina wouldn't be deterred. "We're almost past it!" she cried. "Please, Pappa."

Nonna was standing near the door. Now she came to my bedside. "Enough, Caterina." My sister scuttled off the bed. "The doctor was very clear about this. The sea air is bad for a consumptive's lungs." The old woman looked at me. "We're almost to America. We don't need any more problems."

My face flushed. Nonna's meaning was clear. I'd already brought trouble down upon my family. "Rest, now." Nonna smoothed my covers.

I closed my eyes. When I dreamed again of the beach at Marsala, I was no longer emerging from the water, sun on my face, gulls squawking overhead. No. I was far from land. Caught in a spiral of seaweed. Unable to get free.

CHAPTER 16

"You need to come for lunch today," Pappa told Nonna when he returned later. "You've taken every breakfast, lunch and dinner in this cabin. The other guests are asking for you. Wondering if you're well."

"Let them talk."

Pappa took her hand. "We need to think about the agents in New York." His voice was quiet. "It's got to go smoothly."

"My age. I understand. But haven't we already given that doctor enough money?"

Something seemed to pass between them.

Nonna nodded. "I'll be at lunch."

The plan came together all at once, the way it did sometimes when I was painting. The moment after Nonna left for lunch, I slipped out of bed. I pulled on the navy dress I'd worn from *Binvinutu* and drew my shawl around my shoulders. I tucked the sketchpad under my arm. The *Sargasso*. Caterina said I didn't have much time.

The hallway was deserted. To my left, I heard the clatter of silverware and the low rumble of conversation. I turned right. Ahead, a cabin door opened. I quickly stepped through a door marked *STAFF ONLY* and found myself on a narrow staircase landing. One flight up was the First Class Deck and a birds-eye view of the sea. Below was Steerage. Not such a good view, but I probably wouldn't be noticed down there. I started down. The steps were steep. I grasped the rail to keep from falling. I was midway down when the door at the bottom opened. I pressed myself against the stairwell wall to keep from being seen. Stupid, I know. There was no hiding here.

"Signorina Inglese?"

Hans. He was holding a silver tray against his hip.

He put the tray on the landing and moved quickly up the steps. "Let me help you." He held out his arm. I took it.

"Your father mentioned you were feeling under the weather. Are you better now?"

"Yes." I let myself be led down the steps. At the bottom, I turned to him. "Thank you, Hans."

He gave a small bow, then motioned toward my sketchpad. "Are you going to draw something?"

"My sister was telling me about the Sargasso. I hope we haven't passed it yet."

"You haven't missed it. Come. I'll show you." We stepped through the stairwell door and down the hallway. At the end, Hans opened another door. There was a whoosh of air and the smell of the sea as we stepped out onto a small deck.

"Is this Steerage?"

Hans shook his head. "That's one flight down. This is Deck D. The galley. And the crew members' cabins." He motioned around the deck. "This is our promenade."

The floor was littered with cigarette butts and crumpled newspapers. Two deckchairs with broken slats, each missing an armrest, were pushed up against the wall.

Hans didn't seem to notice. "Come, Signorina." He guided me toward the railing. "There, just behind the ship. See where the water looks different? That's the Sargasso Sea."

The water was flat, surrounded by a shimmering ocean. There was no swirling seaweed. No light filtering through the darkness. I stood on my tiptoes. Still, I could see nothing. Maybe if I were higher up, I could see better. There was a narrow ledge, below the railing.

I slipped my sketchbook into my skirt pocket. "Will you help me up?" Hans put his hands on my waist and lifted me. He held me lightly, but I could feel the warmth of his fingers. My toes found the ledge but I had to grasp the railing to stay upright. Hans gripped me more tightly, his fingers pressed into my sides. The sea spray was on my face; I tasted the saltiness with my tongue. Somewhere distant, there was a warning that I shouldn't breathe in the moist air. I ignored it.

"Do you want your sketchbook?" Hans's voice was husky.

I nodded.

With one hand on my waist, he slipped the other into my skirt pocket. He ran his fingers over my hip crest and down my thigh. I wasn't wearing a corset—Hans could feel how narrow my hips were, and how bony my thighs. Still, he held me, our bodies pressed together.

The door behind us opened. There was the sound of a man coughing. The door closed. My heart was beating fast, but I told myself he'd seen nothing but Hans's back.

Hans slipped his hand out of my pocket. Still holding me tightly, he handed me the pad.

"Can you see it there?" he asked, his voice low.

"I see only a kind of flatness."

"That's the Sargasso."

"It's so black."

"That's from the seaweed. It gets churned up by the storms and then it's caught in the Sargasso currents. Watch closely. Do you see it moving?"

I tried to ignore the warmth spreading through my lower belly, focusing my eyes on the blackness. There it was—a slow circular movement, independent of the waves rising and falling around it.

"I see it."

"It'll spin round and round until it reaches the Labrador currents. Then the Sargasso will let go. The seaweed will break apart. It'll be like the Sargasso was never there at all. Like it was a dream."

"Yes," I whispered, leaning my head against his. "Like a dream." I released my grip on the railing and let myself settle back onto Hans. I started to sketch: The sun high in the noontime sky; the horizon flat, with only the hint of waves rising and falling. In the center, the Sargasso, holding everything in place. A gust blew across the deck, scattering the crumpled-up newspapers. I shivered.

"You're cold, Signorina."

"Just a moment longer." I made more horizontal marks, shading them dark in the foreground, so they looked closer. Further back, smaller horizontal lines. These, I'd keep lighter, blending them with white pencil so they'd look further away. Around the patch of horizontal lines, I made diagonal marks to suggest the more turbulent sea surrounding the Sargasso.

I drew until I was shivering so badly I could hardly hold the pencil. Hans helped me off my perch.

He pulled off his waiter's jacket and draped it around my shoulders. He rubbed my arms, then led me to one of the broken chairs. When I was seated, he took a blanket from a basket nearby. It was stiff from sea-spray—its folds rising in tiny crests—but he did his best to settle it across my legs. We sat in silence for a moment, the ship gently rocking.

Hans looked out at the sea. "It's getting cooler now. The wind's blowing in from the Labradors, in Canada. See the ripples on the water?" The wind was whipping at his shirt sleeves. Through Hans's starched white shirt, I could make out his lean belly and broad chest.

"You can tell most anything from the way the wind moves across the water." Hans's English was flawless, but his voice had the tendency to lilt upward. "Whether it's going to rain. How far offshore you are. Where the big fish are."

"Did you grow up by the sea?" I asked. Mamma would say I was being too forward. Hans didn't seem to mind.

"Yes. In Finland. Near Helsinki."

"Do you want to go back there?"

"To Finland? No. There's nothing for me there." He took my hand. "Tell me about you. Your Pappa says you're a famous engraver. He says you have a big job waiting for you in America. Working for an import/export company."

A famous engraver. A big job. It was too much to take in.

"My father likes to exaggerate."

Hans pointed at my sketch. "You're too modest, Signorina Mimi."

Hans pointed at my sketch. "Your work is good. Anyone can see that."

I should tell him about the tuberculosis. But he was talking to me like I was a regular girl. His jacket was around my shoulders. It smelled of citrus and pine.

"In my country," Hans continued, "one of our best artists is a woman. Helene Schjerbeck. Do you know her work?"

"Yes, of course." She'd been one of the first women artists to study in Paris, though it had been at a private studio, not the *Beaux-Arts* or the *Académie Julien*.

"You could be like her."

I didn't know what to say.

"You'll make it in America," Hans continued. "I have a feeling in my bones. You'll be as famous as Matisse. Or Picasso."

Mamma liked to say that I was no da Vinci. But Hans's expression was kind. Sincere.

He continued. "Maybe your drawing of the Sargasso will hang in a museum in New York. Or Chicago."

I held up the sketchpad. "This drawing?" I couldn't help but smile.

"Yes. And when I come to see it, I'll tell everyone I showed you the Sea."

I laughed.

"I'm serious." Hans stood up taller. "I won't be on this ship forever. I almost have enough money saved for a railroad ticket to California. They have big trees out there. Like Finland. I'll cut down a whole forest. Sell the wood. Get rich."

I stammered something about how exciting his plans were. Hans leaned over and took my hand.

"Come with me out west. You could do your art. Partners, that's what we'd be." When I didn't respond—because how could I, when my heart was pounding in my chest? Hans looked away. "But of course. You have a groom waiting for you in America."

I squeezed his hand. Before this went further, I should tell him. But since Teo, no man had looked at me this way. Like I was a woman. Not an eccentric artist or a wretch with tuberculosis.

Just then, the door swung open, so hard that it hit the wall behind it. Hans jumped up. The blanket fell to the floor.

"There she is, sir." A waiter I'd never seen was pointing at me.

Pappa stepped out from behind him, red-faced, his hands balled into fists. "We thought something had happened to you." Pappa took in Hans in his shirtsleeves and me, sitting on that broken chair, his wait-jacket draped over my shoulders. My sketchbook, lying open at my feet.

Slowly I stood.

Pappa ordered me to take off the jacket.

I slipped one arm out. Then the other. I gave it to Pappa. My face burned in shame. He turned to Hans. "I'm taking my daughter to her cabin. You, I'll deal with later."

"But Signore. I can explain." Hans's sing-song accent had returned. "I found her wandering on deck. She asked me to show her the Sargasso. I was just doing what she wanted."

Pappa sneered at him. "What *she* wanted? My daughter is a proper noble girl. She doesn't *want* anything. You took advantage of her. She's innocent. A consumptive."

I watched Hans's jaw go slack. I saw him take in what must now be obvious to him. I wasn't an artist. Or a girl who had seasickness. I was an invalid with an incurable, wasting disease. He stepped back.

Pappa glared at Hans. "Captain Smith will hear about this. He won't take kindly to you taking advantage of a Second Class passenger's daughter."

Hans repeated that it was me who'd asked to come here. He was saying something else, too—about how he'd been humoring me since I obviously was an invalid. But Pappa turned away. Taking my arm, he led me back to the cabin.

Nonna was perched on the bed, her fingers entwined in her rosary beads, when Pappa opened the door.

"She was on the servants' deck. Looking at the sea."

Nonna waited until Pappa had latched the door. "I assume she wasn't alone?"

Pappa shook his head. "She was with a waiter."

Nonna stared down her nose at me, so long and so hard that I couldn't catch my breath.

"I wanted to sketch the Sargasso," I stammered. "Caterina kept talking about it. I wanted to see it. The whirlpool. The seaweed—."

"And was this 'sketch' worth it?" Nonna poked me in the arm, hard. "To risk your health? To endanger yourself and your family by getting sick?"

I should say that it wasn't. But I thought of my sketch. How I'd captured the stillness, and expectancy, of the sea.

Pappa put out his hand to me. "Give me the sketchpad."

When I didn't act quickly enough, he thrust his hand into my pocket. He drew out the pad, holding it by one corner, like it was contaminated. He leaned over and unlatched the porthole. In one motion, he opened the window and tossed out my pad. I rushed to the window. Below, the frothing sea. No sign of my book.

Pappa turned to Nonna. "What should we do now?"

Nonna pocketed her rosary beads. Her eyes were clear. "We have five more days until New York. We can't have her sneaking around until then."

Pappa shook his head. I wanted him to yell at me. To slap me or tell me I was bad. Anything but that disappointed look on his face.

"Go to the doctor," Nonna said. "Get enough belladonna to last the rest of the trip. Tip him well. That'll keep him from blabbing to the people in New York."

I didn't protest when Pappa returned. I swallowed the pill with a gulp of water. As I was drifting toward oblivion, I thought of Persephone, cradling her pomegranate. Those seeds that let her escape the heavy chains of her mother's love, even if it was only for six months of the year. Her penance was that she was forced to breathe in the sickly scent of Spring—the scent of confinement—and partake of the sweet fruit of Summer, more bitter than any pomegranate seed.

As the spiders crawled over me, biting my buttocks and breasts, I knew I'd paid, too. But it was worth it. Because I'd seen the Sargasso Sea, the seaweed spinning in lazy circles, guided by some force I couldn't see. I'd felt Hans against me, reminding me that my body, small and vulnerable, my lungs wrecked and my skin scarred, could still feel, and want, and be.

CHAPTER 17

CATERINA WAS HELPING ME with my blouse when I heard the rapping on my parents' cabin door. Maybe it was Hans, come for me.

The knocking got louder. More insistent. Hans wouldn't knock like that.

"Signore Antonino Camastrino, alias Inglese?" A stranger's voice through the door. English, like our London tutor taught me and my sisters, but the pronunciation was different: the vowels, drawn out and the *r*'s clipped. Either way, though, they'd used Pappa's old name. That happened sometimes. Like that shopkeeper in Palermo. Pappa had been so angry he'd vowed never to return. But now, Pappa was quiet.

The door creaked open and quietly closed.

Nonna put her finger to her lips. She edged closer to the wall adjoining my parents' room. I did, too. As usual, Caterina was oblivious, stitching and restitching some bit of embroidery.

"We are Officers Watkins and Baker," I heard through the wall. "From the American government."

The government? But this morning, the ship's doctor had signed the affidavits saying we were all well. He'd changed Nonna's birth year to make her younger. There was no mention of my consumption. When Pappa slipped him the bills, the doctor feigned surprise.

Now, Pappa asked if he could be of assistance.

One of them answered that they just needed to clear things up. "We have reports that you work for Vito Cascioferro."

Zio Vito?

"His father worked for my grandfather, the Baron Inglese. I hold that title now." There was a slight glitch in Pappa's voice.

"So, Mr. Camastrino," — it was like the first officer didn't care about Pappa's name or title — "You're saying you don't work for Cascioferro?"

"I work for myself."

The second officer laughed. "We know Cascioferrro bought your tickets. You're here to do his bidding."

"The tickets were a gift. So that we could attend our daughter's wedding. In New York."

The first officer returned the volley. "Your association with Cascioferro raises suspicions."

"He's a wanted criminal," the second added. "A fugitive. He killed a man. Stuffed his body in a pickle barrel. There's an electric chair waiting for him at Sing Sing."

But Zio was respected. Loved. Pappa should tell them they had the wrong person. Instead, Pappa just repeated that Zio was a casual acquaintance.

"You're a liar," the second officer continued. "He's passing bogus money. You know that."

"Bogus money? I don't know anything about that." Pappa's voice was strained.

"Well, this is a puzzle," the first officer said. "We intercepted a telegram sent by one of Cascioferro's agents, saying that 'the artist' was arriving on this ship."

My stomach dropped. Were they talking about me? I caught Nonna's eye. Again, she put her finger over her lips.

"Me? An artist?" Pappa laughed. "I can't even draw a straight line. And if I could, I wouldn't be messing around with fake money. No, officers. I'm not your man. But I wish you luck finding him."

"Oh, we'll find him," the second officer added. "Until then, you'll be a guest of the United States government."

"That's not necessary. I've secured a home for my family in Manhattan." Pappa's voice was tremulous.

"Sir, you misunderstand. It's not an invitation. It's an order." There was the sound of paper unfolding. "When we reach Ellis Island, you'll be taken into custody. There will be a hearing. The judges will decide."

"What about my family?" Pappa asked so quietly I almost couldn't hear it through the wall.

"There are women's dormitories." The officer's voice was monotone, like he was bored.

"I've done nothing wrong."

"Then the judges will let you go."

"If they don't?"

The second man continued. "You'll go to jail. And your family will be sent back to Sicily."

That, Caterina heard. She came to stand next to us. "We're going home?" For her, there was the convent. For the rest of us, though, there was nothing. *Binvinutu* had been sold, the money wasted on fancy gowns for the voyage and wool coats and thick shawls for the New York winter.

The first officer continued. "When the Captain announces the departure of Second Class passengers, you'll stay in your cabins. After about an hour, the ship will dock at Ellis Island and you'll go ashore with the rest of Steerage. You'll find an officer and give him this paper. He'll direct you to the dormitories."

The cabin door opened and closed. After the men were gone, Mamma started in. About how Zio was an idiot and should go *affanculo*.

Pappa came to our cabin a few minutes later.

Before Pappa could tell us, Nonna said that we'd heard what happened. Pappa's shoulders slumped forward.

"You'll get word to Vito," Nonna said. "Isn't that what you agreed to do if there was a problem?"

Pappa nodded.

Caterina started to ask if we were going back to Sicily. Nonna shot her a glance that stopped her cold.

"Will Zio be able to help us?" I asked.

Nonna didn't even look at me. "Vito helps those who help themselves."

CHAPTER 18

As I walked onto the Second Class deck behind Nonna and the rest of my family, I glanced around for Hans. The deck was deserted. It felt so long ago that he'd told me about the giant trees that grew in California that I thought maybe it had been a dream, like those spiders.

Pappa led us to the embarkation area. The ramp we'd used to board the ship in Palermo was gone, the gate locked. A harried cabin boy directed us to a staircase just behind the first smokestack and continued stacking glasses on the tray. "Two floors down. That's the only way off the ship."

The staircase was steep, like the one I'd been on with Hans. I grasped the handrail, feeling for the edge of each step. Pappa had returned my burin case to me that morning. It was in my satchel, knocking against my hip and threatening to unbalance me. I kept my eyes on Nonna's hunched back. At the bottom of the second flight of stairs, we exited through a steel door.

I'd seen them at Palermo Harbor, tossing their balls of yarn to their well-wishers. And I guess they'd been there at the Sargasso, marveling at the gyre circling slowly in place. Here were the *puviri* in the flesh, craning their necks to see. Hoisting each other up, on shoulders, on deck boxes, on railings, all trying to get a look at America. I didn't know it at the time, but these were the survivors. More than a hundred had died on the voyage, their bodies pitched into an indifferent Atlantic.

Soon we were swallowed up, the stench of two thousand unwashed bodies making it hard to breathe. I fell behind. At one point, I could see my family in front of me. Pappa, his arms swept out in front, clearing the path; Mamma, clutching her skirts in a feeble attempt not to touch the *puviri*; Nonna, her eyes down and her lips moving in prayer; and Caterina, held in place between Mamma and Nonna. The crowd surged forward. The gap between me and my family widened. I should have been panicked, searching for the blue and yellow bands on Pappa's boater or the purple ostrich plume on Mamma's hat. But I just kept my eyes on the deck in front of me.

I fell into step beside a woman about my age. Her skirt hem was torn, the fabric grimy from being dragged along the ship's deck. I glanced around for a brother, a father, a husband. She seemed to be alone. What would that be like—to travel across the ocean by yourself, with only a few lire in your pocket? To live on your own, answering only to yourself? The woman forged ahead, her eyes already searching the shoreline, looking for something I couldn't see. For a moment, I imagined I could disappear into the crowd. Give myself a different name. Make my way creating logographs.

After being pushed and prodded, I reached the ship's ramp. The young woman rushed ahead. I was alone again. But there on the dock was Pappa, hat in his hands, scanning the crowd. While I'd been thinking of running off, my family had been here, worrying. I was a selfish daughter—Mamma had always said so. I hurried off the ramp to my family, apologizing for keeping them waiting. We started toward the main building, a colossus as big as the opera house in Palermo. Throngs of *puviri* were moving through chutes toward the entrance. Pappa stopped an officer and gave him the paper, as he'd been instructed.

The officer pointed to the side of the building. "Go that way."

There was a sign for *DORMITORIES*. Beneath it, a right-facing arrow marked *MEN'S* and a left-facing one with *WOMEN'S*. We followed the sign through another door where a uniformed man and a plump matron waited. Pappa gave the man the paper, now dog-eared from being passed between so many people.

The officer read the paper, looking at Pappa as he did. "Your hearing is this afternoon. You'll wait at the dormitory. Come along." He turned toward the right arrow and started walking. Pappa scampered after him, struggling to catch up.

The matron hooked her finger at us, like you'd do with a dog or a servant. We followed down a hallway lit by one sputtering overhead light. At the end was a steel door. The matron extracted a heavy ring of keys from her apron pocket. She turned one of them in the lock and pushed open the door. Once inside, the matron took some dingy sheets and blankets from a dolly and divided them between the four of us.

She started toward the back of the room. Nonna put her hand on the woman's arm. "Excuse me, Madame? We'd like to be close to the bathroom." Nonna gestured toward the entrance to the lavatory, with its black and white checkerboard tile floor.

The matron ignored her until Nonna took a bright green bill from her pocket. "For your trouble." Nonna held out the bill. There were 5s in each corner.

The woman pocketed the bill. Without a word, she led us back toward the lavatory, stopping at some bunks just outside. She raised her hand to the woman lying on the middle bunk. That woman rose quickly, along with the others in her bunk and the next, pulling their sheets from their beds and scooping up whatever meager possessions they had, before retreating to the back of the room.

Nonna put her sheets and small valise on the lower bunk.

The matron folded her hands over her round belly. "Lunch is at 12."

My grandmother drew a second identical bill from her pocket. "I need to get a telegram to this person. As soon as possible." She pulled a folded paper from her pocket and handed it, along with the lime-green bill, to the matron. My Nonna, the old woman who sometimes forgot what day of the week it was, and confused words for each other, was nowhere in sight. In her place, this decisive, hard-hearted person. I thought again of the life Nonna had when she was a young woman, working alongside bandits and revolutionaries up in the hills of western Sicily.

The matron took the bill and the paper and hurried away.

"To Vito?" Mamma asked. When Nonna nodded, Mamma snorted. "A fat lot of good that'll do," Mamma said.

"Have faith, Maria." Nonna tipped up her chin. I saw a hint of the proud and maybe even arrogant noble girl she'd once been.

Mamma flopped down on the bare cot next to Nonna's. She laid her hands across her eyes and sighed loudly. Leave it to Mamma to make everything into a scene.

Nonna unfolded her sheet. "We'll only be here a day or two." I wondered how she could be so sure. "Mimi, you have your burin case?"

I touched my handbag.

"Keep it with you at all times. Under your pillow when you're resting, in your skirt pocket the rest of the time."

I said I would, though looking around at those women, disheveled, their eyes vacant, I couldn't imagine any of them stealing my burins.

A bell clanged. Before the four of us could collect ourselves, a queue had already formed.

"Meals and bedtimes," Nonna explained. "In a place like this— everyday exactly the same—that's what helps you mark time." Maybe she was thinking of the convent where she'd stayed all those years. But there was no bitterness in her voice. No sense that her true life—the one she'd been destined to live—had been stolen from her.

We followed the others to a dining room with mahogany walls and apron-clad waiters. Pappa wasn't there. This, too, Nonna took in stride, leading us to a table on the side. We passed a woman who was visibly trembling, her arms crossed like she was holding a baby. Her arms were empty. An X was chalked onto her blouse.

"Lunatic," Mamma muttered, just as we passed her. I hated when Mamma acted like that—as if these people were too stupid to understand. Didn't she see how the man with that poor woman had lowered his gaze? He'd understood.

I turned to apologize, but Nonna tucked her hand under my arm, urging me forward. When we were out of earshot, Nonna told me the woman was sick. "That's why she has the X."

"But they didn't leave her on the Quarantine Island. Or make her go back to wherever she came from." I looked down at my own blouse, half-expecting to see a C, for consumption.

"Some illnesses are more easily concealed." Nonna touched her own temple. "But they can't be hidden forever." For a moment, I thought she was talking about her own confusion. Then I remembered all those lime-green bills Nonna and Pappa had slipped the ship's doctor to ensure there would be no problems with our health affidavits. Still, maybe someone had told the truth about me and that's why Pappa was in trouble.

We sat. A waiter placed several dishes on the table. Nonna picked up one of them and slopped some of the white, pasty food onto my plate. "Potatoes. Eat, Mimi. You're skin and bones." She picked up a plate of meat and peas. These, too, she shoveled onto my plate. The meat was covered with a disgusting, rainbow-hued sauce and the peas tasted metallic. I choked down all of it.

Near the end of the meal, an older man with salt and pepper hair like Pappa's approached Nonna, his hat in his hands.

"Baroness Inglese?" The man pulled off his hat. "I'm Giacomo Baladucci. My mother was seamstress to your mother. Signora Agata Baladucci."

Nonna nodded, though it had to have been decades ago.

Baladucci glanced around the room. "Is Signore Inglese traveling with you? I'd like to give him my regards."

Mamma blurted out that Pappa had been taken away. Nonna's top lip curled back. You didn't talk about family business to outsiders.

"I'm sorry to hear this," Baladucci said. "But as Signore Cascioferro always says: 'Rough seas make good sailors.'" That sounded like one of Zio's sayings. Then Baladucci bowed and was gone.

I thought Nonna would chastise Mamma. But for the rest of the meal, Nonna sat, seemingly lost in thought, fingering her rosary beads.

Mamma made some more insipid comments—about the quality of the meat (it probably came from a dog) and the length of the waiters' aprons (ridiculous, given the filth all around), but Nonna stayed quiet as a monk. I tried not to think about what would happen if Nonna became confused again, as she had been back at *Binvinutu*. Thankfully, as the waiters began to clear the table, Nonna seemed to decide something. She stood and walked to the front of the room. The matron from the dormitory was there. Nonna slipped another green bill into her hand. The woman leaned in close, covering her mouth with her hand. When she was done, Nonna nodded and returned to the table.

"The hearing's tomorrow. Vito's arranged things."

Mamma wrinkled her nose. "He's 'arranged' things?"

After a long time—in which Nonna glared at her and Mamma sat, not meeting her gaze and tugging at her collar and the cuffs of her blouse—Nonna finally spoke.

"You seem to forget," the old woman said, though it was she who sometimes struggled to recall the word for pen or clock. Last week, she got lost in the Rose Garden, a place she'd tended since she was a little girl.

Nonna continued. "Without Vito, you'd still be Camastrino—you and your daughters. Living above your father's butcher shop. Praying that your daughters would be lucky enough to marry a dairyman or goatherd."

I'd always thought the clerk was correcting a mistake when he changed our names. But Nonna was saying that Zio had made it happen. Without him, we'd still be Camastrino.

Dinner came and went without Pappa. Night fell. Somewhere, a clock struck ten. The gas lamps were extinguished. Under the cloak of darkness came the sound of muffled sobbing. Like breakers on the shore, the remains of one wave feeding the next. When sleep finally came, I dreamed of Pappa lying on a cot—or maybe it was his coffin—an X on his shirt like that poor woman. Unable to move or utter a word. Unable to say who he was—Inglese or Camastrino. I awakened to the cawing of birds outside my window. Here, even birdsong was ugly.

At dinner the next day, the matron approached Nonna. She crouched down next to the table and spoke quietly. Amidst the clatter of forks and the hum of voices, it was hard to hear her words. But I could make out the most important thing, which was that Pappa was being released. We could leave in the morning after breakfast.

The matron stood. "My friend, the bailiff—said he'd never seen anything like it. One judge apologized to Signore. Said it was all a misunderstanding."

Nonna nodded. She reached under the cuff of her sleeve and drew out another lime-green bill. After pocketing it, the matron withdrew. Nonna exhaled deeply.

I awoke early the next morning, the sun still hugging the horizon, an anemic white-yellow ball. The small voice inside whispered that today was the day our lives would finally begin. But I'd been here before: when we left my grandfather's butcher shop for *Binvinutu*; then again, when I headed for Monsieur's *atelier* with my easel and paints.

The first ferry off Ellis Island wasn't until nine, so we packed our bags and set off for breakfast. I heard Pappa's laughter from the hallway. Then there he was, dressed in his best suit, his mustache perfectly waxed, his shirtfront pressed immaculately. He hugged Nonna and kissed Mamma and Caterina on the cheek. When it was my turn, I breathed in his scent—bergamot and orange—and felt my heartbeat slow. How could I have thought about leaving my family back on the ship? My place was with them.

We sat at a table near the front. Pappa talked about all the people he'd met while he'd been away, like he'd been off on a jaunt. It didn't matter. Everything had come out right in the end. The waiters were about to serve the meal—bowls full of scrambled eggs and porridge, and pitchers of milk—when the doors burst open and four officers stormed in.

With an ache in the back of my throat, I watched as they approached our table. The judge must have changed his mind and Pappa was going to be arrested again. We'd all be deported. Like a field mouse frozen in fear beneath the shadow of a hawk, I sat there, unable to do anything.

The officers moved past us. They stopped at a table near the back. One ran his finger across the clipboard. "Giacomo Baladucci. Alias Bartone. Alias Martino. You're under arrest."

I craned my neck to see. It was the same man who'd approached Nonna yesterday. He'd been so confident then. Now he cowered in his seat.

Baladucci shook his head. "Is mistake. You have the wrong person." He pointed to himself. "Baladucci. No aliases."

The officers snickered. I felt sorry for the man but I couldn't look away. One of the officers ordered him to stand up. The other diners quietly left the table, deserting their companion.

One officer slipped a club from his belt. He rapped it on the table. "Hiding in plain sight. So slippery. Tell me, Baladucci. You were going to just slither in, weren't you? Like all your other oily friends."

"Is this about the gambling?" Baladucci looked from one officer to the other. "I didn't know it wasn't allowed on the boat."

One of the officers laughed. "You think this is about gambling? No, it's about the funny money."

"The funny money?" Baladucci's voice cracked.

The officer turned to his colleague. "Do you fucking believe this?" He looked at Baladucci again. "Running your own personal money exchange. Getting the other guinea wops to give you their lire for fake bills. You can cheat those idiots as much as you want. But you can't shit on the legal tender of the U.S. of A."

The other officer chimed in. "Yeah. That's against the law."

"I'll give it to you," the first officer said. "It was a brilliant plan. The only problem was that the bills were clearly fakes."

He leafed through the sheaf of papers until he came to a lime-green bill, then put it on the dining table in front of Baladucci. I got a funny feeling in my stomach. That color. The same shade that I'd seen at Zio's factory and the ones Pappa and Nonna gave to the ship's doctor and dormitory matron.

The officer poked at the bill. "The eagle looks like some school kid drew it. And it's too green."

Everyone in the room was looking now. I wonder if they were as curious as I was about the drawing.

"Is mistake," Baladucci repeated. "Someone give me those bills in Palermo. I don't know American dollars. I couldn't tell they were— what did you say?—funny money." He reached into his pants pocket and pulled out his wallet. "I make it right." He pulled out some bills and tried to hand them to the officer. "These bills—they're better?"

The officer smirked at him. "So we'll add bribery to the list of crimes." The officer with the clipboard wrote something on top. The officer who had been quiet unclipped a pair of handcuffs from his belt.

Baladucci started to get up. "You're sending me back to Sicily?"

The man with the cuffs pushed him back down. "What? So you can just send another wetback here to try this again? No. You're going to prison. Ten to fifteen years, minimum. Now get up!"

I guess Baladucci didn't move quickly enough because the fourth officer brought his club down hard on the table. Plates and glasses rattled violently. My heart was racing.

Baladucci stumbled to his feet.

The first officer pointed at Baladucci's chair. "Look at that! He's pissed himself." The other officers laughed, but not the one with the billy club. He grabbed Baladucci by the shoulder.

"Clean that up," he ordered.

Baladucci didn't move.

With one hand still on Baladucci, the officer raised his club over his head. I looked away, sure he was going to bring it down on the man. Instead, in a voice eerily calm, the officer said, "Clean. It. Up," accentuating each word.

When the poor man still didn't respond, the officer pushed him onto the table. Brown gravy and milk splashed across the front of his fine worsted. His seamstress mother had probably sewn that jacket for her son.

"I need a rag," Baladucci mumbled.

The officer pointed at Baladucci's fine jacket. "Use that."

For a moment, Baladucci looked confused. But when the officer moved toward him menacingly, Baladucci took off his jacket. He folded it neatly, one sleeve, then the other. When it was a perfect rectangle, Baladucci got down on his knees and began to wipe up his urine with it.

When Baladucci finally finished, the sound of his crying holding us all in place there, witness to his humiliation, an officer cuffed his arms behind his back. He looked so pathetic—so vulnerable—standing there in his shirtsleeves. I don't know why, but my fingers went to my left ribs and found the scars there.

CHAPTER 19

I WAS STILL THINKING ABOUT Baladucci's fake bills when we boarded the ferry. Maybe I should have worried about all those lime-green bills Pappa and Nonna had been passing out since we'd left Palermo. But I never stopped to consider they might be an issue.

The boatmen cast off their lines. The ferry shifted into reverse, dark smoke engulfing the deck. Pappa gestured ahead to the jagged skyline. "Isn't it beautiful?"

As we approached, though, anyone could see New York wasn't beautiful. All straight lines and sharp angles, like something a child would build with wooden blocks.

"My associates are waiting for us on the other side," Pappa continued. "We'll travel in a motor car. No old-fashioned horse and carriage for us."

Mamma grabbed Pappa's sleeve. "A motor car? Oh, no, Nino. It's not safe."

Pappa just laughed.

"Where are the horses?" Caterina asked, her voice small.

Pappa made up some story about how the horses didn't need to work anymore. They'd been sent west on railroad cars. They could run free out there, like horses were meant to. Pappa was clever like that. He could make up things on the spot. Had he not winked at me, even I might have believed that the horses were living their best lives out west.

As the ferry approached Manhattan, there was the blaring of horns and the awful screech of metal on metal. Then the smell—a noxious mix of rotten eggs, manure, and kerosene that made my eyes tear. The ferry's engines roared into reverse. We passed under the shadow of the skyscrapers. It turned dark as dusk.

Pappa hired some dockworkers to move our trunks from the ferry to the dock. As he reached into his pocket and peeled off more of the lime-green bills, I felt sick inside. What would these burly men do if they discovered Pappa had tipped them with fake money?

The street was a mass of confusion. Automobiles everywhere, horns honking, tires screeching. Pappa had been wrong—there were horses, too, neighing and pawing at the pavement, probably in a panic over the noise and traffic. Drivers leaned out of cars and carriages marked *TAXI*, calling to pedestrians in unfamiliar languages. One taxi pulled up next to me and Caterina as we stood at the curb.

"Need a ride?" He leaned out, reaching for Caterina as the bandits had. "Come on, girl. I can take you anywhere."

Nonna stepped in front of my sister. "Go on." Her tone was the same as the Cook's when a mangy dog lingered too long at the kitchen door. Smirking, the driver pulled back into the street. A little further on, he stopped to solicit another young woman.

Pappa slipped his watch into his vest pocket. "1:15. They're late." The crowd pressed on us. Someone elbowed me in the ribs, the pain from my old scars excruciating. For a long moment, I teetered on the edge of the filthy gutter. When I managed to stand, Pappa's hand was in the air.

A car slowed and pulled to the curb in front of us. It was red and the length of two carriages, with headlights that looked like bulging eyes. The driver man with a pencil-thin mustache. As the car glided to the curb, I could see he was driving one-handed, his right arm tucked into his coat. Two passengers were in the front seat next to him.

Pappa thrust his hand inside the passenger window toward the brute. "I'm Nino Inglese," Pappa said to the man closest to him, a brutish man with a heavy brow. "You must be Ciro." The man curled his upper lip and ignored Pappa.

"Nicolò," the man in the middle seat said, flashing a smile. Even from the curb, I could see he was young. And handsome. Nicolò motioned toward the driver. "My oldest brother, Clutch."

Pappa reached across the car. "It's good to meet you, Clutch. Vito's told me a lot about you."

Ciro snorted. "Oh, yes. Vito. He keeps his hands clean and his shoes polished while the rest of us do his dirty work."

I waited for Clutch to say something more—no one talked about Zio that way—but he just waved toward the back. "Luggage goes in the trunk." None of the men offered to help. We managed to get the luggage onto the trunk rack, Pappa using his belt to secure it to the car. By the time we'd settled into the back seat, Mamma was cursing under her breath about manners and gentlemen.

The car lurched forward, then ground to a stop. I swallowed my bile, praying I wouldn't be sick all over Clutch's burgundy leather seats.

"Fucking Canal Street," Clutch grumbled. "All these Chinks selling their crap." He struck the steering wheel in frustration. That's when I saw it. Where his right hand should have been, there was a grotesque claw. Just two fingers. One a thumb, the other, a monstrosity that looked like all the other fingers fused together. I'd seen a crab with a claw like that at the beach, using its pincers to tear the flesh from a washed-up fish. My stomach lurched again.

Pappa asked if the traffic was always like this.

"Morning, noon and night," thick-browed Ciro said. "Between the Chinks on Canal and the Kikes on Delancey, it's impossible to get across town."

"Goddamn it!" Clutch slammed his claw-hand against the wheel again. It must have been secured to the gold chain around Clutch's neck because now it bounced against the wheel. The skin was shiny, like it had been stretched too taut over bone. Clutch saw me staring. His eyes in the rearview mirror were cold. Reptilian. I saw myself as he must have seen me. A pitiful consumptive with lungs as wrecked as his terrible claw. When he smiled, though, I felt a kind of kinship with him.

We turned onto another street. Stalls lined both sides. In Palermo, the hawkers sold chickpea fritters and lamb on skewers. Here, though, they sold all kinds of things—pots and pans, blouses, skirts. One even had lingerie—the kind that Sicilian shopkeepers kept in blue silk-lined drawers. Women walked together or alone, no male chaperone in sight. My first thought was that it was dangerous. But that was Mamma's voice, not mine. Because here, no one seemed to notice the women as they walked along. Their long skirts swishing. Their heads uncovered. The hot breeze pulling at their blouses. Maybe it was like Zio had said: Things were different in America.

We inched along. Every once in a while, I'd catch Clutch looking at me, his eyes narrowed, like he was puzzling over something. After a long time, we turned onto another street. Metal scaffolding ran above us.

Clutch motioned toward the scaffolding. "The elevated train. Proof that everything's for sale in America."

Ciro grunted.

Pappa asked what Clutch meant.

"Money talks. How else could something so ugly be built?"

But the sunlight eking through the metal cast intricate, honeycombed patterns onto the cobbles, like the ceilings in Moorish churches back home. I reached into my satchel, forgetting for a moment that my sketchpad lay at the bottom of the Atlantic. My fingers found the burin case, and at the bottom, my torn ticket stub from the ship. My mind was already forming the image—the intricate weave of octagonal stars and crosses. I had no pencil, so I used the straight edge of a burin. The gritty steel stilts; the spans, pocked with rivets; the arches, connecting the columns and beams; the tracks laid across the open floor.

I drew lightly, the V-shaped edge whispering against the paper. I kept my eyes on the scaffolding as the sketch took shape. I'd finished the outline when Clutch finally turned onto a street with rows of gold-hued stone houses. For a moment, the sunlight was blindingly bright.

In a self-satisfied tone, Pappa announced that this was Doctors Row.

My cheeks burned. I wanted to cry out—I was well. I didn't need a doctor.

Pappa didn't notice my distress. "I told Vito—my family is accustomed to living amidst elegance," Pappa continued. "He assured me this is the most exclusive neighborhood in the whole city. It got its name from all the *prominenti* who live here."

Ciro laughed sharply.

"Don't be like that, brother." Clutch's voice was teasing. "You know that the best people live here." Clutch turned his wheel sharply toward the curb and stopped in front of a house with ornate, carved lintels above the doors and windows. "Here we are."

The men got out of the car. Pappa opened Nonna's door; Clutch came to mine. After he'd helped me and Caterina out of the car, Clutch leaned close to me. "You were sketching." He smiled, his gold eye teeth glinting.

He motioned to Ciro and Nicolò to follow my family inside. When Clutch turned back to me, he wasn't smiling anymore. "Let me see the sketch."

There was a pit in my stomach. Clutch thought the Elevated was ugly. He wouldn't like my sketch. For some reason, it felt very important that he did.

"I didn't have any paper." I handed him the ticket.

Clutch held up his hand, silencing me. He looked at my sketch for a long time. Finally, he whispered, "It's the train."

"Yes." I stopped myself from prattling on about how I'd been intrigued by the intricate designs and the play of sunlight on metal.

"It's perfect. The lines. The proportions. The scale." Clutch laughed. "So Cascioferro wasn't exaggerating. You're the real deal." A warmth washed over me. Clutch was pleased. "He had the burins made special for you."

I listened for a hint of reproach—for Zio, for spoiling me; for me, for accepting such an extravagant gift. Hearing none, I asked if he needed another logograph.

He raised his eyebrows. "Another *what?*"

"Another logo—like the pomegranate. For the crates."

Clutch slid his claw hand up and down the neck chain. It made a quiet clinking sound. Then he laughed, sharply. "Logos are Cascioferro's thing, not mine. He uses them to keep track of shipments. Doesn't want any of the shopkeepers thinking they've been shortchanged. 'Discontent breeds disloyalty,' that's what he says. The same kind of horseshit he's always shoveling. Me—I keep things simple. Like you and me. You're an engraver. I need some engravings. You work for me. I pay you. *Mi capisci,* Mimi?"

It was on the tip of my tongue to correct him: I wasn't an engraver. I was an artist. But Zio's words came to me—I should stay open to the possibilities. America was my destiny.

I nodded.

Clutch slipped my drawing into his pocket. "We'll meet tomorrow. At my saloon downtown. Bring your tools." Pappa was waiting for us at the door. "Noon," Clutch told Pappa. "Don't be late."

After Clutch left, Pappa closed the vestibule door and locked it.

When he turned to me, he sighed, deeply. Then he pointed toward the wide, winding stairs. "Your bedroom is upstairs. In the back. With your sister."

I was annoyed. Caterina's constant devotion to the Madonna; the smoky smell of votive candles, never left unattended. The whisperings—*pray for us sinners, now and at the hour of our death*—repeated at all hours of the day, not only during matins but when she pulled on her hose, or picked up her fork to eat, or sat on the toilet. I couldn't imagine sharing a bed with her.

"It's just until the wedding," Pappa promised. "Two or three months, at most."

That was scarcely enough time for the priest to read the banns. Maybe it didn't matter. There was no one here to object, anyway.

Pappa seemed to read my mind. "I know it's fast. But Signore Amoruso is eager. And it'll be good to have things settled."

As I made my way upstairs, I could hear the jingling of Pappa's lucky coin against his watch chain. At the top of the steps, I turned right into the bedroom. Caterina was—as I'd expected—on her knees at a makeshift altar near the window. Just beyond was a small study with a tall window. There was a desk, too, with a new sketchpad and a set of pencils. Outside, cherry blossoms lay scattered on the concrete. I picked up a pencil and was laying out the composition—the carpet of curled-up leaves amidst cast-off cigar wrappers and newspapers—when I heard a loud bang, coming from close by.

I ran from the study, past Caterina, still on her knees, and into the hallway. Another bang. This time, from the small bedroom next to ours. Nonna's room. I pushed open the door, expecting to see her on the floor, like we'd found her last year. That time, she insisted she'd lost her footing on the wet parquet, though the maid hadn't gotten to washing that part of the floor yet. Now, though, she was pacing, her shawl dragging behind her. Clothes were strewn everywhere. Her prayer book lay face down on the carpet. I asked if she was feeling well—a stupid question in light of her disarray.

She ignored me, going straight to her night table. She picked up the Madonna statue she'd brought from home. She raised it overhead, then pitched it toward her half-empty satchel. As it landed, the Madonna's head broke off and rolled under the bed. When she turned toward me, her eyes were vacant.

"Let's put away your things," I said, stooping to pick up her prayer-book. As I closed the book, the back cover fell away, like the broken wing of a bird. I gave it to her. This, too, she pitched toward her satchel. It landed with a sickening thud.

Only then did she seem to notice me.

"I'm ready to go. My things are packed." She was eerily calm.

Gently, I tried to explain that we'd arrived at our destination. "We're going to be living here now."

She turned on me. "Don't lie to me again," she hissed. "This isn't home."

"We left *Binvinutu*." My voice was shaking.

"Not *Binvinutu*. Santa Maria."

"The convent? No. Remember? The family's going to stay together."

"My family—" She curled her lip in disgust. "They hoped I'd die in childbirth."

What was she talking about?

"My mother prayed for it. She told me death would be better than giving birth to a bastard. But the Madonna is protecting me and my baby." Nonna ran her hand over her belly. "Mother Superior says so."

Maybe it had been the long ocean voyage, or the stress of waiting for Pappa to be released. Or maybe it was the newness of it all—the city, the automobile, the house—that had unmoored Nonna. All I knew was that this wasn't like her occasional forgetfulness or confusion. Nonna was lost in time.

Before I could figure out what to do—find her a newspaper and show her the date, or just get Pappa—she crossed the room to her satchel. "They're waiting at Santa Maria. I have to go. Before Father realizes." She picked up the satchel. It fell open, fabric spilling from its gaping mouth.

Trying to stay calm, I eased the handles from her grasp. "I'll help you. But first, we should pray for safe travel. For you and your baby."

We prayed seven rounds of rosaries before Nonna's eyes grew heavy and she allowed me to lead her to her bed. When I was sure she was asleep, I slipped out. Maybe I should probably tell Pappa about this. But he had so much on his mind. Anyway, Nonna would be better when she awoke from her nap. If she wasn't—well, then, Pappa would see that for himself.

CHAPTER 20

CLUTCH'S SALOON WAS ON Prince Street. After the pretty row houses
with the manicured gardens on Doctors Row, I expected Prince Street
to be the home of, well, princely, or at least well-appointed buildings.
But the buildings were run down, with broken windows and crumbling
masonry. Children in rags ran up and down the street, shoeless, their
faces smudged with dirt.

Pappa pointed to the shimmery ooze of sludge that ran along the
curb. "Pick up your skirts."

We looked up and down the street until he pointed to a storefront
with a sign with *Saloon* above the door. "That must be it."

Inside the bar, a haze of grit and smoke hung just beneath the low
ceiling. Wallpaper hung down in strips. The floor was littered with saw-
dust and broken glass.

Nicolò appeared. He smiled at me. "I'll take you back to Clutch."
He held out his arm. I took it.

We made our way through the crowd. A few minutes later, Pappa
and I were standing before Clutch in a back room several times larger
than the bar. Ciro was there, brooding by the back window; Nicolò
joined him.

There was a soft tinkling as Clutch ran his terrible claw up and down
his gold chain. "I'm honored that you're here," he said. "Imagine, the
Baron Inglese in my bar. And Mimi. It's good to see you again." I willed
myself not to stare, but I couldn't help but take in that terrible claw.

Pappa cleared his throat. "Before we start, we need to clarify things."
Ciro snarled at him. The others looked to Clutch to see how to
respond.

Pappa fumbled in his vest pocket. "This is from Vito. Instructions
about stocking the new store. My store." He held out the letter. When
Clutch made no move to take it, Pappa set it on the table in front of him.

"Vito wants to know if we've secured a storefront," Pappa continued.
"We need to get things going. Another shipment will arrive any day."

All those crates outside Zio's factory. Where would they go if there
was no store?

Clutch pulled out an ebony-handled pocket knife. "You're trying
my patience, old man." He flicked open the blade and began turning
it tip over handle, the harsh overhead light glinting against the metal.

When Pappa spoke again, his voice was quiet. "Vito sent me with
specific instructions. We need to use his product first, before we change
anything."

All eyes shifted to me. Whatever they were talking about, it
involved me.

Clutch picked up Zio's letter. For a moment, I wondered if he
was checking to see whether Pappa was telling the truth. He glanced
at it, then tossed it on the desk. He nodded toward his brothers—
some message, exchanged—then turned to Pappa. "You know the
product's inferior?"

Pappa shrugged. "I used it on the way over. I had no problems."

Clutch took his feet from the table. He motioned toward me. "Let's
ask the artist. Nino, give your daughter one of Vito's bills."

Pappa hesitated. But when Ciro started to get up, Pappa took the
money roll from his pocket. Pappa drew one of those lime-green bills
from the roll. He handed it to Clutch, who placed it on the table in
front of me.

Clutch used the heel of his good hand to flatten the bill.
"Cascioferro's product." Ciro handed him another bill. This, Clutch
placed next to the first. "And a real five-dollar bill."

I could see the difference right away. The print on Zio's bill was fuzzy, like someone had smeared the ink before it was dry. The man on the front didn't look right—his face was too round and his eyes too close together. The bottom of his ears didn't line up with the bottom of his nose, making it look like someone had tugged on his earlobes. The color was wrong, too. Lime-green—like the color on the artist's palette at Zio's factory—not jade, like the real bill.

What do you think, Signorina Artist?" Clutch asked.

I glanced at Pappa. I should lie and say the bills were indistinguishable. That's what Pappa wanted. But my face gave me away.

Clutch pointed at me. "See? They're no good. The girl knows this."

Pappa repeated that he'd had no trouble with the bills.

Clutch laughed. "You said that. But there's a big difference between palming a few fake bills onto people who've never seen a five-dollar bill and actually using them—lots of them—in business. People can tell the difference—right, Mimi? You could tell."

What could I say? I nodded.

Pappa shook his head. "Vito was clear in his instructions. First, the Palermo bills. When he moves to New York next year, he can decide about manufacturing the product here. Maybe hire a professional engraver." He drew out the word *professional*.

"We're going to keep with the original plan," he continued. "We have plenty of product to start with."

Clutch smirked. Ciro lunged toward Pappa. "Where do you get off trying to tell us about our business?" If Nicolò hadn't grabbed him, I don't know what he would have done.

"Ciro. Sit." Clutch said calmly. "No one needs to be upset. We're all friends here."

But Ciro was clenching and unclenching his fists.

Clutch stood and came to where Pappa was standing. "Let's do it this way, Don Inglese. You'll get your store. Ciro thinks there may be something uptown. Not far from your fancy new house."

Clutch put his claw hand on Pappa's shoulder. It sent shivers down my spine. "You'll get what you want—the chance to play a big shot store-keeper." Using that terrible claw, Clutch drew Pappa close. "We'll see how Vito's bills do. You think they're so good?" The claw slid up until it was around Pappa's neck. "It'll be your ass on the line."

Clutch released his grip. Pappa fell forward. Clutch asked Nicolò how quickly they could stock Pappa's store.

"A week. If we start moving stock from the warehouse today."

"Good. And be sure to include lots of Vito's special crates." Clutch gestured toward my crates. "The ones with the pretty pome-granate pictures."

They all laughed, except for Pappa.

Clutch pushed the five-dollar bill—the real one—toward me.

"Start practicing, Mimi. If you're as good as I think you are, you'll be working for us full-time."

Maybe it was Clutch's black eyes, or maybe the way he commanded all those men. Or maybe it was my own curiosity. Or my own ego—I knew I could do better with that bill. But I plucked that bill from Clutch's claw and put it in my bag.

Clutch lowered his claw. "Good. Now we begin."

CHAPTER 21

SWEAT TRICKLED DOWN the backs of my legs. I'd taken off my stock-ings—I was alone, so what was the harm?—but it hadn't helped. Indian Summer. As if those poor Indians had played one last, ironic trick on the people who'd driven them from this land.

I put pencil to paper again. I'd started with the man on the front of the five-dollar bill. President Harrison, it was written beneath his image, though maybe I should have started with the back—a small boat at sea, with men in tall black hats and women and babies huddled together as waves crashed over the bow. *Landing Of The Pilgrims*, the caption beneath read.

I leaned in closer to the image of President Harrison. His expression was hard to capture: A half-smile that softened his brows and creased forehead and played on his lips. I'd thought the beard would make it easier, but it only obscured the shape of his mouth. I picked up my hand mirror and tried to make my expression match Harrison's. But my crooked smile—the left corner of my mouth lower than the right—made this impossible.

Every line I drew, I quickly erased. The paper felt grubby, its sur-face worn. I tore it from the book and added it to the crumpled pile. Maybe I should give up. Not because it was difficult—I knew I'd master it, eventually—but because Pappa didn't want me doing this. I don't know. Maybe it had something to do with that poor Baladucci, with his urine-soaked coat. But I couldn't bear the idea of Clutch finding some-one else to make the bill. I was the artist. The engraver.

I stood and gathered up the balled-up papers and went to the bed-room to put them in the trash. It was quiet upstairs. Nonna must be nap-ping. Since that terrible first night, there had been no more outbursts. No mention of a baby or a lover. Most of the time, she kept to herself, either napping or resting in her small room.

I'd just drawn a new oval for Harrison's face when I heard Mamma's angry voice coming from downstairs. She was starting in on Caterina again.

"Sit up straight," she hissed. "No man wants a hunchback."

Bartolomeo, Caterina's intended, was coming for lunch. Mamma had been criticizing her all morning.

Caterina mumbled that she was sorry.

"Don't start crying again."

Maybe I should go downstairs and help my sister. She'd been on edge for days, picking at her skin and pulling on her eyelashes. Who could blame her? A woman's whole world was her husband, and none of us had yet met her betrothed. He might be hideously ugly. Or uncouth. She'd have to marry him anyway. I could go downstairs. Draw Mamma's ire. It wouldn't be hard. Mamma had been furious with me lately. Then Caterina could get a moment's peace.

But I looked at my sketch, an oval drawn faintly. Why should my sister get a break when her only job was to be a bride? Nothing else was expected of her. All she had to do was to show up in her gown. No one was depending on her. Not Pappa, or Zio Vito, or Clutch. I could have felt sorry for myself. After all, I was just a girl. What did I know about sketching those stupid bills? Instead, I put pencil to paper and darkened the lines of the oval.

A moment later, Mamma called up to me and Nonna. "It's time for Mass. I don't want to be late." The old woman's door opened and she started down. But I had work to do. I went to the banister railing and told Mamma I wasn't feeling well.

"You better not get anyone else sick," Mamma warned, her meaning clear. I'd brought the tuberculosis from the *atelier*. It was my fault Rosalia was dead.

"I'm going to rest," I lied.

A few minutes later, the door closed behind Mamma, Nonna and Caterina. I returned to my sketch. An hour later, I'd blocked in Harrison's eyes and nose. I heard the creak of the garden gate and looked down. Pappa was there, with a young man. Bartolomeo. He was tall, with jet black hair that shone in the sun. I looked at the clock on my bed table. Just before one. Mamma, Nonna and Caterina wouldn't be back from noon-time matins for at least an hour. Mamma would be angry to find Bartolomeo here. She thought that the first meeting between betrotheds should be carefully planned. Choreographed, like a ballet.

The men were in the dining room. I went to the hallway to hear what they were saying. Pappa thanked Bartolomeo for his help. With what, I didn't know.

"Don't mention it," Bartolomeo responded. "We're family. The location is good, right? Perfect for a grocery. Lots of foot traffic. Big windows to showcase your olive oil and what-not."

I was confused. There'd been no word about a storefront since the meeting with Clutch and the others last month. Here was Bartolomeo— my sister's intended—saying he'd found a place. But Bartolomeo was a barber. What did he have to do with Pappa's grocery? The men were speaking quietly now. I leaned over the banister. I still couldn't hear. I was about to return to the sketch when Pappa called my name. I don't know why, but I didn't respond.

"Mimi!" he called, louder.

I counted to five, willing myself to be patient before I answered. "Yes, Pappa?"

"Come hear about the store."

The store. I'd have to pretend to be excited when all I wanted was to finish my sketch. But Mamma would tell Pappa I'd been too sick to go to

Mass. I didn't want to give Pappa any reason to say I wasn't well enough to work. I put down my pencil and started downstairs.

I saw Bartolomeo the moment I entered the smoke-filled parlor. Like a Greek god—Adonis, maybe—with his aquiline nose and long arms and legs, though up close, he had the high forehead and deep-set eyes of one of those Moors who'd conquered Sicily long ago. Mamma always told us to steer clear of them. They were lustful. Barbaric.

Pappa's arms opened wide. "Mimi! Come meet your future brother-in-law. Bartolomeo."

"Bartu, please." When he turned to me, I felt a stirring in my belly. *Amoruso means lover*, Zio had said. I reminded myself. This was the man Caterina was going to marry.

Bartu took my hand. "Sister, dear." He pressed it to his lips, then stared at me in a way that told me he knew what I'd been thinking.

"Come sit with us." Pappa gestured towards Nonna's chair. "We were just talking about the grocery."

Bartu released my hand, but his eyes stayed on mine. "You must see it, Signorina. I'll bring you tomorrow. In my motor car."

My cheeks felt hot. It sounded like he meant just the two of us.

Pappa waved his hand dismissively. "Another day. You were going to introduce me around that market. The one with the funny name."

Bartu touched his forehead. "Of course. The Wallabout. My pardons, Don Inglese. It went right out of my head. I was starstruck. The artist with the pomegranate. Don Cascioferro has told us so much about you."

Pappa went to the dining room for more grappa.

Bartu leaned in. "How's the sketch coming?"

I should have asked how he knew about it. But he was close, the smell of citrus and tobacco making me lose myself.

I mumbled something about making progress.

"I could look at it for you," he offered. "I know American money. Not like those guys in Palermo. I handle the bills every day."

Pappa returned with two glasses at the bottle of grappa, sunlight glinting through the amber liquid. He put a glass in front of Bartu, then poured out the liqueur. He asked what we were talking about.

Bartu answered before I had a chance. "Mimi's drawings."

Pappa gulped his drink, then slammed his glass on the table, the remaining liquid sloshing onto the white cloth.

"Let's take it one step at a time, eh?" he told Bartu. "First, the grocery."

"Of course, Don Inglese. Anyway, we need to move the Palermo dollars first. With your store. *Verù?*"

Pappa downed the rest of his drink.

I know it was disloyal, but I couldn't help but wonder if the store was an afterthought, and my drawings the most important thing.

Pappa poured another drink. This time, he downed it in one swallow. He might have refilled his glass a third time had the front door not opened and Mamma, Nonna and Caterina swept in.

Mamma's voice rang out from the foyer. "That hat! It might be the latest Fall fashion, but it was ridiculous. An enormous bird. Like something you'd serve on a platter." Mamma, the fashion maven, insulted by something someone had worn.

Other than the rustling of their skirts, Nonna and Caterina were quiet. Bartu looked excitedly toward the foyer, like a child waiting for a gift.

Mamma was the first into the living room. She stopped short when she saw Bartu.

Pappa put his arm around Bartu's shoulders. "This is Bartolomeo Amoruso."

Caterina's mouth fell open. I couldn't tell whether it was from shock or the lightning bolt. Maybe there's not much difference.

"Donna Inglese." Bartu bowed first to Nonna, then Mamma. He didn't look at Caterina. "I must apologize, Donna Inglese, for coming early. I was eager to meet my new family."

Mamma put out her hand. Bartu kissed it. I saw how Mamma looked at him—the smart suit, the perfectly coiffed hair. She closed her eyes for a moment, pleased.

Nonna pushed her way forward. Ignoring Bartu, she asked if Pappa had seen the storefront he'd set out for that morning. Nonna's world had grown smaller since we'd arrived on Doctors Row. Most of the time, she was quiet. When Nonna did speak, it was almost always to inquire about my health or Pappa's work.

Pappa didn't seem to notice. "It's on Madison Avenue," he said. "Very fancy."

"It has excellent visibility," Bartu added. "The subway station is on the corner; the school is down the block. There's lots of foot traffic."

"And the best part is that Bartu found it!" Pappa squeezed Bartu's shoulder. "And he negotiated a good deal on the rent."

His arm still around Bartu, Pappa gently reached out to Caterina, like she was a skittish horse. "Come, my dear."

Caterina stood still as a statue. Mamma pushed her forward. Unbalanced, Caterina lost her footing. She would have fallen had Bartu not reached out and caught her.

"Are you all right?" He seemed genuinely concerned.

She nodded. Even from across the room, though, I could see the rapid rise and fall of her chest and her pale skin. Bartu tightened his grip on her. Nonna motioned to the daybed. Bartu lifted Caterina in his arms and carried her across the room.

I'd never wanted to marry, not even after the consumption had taken that option from me. But watching Bartu lay Caterina on the daybed, smiling shyly at her, I was jealous. He'd love my sister for who she was, not what she could do or make. Pappa was beaming at Bartu. The ground shifted under me. Pappa had his son now. My place in the family would depend on how well I could make those bills.

CHAPTER 22

I SAT ON A STOOL in the back room of Pappa's store, surrounded by stacks of still-unopened crates, all marked with my pomegranate. Clutch had summoned me there that morning—sending a note to Pappa that read, simply *Bring the girl*. Nonna had shook her head. "The weather's terrible," she said, motioning toward the window. She insisted I wear three sweaters under my overcoat —hers, mine and Caterina's. When I stepped out into the frigid landscape, the snow blowing in every direction, I was grateful.

Now, Clutch and Pappa sat across from each other at the desk. So far, no one had said anything to me.

Clutch rapped on the polished chestnut desktop with his claw. "Distribution is going too slowly."

"Perhaps we opened prematurely. Things take time to get established."

Clutch sneered. "You could sell a thousand jars of caponata. The store owners still wouldn't be able to move those bills."

My pulse quickened. I'd finally gotten Harrison's expression down. When I'd shown Clutch the sketch last week, he'd been so pleased that he'd given me a real five-dollar bill to keep.

Pappa's eyebrows drew together. "They were moving them before. What's the problem now?"

"It was a small-scale operation. It wasn't hard to slip a five-dollar or two into the cash drawer. But now it's a drawer full of Vito's bogus bills. Harder to move, even if it is to pay the suppliers, who don't want them."

"Maybe they shouldn't have a choice." Pappa's voice was cold.

Clutch laughed. "So you're the boss now? Listen, Nino. No one wants to go to jail for pushing those lousy bills. It's time to make a change. That's why I wanted her here." Clutch motioned toward me with his claw. I tried not to think about poor Baladucci. I reminded myself: I'd only made a sketch.

Pappa waved off Clutch. "You talk about jail. But don't we have friends in the police department?"

"Not everything can be fixed by paying off the cops. Especially with all those new crusaders in charge. No. We need to take charge of things."

Pappa stood and went to the tower of crates near the back door. Just under my pomegranate logo, the words *OLIVE OIL* had been stamped. "This is the latest shipment," Pappa said. "Vito promises the bills are better. Shouldn't we at least try to move these first?"

Clutch smirked at Pappa, then gestured toward the crates. "Okay. Let's see them."

I thought Clutch would help with the crate. Pappa was an old man. A crate filled with olive oil tins had to be too heavy for him. But when Pappa picked it up, it was like the crate weighed nothing. He put it on the desk and pulled it open, the wood splintering.

"Come, Mimi." Clutch motioned me over.

Inside were eight olive oil tins. Clutch pulled one out. In a single motion, he took a knife from his pocket and pried open the lid. I was still wondering what olive oil had to do with the bills when he reached inside and pulled out a roll of fives. Like the one Pappa had brought from Sicily, but bigger. He put the roll on the table and took out another. And another. And another. When he was done, rolls covered the top. There must be a fortune here. Judging by that lime-green color, though, all of it was fake.

Clutch peeled a bill from one roll and handed it to me. He didn't need to ask. I knew what he wanted from me.

I told him what I saw. "It's still too green. The print is clearer but the proportions are still off—the name of the bank, the signatures, the blue seal. And the drawing is wrong, too. Especially in the eyes."

Clutch nodded. "Yours is better."

I tried not to look at Pappa. He'd be surprised, probably even hurt. Because he hadn't been in the room when I'd shown Clutch the sketch. He'd been upstairs, retrieving some invoice Clutch said he needed.

"Who's really going to see that kind of detail?" Pappa snarled.

For one long moment, Clutch said nothing. Then he asked me if I could get the color right.

I nodded. "I've worked it out." Leek green. Emerald, mixed with brown and a bluish gray.

Pappa interrupted. "The ink won't be good for you. Remember Dr. Florio's warning."

"But it's ink, Pappa. Not paint."

Clutch hitched his claw up higher on its chain. "Is there a problem? Cascioferro told me the girl was cured."

Pappa shook his head. I wanted to tell him to shut up. The tuberculosis had stolen so much from me. Here was a chance for me to have something of my own. Something that mattered.

I stepped forward. "I'm fine." I spoke loudly, so Clutch would look at me, not Pappa.

Clutch nodded. "For the time being, we'll do what Nino wants. The product's coming out of his stores, so he's taking the risk. But Mimi will keep working on the bill."

Pappa shook his head. "This is a mistake."

Clutch turned to me. "It's time you met Stella. She'll be doing the production."

"Stella Frauto?"

Clutch smiled. "The one and only."

We'd been here almost a year. At the beginning, I thought of her all the time, this independent woman Zio told me I had to meet. But when she hadn't materialized, she became like a chimera or a hippogriff—a fantastical creature that existed in some other realm.

But she wasn't some imaginary being. And I was going to meet her.

CHAPTER 23

"I CAN'T TALK ABOUT THIS RIGHT NOW!" Mamma's voice, shrill. "The wedding is in less than a month. I have too much to do!"

The matchmaker—a woman I'd never met—looked at Mamma impassively. "If you don't deal with this problem, there won't be a wedding."

I'd been called me down to sit with Caterina while they sorted this out. My sister's expression was blank.

"Who made the objection?" Nonna asked the matchmaker, the first time I recalled her having any interest in my sister's match.

"A woman. Monsignor says she wasn't a regular parishioner. She claims she and Signore Amoruso have an understanding."

Mamma demanded her name.

"Oh, I don't know." The matchmaker waved the air in front of her. "Murphy or Kelly. Something Irish."

"Impossible!" Mamma said. "No Sicilian man would promise himself to an Irish girl. The woman is lying."

"Maybe. But Monsignor has postponed the wedding until it's looked into."

"What kind of place is this?" Mamma sputtered. "Where the claim of a woman like that is believed over a gentleman's word?"

The matchmaker arched her brows. "The problem is that Signore Amoruso hasn't denied it."

We all looked at Caterina, bracing for her reaction. It was as if she hadn't even heard.

Nonna said she'd send word to Zio. He might be three thousand miles away, but he'd arranged the match.

I squeezed Caterina's arm and whispered that it would be all right.

"*Puttana*," Mamma spat out. "She'll ruin everything."

"I've let Clutch know, too," the matchmaker said.

Mamma turned on the woman. "Why him?"

"Bartu is his cousin." Signora's tone left no doubt about how stupid she thought Mamma's question was.

I don't know who fixed it—Zio or Clutch—but at dinner two days later, Pappa announced that the wedding would proceed.

Pappa was refilling his wine glass for the second time when he announced that no promises had been exchanged between Bartu and the woman.

Nonna looked up, her eyes clear. "Bartu said this?"

"No. Clutch. Bartu confided in him."

"Bartu was there but said nothing?" Nonna asked.

Pappa gulped down half the glass. "He lost his head. He said things he didn't mean."

In Sicily, prospective grooms were encouraged to sow their wild oats; brides were expected to be virgins. But I'd seen the magazine covers at the newsstand on Lexington. The Gibson Girl with her haughty expression and breasts bursting out of her too-tight blouse. I'd heard the music—"Peg of My Heart" and "Let Me Call You Sweetheart"—about men helplessly in love. Here, women could tilt the scales in their favor in romantic relationships.

"She'll be compensated," Nonna said.

Mamma's head whipped back around to Nonna. "What?"

"The young woman. She'll be compensated." Nonna turned to Pappa. "You'll make sure of it, won't you?"

Mamma was furious. "Matri! This isn't Sicily. The girl let herself be used. She chose this."

Pappa sighed. "Enough, Maria. The girl will live with the conse-quences. But for Bartu, this was a lapse in judgment. A mistake. In cer-tain situations, a man stops thinking straight."

I thought of Teo, on the loft floor with me; Hans, beneath the scratchy wool blankets on the ship's deck. Could I have had that effect on them?

"So we'll go ahead with the original wedding date?" Nonna asked.

Mamma gasped. "That's less than a month away."

"Just get it done." Pappa didn't even look in Mamma's direction.

Mamma began to cry, big round tears that rolled down her cheeks.

Pappa poured himself another glass of wine. After he'd taken a few sips, he went to her. Grazing his fingertips along her damp cheek, he said, "*Cara*. Bartu wants to marry Caterina as soon as possible. We can understand, *verù?*

Mamma—my haughty, big-talking Mamma—leaned into Pappa's hand, like a hungry street cat.

Pappa smiled at Caterina. "Bartu's a romantic. You're the woman he's chosen."

Caterina's shoulders relaxed. It shouldn't have mattered. She'd been raised to think of marriage not as a matter of love, but as a duty. Still, she believed Pappa when he said Bartu wanted her and no one else. Maybe things would have been different if my sister hadn't been told to expect so much.

CHAPTER 24

IT SNOWED THE NIGHT before the wedding. On cats' paws the snow-flakes came, covering the filthy streets. Ice encased the tree branches, some still clinging to their leaves even though it was February. Beautiful but fragile. Like Caterina. At dawn, Nonna gave her a bromide-seltzer to calm her nerves. Thankfully, Caterina fell back to sleep. When Signora Cassata had arranged Caterina's first betrothal, back in Sicily, she assured us that marriage and motherhood would make my sister calmer. I don't know if I believed that. But after today, Caterina would be Bartu's prob-lem, not ours. I'd like to say that I would miss her, like I did Rosalia. Already, though, I'd been thinking about how quiet it would be without her constant prayers and murmurings.

I started down the stairs, past the vase of gardenias from Bartu, their cloyingly sweet fragrance wafting from the alcove shelf. Mamma was in the kitchen with a metal frame balanced atop her head. She had insisted on a pompadour—the latest fashion from Paris—and a beautician from downtown was piling Mamma's hair as high as she could atop her head.

"Tea for your sister," Mamma ordered. "And a biscuit. We don't need her fainting at the altar."

It took forever for the water to boil. I tried not to listen as Mamma jabbered with the beautician about her latest trial—how the dressmaker had used grosgrain instead of satin ribbons on her gown. I was in such a rush to get away that as I poured the water into the kettle, it scalded my hand. Before Mamma could yell at me for being clumsy, I made my way back to the bedroom. Caterina had awoken and was on her knees next to the bed, her Book of Days before her. I placed the cup and biscuit on the bedside table. The Book was opened to St. Agata. She held a platter and on it, her bloody, severed breasts, the price of refusing the Roman prefect. I thought, not for the first time, about the ridiculous sacrifices some made for goodness or piety.

The bedside clock read eight-fifteen. The ceremony was at eleven. I placed the Book on the table. I helped Caterina wash, then slipped the silk chemise over her head, secured her pantaloons with the satin tie, and fastened the dozens of pearl buttons that ran down the back of her gown. Through it all, she stood, arms stiff and body wooden, like one of those life size puppets in the Opera dei Pupi. Not Angelica or Orlando—for them, lack of movement was momentary, unwanted. No. She stood in the wings, a minor character, reluctant to join the fray. Insensible to conflict. To glory.

When I was done, Caterina was trembling in fear. Rosalia had always had a way with Caterina. If she were here, she'd reassure our baby sister. Tell her everything would be all right. But I never had that connection with Caterina. So, like a condemned man who goes to his death without comfort, Caterina set out for the church.

Our Lady of Mount Carmel was down by the river. Its white brick façade so new, so pristine, that it hurt my eyes to look at it. Nothing like the yellowed and moldering exterior of Our Lady of Freedom in Partanna. But maybe there was magic in being wed in a new place like this: everything still possible; no lingering regrets carried over from one generation to the next.

At the church door, Caterina hesitated. I slipped my arm through hers and nudged her forward. At the end of the side chapel, Pappa offered his arm. Together they made their way to the altar. Bartu was already standing there. I thought I saw him glance around the pews, as if looking for someone. I followed his gaze to the back pew, where Clutch was sitting with a woman I'd never seen before. She wore a hat with an enormous ostrich feather. Could this be Miss Murphy, come to stop the wedding? But when the priest asked for objections, there were none. Whatever had happened with the mysterious Miss Murphy, Caterina had won out. I felt a strange kind of victory in that.

After the wedding was done, I turned to see Clutch holding court at the back of the church, the other parishioners listening, rapt, as he carried on about how important marriage was. The woman he'd been seated with was near the votive candles. Now I could see that she wore a man's vest, purple with a gray pinstripe. I would have liked to have a vest like that, for my pencil stubs and graphite erasers.

"Thanks to the Madonna," Clutch said, "I've been blessed twice." He made the sign of the cross with his claw hand. "My first wife, Marialisa, God rest her soul. And now my Lena. She cares for Calogero like he's her own. She's my wife. My partner." The woman in the vest must be his wife. As I stood there, thinking it was strange that she'd wandered off from him, the woman began walking toward me.

She held out her hand. "You must be Mimi." I'd never shaken a woman's hand. The bones were delicate, like a bird's.

"Are you Clutch's wife?" I asked.

"His *sposa*?" She threw back her head and laughed. Then she leaned in. "I'm Stella Frauto."

I mumbled something about how Zio had told me about her. It sounded accusatory.

"Really?" she smiled, one corner of her mouth lifting. "What did Don Vito say?"

I tried to remember his exact words. It felt important that I get it right.

"Just that I should meet you."

Stella took a cigarillo from her vest pocket. "I've also been wanting to meet you. There aren't many of us, you know."

I must have looked confused. She explained. "Women who they let play the game." She gestured toward Clutch, then lit her cigarillo. "Women with skills no one else has." The tip of the cigarillo burned as red as the flickering votives. "Like you and your drawing." She took a drag, then exhaled, smoke filling the small vestibule. "I thought Vito was lying about your talent. He does that. I should know. I've been caught in some real doozies."

She took another drag.

"I told him: Artists are a dime a dozen. Why import one from Sicily when you can hire one off any street corner?"

But I wasn't like other artists. I should tell her about Monsieur Laurent's studio. How, before I'd gotten sick, I was going to be the first woman admitted to the Palermo Art Academy.

Before I could say anything, though, she continued. "But then I saw your work."

She took another drag. "Vito likes to think he's in charge—that he calls the shots. But you can't run things from three thousand miles away. Not anymore." She poked her lit cigarillo into the reservoir of melted wax below the votive candles. "Clutch is the boss here. Lucky for you that he likes you."

The wedding guests began moving outside. Some were pulling fistfuls of rice from their pockets. Stella paid them no mind.

"You have the final sketches?" she asked.

I nodded. "The bill is done."

Stella put her finger to her lips.

I looked around—old ladies dressed in black, lace veils covering their faces. Exhausted mothers grasping the hands of their reluctant children. I couldn't imagine any of them were eavesdropping on our conversation. I lowered my voice anyway.

"We're going back to the house for the reception," I said. "I can show them to you."

"I don't like weddings." She adjusted her vest. "We'll meet next week. You'll bring the sketches. We'll talk about things."

As I watched her walk away, I noticed how small she was. An inch or two shorter than me, she quickly disappeared into the crowd. In her wake, though, she left a disturbance, like the ripples of a far-off wave that can only be felt when it crashes upon the shore.

I made my way down the church steps to where Pappa was standing with Nonna. The snow had melted into dirty slush. We watched Bartu help Caterina into his new Model T.

"New wife, new life," he'd said when he came by the house to show it to us last week. The car was extravagant: forest green with yellow spoke wheels and shiny brass lamps. Pappa told us it cost eight hundred fifty dollars—twice what Bartu earned as a barber in a year.

Bartu pulled away from the curb, filthy slush just missing me. I helped Nonna onto the bench in Pappa's truck, between Mamma and Pappa. I sat on a bale of hay in the back.

Twice, Pappa stalled the car engine. By the time we arrived home, Clutch and his brothers were already there. There was no sign of Bartu or Caterina. When Mamma asked, Nicolò smiled slyly. "They're upstairs." There was something like triumph in his voice. Mamma's cheeks flushed. She disappeared into the kitchen.

Pappa told me to bring Nonna to her room, saying she needed to rest. I tried to object—the new couple would be just next door, in my room. Surely, they needed privacy. But Pappa insisted.

As I started upstairs with Nonna, Clutch called out to me. "Come right down, Mimi. We have to talk."

About halfway up, I heard the creak of the bed. The slap of skin. Bartu, grunting.

Nonna looked up, like an old dog catching a whiff of some long-lost scent. We were almost at the top when she pulled away and started toward the bedroom. I ran after her and tried to pull her away. She shrugged me off, like a petulant child.

"I need to see Curro." She pointed toward the room. "He's here."

Curro? I'd never heard that name.

"Don't act like you don't know." Nonna crossed her arms over her chest. "He's waiting for me."

Curro. Did Nonna have a brother with that name? I don't think I'd ever heard her talk about her family. I struggled to make sense of this. Nonna had a life I knew nothing about. It had been long ago, but now it was seeping through, like the faint hue of color on a painted-over canvas.

"We're going away together." Nonna ran her hand over her belly. "Our baby, too." She smiled.

Another groan from the bedroom. This time, longer, like an animal in its last throes. Nonna turned toward the sound. "Curro!" She darted away. I lunged for her but fell short, landing hard on my knees.

Nonna threw open the newlyweds' door.

I heard her cry, "You're not Curro!"

Bartu began to laugh. At that moment, I hated him.

"Father!" Nonna screamed, running down the steps. "What have you done with Curro?"

I found her in the parlor, head in her hands, weeping. Pappa had his arm around her shoulders. He was crying, too.

Clutch walked to where I was standing. "This is what comes from love. Consider yourself lucky that you're not mixed up in all that." He pulled at his mustache. "You met Stella?"

I nodded. "We're getting together next week."

"*Bene. Bene.* The two of you are going to do great things together."

I nodded, unsure how to respond.

Clutch leaned in, his face close to mine. "You know, Mimi, you and I are alike. People count us out—you because of the consumption, me because of this." He raised his claw. "But these things make us stronger."

He was quiet for a moment before he continued. "Calm seas never made a good sailor."

Zio's old saying. I hoped it was true. Because the course of Nonna's and Caterina's lives had been set by someone else: Nonna, by her father and lover; Caterina, by Bartu. The consumption had stolen the future I had hoped to have.

With my burins and those engravings, I might find a way to wrest back some control.

CHAPTER 25

STELLA STOOD IN THE BACK ROOM of Pappa's store, examining the copper sheets Clutch had provided. It was Sunday. The store was closed, and we were alone. I'd just finished preparing the surfaces, filing the edges down then polishing each sheet with a resin that made my chest hurt. I waxed them and then lit a candle and smoked the surface to make it easier to make out my sketch.

"Now what?" Stella asked. In the weeks since we'd met, I'd come to understand that she liked to know how things worked.

Maybe Nonna had been like this when she was young. She'd taught herself to be a nurse and had lived in the hills for years, ministering to both rebels and soldiers. It was hard to reconcile this past Nonna with the present one. Since the wedding, she'd hardly spoken at all. Even more concerning, she'd somehow forgotten how to pray the rosary. I'd spent most of yesterday morning showing her how to move her fingers over the well-worn beads, repeating, over and over, the Hail Mary.

I couldn't think about that.

"Now, I transfer the sketches I made to the copper," I said.

"Like tracing?"

Stella made it sound easy. She didn't know about all those pencils sharpened down to their nubs that it had taken to get those reverse images right. Eight mirror images. But I'd finally captured them.

I smiled. "Yes. Like tracing."

Stella motioned to the leather case with my initials on the outside. "Do you use the burins to make the tracings?"

"No. That would ruin the drawings." I tried not to think of my pomegranate in tatters. I picked up a wax pencil. "I use this. That way, I can make another plate if I need to." Stella had hinted that it would be a big operation. I didn't want to worry about having to redraw the images.

I placed the drawing on top of the copper, then secured the corners with small dress weights. I used the tip of the pencil to gently press the images onto the soft copper. I worked through the morning and into the afternoon, concentrating on the elements: the outline, then all those dots and dashes and the cross-hatching. When my belly began to grumble, Stella went to get the burlap bag she'd brought. She pulled out a bottle of wine, then went to the front of the store and got a wheel of cheese and a baguette. She poured a glass of wine for each of us. I sliced the cheese and bread.

After we'd finished eating, she leaned back against the desk and put her hands on her belly.

"Gotta hand it to Vito. This is some of the best cheese I've ever eaten. I'm going to miss it when we move to the farmhouse."

The farmhouse. The second time Stella and I met, she'd mentioned it. Located across the Hudson River, someplace in New Jersey. She was the only one who knew where it was. This seemed odd. With an operation as big as this, with all those copper plates, the inks and the paper, I'd have thought Clutch would be involved. But Stella insisted Clutch couldn't be bothered with the details.

"He trusts me." She smiled slyly.

I asked how long it would take to get to the farmhouse.

She held up one finger. "The subway to the piers." Then a second and third. "The Hudson River ferry and an automobile ride. About two hours each way."

I was surprised. "We'll be there all day?"

Stella drank down her wine. "We'll stay one or two days at a time. That'll make things easier."

"You mean overnight?" I heard the alarm in my voice.

"You're worried your Pappa will say no?"

There was no sense in lying. I nodded.

She waved her hand in the air. "Clutch will take care of him." She poured another glass of wine.

"Will it be safe?" The moment the words left my mouth, I hated myself for asking.

"Sure. No one would mess with Clutch."

"And the cops?"

She took another piece of cheese and plunked it in her mouth.

I thought of Baladucci, led away in handcuffs.

"Is this legal?" I gestured to the copper plate before me.

"What? Copying a picture? Don't artists do this kind of thing all the time? I thought it was part of their training."

I nodded, though I'd never tried to pass off a Rembrandt or da Vinci as my own.

She reached across the table and took my hand. "For now, just concentrate on the engraving. You can't control what someone else might do with them," she said, with mock earnestness. "You're an artist. This is art. No one's ever gone to jail for drawing some pictures."

I returned to the copper plates. I finished cross-hatching Harrison's face and the knotty pine of the Pilgrims' small boat. When I was done, I lifted the two sketches off the paper, revealing the copper. The engraving was perfect.

Stella saw it, too. "This is going to work. It's really going to work."

"We'll need the ink soon."

Stella fished out the slip of paper where I'd written the ink colors I'd need. "I just give them this list at the store on Canal?"

"Yes. But I can do it." The truth is that I wanted to go. It had been so long since I'd been in an art store.

She shook her head. "Your father doesn't want you out in public."

I started to protest but she held up her hand. "This is a small thing, Mimi. Let him have his way. For now." She shook her head. "I wonder sometimes, though. About what it was like for you in Sicily."

"What do you mean?"

"You were sequestered, in the old Arab way—?" Stella's voice trailed off.

"Yes, but only until I started art lessons in Palermo."

"That must have been eye-opening."

"Yes." Monsieur Ateleier's studio. Teo. Matisse's *Joy of Life*.

"And Vito arranged it all?"

"He's my godfather," I said. "He and Pappa are *compari*."

"Did you ever wonder why he took such an interest?"

"I was a good artist."

Stella took out a piece of muslin and started wrapping the finished plates. When she was done, she looked at me. "You are a good artist." She laid her hand upon the muslin-wrapped package. "When he was here, Vito kept calling you his little Michelangelo. I see why. But he's a counterfeiter, Mimi. He needed you." She paused to light a cigarillo. "That's why I'm surprised that he's dragging his feet on your bills. He knows they're good. And there's money to be made."

My bills. I liked the way that sounded.

She started to pace across the small back room, still smoking her cigarillo. Stella was hardly ever still, especially when she was trying to figure something out. "I guess he doesn't want to lose control of things. With the new operation here, and him still in Sicily."

"But he'll be here soon." I remembered how excited he'd been about returning to America.

"Not now," Stella said, shaking her head. "Maybe not ever. Unless he wants to go to prison. There's a warrant for his arrest. For murder. So, instead he keeps sending those shitty bills. Insisting that they get moved before we start on the new ones."

"There are so many," I said, looking at the towers of crates, stacked from floor to ceiling.

"Clutch insists on going slowly. Too many bills and the cops start poking around. He doesn't need that. Not with all the attention his protection racket is getting these days. But at this pace, it'll be years before we get going. I don't want to wait that long."

"What are you saying?"

"We need to dump the bills," Stella said.

"Without Vito's permission? How would we do that?"

"Burn them. Shred them. It doesn't matter. They just need to disappear."

Those flames would make a huge bonfire. That would attract attention, too.

"What does Clutch think?" I hated myself as soon as I spoke those words. As if Stella's words only had legitimacy if Clutch agreed.

"We need to keep Clutch away from this. He's reckless. Short-sighted. He's sitting on top of an empire but he's still writing those stupid Black Hand letters."

"Black Hand letters?"

"Extortion letters. Demanding money so the person isn't harmed. Signed *Mano Nero*, with an imprint of his hand."

"The claw hand?"

Again, Stella laughed. "That would be terrifying on its own. But no, with his good hand."

"Do they pay?"

"Oh, they pay. There have been enough stories of pipe bombs and fancy houses set on fire to know he means business. They even cut off a young boy's foot when they thought his father wasn't paying quickly enough—"dragging his feet" was how Ciro put it. Brutal. Unnecessary. The man would have put the money together. He just needed more time.

"Men like Clutch are dangerous," Stella continued. "They tend to take people with them. Like my Salvatore ..." Stella looked out the window at something I couldn't see. I'd overheard Pappa say Stella was a widow. I never considered that Clutch might be somehow responsible.

Stella went to the window. "It's almost time to cut ties with them. Be my own person, without Clutch or Vito or anyone else getting in my way."

To be your own person. What would that be like? To decide for myself whether to paint, or draw, or make engravings of five-dollar bills.

To take a chance, knowing I might relapse and that this time, the tuberculosis might kill me.

"I'll keep the plates for now," Stella said. "It's safer that way." She brought her satchel to the worktable and tucked the muslin-wrapped plates inside.

Just outside the window, a bird was making a nest of twigs and cigar wrappers on a low-hanging branch. She probably should have found a more auspicious place, safe from the hungry tomcats. A higher branch, or perhaps the curve of a downspout. But there was such hopefulness in that small bird's decision that against all odds, I had to root for her.

CHAPTER 26

WHEN BARTU APPEARED at our door on Christmas Day, balancing all those boxes and an enormous fir garland around his shoulders, my first thought was that he looked like one of those jugglers I'd seen at the park, hawking tickets to the circus. He had the perfect audience. Mamma, clapping her hands with delight. Nonna, eyeing him from her perch in the corner. Pappa, whose effusive embrace threatened to topple everything.

While Bartolomeo showed off what he'd brought—a Yorkshire pudding and buccellato cake speckled with figs and candied pumpkin—Caterina stood apart. Her cheeks were hollowed, her eyes haunted, like a creature caught between two worlds. They'd been married almost a year, but she still was not with child. This was surprising. Until baby Nino, Mamma always seemed to be pregnant or recovering from childbirth. Eight babies in twelve years—two stillborn boys, two babies born too soon to tell what they were, baby Nino, Caterina, Rosalia, and me. Nonna, too, must have gotten pregnant easily. I can't imagine there were many opportunities for her to meet with her clandestine lover.

Caterina fell onto the daybed and sat there, slumped.

I sat down next to her. "You weren't at Mass this morning. Did you go to St. Ignatius instead?" I whispered, so Nonna wouldn't hear. Bartolomeo's church had a Jesuit priest, and Nonna hated the Jesuits. She never really explained why, saying only that they made things up as they went along. I would have liked to know more but the time to ask had passed. I suspected it had something to do with what had happened in the hills of Sicily, so long ago.

When Caterina didn't respond, I put my hand on her shoulder. "Did you go to church today?"

She shrugged me off, then turned to her cuticles. The skin, torn and weeping, they were as bad as I'd ever seen them.

"It doesn't matter," I said, quietly. "You can pray at home. You have your Book of Days." Those grosgrain ribbons. A rainbow of color amidst all that torture and death.

After a long while, Caterina spoke. "Bartolomeo says religion is a waste of time. He wants me to be an American wife. To read *Lady's Home Journal*. To keep up with the latest fashions." Religion had always been a comfort to my sister. But if Bartu forbade her from going to church, Caterina would never defy him.

From the adjoining dining room came laughter. Bartu was making fun of a customer in his barber shop—a man who'd recently lost his wife, leaving him with a gaggle of small children. He was off to meet the matchmaker and wanted Bartu to find a way to cover his bald patch. I winced, hearing the cruelty in Bartolomeo's voice.

Mamma came into the parlor, looking for a vase. "What are the two of you gossiping about? Caterina, you should be in there, looking after your husband." Caterina followed Mamma into the dining room, like a beaten dog. I went, too.

"Mimi! Come sit." Bartu pulled out a chair, like this was his house. "We were just talking about you, Sister Dearest."

"About what?"

"Your Pappa says you and Stella have been seeing each other."

"What's it to you?" I asked. Bartu was a lout. A bully. Anyway, Stella wanted to keep the operation between us, at least for now.

Bartu smiled, amused. "I like it when you're plucky." He stretched out his legs. "So tell me: What did she say?"

"We just talked."

"About what?" His smile faded.

"Oh, you know. Girl talk. Fashion. Keeping house."

Bartu pressed his lips tightly together. He was angry. I wasn't sorry. I liked making him uncomfortable.

"Come," Pappa said. "Dinner is ready."

We sat down for a Christmas dinner of roast beef and mashed potatoes. No sign of the monstrous king crab legs, or the clams, still buttoned up in their shells, that filled the market stalls last week. Most Sicilians feasted on the seven fishes, but not us. We were Inglese. Our ancestors were British, my parents always reminded us (Mamma forgetting about her Sicilian roots), so we ate British fare. I thought again of how we belonged neither here nor there. Not quite British, despite our name. But not Sicilian, either.

Bartu was talking business before we'd even finished dinner.

"We had some more trouble with Vito's bills," he said. I'd suspected Bartu knew about the bills. I was right.

Pappa stopped chewing and swallowed hard. "What happened?"

"They were supposed to pass them at the Christmas Fair. But those Krauts are too suspicious. We managed to move about a hundred dollars when the cops showed up."

Pappa's mouth fell open. "A hundred? But Clutch said he was going to get rid of two thousand dollars."

Bartu shrugged. "The passers did what they could. Using fives to pay for small items. Asking for coins and small bills in change. But it was like someone had warned the merchants. One of the passers was arrested."

"Arrested?" Pappa asked.

Bartu emptied his glass of wine. "He was just a small fry. A kid from the neighborhood."

"This neighborhood?" Pappa's voice was suddenly shaky.

Bartu nodded.

"So he got the bills from my store?"

Again, Bartu shrugged. There was no need to answer. Pappa's was the only grocery in the neighborhood. Bartu picked up the wine bottle from the silver caddy. After he'd poured himself another glass of wine, he put the bottle down directly onto the lace tablecloth. A trickle of wine slid down the bottle onto the lace. Bartu didn't notice. "He won't snitch."

"How do you know?"

"Clutch's guys got to him."

After a moment, Pappa asked how it could have happened.

They were careless, I thought, watching the wine stain spread on the white cloth.

"It's the cops," Bartu said. "That Officer Petrosino. He's got a hard-on for Vito."

Mamma's jaw dropped but she stayed quiet.

Bartu continued. "He knows the boy works for Clutch. And Clutch works for Vito."

"So the boy was at the Christmas Market. How did they know he was connected to Clutch?" Pappa asked.

"They followed him from Clutch's saloon. They've got cops watching that place."

Pappa hit his forehead with the heel of his hand.

Bartu told Pappa not to worry. "They don't know about your store."

"But they could find out. I've got thousands of bills in my back room. What if they find out? I can't go to jail. What would happen to my family?"

Bartu took a long swig of wine. "I would take care of them. But that's not going to happen," he added, quickly.

"I don't understand. Vito said America was like the Wild West. Billy the Kid and Jesse James. He told me the law was irrelevant. That the cops were only interested in lining their own pockets."

"Petrosino's a crusader. He wants to prove he's a real American, though the other cops call him 'wop' and 'greaser' right to his face. He'll be gone soon. The others will lose interest and start chasing after the next shiny thing the newspapers wave in front of them."

Pappa put his head in his hands. "What do we do until then? Vito keeps asking for his money."

"Fuck Vito. It's because of him and his crappy bills that this is happening. We need to start making our own money." He turned toward me. "Are you almost done with the drawings, Mimi?"

Not just the drawings, but the engraving plates, too. Tucked inside the muslin and secreted in a hiding place only Stella knew about. I'd be damned if I was going to tell him.

"Why should I tell you?"

All eyes at the table turned to me.

"Mimi!" Mamma pressed her hand to her mouth.

"I'm just asking." Bartu raised his eyebrows in mock innocence. "You're my sister. I care about you."

Bartu had insinuated himself into our house, like a snake that wraps itself around the brazier, slowly robbing a room of its heat.

"They're not done yet," I lied.

"You should get to it. This isn't just arts and crafts. Those drawings are important."

CHAPTER 27

CLUTCH TOSSED AN ENVELOPE marked Western Union Telegram onto the store counter. "Vito wants his money."

Pappa picked up the envelope and slipped it into his pocket, though there were no customers to see. There hadn't been any customers, in fact, the whole morning. From where I sat, next to the register, I could see the layer of dust covering the tomato cans. Pappa had brought me with him this morning, ostensibly to help with the displays. But I was here because Clutch insisted.

Clutch propped his claw on the counter. "We're going to have to get creative. The cops are breathing down our necks. Petrosino. Flynn. A fed named Bonaparte—they say his great-grandfather was Napoleon. Little men, all of them. Out to prove themselves."

Clutch used his claw to pluck a cigar from his vest pocket. He struck a match across the sole of his scuffed shoe and lit it, inhaling in and out quickly, until the room was filled with smoke. Desperate to not start coughing, I put a hand across my mouth and nose.

"We have all these bills to pass," Clutch continued. "Mimi, any ideas about how we do this?"

My cheeks felt hot. I still hadn't gotten accustomed to being invited into the men's conversations.

"We could try a different neighborhood," Pappa blurted out. "Mulberry Bend, near your saloon? Or Pigtown in Brooklyn?"

Clutch turned toward me. "We're hearing that the bills don't feel right. Like new bills, but without the bumpy texture."

Stella said the government printed its bills on special paper from a company in Boston. She'd been trying to get hold of some of it. I didn't offer this.

"We could bleach them," Clutch offered. "Would that help?"

I shook my head no. "It would take away the color. They'd be even more faded than they are now."

"But you said the color's off. Maybe bleach would make it better."

"It might, if the ink was emerald or jade-colored. But Zio's are lime-green. Bleach would only turn them yellow."

"So what do you recommend?" Clutch asked this like he valued my opinion.

I shook my head. "I don't know."

Clutch rubbed his good hand over his claw, like he was concentrating. Then he said we should start printing the new bills.

"What do you mean?" Pappa asked. "Now? Before we pass the Palermo bills?" He touched the pocket where he'd put Vito's telegram demanding payment. "Vito expects to be paid. It's his operation."

Clutch sneered. "They might be his crappy bills. But it's our necks on the line. I say we go forward."

"What'll happen with the old bills?" I asked.

He shook his head. "That's the challenge. Short of a miracle, I don't know how we'll get rid of those damned bills."

A few days later, he got his miracle. That is, if you call a massive earthquake a miracle.

Pappa's newspaper lay on the table. The headlines screamed that there'd been an earthquake in Sicily, deep under the Straits of Messina. There were explosions. Fires. Then a great surge of water that leveled buildings and swept thousands of people out to sea. Caught between the Scylla and Charybdis, but instead of a six-headed monster and an inescapable whirlpool, it was an earthquake and tidal wave. Almost 200,000 were killed.

The next morning, Clutch sent word that we were to meet at the store. When Pappa and I arrived, he and Stella were already waiting inside. I didn't know Clutch had a key.

Clutch didn't even wait for us to remove your coats. "This business in Sicily. It might work to our advantage." He motioned to Stella. "Go ahead. Tell them what you told me."

"I passed Western Union last night. The line snaked down the block and around the corner. There must have been two hundred people, all waiting to send money to Messina and Calabria. I got to thinking about Vito's shitty bills."

The bills? What about all those terrible photos in the newspapers? Whole blocks reduced to rubble. Charred bodies floating in Messina Harbor. Towns obliterated by the tidal wave.

Pappa leaned in.

Stella continued. "We can use Western Union to get rid of Vito's bills." Her lips were parted. She was excited.

Pappa asked how.

"We'll buy money grams with them and send the funds back to Vito. That's all he really wants—to be paid. So we'll pay him." When no one spoke, she continued. "Five-dollar money grams. Until we've used up all the bills."

Clutch smiled broadly. "It's genius."

Stella went on. "We'll start a relief organization. A bogus one. Like the Fraternal Order of Hurricane Relief—something whose purpose is clear. We'll wire everything back to Sicily. Fake dollars sent through Western Union; real lire delivered to Vito. It'll work."

"But the cops are on the lookout." Pappa's voice cracked. "We'll get caught."

Stella said she didn't think so. "The cops have been looking for the bogus bills in groceries and bars. Whorehouses, even. As long as we don't try to send too much money at once, they won't even look at the wires. Western Union will be so busy with all those desperate relatives that they won't even try to monitor the bills coming in."

"So all the money will go to Vito's factory?" Pappa asked. "Won't that look funny?" Pappa was looking at Clutch, but Clutch motioned to Stella that she should answer.

"It doesn't matter," she said. "The money'll be Vito's problem then. From our end, we'll be done. We can start fresh."

Clutch nodded. "An inspired plan. Just one question. When Western Union realizes it's been scammed, what's to keep it from tracing the bills back to us?"

"We won't be directly involved. If anything, they'll try to find the bogus relatives. But we'll pay them enough to keep quiet. Let's say 50 cents for each telegram."

Pappa asked what would happen if they changed their minds and decided to tell.

Clutch smoothed down his mustache. "They won't change their minds. My brothers will make sure. So it's decided. We'll send the messengers out all over the city," Clutch continued. "Divide them between Western Union offices. How many people would you need?"

Stella closed her eyes, calculating. When she opened them again, she had an answer. "If we have ten thousand dollars and send five dollars each time, we'll need two thousand telegrams. Fewer if we send more money."

"Oh, Madonna." Pappa shook his head. "And who's going to write all those telegrams?"

"Mimi and I can do it," Stella offered. "Work back here in the storeroom. It's a lot, but we'll keep it simple. Vary the scenarios and the names. We can be creative. Can't we, Mimi?"

I nodded.

But Pappa said it was too dangerous.

"Nino," Clutch smiled, his gold tooth glinting in the lamplight. "Let the girl do it. She wants to. Right, Mimi?"

I should have refused. Pappa clearly didn't want me to do it. Instead, I agreed.

Pappa folded his arms across his chest. He opened his mouth, like he was going to say something, but then closed it again.

CHAPTER 28

I STEPPED INSIDE the vestibule at Doctors Row and brushed the snow from my coat and shawl. I heard Bartu's voice, full of its usual bravado. I pulled off my gloves, bending and stretching my fingers. I'd been hunched over a desk every waking hour over the last three weeks, writing telegraph messages.

> *FOR MY DEAR MAMMA. FIVE DOLLARS TO BURY PAPPA AND LITTLE FRANCESCO.*
>
> *FOR MY WIFE. FIVE DOLLARS. ALL I HAVE FROM LAYING SUBWAY TRACK. USE TO REBUILD HOUSE.*
>
> *TO NONNA. FIVE DOLLARS IN MEMORY OF PAPPA. SWEPT OUT TO SEA IN FISHING BOAT.*

Messages of despair. Grief. Resignation. Drawn directly from the pages of the *Progresso* and *The New York Sun*. Who would have believed that death and destruction came in so many different forms?

Cook would have said I was tempting fate by writing those messages. Maybe she was right. But slowly, the stacks of bills in Pappa's storeroom got smaller. We moved eight thousand dollars and might have gotten rid of the remaining two thousand, too. But the lines at Western Union began to shrink, as the bereaved got back to their more mundane concerns—jobs, rent, food.

With fewer real telegrams, Stella said our bogus ones would be more conspicuous. Stella was like that—always weighing what she called the risks and rewards. Anyway, she said it was time to start on our own bills. Like it was our decision and no one else's. Which I guess it was, though I still couldn't believe that Clutch or his brothers would let us be.

My fingers were stiff but I finally managed to unbutton my coat. After I hung it up, I started down the hallway toward the kitchen. I was tired. But a cup of tea first. Maybe some figs.

Just then, Bartu came toward me, his arms out. "Sister! Finally, you return!" He guided me toward the dining room.

"Sit down, Mimi." Mamma was smiling. "Bartu has news."

Caterina was gaunt and pale. Her eyes, fixed on her plate of untouched *biscotti*, their S-shape so perfect that there was no mistaking that they'd come from the bakery.

Bartu hitched his thumbs inside his suspenders. "We're having a baby!"

As if on cue, Caterina put her hand over her mouth and ran from the room. The sound of retching came from the hallway bathroom.

Bartu sat on the edge of the dining room table. "She's been sick for two weeks. Morning, noon and night. She's very pregnant." As if my sister's suffering was testament to his virility.

From her chair near the window, Nonna spoke. "A baby is a gift from the Madonna." She'd been more and more confused these days. Bartu's words, though, she seemed to understand.

Bartu rocked back and forth on his heels. "The first Amoruso born in America. I'm sure it'll be a boy. When a man makes his wife this pregnant, it's always a boy."

I was about to tell Bartu he was wrong—Mamma hadn't been sick at all with any of her boys, though none of them had survived infancy. But before I could, Nonna had stood and had begun to pace, her hand over her belly.

She muttered something about someone taking her baby, that same worry that had sent her into a panic at the wedding party.

I approached her. She backed up against the window. "Leave me alone, Sister!" she screamed. I had a vision of her falling through the plate glass to the sidewalk below.

"It's all right," I said calmly, as much to Nonna as myself.

"Get her out of here," Mamma snarled.

I took Nonna's hand, easing her away from the window. "Let's go upstairs. We can decide where to put the cradle."

Bartu laughed.

Nonna turned toward him, her eyes clear. "You won't take my baby. I won't let you."

I shot a warning glance at Bartu, then pulled Nonna along. As we walked up the stairs together, I heard the downstairs hallway toilet flush and Caterina shuffling back into the dining room.

"You sure took your time in there," Bartu barked. "My coffee's cold. Get me another cup."

Nonna stopped on the middle stair. "I hate Father," she hissed, gesturing toward Bartu. "He wants to kill my baby. But I won't let him." She dug her fingernails into my arm. "You'll help me get away, won't you, Sister?"

Poor Nonna. Betrayed by the people who were supposed to love her. "Come," I said, urging her forward. "You need to rest. You and your baby."

Nonna slipped her olivewood rosary beads from her pocket. She wrapped them so tightly around her hands that her fingers began to turn white. "I'll pray for Curro." She laid down on the bed and ran her hand over her belly. "And my baby." She closed her eyes. Thankfully, she was soon asleep.

I returned to my room. I couldn't bear to be around Mamma, tutting over Caterina. Or Bartu, boasting about his manhood. Or Pappa. Happy. Proud in a way I hadn't seen him since Monsieur Laurent assured I'd be admitted to the Art Académie. But I reminded myself. My life could be my own. I wasn't bound by a husband or a baby. I thought of the farmhouse Stella had described. The fancy paper. My engraving plates. And Stella's promises: We'd be rich. I'd have my own studio, with canvas and paints. Surely that was better than a selfish husband and squalling baby.

When I awoke that night, I reached for Caterina, though she'd been gone for more than a year. I rose from bed, the wood floor cold under my feet. It was quiet, the radiator cold. Silent. Had we run out of coal? But no. Just a few days ago, the coal man had made a delivery, a cascade of shimmery black rocks tumbling down a chute into our basement. Like the sulfur mines in Partanna. The cartloads of yellow-flecked rocks. The *carusi* boys, baskets strapped onto their backs. Their bodies, impossibly small.

I wrapped my shawl tightly around myself and headed downstairs. The grandfather clock struck half past four—that time of the night between Nonna's nighttime wanderings and Pappa's first trip to the water closet. Soon, the lamplighter would extinguish the streetlights, though the winter sun would stay low in the sky, giving little warmth or light to the frigid city streets. I held fast to the banister and made my way toward the kitchen. I put the kettle on and opened the tin of *finocchio* tea, breathing in the sweet anise. I stirred the seeds into my cup and poured the water on top. My hands warming, I went into the parlor. I settled into Nonna's chair. My fingers found those old scars.

I must have nodded off because I was awoken by Pappa's voice.

"Who's there?" he demanded. "Show yourself." There was a loud clicking sound. "I have a pistol."

"It's me, Pappa."

The gaslight beside the fireplace blazed into life. Pappa stood there, pointing a gun at me.

"Show yourself," he demanded.

"It's Mimi. Your daughter." I stood and put my hands in the air, as I remembered Baladucci doing at Ellis Island.

"Mimi?" Pappa lowered the gun.

"I couldn't sleep."

"Why are you skulking around? I could have—hurt you." In the lamplight, Pappa looked ghoulish, deep shadows under his eyes and mouth. He dropped the gun to his side and stumbled back. His breath was ragged. "There's been trouble," he mumbled.

Trouble. I saw it in a flash: the powdery fungus on the wheat, the shuttered sulfur mine, my paintings and art supplies, up in smoke. Zio's words—Pappa was unlucky.

I didn't ask. Pappa continued anyway. "An American policeman was killed in Palermo." He paused before he continued. "Petrosino. He went over to find out about the Black Hand. I told Clutch to stop sending those damn messages. He wouldn't."

I pointed to the gun. "Why do you have that?"

Pappa just shook his head. That was more terrifying than anything: that Pappa was afraid, but he couldn't—or wouldn't—say why.

"What will we do, Pappa?"

He sighed heavily, then put the gun into the waistband of his pants. "What can we do? We wait and see what happens."

We didn't have to wait long. Three days later, Bartu brought word that two of the men he'd hired to send telegrams had been taken in for questioning. "I trust these guys. They'll keep their mouths closed."

Caterina arrived the next day. After she'd dragged herself upstairs and Pappa had settled her into a chair, she told us Bartu had been taken. "Two police officers. Early this morning." She turned white, then put her hand over her mouth.

I hurried Caterina into the water closet and stood by, helpless, as she dry heaved into the toilet.

When we returned to the living room, Pappa was gone.

Mamma was chewing the inside of her lip. "He went to send word to Vito. But what Vito's going to do from over there, I don't know."

When Pappa got back home, Clutch was with him. I heard them in the hallway.

"A stupid move sending that telegram to Vito," Clutch hissed. "The cops are falling over themselves trying to tie us to the Petrosino killing. You just made it easier for them."

Pappa insisted it would be fine. "I spoke in code. They'll never figure it out."

The two men came into the dining room. Clutch's clothes were wrinkled, like he'd been sleeping in them.

"Code?" Clutch asked. "What does that mean?"

Even I heard how ridiculous Pappa sounded.

"I told him everything was fine," Pappa continued. "That he should expect another delivery."

"Another delivery?" There was a sharp edge to Clutch's voice. "But we're not sending any more money."

I'd been there when they agreed with Stella that it was too dangerous to send more wire transfers. But here was Pappa, telling Zio to expect another delivery.

Clutch leaned in menacingly. One-handed or not, he could hurt Pappa. Maybe even kill him. "You're an idiot," Clutch said. "The cops are looking for a way to connect you with Vito. To show that you had a way of telling him that Petrosino would be in Sicily."

"But I didn't tell him—." Pappa said.

Mamma hurried me from the room. I could still hear Clutch raging.

"Do you really think that matters?" Clutch slammed his good hand on the table. "That fucking Cascioferro! He had to have the last word, like with everything. But killing Petrosino—that's going to bring everything down on us: The cops, the feds, every ambitious politician. If they tie us to the bad bills, it'll be worse. Counterfeiting is serious here. You can go away for twenty, thirty years."

I should have known this. I'd seen Baladucci hauled off to prison. But I guess because no one had talked about it—not Zio or Clutch or Stella—I'd foolishly thought I was safe.

"I'll tell you, Nino," Clutch thundered. "I've already gone to prison for Cascioferro's fake coins. Someone else will have to take the fall this time."

I was thinking of Clutch's words the next day, when the cops arrived at our door, their knocking too insistent to ignore.

Pappa opened the door a crack. "Antonino Inglese?" one asked. I thought of those officers on the *Sofia Hohenberg*. Maybe Pappa was thinking about it too, because he hesitated before answering.

"I'm Antonino Inglese."

The officers pushed their way inside. They slapped handcuffs on Pappa's wrists. Then they took him away.

I ran the five blocks to Stella's apartment. When I finally got to her doorstep, I was wheezing.

"The cops took Pappa."

Stella helped me off with my coat and hung it on a nail behind the door.

I started to repeat what I'd said. She stopped me. "I know." She stood to light a match on the stove burner. "Sit," she said. "Rest."

I sat there, taking in the small room with its solitary chair and table. In the corner was a bed roll. Over it was another striped vest and shirt, identical to what Stella was wearing. The water boiled. She brought the tin saucepan to me, the smoke rising.

"Try to breathe this in," she said. "For your lungs." She pulled a shabby shawl from the back of her chair and wrapped it around me. "I told them we should go to New Orleans. It's warmer there. Better for you."

What was she talking about? We came to New York because that's where Pappa's store was going to be. No one had said anything about New Orleans.

Stella continued. "Clutch refused. He and Vito hated that city. They said that Sicilians were treated like Negroes there." Stella went to the sofa and pulled off a blanket. Like the shawl, it was threadbare.

"I told them there were other cities, where it wasn't so cold," she continued. "St. Louis. San Francisco. They wouldn't even consider it."

I shook my head. "We came here for Pappa's store. And so Caterina could marry Bartu."

Stella smiled sadly. "You still don't see it, do you? Your family was brought here because of *you*. Not so your father could open a store or Caterina could marry Bartu."

"So it's my fault Pappa's in trouble?"

She crouched down in front of me and took my cold hands in her warm ones. "Listen to me. Your father's in trouble because he was stupid. Sending that telegram to Zio, even though we told him to lay low and let the trouble with Petrosino pass. I don't know why he did that. Maybe because of a misplaced sense of loyalty to Vito. But he brought this trouble down on himself. And all of us."

If what Stella said was true, I should be angry at Pappa. But I couldn't help but think of him in manacles. He looked old. Pathetic. I quietly asked what would happen to him.

"That depends on what Bartu told them," Stella said.

Pappa's fate, in the hands of that baboon.

"Will he go to jail?"

Stella shrugged.

"But we wrote the earthquake telegrams."

"The cops don't care about those telegrams. They're more concerned about how the counterfeit bills got into the country in the first place."

"Through the crates," I whispered, thinking of all those boxes labeled *Mercantini Import/Exports* with my pomegranate logo on front.

Stella nodded. "They tracked the bills of lading and discovered almost every crate was delivered to Antonino's store."

"But Pappa didn't know what was in those crates." I said, though I knew that wasn't true.

Stella snorted. "You don't really believe that, do you? Your father knows who Vito is. What he does. He knew what he was getting into when he agreed to let Vito send those shipments to his grocery. Your Pappa wasn't the mastermind, but he understands the operation. The cops will pressure him to tell them."

"My Pappa would never betray Vito."

"I know. I'm more worried about what Antonino might tell the cops about Clutch and his brothers. Let's just hope he keeps quiet. Because Clutch is dangerous when he's angry. And he never forgets."

CHAPTER 29

I WOKE UP SHIVERING, immediately afraid I had a fever. I probed my old scars, as if I could tell by feel whether the consumption had returned. I eased myself into an upright position, waiting for the cough that would signal a relapse. When I didn't start coughing, I stood and went to the radiator. It was cold. There were ice crystals on the inside of the window. I tried to remember the last time Pappa had gone to the cellar to fill the hopper with those shiny black rocks. It must have been before he'd been taken, more than two weeks ago, now.

I slipped into my boots and went to the hall. Past seven, but it was still quiet. Nonna had been up again during the night, wandering. Confused. Thankfully, there was a deadbolt on the front door.

Mamma was lost, too. Since Pappa had gone, she'd hardly left her bed, not bathing or even brushing her hair. It was like the melancholia she'd suffered after little Nino died.

I crept downstairs to the kitchen, then went to the cellar stairs. My shoulder pressed against the damp stone wall, I descended, careful not to trip on the too-shallow bottom stair. I made it to the coal scuttle. My fingers grazed the bottom, coming away with dust that shimmered even in the dim light that eked through the splintered frame of the coal chute door. I reached up into the chute. Like the scuttle, it was empty. February in New York City. Too cold to be without heat, and I had no idea how to make the coal man come.

Stella would know. But the last time I'd seen her—on the day Pappa was taken—she told me not to contact her until after the cops finished their investigation.

"The cops are watching everything. Looking for some way to pressure your father. To make him say what he knows."

I tried to assure her that I'd told Pappa nothing about the farmhouse or the fancy paper or her plans to start making our own bills. She waved me off, saying this was the only way to stay safe.

But with the coal bin empty, I needed her help. I went upstairs and dressed quickly. Before I stepped outside, I looked up and down the sidewalk, as if I might see some cop there, waiting for me. But the residents of Doctors Row slumbered, dreaming about whatever the rich dream of. A new car. A fancy dinner downtown. Tickets to the Spectacular. Not so different from what the nobility had wanted. I turned onto Lexington and joined the throngs of workers off to their factories, or their construction pits, or their employers' fancy houses.

I'd rung Stella's bell several times when the living room curtain rustled. The door opened and Stella pulled me inside.

Before she could be angry, I told her I hadn't seen any cops.

"You wouldn't have seen them, Mimi. They're detectives. They're not in uniform," she sniped. "Why are you here?"

I told her about the coal. I half-expected her to criticize Pappa or to tell me to ask Zio. Instead, she told me she'd take care of it. Then she pressed a ten-dollar bill into my hand. "For food. And rent."

I tried to give it back. "Pappa will be back soon."

She shook her head. "I'm not sure about that. If the cops want to make an example of him—to show what happens when you throw in your lot with someone like Clutch—he could be going to prison for a long time."

"He's an old man!"

She shrugged. "People die in prison." Unspoken, that her husband, Salvatore, was buried in a potter's field somewhere.

I folded the bill and tucked it into my satchel. If Pappa was sent to prison, I'd need more than this to keep the household going. I asked when we could start making bills.

"Not yet."

"When?"

"Once the cops decide whether to arrest Clutch. After that, they won't be watching so closely. For now, don't tell anyone about the plates."

Who would I tell? Not Mamma—she'd run to Bartu. Not Nonna—she was too confused. And not Caterina—since she'd become pregnant, she'd drawn in on herself, like a snail to its shell.

"How's your sister?" Stella said, reading my mind.

I shrugged. "Pregnant."

"She should lay off that shit Bartu's giving her."

"What shit?"

"The *Vin Mariani*, or whatever they're calling it these days. Wine laced with cocaine."

"My sister doesn't drink." But I thought of the last time I'd seen her. Her eyes had been glassy; her head lolled to the side.

"Bartu says it keeps her manageable."

"She is manageable."

Stella laughed. "Don't get defensive, Mimi. I'm just telling you what I've heard at Clutch's place. I wouldn't care. What people do behind closed doors is their business. But that stuff hurts the baby. And a sick baby will make things hard for you."

My stomach turned. "What do you mean, sick?"

"Born hooked on the stuff. Doesn't stop crying. Up at all hours of the night. Won't eat. Has trouble breathing. With your Nonna's senility and your Mamma being—well, your Mamma—it'll fall on you."

"But I have the consumption." Though I knew I was only contagious when I was sick.

Stella laughed. "Bartu and your sister will be so desperate for your help that they won't care if you cough all over their brat. So get your sister off the juice. I'll see you again when things resolve themselves with the police."

By the time I arrived back home, my concern for Caterina had turned to fury. Why should I have to take care of her and her sick kid? Those engraving plates were my chance to start again. To have something of my own. I wouldn't let it be stolen from me the way my painting had been.

CHAPTER 30

CATERINA'S HOUSE WAS A MESS. Dishes piled in the sink, curdled milk on the counter, dirty clothes, left where they'd dropped. All of Mamma's lectures—about the proper fork to use for *pasta con sarde*, the exact shade of pale consomme, and how to wash *alençon* lace (with just the fingertips, using tepid water)—and this was how Caterina lived.

"Were you asleep?" I asked. It was after eleven but there were creases on her cheek from her pillow. "Sleep is good for the baby."

She eyed me suspiciously.

I asked if she'd eaten.

No response.

"I'll make you some tea." I went into the kitchen and brushed the mouse droppings from the stove top. I turned to fill the kettle. There, above the sink was a small bottle, empty but for a swallow of amber liquid. *Vin Mariani.* I slipped the bottle into my satchel, then put the kettle on the boil.

I returned to the bedroom. Caterina was on her side, facing the wall. I placed my hand on her shoulder. "Come and have some tea."

She mumbled that I should go away.

"Come on, Caterina."

I pressed down on her shoulder. She flailed at me. "Leave me alone!"

"I will," I said, trying to stay calm. "After you have your tea." I took hold of her arm and gently pulled her from the bed. She sighed heavily then dragged herself to the table. She sat. I poured her tea, then mine.

"Sugar?" I held up the nearly empty bowl. She waved me off. I continued. "I saw an article in *Il Progresso* last week. About making a window garden for growing American vegetables. That way, the baby can get used to the flavors. Corn, turnips, peas. You can put it right on that sill." I pointed to the narrow ledge next to the table.

"We're moving soon. To a big apartment on Park."

I nearly choked on my tea. "Where did Bartu get the money?" I sputtered.

She shrugged. "He's starting something new."

"Oh?"

"Something with that woman, Stella."

My heart started beating so hard I thought it would explode. I took a breath. Then two. When I was calmer, I asked what he'd be doing with Stella.

Again, she shrugged.

I told myself: Bartu liked to talk. Anyway, I was here to speak with Caterina about the cocaine.

"How are you feeling?" I asked.

She looked at me like I was an idiot. "I'm pregnant."

"Isn't that a good thing?"

"For Bartu, I guess. And Mamma. It's what they expect."

"And you? You must be excited to be a mother."

"I'm tired all the time."

"Are you drinking wine? Alcohol can make you tired." I tread carefully.

Caterina's mouth twisted into a sneer. "Did you read that in *Il Progresso*, too?"

"I'm just looking out for you. I want the baby to be healthy."

Her lower lip started quivering. "I've been praying for forgiveness. But it doesn't make the feelings stop."

My stomach dropped. "What feelings?"

"I hate it," she hissed, looking down at the swell of her belly. "I wish it was gone."

"What? The baby?" I could have reminded her—the point of

getting married was to have babies. But the two of us had seen the same things on the streets of New York City. The exhausted mothers, babies on the breast, holding fast to their toddlers' wrists while their older children lugged sacks of garbage or silk flowers or rags behind. Maybe Nonna was right when she said so long ago that Caterina was meant for the convent. She wasn't strong enough for this.

I put my arm around her shoulder. "We have to make the best of things, you and me. That's all we can do."

We weren't an affectionate family. Mamma said that was for the *puviri*. But as I held Caterina, her body softened into mine.

I'd talk to her about the *Vin Mariani* later.

CHAPTER 31

My first thought when I saw the newspaper photo of Clutch, police flanking him and his one good hand cuffed to a chain around his waist, was that Stella and I could finally get back to work. Of the ten dollars Stella had given me, only some coins remained. That afternoon, I'd gone to the market, returning only with a head of garlic and some escarole. It was strange to be living in this fancy house but have nothing in the cupboards. Kind of like living at *Binvinutu* with its stained ceilings and threadbare draperies.

As I was slicing the garlic, Mamma appeared in the kitchen. She was holding a telegram.

She put it on the table in front of me. "What does this mean?"

I read the message. It was in Sicilian. We spoke mostly Italian at home. Sicilian was like a code, with all its z's and u's. "It's from someone named Puccio," I said. "He's Pappa's lawyer." I reread the second sentence, not quite digesting it. "He's arranged for Pappa to come home to settle his affairs."

"What do you mean, 'settle his affairs?'"

If I had the energy, I might have finessed that second sentence. But Mamma stood there, demanding an answer. I kept it as simple as I could. "He's going to prison. Five years. To Atlanta."

Mamma grabbed the telegram out of my hands, the edge of the paper cutting my hand. "I can read the words!" she screamed. "But what does it *mean*?" *Melodrammaticu*, for sure. But I had to admit that five years in prison, thousands of miles away, was cause for alarm.

I tried to convince Mamma that this was better than the twenty-five to thirty years Pappa might have been sentenced to. I don't think either of us believed it.

"How will we live?"

"It'll be all right, Mamma."

"How? How will it be all right?" she turned on me, like an injured animal. "And there's still nothing from your godfather. Not a postcard. Not a telegram."

I relayed to Mamma what Stella had said. The cops were still trying to figure out who had sent word to Zio that the murdered officer would be in Palermo. The less communication between Zio and Pappa, or any of us, the better.

Mamma scoffed. "That would be a first—Vito looking out for Nino. He's always been jealous of your Pappa. His title. The estate. He knows that he'll never be more than a peasant, even if he's as rich as Midas."

Before we left Partanna, Zio said the nobility were finished in Sicily. Mamma might be the only one who didn't realize it.

I read the telegram again. "This was sent today. Maybe that means Pappa's coming home."

Mamma jumped up and ran to the cupboard. She threw open the door. "It's empty!" she screamed. "How did this happen?"

As if this was a new development. But over the last two months, we'd been steadily eating through all our stores.

"We'll have escarole and beans," I said.

"That's peasants' food. We need veal. You should go now, before the best cuts are gone." Mamma thrust the shawl into my hands and headed upstairs. A moment later, I heard her in her bedroom, opening and closing her dresser drawers. Probably searching for just the right oufit to wear for Pappa's homecoming.

I wandered the frigid streets, my purse empty, returning only when I could no longer feel my toes.

When I got back, Pappa was in the parlor, speaking quietly to Nonna, an empty wine glass in front of him. He rose quickly when he saw me.

Nonna pulled him back down. "Don't leave me, Curro." Lately, Nonna had been calling me Rosa. Confusing me with some long lost sister or my Rosalia. But this—thinking Pappa was her lost lover—this was pathetic. I couldn't help but feel sorry for her.

Pappa kissed her hand. He whispered something in her ear. A few minutes later, he motioned to me that I should help her upstairs for her nap.

Nonna let herself be led to her small bedroom. As I turned to leave, I looked back at her, curled up on her bed, her rosary beads tangled in her fingers, a beatific smile on her face.

I returned to the parlor. Pappa had refilled his glass. Mamma was sipping sherry. Her lips were stained crimson.

"This has been a good house." Pappa waved around the parlor. "I'd hoped to buy it someday."

Mamma narrowed her eyes. "We will buy it. You promised."

I somehow resisted the urge to shake her. Pappa was headed for prison. We'd be lucky to keep a roof—any roof—over our heads.

Mamma began to pout. "You promised we wouldn't have to move again."

"It's just for the time being." Pappa drained his glass again. "When I get back, we'll buy a house in Westchester. Near the sea. You'd like that, wouldn't you?"

But Mamma wasn't having any of it. "I won't move." She folded her arms across her chest.

Pappa drew Mamma close. "*Cara mia*. You'll see. Things will be fine."

"How will we get by?"

"Bartu's doing well. He'll help."

Mamma pointed at me. "What about Mimi? Didn't Vito say there'd be work here for her?"

"A few pretty drawings won't pay the rent."

But it wasn't just a few drawings. Stella and I would have our own counterfeiting operation. We wouldn't get caught because my bills would be perfect.

"Stay away from Stella," Pappa said, like he was reading my mind.

"You can't trust her."

Who was Pappa to speak of trust? Stella told me he'd snitched on Clutch, giving the cops information about his protection racket in exchange for a lighter sentence.

Pappa polished off another drink and staggered to his feet. "Let's go to Bartu's. I want to see Caterina."

Bartu greeted us at the door. He and Pappa hurried up the steps, with Mamma at their heels, leaving me alone to manage Nonna, who walked hesitatingly, like she couldn't quite remember how to put one foot in front of the other. When we finally reached the second-floor apartment, Pappa was holding Caterina's hands.

"Beautiful daughter," he said, his speech slurred. "Your pregnancy is a gift from the Madonna. The first Inglese born in America."

Bartu quipped that it was the first Amoruso, too.

"Of course!" Pappa slapped Bartu on the back.

"My mother told me it'll be a boy," Bartu added. "You can tell by the shape of the stomach."

"There's no greater joy for a man than to pass his name onto his son," Pappa said, though he'd always said he was happy with us girls.

"What do I need with a son?" Pappa had said when the midwife told him that Mamma would have no more babies. "I have my girls. I'm a king among men."

Now, Pappa squeezed Bartu's neck affectionately. "I'm trusting you, Bartu. To take care of that baby. While I'm—away. The rest of the family, too."

"I'll do my best." Bartu eased away from Pappa—it was subtle, but I saw it. "But two apartments—it'll be expensive." He rubbed his forefinger and thumb together.

Maybe it was Pappa's comments about sons, or Bartu's offhand response. I couldn't help myself. "I'll work," I said. "I can make logos, like the one I made for Zio Vito."

"And the engravings," Bartu said. "You'll get started on those."

Before he could, though, Pappa put up his hand. "Enough. You won't have time for any of that, Mimi. Your sister's going to need you. Bartu will provide." Unspoken was that this should be enough.

Bartu sneered at me. "A good woman is a silent woman."

There was a pounding in my head. The Vin Mariani, intended to keep my sister docile. I wanted to hurt Bartu. Make him suffer. Pappa must have seen because he shook his head.

"Sooner or later, Mimi, you're going to have to accept your lot. You're a girl. For once in your life, act like one."

Act like a girl? From the moment I picked up my first crayon, Pappa had been telling me it didn't matter that I was a girl. I was an artist. I had a vision to follow.

"Mimi. Do you hear me?"

It was impossible not to hear. I nodded.

I glanced toward Bartu. He grinned, like he was taking pleasure in my humiliation. Stella was right. He was a small, grasping man. Caterina might be his puppet. I wouldn't be.

When we finally left Bartu's, it was night. We walked home, Nonna's hand in mine. The house was dark—we must have forgotten to leave the parlor lamp lit. In the vestibule, Pappa turned the gaslight, the click and spark intruding on the quiet. When the light didn't catch, Pappa said the pilot in the cellar must have gone out. "I'll need your help with it," he said to me. "Get your Mamma and Nonna settled in the parlor, then come back to the kitchen."

A few minutes later, I made my way to the darkened kitchen and called Pappa.

"Are you near a light?" Pappa's voice sounded from below.

"Yes," I called. "I'm here."

"That's strange. The gas supply valve is turned off." I heard Pappa grunting. "All right. I got it open. On the count of three, flip on the light."

"Okay."

"One. Two. Three. Now!"

I turned the switch. In a flash, it was light.

It took a moment to register what I was seeing.

Two rows of rats, their bellies cut open, their entrails splayed on the linoleum. And beside each one, a tiny pink tongue.

I lost my balance and fell backwards, hitting my head against the oven.

Pappa was on the cellar stairs. My first thought was that I didn't want Pappa to see the rats. Maybe I was trying to protect him from the terrible scene. Or maybe him seeing would make it somehow more real. Pappa was at the top of the stairs. The cellar door swung open.

"*Che cazzo?*" he cried, in an instant, taking in the carnage. He rushed to the sink and was sick.

After he'd finished retching, and I washed his vomit down the drain, he took a burlap bag from under the sink. Then one by one, he started picking up the rats and dropping them into the bag.

"Who did this, Pappa?"

Pappa didn't respond.

"Should we call the police?"

"No!" he screamed. The rat he was holding pitched forward.

"We locked the door before we left for Caterina's."

When Pappa didn't respond, I asked how this could have happened. But I think I already knew.

Pappa opened the sack and stuffed the rat inside. He bent to pick up another.

My heart was pounding. "Does this have something to do with Clutch?"

"Shh!" He stood and exhaled deeply. That's how I knew that Stella was right: Pappa had turned on Clutch.

I moved closer. I was so near now that I could reach out and touch his shoulder. I didn't. "What will happen when you go to prison?"

Again, no answer.

"Will we be safe here?"

When Pappa still didn't respond, I wondered if he'd been struck dumb. That happened to people sometimes when they suffered something traumatic. Something like this, I thought, looking around at the rats still laying on the floor, their bellies split open, their tiny tongues ripped out.

"What will we do?" I whispered.

He dropped the sack on the floor. The dead weight landed with a sickening thud.

"I'll get word to Zio," Pappa said. "I'll be discreet. Use a go-between. Everything will be all right."

As always, Pappa would run to Zio, expecting he'd make things right. This time, though, I knew we were on our own.

But I had Stella. And those five-dollar engraving plates.

CHAPTER 32

PAPPA'S LAWYER SHOWED UP the day before Pappa was to leave for Atlanta. My first thought was that Puccio must have figured out a way to keep Pappa out of jail. Listening at the butler door, careful not to set it to swinging, I soon realized that wasn't why he was here.

"That damn judge," Puccio said. "He should have let you go. You made their case for them."

I heard the tinkling of a spoon against a cup. Puccio continued. "I rely on you to tell Don Cascioferro that I tried my best to keep you out of jail. But the cops are falling all over each other to prove how tough they are on crime."

Pappa said nothing.

"I used my influence to get you a good job down there. Shelving books at the library."

I thought I heard something about a contribution.

"Fifty dollars to the Warden's pet project—the prison baseball team," Puccio said. "No brickmaking or turpentine factory for you. No. You'll be in much more genteel company."

Pappa quietly asked about Clutch.

"What we heard is true: He'll be in Atlanta, too. But you don't need to worry," Puccio assured. "Clutch will be doing hard labor on the rock pile or in the cotton fields. You'll be safe."

When I came down for breakfast the next morning, Pappa was already at the dining room table. The kitchen carving knife was next to his espresso cup. The ashtray was heaped with cinders. Pappa had been up all night. I didn't want to think about what he'd been standing guard against.

"Are Mamma and Nonna awake?" I asked.

"Let them sleep. Sit."

I sat.

He plucked his lucky coin from his vest pocket. "When you move next week—tell no one, and I mean no one, about where you're going."

I must have looked afraid because Pappa mumbled some drivel about Bartu protecting us.

My eyes moved to the knife.

Pappa slid it off the table and onto his lap, like he'd just remembered to hide it from me. "The important thing is that you lay low. Until things die down."

"Should we leave New York?" I asked, thinking of Stella's farmhouse in New Jersey.

Pappa misunderstood. "You can't go back to Partanna. There's nothing for us there. And Nonna needs to get stronger."

I didn't have the heart to point out the obvious—the way her gaze darted from one person to another, as if we were strangers to her. The smell of decay that hung around her, even after I'd scrubbed her urine-soaked clothes and bedding. Nonna wouldn't get stronger. She was dying.

"When I return, I'll find work. Legitimate work," he said in a rush, as if saying the words quickly would make them true.

"Yes, Pappa." I wanted to believe him.

The doorbell buzzed. Once. Twice. Three times. The sound was so jarring it set my teeth on edge.

Pappa nodded to me.

I stood and went to the vestibule. I saw them through the front doors. Two square figures with ridiculous bowler hats. Impatient now, one knocked again, so hard he rattled the glass.

I opened the door. They were dressed in dark blue uniforms, their jackets set with two rows of shiny brass buttons, a six-sided silver star at each man's breast. Thugs dressed like cops. Like those men who'd taken Pappa from the *S.S. Sofia Hohenberg*, or the ones who'd terrorized poor Baladucci.

Close on my heels, they followed me inside.

One officer pulled a piece of paper from his pocket. "Anton Ingels?"

I expected Pappa would correct the mispronunciation. Instead he stood. "I am he."

The officer brusquely folded the paper and put it into his jacket pocket. "Let's go. We have a long trip ahead of us."

The second officer took a pair of handcuffs from his belt. Pappa held out his wrists like he'd expected this. The officer pulled a length of chain from his pocket, slowly, like a magician's reveal. "Are you going to behave?" He smiled indulgently, like Pappa was a naughty child. "Or am I going to have to chain your feet?"

My nails dug into my palms. Those goons. Anyone could see Pappa's stooped back and pathetic comb-over. He was an old man. He wasn't running anywhere.

"Say your goodbyes," the first officer said. "We have a train to catch."

Suddenly frantic, I asked if I should get Nonna and Mamma.

"Don't bother them." Pappa moved toward me but the cuffs were in the way. We kissed on the cheek—only once, though. The American way.

"Very touching. Now let's go." He grabbed Pappa by the cuffs and pulled him away.

Before the door slammed behind Pappa, he told me to be a good girl. "And listen to Bartu."

Sitting on a park bench the next day, I told Stella about Pappa's parting words. She stretched out her arms and legs like a cat.

"Bartu's an asshole. We're not telling him anything. Especially about the printing press. We don't need a partner. Especially one who can't keep his mouth shut."

I looked out towards the river. An icebreaker was powering through, leaving leaving behind jagged gray-blue slabs of ice. Stella pulled her coat around herself. It was too big—a man's coat, it seemed—and threadbare. "Cold as a witch's tit, this place. Everyone scrambling to put a few dollars in their pockets. And what for? So they can pass that misery on to their children? I never wanted that for myself. Or my daughter."

"You have a daughter?" All that time we'd spent together writing the earthquake telegrams and making our engraving plates, and she'd never mentioned a daughter.

She nodded. "Christina. Fifteen last October. They took her when I went to prison." She looked out, beyond the river. "Told me I wasn't a fit mother. That she was better off with someone else. She was only four. I heard a family on Long Island adopted her. There are farms out there. Miles and miles of potatoes." Just then, a gust swept through, scattering scraps of newspaper and tattered leaves.

Stella asked about the new apartment.

"It's on Lexington and 110th. Over a drug store." I forgot all about my promise to Pappa to keep it a secret.

Stella's lips turned up at the corners. "It'll be hard for your mother. Going from Doctors Row to that. But you know what they say: 'Fortune turns like a wheel, this way and that.'"

"Maybe." Though after losing those three boy babies and *Binvinutu*, Mamma would probably say she'd suffered enough misfortune for a lifetime.

"And your Nonna?" Stella asked. "How is she now that her Sonny Boy is gone?"

I felt suddenly very angry. What did Stella know of Nonna or her life? She hadn't found her in the middle of the night, curled up on the floor, whimpering and clenching one of Pappa's shirts.

"She's fine."

Stella shook her head. "You need to get away from them."

"Who?"

"Your family. Your sister, your mother, your Nonna. They're eating you alive."

"They need me. I can't just leave."

Stella continued looking at the river. "You're always going to feel that way."

"What way?"

"That they can't do without you. With every baby Caterina pops out, it'll get worse." The wind gusted, blowing off her scarf. She didn't move. "It'll be like those poor suckers digging out that tunnel." She gestured toward the East River. "A stickiness under their boots. Then, mud up to their ankles. Their knees. Trapped. With no one to rescue them."

I tried not to think about what that would feel like. Knowing that where you stood was where you'd die. And that there was nothing you could do about it.

"No. I'm an artist."

"And a damn good one. Those engraving plates are some of the finest work I've ever seen. But you're a woman, too. A Sicilian woman. And this is your sister's baby."

"Mamma can help." I tried not to hear the desperation in my voice. Or feel that stickiness under my feet.

Stella laughed. "We both know she'll be useless. It'll fall to you, Mimi. The only thing you'll be drawing is stick figures."

I felt the mud, creeping up my ankles. The suck of it, pulling me down. I tried to stand up straight. "That won't happen."

"Good. Remember, your sister made her choices."

Not exactly true. Caterina wasn't strong enough for that.

Stella continued. "The plates are already in Hackensack. Hidden under the biggest manure pile around." I thought of that muslin, the cow shit soaking through. It didn't matter. They could be cleaned.

"Things are almost ready," Stella continued. "The paper came in last week. I'm just waiting on the inks. You're sure we need all three? The green looks about right."

About right would land us in jail. "No," I said. "We need the red and blue, too."

"Okay. But I'll have to use a fake name to order it—the feds are paying attention now. It's expensive, too."

If we got this right, we'd never have to worry about money again.

A blast of cold air blew in from the river. I tucked my nose and mouth under my coat collar. The cold seeped in anyway. I should have brought my shawl. I couldn't get sick now.

CHAPTER 33

Bartu had grudgingly agreed to help us move our belongings: The satchels and trunks we'd brought from *Binvinutu*, along with the useless things Mamma had bought since we'd moved to Doctors Row. A crystal punch bowl, an ornate silver tea strainer, the set of seafood forks—these told the story of the life Mamma thought we'd have in America. I wrapped each item carefully and placed it in a packing crate. Not because I thought we'd use them—I couldn't imagine ever needing twelve tiny sterling silver forks—but because the sign in the pawn man's window promised top dollar for items in excellent condition.

Our things lay in a heap on the sidewalk while Bartu went into the drug store to get the apartment keys. He'd brought a buddy to help: A hulk of a man with no hair and overdeveloped biceps. The man was picking up each satchel and box, shaking it like an overzealous child at Christmas.

Bartu finally emerged, keys in one hand, a paper bag in the other. Could that be the *Vin Mariani*? But no. With Caterina about to give birth, surely he'd stopped giving her that poison.

Squeezed in between the drug store and a Chinese laundry was a nondescript door. Bartu unlocked it and stepped inside. His partner followed. I slung the satchel over my chest. Inside was my burin case and Nonna's most precious things—her prayer book and repaired Madonna statue, the crack at her neck still visible. The tenement door swung closed before Nonna, Mamma, and I could step through. We huddled, Nonna shivering in the cold, until the two men returned. They paid us no mind, just went to the trunk. Each man taking hold of a handle, they started up again. This time, though, I stuck out my foot before the door closed. I considered our remaining satchel—battered and patched—and the two crates. Surely, no one would steal them in broad daylight. We started up, Mamma in front and Nonna and I following.

The building was only a few years old, but the stairwell smelled like old cabbage and the masonry walls were covered with spiderweb cracks. Our apartment was on the third floor. At the second-floor landing, Nonna began to weep. I thought we might have to cover her eyes—like the coachman at *Binvinutu* sometimes had to do with the horses during lightning storms. But drawing her rosary beads from her pocket, she seemed to gather her courage.

"Pity me, St. Jude," Nonna whispered, appealing to the patron saint for hopeless causes. It was the most she'd said in months. I leaned in close to hear more. But there was too much noise in the hallway—too many doors slamming and people laughing and arguing—for me to make out what she was saying.

On the third-floor landing, Bartu and his buddy rushed past us.

Bartu asked where the satchel and crates were, as if we could have somehow managed those, too.

"When you're rich, you can be careless," Bartu muttered. But when we stepped through the door of our apartment, I knew that no one would ever mistake us for being rich. It was wedged between the apartments to the front and rear, the only window in the small galley kitchen. The parlor—such as it was—opened to an air shaft; the bedroom was little more than a closet. The air was fetid. I'd have to get used to it. The furniture left by the prior tenants—a stained mattress and a daybed, a spindly table and three mismatched chairs—looked like they'd fallen from the junkman's truck.

Bartu returned, he and his partner carrying a carton. There was no satchel. He took one look around and gave a low whistle. "What a shithole." Though it was he who'd found the place.

"Where is my satchel?" Mamma asked.

In my mind, I did a quick inventory of what was inside: clothes; some silverplate and crystal. Nothing truly valuable. I pulled my own bag closer.

Bartu brushed the dust from his lapels. "That's all there was."

Mamma looked at me accusingly. "We left it on the sidewalk." Her chin began to quiver. Any minute, she'd start to cry.

"It'll be all right, Mamma," I said, gently. Pappa's words in my mouth.

"How?" she snarled. "How will it be all right?" She broke down, her crying so mournful that I wanted to tell her about the engraving plates. Soon, I'd be making money. I'd find us a decent place.

Bartu smiled, amused. "Good luck unpacking." As he and his side-kick headed downstairs, I heard them laughing.

After a long time, Mamma dried her tears. She went to the bedroom. When she returned, she reported that there was only one bed. "Where will you and Nonna sleep?" she asked.

Here was the self-centered Mamma I knew. Assuming the bed was hers. "You and Nonna can share the bed," I said. "I'll sleep on the daybed."

Mamma's lip curled in disgust. "I don't want to sleep with her. She wets the bed."

Mamma was talking like Nonna wasn't there. But looking at the old woman, rocking back and forth and muttering gibberish, I felt sorry for Mamma.

At least we could keep track of Nonna in that tiny space. Her night-time wanderings had gotten worse since Pappa had been taken. A few days ago, I found her fiddling with the deadbolt on the front door. I didn't want to think about what would have happened if she'd gotten out on the street. Now, I hooked my hand under Nonna's elbow and guided her toward the bedroom. I opened the satchel and pulled out the Madonna and prayer book and put them on the radiator. Nonna slipped a small votive candle I didn't know she had from her pocket. I pinched off the wick so it couldn't be lit. A fire in a cramped space like this would be dangerous.

I woke several times that first night. But I had not a moment's confusion about where I was. People coming and going, with little regard to the hour, the downstairs door slamming behind them. Arguing next door—was that Russian I heard?—and the rhythmic sound of bed boards creaking. Strangely, though, Nonna stayed asleep. Maybe she was comforted by all those nighttime sounds and the fact that others were awake, too, through those long, dark hours.

The next morning, I felt calmer. Bartu didn't really care what happened to me, Nonna or Mamma. That was fine. Soon I wouldn't need Bartu or anyone.

CHAPTER 34

EVEN IN OUR SORRY STATE, Mamma insisted on Sunday family dinner. "It's tradition," she said that first week, as she placed the discounted fruit—bruised apples and overripe pears—into her crystal bowl. "For Caterina's children. To know where they come from."

I wanted to shake Mamma. Hadn't she seen Caterina, rail-thin, her eyelashes plucked bare, burn marks and cuts covering her hands and wrists? It would be a miracle if she delivered one healthy baby, let alone a whole brood. But Mamma lived in a fantasy world, like Nonna's heaven and Caterina's morphine-stoked haze. Wealth. Respect. A perfect family. She assumed all of it would be hers. One of us had to live in reality. I guess that was me.

By the time Caterina and Bartu arrived, Nonna had wet herself twice. Mamma had lost her temper with the old woman, screaming that the apartment smelled like urine (it did) and that Nonna had done it out of spite (unlikely). I needn't have worried. Neither Caterina nor Bartu seemed to notice.

Bartu wasn't there long. He dropped a square bakery box on the table and announced he had a meeting.

"I'll see you at home." He kissed the top of Caterina's head. Her eyes were glassy. Her mind, far away. I thought of the package Bartu had gotten from the drug store the day we'd moved in.

"You're leaving?" I asked him, gesturing toward Caterina.

"She's fine."

"She's pregnant." Nine months pregnant, I wanted to say. And high.

"Women deliver babies all the time." Bartu waved his hand dismissively. "But if you're worried, you can walk her home. I have a meeting," he repeated. "An important meeting."

He looked at me like he was daring me to ask who he was meeting with. I didn't.

After Bartu left, we sat down to eat. Caterina picked at her food.

"This is why you're so skinny." Mamma tapped Caterina's plate with her fork. "When I was pregnant, I ate all the time. The richer the food, the better. It'll be the only time in your life you won't have to worry about your figure." Mamma smoothed down the front of her skirt, like she was assuring herself that her belly was still washboard flat.

I had just served the cheese course when Caterina cried out. Nonna stood and came to her, sure-footed for the first time in months. She placed her hand on Caterina's belly. "The baby's coming."

"Should I get the midwife?" I asked.

"Not a midwife," Mamma corrected. "Dr. Casagrande. He delivers babies for all the *prominenti*. In the Lying-In Hospital. The modern way."

I offered to go for him, but Caterina told us she hadn't engaged him.

Mamma was furious. "What do you mean, you haven't engaged him? He only delivers babies for mothers who are in his care."

Caterina said she wanted Nonna. But my grandmother had already retreated: she was at the kitchen window, wringing her hands and staring at something I couldn't see.

Mamma turned to me. She looked panicked. "That Stella woman. Your father says she knows everyone. Go get her." She pushed me toward the door. "Hurry!"

I ran. By the time I got to Stella's, I was soaked with sweat.

An aria was coming from inside. I think it was from *La Bohème*. Stella opened the door. Her face was streaked with tears.

"It's Caterina." I struggled to catch my breath. "The baby."

Stella pulled me inside. "Did you run all the way here?"

I nodded. "She needs help. Please. Do you know someone?"

"A midwife? Everyone I know is out of business. Or in jail."

"Please, Stella."

"Wait," she said, wrapping her shawl around her shoulders. "There may be someone."

"I'll come with you."

"No. It's better if I go alone."

"Why?" I asked. The last thing I wanted was to go back home.

"New people make her nervous. Go back to your sister and wait. I'll bring her."

"I don't know what to do."

"Your Nonna knows. She was the nurse for the convent, right? She saw plenty of births."

"But Nonna is senile..." Nonna had been declining since we'd arrived in New York. But I'd never said that word before.

"She'll remember what to do. People do, in situations like this. So go home. Get Caterina into bed and wait. I'll bring the midwife as soon as I can."

It was late Sunday afternoon. The sidewalks were crowded with young couples strolling arm-in-arm while their older counterparts shuffled along, talking about whatever old people talk about. Women walked together or congregated on stoops, their work done for the moment, gossiping, while boys in packs darted between the pedestrians, prompting the reprimand of their elders.

When I made my way back to the tenement, Nonna was waiting for me in the vestibule. Her eyes were wide.

She bowed her head. "Sister is laboring hard, Mother Superior."

People were passing in and out of the building. Some were amused, seeing Nonna in her faded nightgown. Most were annoyed.

A shriek rang out from above us. More animal than human. My sister. In pain.

Upstairs, Caterina was pacing between the kitchen and bedroom and parlor. Her sleeves were torn, her hair wild. Mamma cowered in the corner.

"The midwife is coming," I told them. "We need to get ready."

My sister rushed toward me. "I thought you were gone." It hurt that she'd think I'd abandon her.

I guided her toward the bedroom. "Let's get you out of these clothes." I helped her off with her skirt and chemise. She kicked off the knickers, all modesty gone. As she swung her legs into bed, I could see her privates. Swollen. Red. I felt woozy. I pulled the sheet over her. She closed her eyes. For a moment, I could pretend she was a little girl again. Worn out after a day of adventuring: rescuing a turtle that had wandered onto the garden path or helping Cook pick fennel blossoms.

Caterina cried out again. Clutching her sheet, she began to writhe. Nonna edged closer. She placed her hand on Caterina's belly. "My baby. Mine."

Caterina screamed. "Help me! Oh, Mother of God, someone help me!" For the first time, I considered that my sister might not survive this. Cemeteries are filled with the graves of young women who've died giving birth.

I heard footsteps on the stairs. *Please Madonna, let it be Stella.* I could have fallen to my knees in thanksgiving when I opened the door and saw her there.

"This is Signora Grassi." Stella stepped aside. The woman leaned heavily on a cane, a battered satchel tucked under her arm.

There was another cry. Signora hobbled into the bedroom. I was surprised at how quickly she moved.

Signora instructed Mamma to get the rags and boiling water. She told Stella to keep Nonna out of the way. "You," she pointed at me. "Help me get her into a squatting position." Signora pulled my sister up by the elbow. As another contraction took hold, Caterina flailed her arms and legs. She hit Signora in the face.

Rubbing her eye, the midwife ordered me to tie up Caterina.

I turned to Stella.

Signora hit my leg with her cane. "Do you hear me? Tie her arms and legs to the bedposts."

"What? Like an animal?"

Stella whispered to me that if we didn't do as Signora said, she'd leave. I glanced toward Nonna. She was curled up on the floor near the window, her arms wrapped around her knees. Lost to us.

After we'd bound my sweet sister, the midwife ordered Stella and me to hold her still. She reached down and forced open Caterina's knees. She thrust her hand inside. Caterina whimpered.

"You had to know this would happen, dearie," the midwife hissed. "There's no pleasure without pain."

Stella muttered something about Caterina being married. I don't know what that had to do with anything. Signora thrust her hand in further. When she finally pulled away, Caterina was ashen.

Signora smirked. "Married, huh? Well, consider yourself lucky. You don't know how many barren women come to me, desperate to be pregnant. And how many of them are abandoned by their husbands."

The midwife turned to Stella. "You lied to me. This isn't an emergency."

"It's her first baby," Stella said, adding that Signora would be well-compensated.

"You'll pay me double."

"Double? But why? She's married. There won't be any—complications."

"Because I said so." The midwife sneered. She was missing most of her teeth.

"But it's legal."

In this country, there were laws against everything. Begging on the street; playing the numbers; even tossing trash on the ground. Could there be a law against helping a desperate woman have her baby?

"That's my fee," Signora said. "Take it or leave it."

Stella shook her head. "You're a piece of work. You know that?" She pulled open her blouse. She was wearing a worn leather pouch around her belly. She unzipped the center compartment and pulled out a bill. I thought I saw a 50 in the corner. No midwife costs that much.

She gave the bill to Signora. Satisfied, the midwife began unpacking her satchel, laying each terrible thing on the dresser. Long needles with stained plastic tubing. A pair of scissors with elongated blades. Black tongs like the ones the blacksmith used to forge metal in the fire.

The midwife picked up a long-handled spatula. "We need to draw the baby down. Both of you," she gestured to me and Stella. "Push on her belly."

I guess I must have hesitated, because Signora snarled, "Squeamish, eh?" I shook my head no. She saw through me.

"If you don't do this, they'll die. Mother and baby." My legs felt too weak to hold me. I made myself go to the opposite side of the bed. Following Stella's lead, I pressed my hands flat against my sister's stomach. I'd taken care of Caterina since she was a little girl. But her body seemed possessed by this sinister, alien thing.

The midwife thrust that spatula into Caterina. When she pulled it out, there was blood on the spat. She tossed the instrument to the floor.

Signora muttered that it was taking too long. "I'm getting the baby out." She was a round woman, but she moved quickly, picking up the tongs. She pressed its handles until the blades opened, like the jaws of a snake. Unable to turn away, I watched as the woman got between Caterina's legs. Too late, Caterina realized what the woman meant to do. She tried to get away, but Stella and I held down her arms.

The midwife thrust the tongs more deeply inside Caterina. "It's a terrible world, *bambinu*. You have to be born, anyway." She twisted this way and that with the tongs. It went on for an impossibly long time. Caterina must have passed out because Signora slapped her hard on the inside of her thigh.

"Come on, girl," she urged. "It's time to push."

When Caterina didn't rouse, Signora slapped her again. My sister's eyes fluttered open. "If you don't cooperate," the midwife hissed, "I'll cut you. And you and your baby will probably die."

Caterina seemed to try to focus.

The midwife directed Stella and me to get Caterina into a squatting position. She thrust the tongs back up into her. Her face and arms glistening with her sweat and my sister's blood, the midwife ordered Caterina to push. She gave one last pull and the baby slithered from his mother's womb. His head, still caught in that vise; his body, covered with blood and something that looked like clotted cream. Arms and legs hanging down like a rag doll. For one terrifying moment, he lay there. Still. Silent. Then the midwife slapped him, hard, on the back. He screamed in protest, hands balled up, face red.

"It's a boy." Signora seemed as satisfied as if she'd birthed him. She swaddled him quickly, then thrust him into my arms.

For months—or maybe years—this child had been only a thought, and not an entirely welcome one. I'd turned my back on the prospect of motherhood and then had it taken from me. Now he was in my arms. Flesh and blood. His rounded bottom; the angles of his elbows and heels. The thick fringes of his lashes. I lowered my head to breathe in his scent. Sweet, like freshly-laundered sheets drying on the clothes line.

The midwife was working over my sister. "Your husband will appreciate this," she snarled. I turned toward her, wanting to agree. Because Caterina had come through hell—the pregnancy, the horrific delivery— to make this perfect person.

But Signora wasn't talking about the baby. In one hand, she held a long strand of sinew. In the other, a thick needle. "He'll want you back the way you were on your wedding night. All men do. Even after four or five babies, that's what they expect." She snickered. "It takes so little to keep them happy."

When the midwife stooped to sew up my sister's privates, sundered like scraps of fabric, I knew she was wrong. Because bringing this baby— this perfect child with his cupid's lips and perfectly shaped brow—hadn't been a little thing.

Stella came to me.

"He looks like Bartu. All this," Stella said, motioning toward the bloody sheets, the midwife kneeling between my sister's knees, stitching her up with that disgusting cat gut. "Just to give him a brat."

I started to say that the baby was beautiful. More lovely than anything I could make.

But she'd gone to the window. "I'll ask Signora to give her something to keep her from getting pregnant again. At least right away. It'll be good for her. And you."

Something to keep Caterina from getting pregnant? Was that even possible?

Before I could ask, Stella said, "You're lucky, Mimi. You only have to worry about yourself. No horny husband or screaming baby. Just you and your art."

"Yes," I whispered. But holding that baby, I wasn't sure.

CHAPTER 35

LATE IN JUNE, I found a chrysalis hanging from the underside of a half-chewed leaf on my way back from the market. Soon, I'd break free of my cocoon. I'd live the life I was meant to live. But not yet. I thought of Baby Sebu, his eyes on mine as I gave him the bottle. The fluttering of his lids, his heaviness, as he drifted off to sleep.

Stella was getting impatient. My plates were still wrapped up, the inks and paper ready. She'd gone over every millimeter of the printing press—cleaning the pad and roller, leveling the feet, and oiling the moving parts. Still I kept putting her off though the pantry shelves were empty and the rent would soon come due.

I plucked the chrysalis from the leaf and put it in my pocket. When I arrived back at the tenement, there were pamphlets strewn on the vestibule floor. *Why New York Men Should Give New York Women the Vote*, one read. The oldest Sugarman girl, our front hall neighbor, carried a messenger bag stuffed with papers like this. I kicked the pamphlets aside and opened our mailbox. Inside was a Past Due bill from the coal delivery man. How could someone think about votes or anything else when they couldn't afford heat?

I opened the door to the apartment. Mamma rushed toward me. She was clutching her handkerchief. Her eyes were red. At first I thought it was Pappa. Then I heard Nonna in the bedroom. Her breathing was ragged. A sputtering exhale followed by a terrible pause. Mamma cried that she'd been like this since morning.

"Where were you?" Mamma demanded. "Your grandmother collapsed!"

I went to Nonna's bedside and whispered her name.

She furrowed her brow, like I'd disturbed her.

"It's me, Mimi."

Nonna struggled to open her eyes.

"Sister," she whispered. "You're here."

"Yes." I squeezed her hands. They were cool and waxy.

"I thought you were dead. There was so much blood."

Like a compass that always points north, my fingers found those scars. The terrible incisions Dr. Florio had made.

"No, Nonna." I pressed her mottled hand to my lips. "You nursed me back to health."

She shook her head furiously. "It's my fault. The letter opener. I'm going to jail. Mother Superior says so." Her words were more fluid than they had been in a long time. "But I had to. Beatrice was my friend."

I laid my hand across Nonna's brow.

"The priest!" she cried out, as if remembering.

"Monsignor Marino was here Saturday," I reminded. "He heard your confession."

"No! Father Rizzo. He told her the Madonna wanted them together. Father lied to her," Nonna cried. "Not like Curro. He loved me."

After a long time, Nonna's crying trailed off. She fell into a deep sleep. I tried to rouse her—rubbing her arms and calling her name—but there was no response. Like the stuttering of the gaslight in the nighttime breeze, her breathing became more erratic. She'd breathe fast, almost like panting, and then so slowly that I placed my hand lightly on her chest to be sure she was still alive.

Deep in the night, Mamma came into the bedroom. Together, we sat vigil, waiting as night receded and the faint rays of dawn eked through the air shaft window. The space between breaths became longer. Unbearable. Until they were no more. I peeled back Nonna's blanket and sheet and laid her hands across her chest.

I rose. "I'll get the priest."

Mamma nodded. "She'll need her finest dress. The one she wore on Sundays. They don't wear funeral shrouds here." Leave it to Mamma to know how to dress for death.

"A funeral plot?" I'd never really thought about what would happen here.

"Pappa arranged it."

"He bought a cemetery plot?"

"He didn't have a chance. Everything happened so fast."

But Nonna was eighty years old. Surely Pappa should have anticipated this.

I asked where.

"Someone offered their family plot. The Locanos or Lucinis—I can't remember. Pappa wrote it down." She hitched her thumb toward the dresser. Amidst Mamma's scarves and stockings and camisoles was the name of the plot where Nonna would be laid to rest. Poor Pappa, leaving for prison and knowing his mother would probably be gone before he returned.

I returned an hour later with the priest. He was a young man, barely out of the seminary. His collar gaped at his neck. As eager as a bridegroom, he entered the death room. His gaze fell on Nonna. He made the sign of the cross and prayed beside her body for a long time.

I don't know who gave me Nonna's rosary, though that wooden nun's crucifix with its tiny pewter Jesus should have been buried with her. It was rough—even splintery—and it smelled faintly of sandalwood and sweat. I fingered the beads and then pressed down on the sharp-edged Jesus. Unbidden, the words came to me: *Hail Mary, Full of Grace. The Lord is with Thee.*

And though I hadn't believed since I was a child, I prayed for Nonna. If there is a heaven, surely she had earned a place there. When I was done, I slipped the beads back into my pocket.

On the way home from Calvary Cemetery—an immense place filled with hundreds of thousands of gravestones pocking the hillside—I fingered the tiny Jesus, feeling the places where the pewter had been worn smooth. We passed the squalid buildings and smoke-spewing factories, the morning fog that lay heavy on the East River. When Mamma and I reached the tenement, no one asked about Nonna. They continued as they had before, arguing and laughing, the sounds echoing in the stair. I took Nonna's Madonna and prayer book from atop the radiator. I'd bring them to Caterina, along with Nonna's crucifix. I'd drop her few pieces of clothing at the church.

Nonna had taken up so little space, both here and in Sicily. She'd suffered—her lover gone, her baby abandoned to the wheel. But she'd kept their memories close, refusing to marry or bear other children. She'd lived a life of meditation and prayer.

A life that she'd chosen.

Later, I'd go see Stella. Apologize for delaying things. Tell her I was ready to start.

CHAPTER 36

WHEN I TOLD MAMMA I'd be working with Stella, she didn't question me about what I'd be doing or if it would be safe. She asked only how much money I'd be bringing in. The same question she'd had for Pappa when we became Inglese and started collecting rent on the land. And again, when Zio asked Pappa to move to America to run his grocery store. Money was what mattered to Mamma. Maybe it was because she was a butcher's daughter. She'd grown up hearing the agonized screams of animals whose only value lay in what people were willing to pay for their flesh.

I left without answering.

It was a sweltering day. By the time I reached Stella's, tiny black spots swam before my eyes.

Stella pulled me inside. "You look terrible." She filled a glass with *zammù*. The milky drink glowed in her dimly lit space.

I put the glass to my lips, breathing in the smell of star anise. I swallowed it down. I felt better.

"I'd started to wonder if I was going to see you," Stella said.

"I want to start work."

"Are you sure you have the time? All those people relying on you. Your addict sister and her baby. Your senile Nonna."

My eyes welled with tears. "My Nonna's dead."

Stella touched my hand. "I'm sorry, Mimi. I liked your Nonna."

I pressed down on my lids. Now wasn't the time for emotion.

"I need to start right away," I repeated.

"What's the rush?"

"We have no money. Mamma's pawned most of her silver."

"I thought Bartu was helping. Wasn't Vito supposed to be sending him money?"

I shook my head. "No one's heard from Zio. Maybe he found out that Pappa gave testimony against Clutch?"

"Bullshit. All of it. Vito doesn't care about Clutch's stupid extortion business. He never has. He's only ever been interested in the counterfeiting operation and your engraving plates."

"So this was always the plan," I said, still trying to accept what Stella had said the day the cops took Pappa."

Stella nodded. "Vito's guy in Palermo was a hack. We needed a real artist. Vito told me about you. Then there was the tuberculosis and all that drama. But I've always wanted you."

"But I was going to art school. Zio had arranged the lessons to prepare my portfolio."

Stella shrugged. "I guess he figured it would help with the engravings."

"But I was going to be an artist," I whispered, only to myself. "Like Matisse." *The Joy of Life*. My painting of *Binvinutu*.

Stella shook her head. "He wanted you to believe that. But this was always his plan."

I thought of Pappa, in prison in Georgia, a place I couldn't imagine.

Stella took my arm. "We'll take control. You and me. We have the engravings and supplies."

"I can't go to jail."

She nodded. "That's why we're being careful. The farmhouse is way out in the sticks. When the bills are done, we'll ship most of them out of state. Even if the cops thought that women could do something like this—which they don't, by the way—they'd never be able to tie it to us." Stella leaned in. Her breath smelled like licorice from the *zammù*.

"Don't worry, Mimi. No one's going to jail."

I'm not sure I believed her. But a terrible realization was dawning on me. If not for me and my art, we wouldn't have left Sicily. Pappa wouldn't be in prison. Nonna would be buried in the leafy cemetery at *Binvinutu*, under her own headstone. Caterina would be spending her days as Nonna had wanted, in quiet meditation, not bound to a man like Bartu. Even if I wanted to walk away, which I didn't, I owed it to my family to help them.

Stella smiled. "Don't look so gloomy. You might enjoy making the bills."

Sure, there would be satisfaction in finally using those plates. But I sensed Stella meant more than this.

"We make money because we *can*," Stella continued. "You'll see, Mimi. It's thrilling. Like sex. When it's good."

I thought of Teo and the loft at the atelier. My cheeks began to burn. I watched as Stella's expression changed from bewilderment to bemusement. "You're a virgin."

I looked away and mumbled that I wasn't allowed to marry.

"I'm not talking about marriage. I'm talking about sex. Surely, you had the opportunity while you were in Palermo."

"I was chaperoned."

She smirked. "There's something you're not telling me, Mimi. That's okay. You're entitled to your secrets. God knows, I've got lots of them. For the record, though, lots of people with tuberculosis get married. They have sex. They make babies. This whole thing—about how you can't marry because of the consumption—it's bullshit."

I drank the rest of the *zammù*, the cool liquid trickling down the back of my throat. When I got home, I pulled out my burin case. I fingered each instrument, feeling the warmth of the handle, the sharpness of the blade. With these burins, I'd made those perfect engraving plates, hidden underground at the farmhouse. Soon, we'd pull them from their hiding place; we'd free them from their shroud of shit and muslin and whatever else lay hidden beneath the earth.

I felt like I was standing at the edge of a cliff—like Icarus before he leapt to flight. The jagged rocks below; above, an unending cornflower blue sky.

CHAPTER 37

"THAT'S WHERE WE'RE GOING." Stella pointed across the river to New Jersey, to a clock tower taller than any basilica. Only in America would keeping time be sacred. Just beyond were mounds of green, ringed by violet-hued hills. If I looked past the wharf and clock tower, I could almost imagine Stella and I were explorers and this an undiscovered land. The burins tucked in my satchel, as important as a sextant; the engraving plates, a buried treasure.

The ferry slowed as it approached the dock, the tar-swabbed pilings shimmering in the morning light. The heat settled around us again like a heavy, damp cloak. We stepped off the ferry along with six or seven other passengers. In New York City, the heat drew the people outside, like ants to a picnic. Here, though, the terminal was deserted. Stella hadn't exaggerated when she'd told me the farmhouse was remote.

We exited into bright sunlight. Stella crossed the street to a field of cattails and parted them like a heavy curtain. She waved me forward and then stepped through. The ground was spongy, the cattails, with their fuzzy-cigar shaped spikes, too dense to see beyond. If I got lost here, I'd never find my way out. Just as my heart was starting to race, Stella reached out from the green and pulled me in. "Be careful. You don't want to be swallowed up."

Like Persephone falling through the earth, to her destiny.

The cattails slapped against my hands and face; weeds and vines tangled around my feet. Stella kept hold of my hand. After what felt like a long time, we stepped into a clearing. Fence posts tilted to one side or another, their rails on the ground. Rusty wheels and parts of machines lay next to them.

Stella had tucked her skirt between her legs. She was holding it from behind. The prostitutes in Palermo hitched up their skirts like that. I guess men liked to see what was hidden from them, even if it was just a pair of ankles or a glimpse of stockinged legs.

"The railroad dumped their crap here," Stella said. "First chance I get, I'm going to have some pants made for myself."

She gestured toward an immense, tarp-draped shape. "Help me with this, will you?" She pulled up one corner. I took the other. Together we folded down the canvas. Underneath was an automobile. A cadmium red two-seater with gold-spoked wheels. So much for being inconspicuous.

"Is this yours?"

Stella laughed. "There's no law against women owning automobiles. At least not yet."

When the canvas was folded into a small square, Stella tucked it under a rock. It seemed like a lot of trouble to hide a car, especially given how few people were out here. But Stella knew what she was doing.

Stella went to the crank and turned it. She wiped her oil-covered palms on her skirt. Mamma would be disgusted. But she'd never had to start an automobile.

After several more cranks, the car started. I settled in beside Stella, the satchel in my lap.

She pointed to the strap. "Hold on."

The road was strewn with boulders and pitted with holes. Overhead, tree branches reached toward each other, casting a deep shadow below. We continued, birds screaming in protest. We finally crashed through the thick underbrush. Cattails stuck to the windshield and side mirrors. Stella turned sharply onto a dirt road.

"It's always a bit hairy, that part." she said, gesturing back toward the brush. But the road ahead wasn't much better. As we bounced over its pitted and rock-strewn surface, I was sure I'd be sick. I was grateful when the car screeched to a stop before a thick oak tree.

Stella got out. "We'll walk from here."

I picked up the satchel and joined her. "Should we cover the car?"

Stella waved her hand in the air. "Not necessary."

The cattails rustled, the susurration louder. More insistent. I hesitated.

Stella smiled. "You're not afraid, are you?"

I shrugged.

She took my hand. "No one knows about this place. We're safe."

It was the kind of thing Pappa would say. But Stella wasn't Pappa. She understood the cruel realities of this world: the way things could seem closer than they were and how people's paths could cross and then diverge, never to meet again.

We walked a little further, through a small opening in the brush. Ahead was an old farmhouse, listing heavily to one side. Several canvas tarps had been tied together over the roof. They blew lazily in the breeze.

"I'll show you inside. Then we'll retrieve the plates." Stella gestured toward a massive dung heap just beyond the tarps.

She went to the door. The paint was chipping, but there was a thick chain and heavy padlock across it. Stella reached into her bag and retrieved a key. A moment later, she pulled off the chain and tossed it on the ground.

Inside was one large room with a vaulted ceiling and a hayloft. The dirt floor had been covered over, and though there were already hairline cracks on the surface, the room smelled of wet concrete. Someone had boarded up the small windows above what must have been horse stalls. But a wire-reinforced skylight ran the length of the space, flooding it with light. At the center of the room was a table covered with a crisp, clean sheet. Next to it were several pallets, piled high with crates stamped *NEW ENGLAND PAPER COMPANY*.

Stella drew back the sheet reverentially, revealing an immense machine. Wrought iron, like the radiators in the tenement. I tried to lift the corner. It was too heavy. Stella laughed.

"Three guys had to move that from the truck."

I was surprised. She'd been saying no one else knew about this place. "Was it Clutch's brothers?" I asked.

She snorted. "Those goons? Ciro and Nicolò would tattle to Clutch like little girls. That kind of trouble I don't need. No. It was some men from Little Africa. Downtown."

Curious, I asked if they were Negroes.

"Yes. Is that a problem?"

I shook my head. In Sicily, San Calogero, protector of the western hill towns, is always brown-skinned. There are so many shades of skin color—from wave after wave of foreign conquest—that people hardly noticed. In America, though, Sicilians seemed to forget this tolerance, calling Negroes *moolinyan* or *moolies*—after the word for eggplant, *milinciana*.

But not Stella.

"I trust them. They won't tell Clutch or any of them." There it was again: Stella's overconfidence. I asked how she could be sure.

"There's no love lost between the coloreds and the *peasani* in New York. Anyway, I promised there'd be something in it for them. Later, when we're moving the money."

That old saying: The enemy of my enemy is my friend. But did we really want Clutch and his brothers as our enemies?

Stella ran her fingers over the printer. "The Pearl. Top of the line. We can run twenty plates a day. Another day to do the backs, that's two hundred bills. Every other day—a thousand dollars. If we're here Monday through Saturday—the ferry doesn't run on Sundays—it'll be three thousand a week."

Three thousand. An absurd amount.

"It'll be less after we pay for expenses," she continued. "Paper and ink. Security. Money to keep the police from nosing around here. Still, probably close to a thousand for each of us."

A thousand a week? Rent on the apartment was twenty dollars a month. I could buy that whole building in a few months. Not that I wanted it, but still.

There was a map of the United States on the wall. Small red pins dotted the surface. Stella went to it. "We'll be starting in New York." She gestured toward the now-familiar coastline. "We'll distribute just enough to cover our expenses. As my husband always said, we don't want to shit where we eat. The rest of the money, we'll send west and south." She spread her hand wide, her fingers like the spokes of a wheel.

How many times had I stood outside Pappa's study, while he and Zio talked? My godfather might have bought me those burins. He might have planned for me make the five-dollar bills. But I always would have been his puppet, following his commands. Pappa's plans were pipe dreams—*Binvinutu,* with its sulfur mines, olive groves and wheat fields; the grocery on Lexington. But Stella and I were partners. Our plans were as real as that Pearl printer. Those stacks of special paper. The boxes of ink, filled with tiny bottles of green, red and blue.

"Now, let's get our engraving plates." Stella turned toward the door. She pulled two smocks and two pairs of gloves from a hook.

She gave one set to me. "There are boots by the door. Take off as much as you can. That manure pile will be disgusting. And hot."

I watched her strip down to her chemise, then, with one sweep, she pulled that off, too. I shouldn't stare, but I'd never seen a naked woman. She looked at me and smiled.

"Don't be shy, Mimi. You don't want to soil your clothes."

I don't know why I should have cared, but I didn't want Stella to see those shiny, puckered scars that pulled at the skin along my left rib cage.

I waited for Stella to bend down to pull on her boots. Facing the wall, I slipped my dress over my head. But I kept on my chemise. I was grateful when Stella said nothing more. Once we were both dressed—smocks, gloves and oversized men's boots—we headed to the heap.

The summer heat made the stench almost unbearable. I breathed through my nose and tried to distract myself. "Where did you get the manure?" I asked, motioning toward the empty paddocks and pens.

"Shipped in. From a farm down south. I told the man I was a widow and wanted to start a small vegetable farm. When he came around afterwards—curious or horny, who knows?—I had the Negroes scare him off. Threw in a few more dollars for his inconvenience." Stella smiled wryly. "Vito's money, or course."

The dung heap was taller than we were. We used shovels and pitchforks at first. The smell was so bad that Stella tore her petticoat into strips so we could cover our noses and mouths. When we got nearer the bottom, we put down the tools and began throwing handfuls to the side. I clawed through the manure, bits of shit falling into the cuffs of my gloves. After a while, I pulled off the gloves and used my bare hands to claw into the dirt.

Stella leaned on her shovel. "It's just a little deeper."

Sweat trickling down my back, I burrowed down, dirt and pebbles wedging under my nails. Finally, I felt the hard, flat surface of the plates. I probed the underside with my fingers, then managed to get one side up, extricating the muslin-wrapped package like it was one of those treasures being unearthed in Egypt. Once the pouch was in my hands, I began fumbling with the knotted ties.

Stella reached down for the package.

I don't know why, but I hesitated. It was only for a moment, and I don't think Stella even noticed. But part of me didn't want to surrender those plates.

Her hand was still out. "We should go inside," she said. "And get cleaned up."

Reluctantly, I handed it to her.

I stood slowly, the heat and stench making me dizzy. By the time I got up, Stella was on her way back to the farmhouse.

When I got inside, Stella was trying to open the muslin package. The ties were caked with bits of manure and dirt. She motioned toward the hallway.

"The sink's in the last feed stall. There is a bucket of water and soap. Strip off everything. Throw it in the barrel. You're never going to get it clean."

When I returned, my skin raw from being scrubbed clean and the smell of manure still in my nose, Stella had managed to extract the plates. She handed me an apron. "I'll finish cleaning the plates. You start with the inks."

I slipped the apron over my head.

Stella pointed to another horse stall. "You can mix the inks in there." The floors and walls were whitewashed. There was a long table, and above it, a rectangular window that flooded the space with light. In the middle were three glass bottles, each filled with ink. Red. Yellow. Blue. I picked up the blue—cobalt blue, the exact shade I'd asked for—and ran my fingers over the label. *Carter's. Made in U.S.A.*

"I went right to the source," Stella explained. "Like the paper. It was expensive. The same materials as what the government uses. I'm doing it right. Not like Cascioferro. The materials. The paper. And a real artist," she said, smiling. "Not one of those amateurs in Palermo."

When Stella looked at me, her eyes were as dark and unknowable as the nighttime sky. *Colpo di fulmine.* The thunderbolt.

She broke the trance. "I taped two bills there, right below the window." She gestured toward the five-dollar bills affixed to the wall. "To get the color right."

"I've already worked out the color," I said, hearing the conceit in my voice.

"I was just trying to help."

A little embarrassed, I fumbled in my satchel longer than I needed to and then pulled out my burin case. Inside was the paper with the formulas for the colors. How many times had I sat in my room on Doctors Row, figuring out the exact shades? Weighing and re-weighing the percentages to make the colors I'd need. Now, I placed the paper on the table and uncorked the bottles of cobalt and cadmium yellow. I added the precise amounts of each to my palette. As I swirled them together, green appeared. I added the carmine red and a bit more of the blue and swished them all together. Like alchemy, jade-green emerged. I held the palette to the bills Stella had taped up. The color could be a little brighter, but it was passable.

I went to the worktable where Stella was cleaning the engraving plates. I laid the palette before her like an offering.

"It's good," she whispered. "It's really good." She looked down at the two plates. "Which side should we start with?"

I looked at my watch. Just past noon. The last ferry back to Manhattan was at 7. I thought of Mamma, her eyes moving between the front door and the wall clock. But this was my work. I'd be home when I was done.

I pointed to the plate of President Harrison. "We start with the front. Let it dry. Tomorrow we do the back. The first run will be finished by the end of the week."

"Is there anyway to speed it up?" Her eyes were wide with something like fear.

"We talked about this. Why, is something wrong?"

"It's the Camorra," she said, finally.

"The Camorra?"

"The Napolitani. Really, Mimi. Don't you ever read a newspaper?"

I felt like I'd been slapped in the face.

Stella reached out and took my hand. "I'm sorry. I'm just tense. The Camorra have been trying to weasel in on the Morello brothers' territory, in Greenwich Village. We don't need them asking questions about the five-dollar bills or Vito's shipments. They need to stay in Brooklyn, doing whatever the fuck it is they do."

"Are you worried?" I heard my voice catch.

"Not yet. But the Camorra are hungry. Nibbling at the edges, like little fish. But little fish grow. Especially if the eating's good. That's why we need to start making the bills. So we can pay for protection here and in New York."

"Protection?"

"Don't worry. I can ask the coloreds. The Bowery Boys. The Tongs. The Camorra has lots of enemies."

The floor felt unsteady beneath my feet. I'd actually begun to think we were safe, with Pappa and Clutch in prison.

"It'll be fine," Stella assured. "Just concentrate on making the bills. That's the key to everything."

I nodded, wanting to believe. I laid the first plate on the machine.

CHAPTER 38

"Stop dawdling, Mimi! Come on."

Mamma acted like we were going somewhere important. But it was only Sunday dinner at Bartu's.

I smoothed out the pleats on my skirt, trying to hide the ink stains. My everyday skirt lay in a bundle under my daybed, ink splattered on the front and sides, already stained by mid-week. Then Thursday, when the ink pad had snapped off the machine just after we'd begun to run the backside of the bills, spraying ink all over me and ruining that skirt. The sheet of bills in the press had been ruined, along with most of the sheets that were drying on the side table. I'd looked at Stella, on her hands and knees, desperately trying to sop up the ink. She'd been so sure this would work. Yet here we were, a broken printing press and an entire week of work ruined.

"Don't worry. It'll be fixed by Monday."

Now, I pressed my hand over the blotch of dried ink. The last thing I needed was for Bartu to realize that we'd started making bills that week. I opened my dresser drawer and rummaged inside for my scarf. As I did, my fingers brushed against Nonna's rosary beads. Maybe I should pray to the Madonna for help with the press. As if those beads—chipped and worn, links tarnished, the tiny Jesus worn smooth from Nonna's constant caress—had any power. I pushed them to the back of the drawer then wrapped the scarf around my waist and went to the kitchen.

"Do you really have to wear that?" Mamma asked, pointing to the scarf.

"It's the latest. I saw it in a window downtown."

"Whatever. Let's go. Get the roast."

I picked up the roasting pan, careful not to spill the juices. Ridiculous. We didn't have enough money for rent, but we still brought the roast every week. Mamma had started pawning the silver seafood forks to buy the meat—one fork, each week. The pawn shop owner must almost have a full set by now. I should be angry. Bartu, with his barber shop and wealthy clients, should be buying the roast.

When no one answered the buzzer for Bartu's apartment, Mamma used her key. Inside, it was eerily quiet. I called Caterina. Sebu. No answer. Momma started toward the bedroom but I hung back, dread engulfing me. While I'd been playing with that stupid press, something terrible had happened to my sister and nephew. I staggered to the table and leaned heavily against it. Finally, I heard Mamma's voice. She was angry. I exhaled, relieved, and made my way to the bedroom.

Mamma was standing over my sister's bed, her hands on her hips. "Why didn't you answer? We kept ringing and ringing."

Caterina muttered something. Her words were jumbled.

"Bartu's out?" Mamma asked.

I walked in the room. Something shimmered amidst the bed table clutter. Could it be the thing the midwife gave her after Sebu was born? A long glass funnel with a bulb at the end, the midwife had called it a douching syringe, and told Caterina to use it after she and Bartu had relations. Stella had slipped her an extra twenty-dollar bill for it. I inched closer. No sign of the syringe, but the tabletop was littered with tiny glass ampules. I picked up one. A residue of white powder clung to its edge. Caterina was passed out, still in her nightgown though it was afternoon. Sebu was asleep on the blanket beside her. He looked peaceful—too peaceful—his chest rising slowly, his tiny arms flung out to the side.

Mamma yanked off the coverlet. "It's past one."

Caterina grabbed for the blanket. Mamma pulled it away from her, an absurd tug of war. "You'll never hold onto a man like Bartu if you keep up like this. Get dressed." Mamma picked up Sebu and slung him over her shoulder. His arms and legs were limp.

"You," she motioned to me. "Help your sister."

I managed to prop Caterina against the headboard. When I tried to get her nightdress over her head, though, I saw that the collar of tiny daisies—the stitches she'd labored over as a girl—was torn. The white muslin fabric was gray, dingy. Mamma would be furious. *Bella figura*. Even if—or maybe *especially* if—the only one who saw you was your husband. I balled up the gown and tucked it under the bed.

Mamma returned. Sebu was in her arms. He was gulping down the contents of a bottle.

"Where did that come from?" I pointed at the bottle.

"I bought it from Rexall. The ladies at church were talking about the benefits of bottle-feeding. It's a good thing I picked up that formula. He's too small. Your sister's milk isn't enough."

Caterina was already obsessing about how she was a bad mother. I didn't want to think about how she'd feel when she woke to find she'd been replaced by a bottle.

"See how well he's drinking?" Mamma smiled at little Sebu. "Sugar. That's the secret. Babies love it."

How Mamma could be an expert on such things, I had no idea. She'd never nursed us or cared for us as small children, leaving our care to a wet nurse or nanny.

After Sebu had fallen back asleep, Mamma laid him down on the bed for a nap. Together, we wrestled Caterina into some clothes and onto a chair. I was feeding her some bread and milk when Bartu sauntered in. I tried not to notice how Caterina flinched as he approached the table.

Bartu rubbed his stomach. "Just in time for dinner!"

He ate three helpings, leaving nothing for leftovers. When he was done, he pushed back from the table. He put his hands into his waistband.

He turned toward me. "So, sister dear, how have you been? Come, talk to me." He tried to grab my hand. I managed to slip his grasp.

"I've been well. And you? How's work?" Maybe it was the way I asked it, or the fact it was usually men who asked each other about work, but Mamma shot me a warning look.

Bartu didn't seem to care. "Good." He slathered his bread with butter. "I'm starting something new."

"Oh? That thing with your clients?"

Ever since we'd met Bartu, he'd been boasting about the tips he got from his Wall Street clients. "They like to talk when they're in the chair," he'd told Pappa.

He shook his head. "No. I'm working with some fellas from Brooklyn. You might be interested."

"Oh?"

"They need some engravings."

Hadn't Stella just talked about some guys in Brooklyn who were asking about Clutch's business? The Camorra. That's what she'd called them.

"What kind of engravings?" I asked.

"Never mind about that. Do you have your tools?"

"The burins? I'm not sure," I lied. I knew exactly where they were, tucked beneath the floorboard under the daybed.

"You're careless. A slob. Like your sister." Bartu gestured around the kitchen, its counters littered with dirty plates and old newspapers. "That's what comes from having servants."

Mamma stood. She picked up her plate and put it in the kitchen. From the set of her mouth, I could see she was furious. It was one thing for him to criticize Caterina. But insulting the nobility—the life she'd been chasing her whole life—that was something completely different.

Bartu leaned in.

"So do you think you can find your burins?" His breath was sour. He wasn't going to let this go. "It could be big money. Do you know how expensive it is for me to keep up two apartments?"

Liar. He hadn't given us a cent.

Bartu mentioned the burins once more during the salad course and then twice over espresso. As we stood at the door saying goodbye, he clasped my hands again.

"Find those burins, Mimi. It'll be good for you." His smile was gone. "And all of us."

I tried to keep my expression neutral. Caterina was under his thumb, not me.

"I'll look," I lied. "They might still be packed."

Then he offered a way out. "Let's just hope they weren't stolen when you left them on the street."

Moving day. The burins had been safe in my satchel. Bartu didn't need to know that.

CHAPTER 39

When I told Stella about Bartu on the ferry the next day, I thought she'd laugh. Instead, she shook her head. "He's a dangerous man."

"He's an asshole," I corrected.

"That's what makes him dangerous. He doesn't know he's playing with fire."

Stella stabbed out her cigarillo on the bow railing. "I hope you didn't tell him anything,"

"Of course not."

"Good."

She was quiet the rest of the ferry ride. When we got to the factory, though, Stella asked me to repeat exactly what Bartu had told me. After I did, she lit another cigarillo.

"So they don't have an engraver." She exhaled. "That's good news."

"Or burins," I added.

"Buying a set of burins is the easy part. It's finding a talented engraver who can also mix paints that's near impossible." I thought she'd say something about how I was that person. Or how happy she was that we were working together.

Instead, she told me to be careful. "New York's a powder keg." Stella flicked her ash into the wind. "With Clutch in prison, his brothers haven't been able to secure their territory. In Sicily, everyone knew who was in charge in a town or a city. Here, everything's up for grabs. It's not just the Sicilians or Italians. The Jews, the Chinese, the Coloreds, the Irish—it'll be war. War takes money. Lots and lots of money. And you, my dear, can make that money."

Stella pulled a small brown envelope from her pocket. She spilled its contents into her hand. A small bracket and some screws. Then she turned to fix the Pearl.

About an hour later, she was done, and the engraving plate of President Harrison was back in position.

"You need to stay away from Bartu," Stella said, like there'd been no interruption in our conversation. "Can you do that?"

I reminded her about Sunday dinners.

She shook her head. "Ridiculous."

"He isn't there most of the time."

"Of course not. He's with his whore."

"His whore?"

"That Mick girlfriend. The one he's been with for years."

"Years?"

"Since before the wedding. She's the one who went to the priest and told him that Bartu had made promises."

I shook my head. "He works late. He's a good provider." I don't know why I defended him.

"The perfect family. What bullshit."

"Will he leave my sister?"

Stella shrugged. "Who knows what these men will do? But in the meantime, make sure your sister doesn't get pregnant."

"She's been sick. Probably not well enough to engage in—relations."

"Bartu doesn't give a shit about how she feels. The midwife gave her that thing to use. Remember?"

The douching syringe. I thought of those empty vials. "I don't know if she still has it."

"She better have it. And she better use it. The last thing your sister needs is another brat. And you," Stella put her hand on mine. "No more Sunday dinners."

"Mamma will be angry." I heard how stupid it sounded the moment those words left my mouth.

Stella shook her head. "You're a grown woman, Mimi. Just tell her no."

"But my sister needs me. To help with the baby."

"Oh, yes, the baby. Just tell them that you're feeling ill. You're worried you're having a relapse of the tuberculosis, and you don't want to infect little what's-his-name."

"Sebastianu," I said. "Sebu."

"That'll buy you some time, right? Once you're bringing in the money, you can say that you're too tired. I'll bet your Mamma won't bug you once you flash her some of that cash."

I nodded. But to myself, I was thinking about how I'd miss Sebu's sweet smell and the way his fingers curled around mine. I'd never thought of myself as maternal—I'd assumed that being an artist would insulate me from that. But there was something about the way he stared into my eyes that made me want to protect him. I thought of Mary Cassatt's painting of a woman gently washing a child's foot in a basin. The tenderness. The love. Cassatt had no children. Still, to create that masterpiece, she must have known those feelings.

Stella broke into my reverie. "Do you hear me, Mimi? Stay away from Bartu. At least until the Camorra are taken down."

"I hear you." I unscrewed the jar of ink I'd mixed last week. I shook, then stirred it. The color looked slightly off—more yellow than green— so I put it aside and mixed another batch of ink. When it was right, I brushed it onto the engraving plate. I turned the flywheel. The clamshell opened. I snapped the front plate onto one side; on the other, I slipped a piece of watermarked paper. Half a turn brought the rollers over the ink pad and then onto the plate. Completing the turn closed the clamshell, pressing the inked plate onto the paper and transferring the engraving. Turning the wheel again opened the mechanism. I removed the paper and checked the images. President Harrison was perfect. I laid that paper to the side and put a new piece in the Pearl. I repeated the process until I had ten sheets of five-dollar bills, the images, sharp and exactly aligned.

The door opened and Stella appeared. "The press stopped. Is everything working all right?"

I looked up from the table and smiled. Stella came to stand beside me. She peered at the bills, studying them. When she stood, she was smiling. "They're spot on."

I felt a lightness inside like I'd had when Monsieur Laurent said I was ready for the Academy. Then that niggling feeling, the one that warned against pride.

"I still need to do the other side. And these," I said, pointing to the last sheet of bills. "These got a little light, though I think I can match the backs."

"It's fine. Better than fine, actually. When they're a little worn-looking, they're easier to pass."

I started to ask about the distribution. But Stella put her hand on my shoulder. "I'll worry about that. Let's just enjoy this, all right?" She slipped her hand off my shoulder and bent to peer more closely at the bills. "They look real. Like they came straight from the United States Printing Bureau."

She turned to face me. "I knew you could do it. Still, it's still a shock to see them all laid out like that."

I laughed. "A shock?"

"Maybe more like a pleasant surprise. I knew you were good. I just didn't know how good."

"Better than Vito's guy?" She'd already said it was. But as I stood there, all I wanted was to continue to bask in the glow of Stella's approval.

She returned her hand to my shoulder and squeezed me closer. "You're the artist. No one else could do this."

I turned toward her and inhaled her familiar smell of tobacco and anise. My fingers grazed her sleeve. The fabric was rough—home-spun like a Sicilian peasant's. I don't know why, but I stepped toward her, closer now than I'd ever been. She started stroking my hair. Her breath was on my face. I reached up and placed my hand on the nape of her neck. She turned to kiss my hand. A warmth spread through my belly.

I'd felt like this before—with Teo and Hans—but this was different. Stella knew me.

We embraced. Her soft lips were on mine. The sun through the sky-light felt warm. Her mouth tasted like strawberries.

Stella shrugged off her jacket and placed it on the floor. "Come."

My mind was racing. "Stella—" I started.

She put her finger to her lips. "Shhh." She eased me to the floor and began to kiss me again. This time, harder.

Her eyes were closed. Was she imagining she was somewhere else? With someone else?

"Just relax," she whispered.

I closed my eyes. Her hands began to wander over my body. First my neck and shoulders. Then my chest. My breasts. My nipples. I arched my back, wanting more. She kissed me again. I wondered if I should be touching her. I reached out and felt the curve of her breasts. Much bigger than mine. Soft. Comforting. She gently pushed my hand away.

"Later. Now, let me take care of you."

Stella unbuttoned my blouse, then reached inside and ran her fingers down my corset and over my belly. I shuddered. She eased off my blouse and began to unlace my corset. I leaned back. The sun was warm. She eased my right hand out of the corset. As she started on the left, my hand went to my scar.

"It's all right," Stella whispered.

I knew it wasn't. I folded my arms over my chest and rolled onto my left side.

"What's wrong?"

How could I tell her about the numbness? The way it felt like that part of my body belonged to someone else. Maybe Teo, with his endless coughing; or Dr. Florio, with his knife; or even Zio, with all his plans.

Stella tried to roll me onto my back. But I hooked my ankles around the table so she couldn't. Holding fast to the legs of the table, I stayed on my side. She exhaled loudly and released me.

"I want you to feel good, Mimi." Her voice was gentle. "You deserve to feel good."

"But my body," I croaked. "The scars."

"Think I haven't seen scars? Salvatore was in knife fights. He'd been cut all over. His arms. His chest. His face. Jagged. Red. Horrible—."

For a moment, she was quiet. When she continued, her thoughts seemed far away. "Then they cut him in prison." She squared her shoulders, as if recounting the brutality of the act might somehow make her stronger. "Ear to ear. With a dagger. The warden said they almost took his head off completely."

I whispered I was sorry.

"Cascioferro arranged it. He thought my Salvatore had sold him out. Fucking *omertà*. The prison wouldn't even send him back to me. He's buried in an unmarked grave in Buffalo. Do you know how cold it gets there?" She fell quiet.

I leaned in close. "You loved him."

"He was a good man, maybe the only good one I've ever known." Her hand fell away from my breast.

"I'm sorry." I repeated. Her warmth was already fading.

"Yeah. Well. That was a different life. I don't need Cascioferro or Clutch or any of them. I'm doing this on my own. I mean, we're doing it. The two of us. Together." She stroked my cheek. I edged closer.

I stiffened as she bent to kiss my scar. At first, it felt like a vague pressure. But as she intensified her stroke, using her tongue and the tips of her teeth, a shudder ran down my spine.

She untied my bloomers, then eased them over my hips. Her mouth moved to my breast. Her fingers ran down my belly, to my folds. Gently, she touched me. Then more urgently, the bud at my center. I arched my back. Her mouth was on me. Licking my folds. Sucking me. As the waves overtook me, I cried out. For the first time since Teo, I felt alive.

"This is what you're made for, Mimi." Stella took me in her arms again. "Not just for your art. But for this."

As I lay there, my pleasure beginning to ebb, I knew she was right.

On the ferry back to Manhattan, Stella hooked her arm through mine. "A good day today."

"Yes." My pulse quickened remembering her mouth on me.

"Ten completed plates. Each with ten five-dollar bills, so five hundred dollars."

Had I imagined the two of us on the floor? Those waves of pleasure?

"You're frowning, Mimi. What's wrong?"

I didn't know how to answer.

"You're thinking about what happened back there," she nodded back towards New Jersey. "Between us."

I nodded.

"Men aren't the only ones who can feel good. There are women all over this city who prefer women. And men who prefer men." She pointed across the harbor. "Over there, in Staten Island, are two women who live like they're married. One is a famous photographer. Alice Austen. Do you know her?"

I shook my head.

"They have a house. They open it up on weekends. Mostly women. Looking for a place to be who they are. To belong."

To belong. That old longing welled up inside me.

Stella took out a cigarillo. Cupping her hand around it, she lit the tip and inhaled. It glowed red.

"It's against the law," she continued. "The cops can throw you in jail for it. Not us, though. They won't be coming within a mile of the farmhouse."

Was she talking about us, naked on the floor, or about the counterfeiting? I decided it didn't matter.

"What if things go wrong?" I asked, because things always seemed to go wrong.

Stella tossed the cigarillo stub over the railing. It disappeared into the frothy, churning water. She didn't tell me not to worry. Or that everything would be fine. Those were things you'd say to a child. "If things change, we'll figure out what to do."

In the distance, the Manhattan skyline loomed. Gray and beige, bits of black. A seemingly endless repetition of squares and rectangles. When I got home, Mamma was out. I went on my knees beside my daybed and felt for that loose board I'd hidden my burins under. I pried off the nails, then listened for any sound of Mamma in the hallway. Hearing nothing, I raised the board. I reached inside and felt the pebbly leather of the burin case and the smooth metal plaque with my initials. Soon this space would be filled with money. Not our fake bills, but real ones.

Enough to take care of Mamma, and maybe even Caterina and Sebu. And enough for me to get free from this place, if that's what Stella and I decided.

Stella and me. The taste of her mouth. The feel of her body, on top of me. The waves of pleasure.

Some might say she took advantage of me. Or tricked me. But I'd made my own decision, like Persephone with those pomegranate seeds. Maybe I'd be damned to hell, or to some earthly prison.

But I'd chosen this. All of it.

CHAPTER 40

I UNLOCKED THE MAILBOX. Inside, the morning and evening mail. Mamma was out again, shopping or at lunch with the church ladies. Sometimes it seemed she spent money faster than I could make it. The space under the floorboard was so crammed with bills that I'd had to pull open another floorboard for my burin box. Still, it would have been nice if Mamma was home when I returned from the farmhouse, at least some of the time. I took the mail from the box and closed it again. I rubbed my hand over the back of my neck. It had been a long week.

Upstairs, I looked quickly through the mail. Mostly store catalogs addressed to Mamma. A bill from the coal man—winter had come and gone, this year, with plenty of heat. I'd be glad to pay for it. A letter from Sisters of Charity, asking for another donation. And a white envelope addressed to Mamma, with a return address from the Atlanta penitentiary. I felt that old panic but reminded myself: if it were serious, they would have sent a telegram. I turned the letter over and fingered the back flap. Whatever this was about Pappa, it would be better if I knew first. I drew my finger under the flap and pulled out the letter. I read it quickly, scanning for those words that would change everything: condolences, grave, cemetery. Seeing none of these, I tucked it back into the envelope, relieved.

I pulled off my coat and put my satchel on the floor next to the daybed. I eased off the nails and lifted the floorboard. With today's receipts, I'd have almost twenty thousand dollars. Less than what

Stella said it would be for a year of work, but still, a dizzying amount of money. And as Stella predicted, each time a finished sheet rolled off the press and I saw those perfect bills—Harrison and the pilgrims, crisp, and the color, the perfect shades of leek green and grass—my pulse quickened, and I felt a kind of breathlessness and excitement I'd only experienced on the farmhouse floor with Stella.

When Mamma finally returned, I told her about the letter.

"Pappa applied for parole."

"What's that?" she asked.

"It's where you get out early. Remember? The lawyer was talking about that before Pappa went away."

"So is he coming home?"

"He's got to pay a fine first. Fifteen hundred dollars."

"Fifteen hundred? It might as well be a million!"

"I know. It's a lot." The truth was that she'd spent at least that much this year in department store charges and charitable contributions to keep up with the church ladies.

"He's been gone for three years," Mamma cried. "How much longer are they going to keep him there?"

"It's a five-year sentence," I reminded her.

"Two more years. How will he survive?"

Like he'd survived so far, I wanted to say. With whatever cushy deal Puccio had arranged.

"Maybe Vito could help?" Mamma asked. But Zio hadn't sent any money since before Pappa went to prison. "Or you could work more?"

"I work fourteen hours a day. Six days a week." Some of that I spent on my back with Stella's mouth between my legs, but still.

"Didn't Zio say you could make more of those pomegranate things?"

"The logos?"

She nodded.

"My burins were stolen." I repeated the lie I'd told Bartu, when he'd first asked about helping the Camorra. "You know that."

"Don't talk to me like that! I'm still your mother. I almost died giving birth to you."

That old story, recycled for effect. This time, though, I didn't feel guilty. "I'm sorry, Mamma." I placed my hand on my chest. "The truth is that I haven't been feeling well lately." Another lie. I'd been feeling so well that I almost believed Stella when she told me I didn't have the consumption anymore. "I'm sorry I was disrespectful."

Mamma jutted out her chin. She could have thanked me for what I'd done—paying the rent, keeping the coal bin filled, making sure there was food on the table. Instead, she told me she'd ask Bartu. "He's making lots of money. I'm sure he'll help with the parole money."

It had been such a long time since Bartu had been at a Sunday dinner. A few months ago, I'd been shocked to find my sister's cupboard shelves bare, but for some salt and a half-empty box of farro. Bartu's chifforobe was empty, too, the bare hangers clanging against each other.

Even if Mamma could track down Bartu—at his barber shop downtown or at his *puttana*'s apartment—I doubted he'd pay Pappa's fine. It was just as well; he'd have expected Pappa's debt to be repaid. With interest. Not by me—from what I could tell, he still had no idea about the farmhouse. But by my sister. I suspected it had been a long time since he'd shared Caterina's bed. That was fine. She hadn't gotten pregnant. And there were days when her melancholy almost lifted. She'd have another spoonful of farina, or give Sebu a wistful smile. If Bartu stayed away long enough, maybe she'd finally return to herself.

In the meantime, Stella and I could continue as before, making love on the hay-stuffed bed while sheets of newly printed five-dollar bills hung drying on a clothesline above us. We didn't need Pappa home sooner.

The next Sunday, as I was climbing the steps to my sister's apartment, I thought I heard laughter. Caterina. Tinkling, like tiny metal bells hung in the breeze. And Sebu's giggling—endless, infectious. By the time Mamma and I reached their doorway, we were both smiling.

The apartment door opened. Sebu spilled out.

"What's going on here?" Mamma asked, reaching out to Sebu. The three-year-old was often shy around Mamma. Today was different. He went to her. She closed her eyes, breathing in his little boy scent. At that moment, she looked relaxed. Content.

I put the groceries on the table.

Caterina came up behind me. "Did you bring the cannoli?" When I held up the bakery box, tied closed with braided red and white twine, she smiled. "Thank you, Mimi." She kissed the top of my head.

We stood there—Mamma holding Sebu, me and Caterina, arms around each other — when Mamma cleared her throat.

"When will Bartu be home?"

Caterina stiffened. Mamma never could leave well enough alone.

"I asked you a question, Caterina. When will Bartu be home? I have something to discuss with him."

My sister began picking at her cuticles. It had been months since I'd seen her do that.

"Caterina! I'm talking to you!"

"He's gone!" she screamed.

"Gone where?"

"To his *puttana*. Margaret." Caterina spat out the name.

Mamma looked stunned. "Margaret? Margaret Kelly? The one who objected to your marriage banns?"

"He says he loves her," Caterina said, quietly.

Mamma laughed, mirthlessly. "Ridiculous. It's sex. Nothing more." Ah, but sex could be compelling. I knew that now.

Mamma turned to Caterina. "Have you been performing your wifely duties? If you were, Bartu wouldn't have strayed."

Caterina's cheeks flushed.

"Have you?" Mamma badgered.

"He doesn't want me." Caterina dropped her gaze to the floor. I could see the pain in her eyes. At least there wouldn't be another baby.

"Have you looked in the mirror lately?" Mamma continued. "A man doesn't want a woman who's let herself go." Her cruel words reached their mark. My sister's eyes filled with tears.

I held out my hand to Sebu. "Let's go make art." I led him into the bedroom and pulled the sketchpad and pack of crayons from the bottom dresser drawer.

"I saw a squirrel today," I said. I flipped past the drawings of cats and flowers and cars that we'd done on other Sunday afternoons. I took a brown crayon. Quickly, I sketched the creature I'd seen scampering up and down the old oak outside the farmhouse. "See? And here's his tree." It was fall, but I drew an oak in full leaf, its branches reaching to the sky.

Sebu's bottom lip stopped quivering. He watched as I filled in the animal's bushy tail and its small, alert eyes and rounded ears.

I handed Sebu the brown pencil. "Can you do his fur? It's soft as velveteen." I made a petting motion, like the animal was there with us.

Tentatively at first, he made a few small marks on the squirrel's back.

"That's right. Fill it in. He had lots of fur. Reddish-brown." I pulled the red and black crayons from the pack.

In the parlor, Mamma continued her assault.

"When was the last time you bought a new dress? Or had your hair done? Just because he's your husband, it doesn't mean you can ignore how you look."

I thought I heard Caterina mumble something about not wanting Bartu back.

Sebu and I both startled at the terrible sound of an open-handed slap.

"Don't be stupid," Mamma snarled. "He's your husband. Of course you want him back. Now stop your crying. The neighbors will hear you carrying on."

Sebu began to whimper.

"Let's draw something else." I opened to a new page. "What should it be? An aeroplane? An automobile?" I tried to put the pencil into his hand. But he shut his fists too tightly. He began to cry.

Outside, the gaslight flickered on. The lamplighter would be climbing down from his post, tucking the ladder under his arm and moving to the next post. So much effort, for just that dim circle of light.

I placed my hand on Sebu's back. After a long time, his crying stopped.

On the ferry the next morning, I told Stella about the visit.

"Caterina's so much better," I said. "Sebu, too." I left out the part about him crying. She already thought he was too sensitive.

The wind blew across the deck. Stella pulled up her collar. "That's because Bartu isn't there."

"I wish I could get them out of there."

"St. Mimi to the rescue again." Stella laughed, unkindly.

"Caterina is strong. She can manage on her own."

"With your help, of course."

What was I supposed to say? She was my sister, trapped in a loveless marriage while I had my engraving. And Stella.

"I don't mind."

"What did I tell you, Mimi? You'll never be free of them."

"I will."

Stella shook her head.

I put my hand around her waist. "I'm free now, aren't I?"

She looked away. "But what will you do when your father is released?"

I thought of that letter. Maybe I should have felt guilty, leaving him there when I could have easily paid that fine. But in two years, I'd have enough money that things would be settled. A house in Westchester. A bank account large enough that Pappa would never again have to try his hand at work. Caterina and Sebu would move in with them. Pappa would finally have his boy; Caterina would be happy, like she was today. Bartu would be a distant memory.

I pulled Stella closer.

"My family will manage without me. Soon, we'll be able to go wherever we want. You'll see."

We kissed. Her lips were chapped. Fall was coming on. But the cold couldn't hurt me.

CHAPTER 41

SOMETIME THAT SUMMER, I realized that the engraving plates no longer lay flat on the bed of the press. After almost two years of having the weight of that roller pressed against the soft metal, the plates had become misshapen. I'd need to carve new plates. But when I pulled the burins out from under the floorboards, I saw they needed sharpening. I had no whetstone, so I went first to the pushcart vendors on Lexington Avenue. Amidst the hustle and bustle of selling, the hucksters wouldn't remember a mousy spinster looking for a sharpening stone. But they had only coarse sharpening blocks, like for axes and saws.

One seller waved up the street. "Woolworth's," he said, not even bothering to look at me.

The Woolworth's on Third and 121st Street had opened a few years ago to great fanfare. A remnant of the banner that had crisscrossed Third still hung from a streetlight. I'd never been inside the place—*THE BEST FIVE AND DIME IN NEW YORK,* according to the board that hung above the entrance. But I'd marveled at the signs that nearly covered the front windows, advertising everything from yarn to screws to ladies' shirtwaists.

Now, I stepped inside. It was a cavernous space with embossed tin ceilings and glass cases that ran from front to back. The counters were mahogany, the wood glassy in the afternoon sun. I made my way down the center aisle, trying to make sense of the jumble of goods being sold here. There were ladies' undergarments; next to them, glassware. Just beyond, linens and towels. Toward the back, a counter for hardware. Alongside, a counter with the kind of satchels and trunks you'd need for a trip.

I went to the hardware counter and laid my gloves on top. Stella told me it was important to do this—to establish your place, especially when people thought you didn't belong. The two clerks behind the counter gawked at me; a customer holding a length of rope smiled at me indulgently. I placed my bag on the counter, next to my gloves, and waited for one of the clerks to approach.

"Sure you're in the right place, Miss?" He pointed to the sign overhead. *PAINTS. HARDWARE. PLUMBING.* "Women's garments are in front." He smiled. His teeth were brown. Rotting. That gave me courage.

"I need a whetstone."

He tilted his head, like he didn't understand.

"For sharpening," I added.

He laughed. "What? Like for needles? That's in *SEWING NOTIONS.*" He waved vaguely toward the left.

I kept my eyes on his. "No. For a blade."

"A blade? What are you needing a blade for, Miss?"

Stella would have said something witty but vaguely threatening—like that she had a switchblade that needed honing—but I'd never been good at snappy retorts.

"My embroidery scissors are dull," I lied. "I need to sharpen them."

"You can bring them to the tool shop out back. They'll do that for you."

I shook my head. "I don't get out that often. It'll be easier if I have a stone at home. My husband can help me," I blurted out, immediately hating myself.

But the idea of a husband seemed to ease the clerk's mind. He crouched down beside a case with dozens of drawers. He ran his hand down the case, then opened a drawer near the bottom and drew out three stones. He stood and laid them on the counter in front of me.

"Coarse. Medium. Fine," he said, touching each stone.

I reached for the fine stone—a shard of charcoal-colored flint. He covered my hand with his.

"That'll be too small." He ran the tip of his obscenely pink tongue over his rotted teeth. "You'll need something bigger."

He pressed his sweaty hand down on mine, his meaning clear. With effort, I pulled away, bringing the flint with me. "This will be fine." I restrained myself from saying something about his faint, moldering smell. The less any of these men remembered of me, the better.

I picked up the stone. "Where do I pay?"

"It's 90 cents." He narrowed his eyes. "Do you have that much?" He looked pointedly at my faded black shirtwaist.

I had three dollars in my purse. Stella said it would be enough. Still, I almost reached into my satchel to make sure the money was there. I kept my eyes on his. "Yes. Where do I pay?"

He gestured toward the center of the store, where two registers sat on identical mahogany counters. A line of customers waited to settle up. A few held hammers and hacksaws; one cradled a travel satchel. I joined the end of the line.

For the short time Pappa had owned his store, he had made a practice of placing items near the cashier that might tempt a customer to add to his or her order. A bowl of lemon drops. A stack of gum. Inexpensive but self-indulgent. Woolworth's must have figured it out, too. Because all along the checkout line were those last-minute, almost-forgotten items—packets of tacks, small bottles of glue, bundles of rags. One wooden rack held dozens of picture postcards. I guess it made sense: They were selling traveling bags here. As I got closer, I saw them: places like Lancaster, Pennsylvania and Batavia, New York, wherever they were. Next to them, a row of cards titled *FAR WEST*, with images of mountains and canyons. There was a river winding through, and something shooting steam out of the ground. Engravings, like I'd been making. But they had a dreamy, otherworldly character and were colored in fantastical hues.

I picked one up. The lettering on top read *Yellowstone and Colter Peak*. A lake, colored in shades of peacock green and lavender blue. Beyond it, a snow-peaked mountain in creamy pink. The image had been composed in such a way that it looked like a window looking out onto the mountain. But instead of curtains, pine trees framed the scene. Like Matisse's *Joy of Life*—a glimpse through the trees and a clearing that promised a heaven on earth. That's what I'd always wanted: to see the world new and capture one small, perfect aspect. Not an exact replica, like the five-dollar bills I'd been making. But something real. True.

The line lurched ahead. I followed, still holding tight to that Yellowstone card. I ran my fingers over the surface, as if I might feel the roughness of that tree bark or the cold of the snow. But the surface was smooth, like my engraved images were. The difference, though, was that while my engravings were worth something—five dollars an image; fifty dollars a sheet of bills—these were a dozen for ten cents. Virtually worthless. Still, the images were beautiful.

Stella said my tuberculosis was cured. When we were finished with the bills, I could return to my painting. For now, though, I couldn't get sick again. Too many people relied on me. Soon, though, there'd be enough money that I wouldn't have to worry. I could return to my oils, or use a different medium—maybe pastels, or colored pencils, or watercolors. Move far away, the small voice inside whispered, like *Yellowstone and Colter Peak*. Disappear into those canyonlands and be the person I was meant to be.

"Next?"

I looked up. The cashier was looking at me, eyebrows raised. He was annoyed that I'd made him wait. I went to the counter and placed the whetstone in front of him.

"That, too?" He gestured toward the postcard still in my hand.

It would be so lovely to have that card tucked beneath my pillow. A talisman, like Nonna's rosary beads, intended to bring good fortune.

I turned and slipped the card back into the rack.

Maybe it was because I didn't believe in luck. Or maybe I was already imagining that the time would come that I wouldn't need a postcard to remind me that such beauty existed.

CHAPTER 42

MID-FEBRUARY. The frigid air slipped through the gaps in the farm-house clapboard, carrying off the heat from the fire Stella had lit in a rusted steel drum.

She gestured toward a bale of hay. "Come, warm yourself." Stella poured black coffee from the thermos. Too bitter to drink, but the heat warmed my stiff, cold fingers.

She took a sip. "Some of our distributors are coming by today."

I glanced toward the place we kept the finished bills. There were only three crates waiting. "Didn't they just pick up?"

She stood and placed a bundle of dried cattails on the fire. They smoldered and crackled, adding to the smoke. "They're not coming to pick up. There's something they want to discuss."

My stomach dropped. Things had gone along well for so long that I'd grown complacent.

Stella must have read my expression. "Don't worry, Mimi, Everything's fine. So good, in fact, that we should think about adding more distributors."

"Are you sure?" I asked.

She took my hand, her face flushed from the fire. "Yes. I'm sure."

Without thinking, I glanced toward the bedroll, just beyond the barrel.

She laughed. "You have a one-track mind, Mimi Inglese! Later. After the meeting. We'll celebrate." Stella liked to tease that I was making up for lost time.

"Who is it?" I asked, trying to get back on track.

"Some Micks. From the Navy Yard in Brooklyn."

"Irishmen?"

"A woman and a man."

"A woman?"

She nodded. "Belle Harrity. One of the leaders of the White Hand."

The White Hand? Clutch had signed his extortion letters with the Black Hand. It couldn't be a coincidence.

Stella guessed at my confusion. "Yeah. The White Hand. The Micks are playing on that whole—'we're white, you're black' thing. Not that Clutch's brothers can do anything about them. They're having a hard enough time holding onto their numbers rackets."

She downed her coffee. "Anyway, Belle's a smart woman. If she's got her hand in the distribution, it'll go well."

I thought of what Bartu had said about the men he knew. "They're in Brooklyn?" I asked. "Are they friendly with the Camorra?"

"Sworn enemies. The Irish, the Jews, the Napolitani—-all fighting over the same shithole. We help the Irish, maybe they'll be strong enough to keep Ciro and Nicolò in check."

"But you said the Morellos were weak." It was hard to keep track of things.

"Never count the Morellos out. Clutch is in jail. But he still has two brothers, and now, his son, Calogero, who are doing his bidding. Nicolò's trying to take control."

"And the Irish are better than the Camorra or the Jews?"

"I don't trust any of them. But I like Belle. And the Micks need us—maybe more than any of the others. We can be partners. They won't try to take over the operation."

Working on the Pearl a little while later, I heard the familiar voices of one of our Negro distributors.

He introduced Stella to Belle Hannity, then left. I wiped my hands on a rag and made my way into the office. A young man blocked the door.

"Excuse me." I gestured inside.

The man had a flattened nose, and a jaw that looked like it had been smudged out of place. He waited for direction from the woman who sat across from Stella.

Stella gestured toward me. "This is our artist. Mimi Inglese."

Belle nodded. The man let me pass.

She looked me over. "The counterfeiter. I thought you'd be a bit more imposing." The woman's accent was strong—her th's, t's and her r's hard. About Stella's age. But while Stella was all grays and beiges, Belle was bright red—her hair dyed scarlet and cherry red on her lips. Stella tried to be invisible; Belle wanted to be noticed.

Belle propped one boot on a packing crate and turned back to Stella. "Thanks for seeing me."

"Of course."

She smiled. Her teeth had been whittled into points, whether by decay or design. "We need help. Me and my friends. Brooklyn's our city. The Navy Yard. That's where we earn our living. Keeping the docks safe from the criminal element."

I had to stop myself from laughing. If they were anything like the Black Hand, *they* were the criminals.

Stella leaned back in her chair. "What can we help you with?" It was the kind of thing Zio would have said.

"We run a legitimate business. Making sure nothing happens to the dockworkers or the shipments that arrive at our piers." Belle stood. "Lately, though, some greasers have been trying to muscle in on the action."

Stella's full attention was focused on Belle. "The Camorra. We've heard."

Belle nodded. "They want the docks for their cocaine business. Especially now that the government's going after it."

All those vials of poison Bartu had brought home from the pharmacy. "Will they stop selling it?"

Belle smirked at me. "That's not the way the world works, little sis."

"People will keep using it," Stella said. "Legal or illegal."

Belle nodded. "But it'll make it more expensive. The Camorra will jack up the prices. Buy more cops. Push us off the waterfront."

Stella interrupted. "Unless you can buy your own cops. That's where you need our help."

Our help? We were here to make five-dollar bills and stay out of jail. Not "help" anyone and certainly not get mixed up in something between those two gangs.

Belle kept her eyes on Stella's. "We need money, fast. You have money to get rid of. What is it your people say? One hand washes the other."

Stella smiled but her eyes were cold. *Your people*. Grouping us in with Clutch and his brothers. "So how many bills do you think you can move?"

Belle gestured toward the man. I'd almost forgotten he was there. He pulled several stacks of bills from inside his jacket pockets and laid them on the table.

"How much will this buy?" Belle asked.

Stella motioned to me. I quickly separated the bills—ones, fives and tens. Not new, like our bills. But real.

I counted them. "Two thousand dollars."

That would buy ten thousand dollars in our bills. I waited for Stella to say that it was too much. We kept our footprint small in the city so no one could trace the counterfeits back to us.

Instead, Stella went quickly to one of the crates of counterfeit bills. She brought it back to the table. "Ten thousand dollars. Can you really move that many bills?"

"If they're good," Belle said. "Are they good?"

Stella pulled open the lid. "See for yourself." She handed Belle a stack of fives.

As she flipped through the bills, Belle's eyes went wide. "You made these?"

"Mimi did," Stella's voice swelled with pride.

"They're perfect."

"She's an artist. Professionally trained."

I don't know why Stella lied. She knew I'd gotten sick before I could go to the Academy.

Belle nodded. "They might just work." She smiled broadly, not caring about her rotten, pointy teeth.

For a moment, I forgot about the risk of moving that many bills. A feeling of warmth washed over me. My bills spread all over New York City.

Later, though, after Belle and her henchman had gone, I asked Stella why she'd given the Irishwoman all those bills.

"It was the prudent thing to do." She pushed my share of Belle's two thousand dollars toward me.

"How was that prudent? All those bills circulating in Brooklyn?"

"It'll keep the Camorra from getting too big."

"Wouldn't it be good if they beat the Morellos?" I asked.

Stella shook her head. "It's not that we want one side or the other to win. We just want to ensure a kind of balance of power. You know, like in politics. Germany, Austria-Hungary, Great Britain—one of them gets too strong, it threatens everything."

Politics? What was Stella talking about?

She placed her arm around my shoulders. "Don't worry, Mimi. I'm just trying to keep us safe."

My stomach dropped. "Are we in danger?"

She brought me close and kissed me on the cheek. "We're fine. I want to keep it that way for as long as possible."

"As long as possible? What's going on, Stella? You need to tell me."

"Nothing's going on, Mimi. But things are always changing. We have to stay ahead of it."

I asked a lot of questions after that, but Stella gave the same answer. The bills were perfect. We were safe. She was just being cautious.

It was only when I was back in the tenement, tucking my share of the take under the floorboard, that I thought of something I hadn't asked Stella about.

Belle was Irish. Could she know Margaret Kelly—Bartu's *puttana*? We'd managed to keep Bartu from finding out about the engraving operation. But what if Belle told Margaret? Would Bartu return, demanding to be included?

I pushed the floorboard back into place. I was letting my imagination get away from me. There were thousands of Irish people in the city. These two women couldn't possibly know each other.

CHAPTER 43

I PULLED MY SHAWL over my coat, wincing as I wrapped it against myself. It had been a long winter. A cold had turned into a nasty cough that I couldn't shake. Whether it was tuberculosis or not, I'd taken to wearing my poultice all the time, the mustard seeds leaving swaths of puckered, blistered skin. In time, it would heal.

I stepped onto the sidewalk. The breeze was mild. Welcoming. I made my way past the sycamores, the sidewalk below littered with small, spiky balls. The canopy above filled with tiny buds, as delicate as flowers, that cast a soft glow of green. While I'd been bent over the press, turning paper and ink into money, winter had surrendered its grip and spring had returned.

I passed Caterina's street and turned toward the river. Mamma was at ten o'clock Mass; I had some time to spare before I was expected to return with sweet buns, penance for not going with her. As I crossed First Avenue, the East River opened before me.

I walked to the railing to watch the boats. A tug pulling an impossibly large barge; a fishing boat that hugged the shore so tightly I could see the men, hats pulled down against the wind. And an elegant sloop, its sails filled with wind. Suddenly the wind kicked up. As I watched, the sails waffled, then flapped wildly. The sloop tipped over, its deck skimming the water. I'd never considered that too much wind could imperil a sailboat at least as much as too little. As I watched, the captain dropped the front sail. The boat began to right itself. The captain drew in the middle sails, tightening the slack until the cloth no longer fluttered. Disaster averted, the sloop continued on its way.

Realizing I'd been holding my breath, I exhaled and set off for the bakery.

Sebu squealed with delight when I arrived with the pastry box.

"Zia!" he cried, reaching for the box. "Give me!"

Mamma stuck her nose in the air. "That boy needs to learn some manners."

In the past, that kind of comment would have sent my sister running, humiliated, into the bedroom.

Now, though, Caterina didn't even turn from the stove, where she was frying rice balls. "Sebu. Show Zia Mimi your picture."

The boy's hands dusted with sugar, he made for the bedroom.

"He's been using the crayons you got for him for his birthday. He draws all the time." Caterina turned over another ball. "Night and day. I had to hide them to get him to go to sleep last night." Caterina scooped a ball from the oil and put it on a towel to drain. She turned toward me and smiled.

Crayola. Wax crayons in eight shades. I'd marveled when I'd seen them in the toy shop window. Made for children. A rainbow of color at their fingertips.

Sebu ran to the bedroom. When he returned, he was grasping a piece of paper. He thrust it toward me. "It's a balloon! You can ride on it all the way to the moon!"

"The moon. That's far away, isn't it?"

"As far as the sun!" He reached his arms out wide.

Mamma looked on, disapprovingly. "You really should correct him. The nuns will think he's simple when he starts school in the fall."

"No one will think he's simple, Mamma." I put my hand on Sebu's head and felt his hair, smooth and thick. "He'll be the smartest boy in his class." I smiled at him. "No. The smartest in the whole school."

Mamma shook her head. "He'll get a big head. Just like you. All that talk about being a famous artist."

I bit my tongue to keep from telling her off. I wasn't famous, like Matisse or Cassattt. But I had so many five-dollar bills stuffed under that one floorboard that I'd soon have to start storing them someplace else. I couldn't say this to Mamma. She'd demand I pay Pappa's way out of prison. I wasn't ready for him to return.

Sebu tugged on my sleeve. "Do you like it?"

I held it up. "It's fantastic. Like in the *Wizard of Oz.*" The little boy's favorite book, I'd already read it to him twice.

"But mine's all the colors." He ran his small fingers over the balloon.

"Yes. A rainbow. Like the one we saw over the East River. All the colors from red to violet."

Sebu wasn't listening. "The Wizard is mean."

"He is?"

"He makes the Munchkins wear those glasses. All they see is green."

"That is mean." I had to bite the inside of my cheek to keep from laughing.

"Why does he do that, Zia?"

"What? Make them wear green glasses?"

Sebu nodded.

I shrugged. "The Wizard says it's to protect their eyes."

"They can't see the other colors."

It certainly didn't seem right, but what could those tiny munchkins do?

"Green's a good color," I said. I hated myself the moment the words left my mouth. Even if green was beautiful, the Wizard shouldn't have that power.

Sebu turned his attention back to his sketch. "Here's the basket Dorothy rode in." He pointed to the brown box he'd drawn beneath the billowing balloon.

Mamma rolled her eyes. "Why do you fill his brain with such nonsense? Balloons. Wizards. Really."

"It's a story, Mamma."

She snorted. "A story. Where's that going to get him? He has to accept things the way they are. Not chase after some—fairy tale."

Like marrying a bastard and expecting to become the Donna Inglese? I should leave it alone. I couldn't. "It's not bad to want something more."

"Oh, really?" She jutted out her jaw, ready for a fight. "And where has that gotten you, exactly?"

I was rich, but I wouldn't tell Mamma. Not yet. But looking at my sister, humming quietly as she scooped another browned rice ball from the pan, and Sebu, tongue between his teeth, happily lost in drawing, I knew it was more that that.

Soon, we'd have a house in Westchester. Maybe not as grand as *Binvinutu*, but I'd own every brick, every plank of wood, every nail. Pappa wouldn't have to work for men like Morello. We'd be free. All of us.

And it had all come from wanting more.

CHAPTER 44

I PASSED THE CORNER where the newsies hawked their papers. "Extra! Extra!" one boy called out. "Gangster's son killed!" he called, in a singsongy voice. I pulled a coin from my pocket. He gave me a paper. On the front page, Clutch's mugshot. Next to it, a body face-down on the pavement, arms and legs akimbo. Something inky pooled under it. My eyes moved greedily across the page, devouring the words. Calogero Morello, Clutch's only son, killed in a shoot-out.

Once the ferry was underway, Stella told me it was the Camorra. "They're making a statement. They want the Morellos out." She looked toward the Statue of Liberty. "It's going to be a bloodbath."

Was this the 'balance of power' she'd been talking about?

A few months later, there was another headline—"Gangland Violence Surges!" and a photograph of Nicolò Morello, Clutch's handsome brother. He'd been killed hunting down Calogero's killer.

This time, Stella didn't wait for the ferry to get underway. "We have a problem," she said, as soon as I stepped onboard. "Calogero—he was a hothead. Probably had it coming to him. But Nicolò was pragmatic. A businessman. He was trying to broker a deal with the Camorra. They didn't want a deal."

Lately, there had been so many shootouts. Every week, another street, blocked off with sawhorses and rope. Another patch of sidewalk doused with bleach to remove the bloodstains. Despite the fact that I'd known Nicolò, I asked why we should care about his murder.

Stella sighed. "Up until now, the Camorra have stayed on their side of the East River. Bushwick. The Navy Yard. Coney Island. But now they're making a play for Manhattan. The Morellos' turf."

"We're in New Jersey. Most of our distributors are out of town—."

Stella pulled a cigarillo from her pocket. Her hands were shaking. "Ciro is still alive. Vito won't allow him and the rest of the Morello crew to be pushed out of Manhattan. Vito's whole legacy—all his plans for returning here—would go up in smoke. He doesn't want that. I heard he's trying to fix things so he can come over."

Zio here? No. He'd find out I was making the bills. He'd try to make me fall in line behind him. "I thought the cops were after him."

"They are." Stella tapped her ashes on the floor. "The *Most Wanted* poster for the Petrosino killing still hangs at police headquarters. But Clutch is in prison and Ciro's too much of a hothead to run the business. Vito needs to be here."

I thought of Pappa and his lawyer. The testimony he'd given in Clutch's trial. I didn't want to think about what might happen if Zio found out.

"Will we be safe?" My voice sounded far away.

Stella took a long drawl on her cigarillo. "We haven't done anything wrong." Her voice was unsteady. "I mean, no one told us not to make the bills, right?"

"But Zio gave me those burins. He expected me to work for him."

"Sure. And you would have, if he hadn't insisted on trying to move those shitty bills and if Clutch hadn't gone to jail. Right?"

I shrugged. "So what can we do?"

She stamped out her cigarillo. "Work. Make as many bills as we can. Hopefully, by the time Vito puts it all together, we'll be gone."

In the last few months, we'd been talking more seriously about leaving. Taking the Pearl and leaving everything else behind. But when I thought about another place—Chicago, or St. Louis, or San Francisco—it seemed as surreal as that postcard image of the Yellowstone.

A few weeks later, just as Mamma and I were finishing dinner, there was a knock.

I opened the door. A man in a uniform stood there. For one agonizing moment, I thought he was a cop, coming to arrest me. But his uniform was little more than a costume—his cap emblazoned with the words *POSTAL TELEGRAM*, his badge, a Western Union patch. I looked closer. His face was smooth. He was a boy, not much older than Sebu.

"Telegram for Mrs. Inglese."

My hand was trembling as I took the envelope.

Mamma made the sign of the cross. "You read it."

My knees went weak. Pappa. He was an old man. I should have paid the fine when I could have. Now he was dead.

I slid my forefinger under the flap. I pulled out the onion-skin paper. It was from Signore Puccio, Pappa's lawyer.

SIGNORE INGLESE RELEASED WILL ARRIVE NEW YORK AUGUST 16

"Pappa's coming home." I glanced at the calendar. The 16th was two weeks away.

Mamma grabbed the telegram and quickly scanned the words. "His prison sentence isn't over. Someone must have paid his fine. Does it say who?" She turned the paper over. It was blank. "Or maybe the government realized he did nothing wrong. All these years in prison and he was innocent!"

"He was set up," Mamma continued, like a train gaining steam. "It was that grocer on Third Avenue. You know, the one who was always complaining that the cans were dented? Well, he'll get his. Pappa will tell Vito to stop supplying him." She was still prattling on about Pappa's innocence when I realized I had to let Stella know.

I pulled on my shawl and opened the door. "I'm going out."

"Now? Where?"

"Just out." I closed the door behind me.

Night was falling as I made my way toward Stella's house on First

Avenue. I knocked on the basement window.

"Who's there?"

"Mimi."

The window curtain fluttered. A moment later, Stella was at the door. "I told you not to come here. Someone could be watching."

The words came rushing out. "Pappa's getting out. Someone paid his fine."

"Cascioferro—."

"Why would he do that?" I knew I sounded churlish, but I couldn't help it.

"With all this uncertainty and no real hope of Clutch getting out, Vito's getting nervous. It's just a matter of time before Ciro's dead. Vito can control your father. And he needs you. And your five-dollar bills."

If only Pappa would finally realize Zio was using him. But that would never happen.

I said, "We can't let Pappa find out what we've been doing." How to tell Stella that everything Pappa touched turned to shit?

She said we should leave.

"I can't," I blurted out. There was supposed to be a house in Westchester—a safe place for Mamma, Caterina and Sebu.

"He'll take over your life when he gets back. You'll have nothing. Just like before."

"But my sister. Sebu..."

"You can leave some money for them. Be discrete. Make sure Antonino and Bartu can't get their hands on it."

"What should we do now?" I asked quietly.

"We have some time before Antonino comes home. Let's finish the bills for Belle. That'll use up the rest of the paper. Then we'll bury the plates again. Until we know what's what."

For the next two weeks, we worked night and day. My fingers and hands were so ink-stained that I didn't think I'd ever get them clean. I worried that Pappa would see my hands and know. Like the blood of the pomegranate had stained Persephone's hands, revealing to everyone that she'd eaten those seeds. But there was so much money under the floorboards now that I told myself it didn't matter.

The night Belle came for the rest of her money, the air was filled with the ammonia smell of printing press cleaner. After Belle and her helpers had gone, leaving a large duffel stuffed with money, Stella poured the grappa. One glass. A second. Stella stood, unsteady. She went to the Pearl and unsnapped the plates, then signaled I should follow her outside. I watched as she dug a hole in the cattail fields, far from the farmhouse and the remains of that old dung heap. She tucked one plate in, then the other. Then she used the spade to cover them up. I know it sounds stupid, but I started to cry, like a part of me was being buried.

Stella put her arms around me. "We'll come back for them if we can. If we can't—well, it'll be a long time before anyone finds them. We'll be long gone." She gave me a handkerchief. I wiped my eyes. "You have the burins somewhere safe?" she asked, not for the first time.

When the space under the floorboards had become too stuffed with bills, I pulled up another board, this time under the window, and put my burins there.

"Yes," I said. "They're safe."

CHAPTER 45

MAMMA BRUSHED PAPPA'S BOWLER again, the sound of the bristles scratching the surface. In those spots where she'd been too vigorous, the fabric was shiny.

She held up the bowler. "This is a winter hat. He should have a straw hat. That's what all the men are wearing. Bartu will take him downtown. He'll buy a new hat."

"Yes, Mamma." No need to remind her that straw boaters were for young men or that we hadn't seen Bartu in many months.

She looked at her wristwatch. "Goddamn that train! Check the schedule."

I'd already checked the timetable. But I checked it again anyway. The Crescent train from Atlanta to Pennsylvania, scheduled to arrive at 12:10.

"It's after 5," Mamma grabbed the paper from me. "Useless! Completely useless!" She crumpled it into a ball.

I should reassure Mamma she shouldn't worry. Trains ran late. Pappa would be home soon. But I was worried that something—maybe my tone of voice or the expression on my face—would betray the truth: I didn't want Pappa to return. I went to the icebox and took out the antipasto I'd prepared as a homecoming. I put it in front of Mamma.

She pushed the plate away. "That's for your father. Where is he? You must have given him the wrong address."

Could I have done that? Written 101st Street instead of 110th? Stella said there were no mistakes. Only ways the brain tricks itself into getting what it secretly wants.

"Go." Mamma pointed at the door. "Look for him."

I stepped outside and looked back at the tenement. Pappa would have walked right by this building, never guessing that we'd sunk this low. Maybe he'd seen the way we were living and just kept walking. As I looked at the pails, overflowing with garbage, and the weeping brick facade with its white powdery streaks, I couldn't blame him. Mamma and I had been living like *puviri*. Maybe Pappa couldn't bear the shame.

I walked quickly, my eyes on the pavement in front of me, until I found myself at Pappa's old grocery. White-marbled slabs of beef hung in the window where the pyramid of olive cans had been. I cupped my hands over the glass and looked inside. A line of shoppers snaked down the center aisle. I'd always assumed the lack of customers had to do with the store's unfortunate location under the elevated train. But neither the screeching train overhead nor the dimly-filtered sunlight kept these customers away. I turned to see if Pappa lingered nearby, his failure amplified by the butcher's success. There was no sign of him.

I wandered through the park. The men sat easily together, laughing and chatting. If only Pappa had someplace like this to belong. I felt that old pain again, Pappa's sorrows and disappointments keener than my own. He'd spent nearly his whole life waiting. And for what? A manor house that was falling down. A sulfur mine left shuttered. A grocery store with no customers. Almost five years in prison. No one could blame him for wanting to start again, somewhere no one knew him.

I'd almost convinced myself Pappa wasn't coming home when I turned the corner and saw him leaning against the lamppost across from the tenement. He was clean-shaven, but even without his mustache, I recognized him. I drew closer. Now I could see how his pants hung down, the hem filthy. He looked small. Pathetic. I wanted to run away. Pretend that sad, old man wasn't my father.

Before I could get away, though, Pappa raised his hand to me. I stood there, unable to move. He crossed the street and put his arms around me. It was hard to breathe. I counted to ten, slowly. Then again. Finally, Pappa released me.

"Have you been out here a while?" I asked. I hadn't seen him when I left the tenement an hour ago. Or maybe I hadn't really looked.

He shook his head. "Not long. I've been out walking. So much has changed. The demolition. The new construction. Out with the old, right?" He smiled, too brightly. "How about you? How are you?"

How to tell him that I'd never felt more alive? "I'm good."

He turned toward the tenement. "So this is the place."

I saw Pappa take in the old woman in rags, standing in front of our building and picking through the trash barrel. The group of Siciliani, hair slicked back, crouched on the pavement, stashes of coins before them, engrossed in a card game. The shoeshine boy kneeling on the ground in front of his customer, a rag in one hand and a bottle of polish in the other.

"It's not Doctor's Row," Pappa said.

"It's the place Bartu found."

Pappa winced. I'd hit my mark. Then he said we wouldn't be living here much longer. He had a plan.

"What do you mean?" I asked.

"Why are you looking at me so serious?" Pappa scrunched up his face, an exaggerated gesture that left no doubt he was mimicking me.

"Is it legal?" I asked, loud even on that busy street.

"Shhh." Pappa guided me toward the tenement door. "Of course it is. Come inside. We'll talk."

Mamma must have recognized Pappa's tread on the stairs because she was waiting at the apartment door.

"Nino!" She rushed to him. He seemed to shy away, but only for a moment. They embraced. When Pappa finally eased away, there were tears on Mamma's cheeks.

"I've been waiting." She smoothed a hand over his hair. "You had me worried."

We went inside the apartment. Pappa took off his jacket. I tried not to notice how the dirt on his pant cuffs left a grimy streak on the wood floor.

"I told Mimi. I've been out walking. Everywhere, there's a hunger. The bigwigs have struck it rich. Now the little people want their chance." Pappa's words sounded rehearsed, like he was repeating someone else's speech.

In the midst of this, Mamma told me to pour Pappa a cup of espresso. Pappa waved her off. "Sit, Mimi." He touched the chair next to him. "I want to talk to you."

Mamma went to the sink. The banging of the metal espresso pot against the cast iron left no doubt that she was angry.

Pappa didn't notice. "How's your art?"

"It's good."

He sat forward in his seat. "Working on anything new?"

"Just some sketches. Nothing important."

"Bene. Bene. It's good to keep up your skills."

I nodded. Where was he going with this?

"Have you heard from your Zio?"

"Zio Vito?" I asked.

Pappa nodded.

Mamma slammed down the pot. I thought she'd say something about how she'd written to Zio, asking for the money he'd promised. She stayed quiet.

"No, Pappa. Not recently."

"I thought you were doing a logo or something."

Had his tone changed with the words "or something"? Could Zio have found out about the five-dollar bills and told Pappa? I waited for Mamma to tell Pappa that I'd been working with Stella. She didn't.

"We haven't heard from Vito," Mamma said. "He abandoned us."

Pappa smoothed his hand over the stubble where his mustache had been.

"You're wrong, my dear," he said. "Vito is the one who paid my fine.

If it wasn't for him, I'd still be in Atlanta."

Mamma narrowed her eyes. "Always, you defend him. A fifteen hundred-dollar fine. What's that to a man like Vito?"

"He's my friend, Maria."

Mamma scoffed. "Some friend. And that match he arranged for Caterina. Do you know Bartu has a *puttana*? He's all but left Caterina and the boy."

Pappa reached out and took Mamma's hand. He pressed it to his lips. "My dear. It's been so hard for you. I'm home now. Things will be better."

Surely, Mamma wouldn't believe those same old promises. But I watched as Pappa pulled her into his lap. Before I closed the front door behind me, I heard her crying softly, and Pappa, as usual, comforting her.

I returned just before dark. The apartment was quiet. I glanced into the bedroom. The sheets were rumpled. The quilt lay on the floor. In the kitchen, my parents sat next to each other. Mamma's bun was undone. Her salt and pepper hair lay around her shoulders.

"Ah, you've returned." Pappa's legs were stretched out, his hands in his lap.

"Pappa's made risotto," Mamma said. "Think of that! He cooked!"

"I learned it from some friends. It's an easy dish. Rice. Broth. Cheese. All it takes is time. And I had lots of time." Pappa laughed, then pulled out a chair for me. "Sit. I'll make you a plate."

Pappa ladled the risotto into a small bowl. He put it before me. It smelled earthy. Like the woods around *Binvinutu* in the fall, when mushrooms sprouted underfoot.

"It's delicious," I said, surprised.

Pappa wiped his hands on his pants. The dirt had dried on his cuffs, pebbly, caked-on grit that clung to the fabric.

"You can learn a lot when you're locked up for almost five years." He slid into his chair. "Mimi. Your Mamma tells me you've been keeping things afloat with some kind of business."

So Mamma had told him about Stella.

"Just something to pay the rent," I say, touching the floorboards with my foot, feeling for the one that was raised slightly.

Pappa smiled. "This is good. I always said you could make a living with your art."

I wanted to laugh. A living? I had a fortune hidden under that board. And my burins, under the floor near the window. "Yes, Pappa," I said, steeling myself for the question I thought would surely come—what had I been doing? I'd already prepared an answer: I'd been working on advertisements for a ladies' magazine downtown.

But Pappa didn't ask about what I'd been doing. Instead, he told me he had a job for me.

"Doing what?" I asked, surprised.

"Sketching. Like you did with Zio's burins."

"I don't have them anymore." I started telling Pappa about how they'd been stolen doing the move.

He waved me off. "No problem. For now, it's only drawing. A building. Some flowers. Simple." Pappa continued. "My associate will be here next week. We can talk about it."

"What kind of business is it?"

"It's a bit complicated. Carlo can explain it better than I can. Carlo Ponzi. We were together in Atlanta. He's brilliant."

If he was so smart, how'd he land in prison? "Why was he there?" I asked.

Mama gasped. "Mimi! What a rude question!"

Pappa put his hand down, like he was calming an agitated dog. "It's all right. Mimi can ask that question—in fact, she should." Pappa turned toward me. "It was a misunderstanding. He was in Canada, waiting to board a train to New York. Some *paesani*—fresh off the boat—approached him because they were having trouble understanding the schedule. He helped them. For that kindness, he was arrested. The cops claimed he was smuggling aliens into the country. It was a miscarriage of justice." These words, too, sounded like someone else's.

"Carlo made the best of it," Pappa continued. "He made friends with the warden. And with Clutch."

"He knew Clutch?" I asked. I'd been thinking about him in leg irons, not out there making friends.

"They were cellmates for a while. The warden put Carlo in there to find out what Clutch was up to."

I waited for a moment for Pappa to continue. When he didn't, I asked what this Ponzi had found out.

Pappa shrugged. "Who knows? It wasn't important. Or if it was, Carlo made the most of it with the warden. He's agile. Smart. He makes it his business for everyone to like him."

"How does he do that?"

"Damned if I know! But the warden had a party for him when he was released. Champagne. Foie gras. Oysters. Imagine that!"

If everyone likes you, in Sicily they'd say you're *si nuddi moscato cu nnenti*—a nobody mixed with nothing.

But that doesn't mean you're harmless.

CHAPTER 46

I SPENT THE NEXT FEW DAYS shuttling between our apartment and Caterina's. Pappa was thrilled to meet Sebu, though the boy hid behind my skirt most of the time, venturing out only when Pappa went to the Western Union office.

Pappa was waiting for a telegram from Carlo Ponzi saying when he'd arrive in New York City. When nothing had arrived by Thursday, I asked Pappa if everything was all right.

"Oh yes. Carlo's just busy. Getting the lay of the land. It takes time in a new place. Don't worry. We'll have work soon."

Stella's voice was in my ear, saying I'd never be free of my family.

We were at Caterina's, getting ready to eat our Sunday roast, when I heard the doorknob jiggle and someone come in. I didn't know when Bartu had last been home, but when he burst into the kitchen—bottle of wine in hand—it was like he'd never been away.

Pappa jumped to his feet. "Bartu, my boy! You got my message."

"You're looking well, Nino." Bartu glanced around the room, taking in the happy scene. Caterina stood from the table and went to the corner of the kitchen, as far from Bartu as she could get. Sebu joined her. Pappa didn't seem to notice. He motioned to Sebu's empty chair. "Come. Sit."

Pappa was at the head of the table, in Bartu's chair. For a moment, I thought Bartu would tell him to get up. Instead, he slid into Sebu's chair. Deftly opening the wine he'd brought, Bartu filled his and Pappa's glasses.

"The best they had," Bartu said. "It cost almost three dollars. But we're celebrating." Bartu raised his glass. "To you, Nino. Welcome home!"

Pappa nodded. "And to our business."

I felt blindsided. Pushed aside. While Pappa had been talking about my art skills, he'd been planning to partner with Bartu.

Bartu refilled Pappa's glass. "I'd hoped Signore Ponzi would be here."

"He will be. He just has to finish laying the groundwork for the operation."

"Where is that again?" Bartu asked.

Pappa downed his second glass of wine. "Down south. Alabama."

Bartu laughed. "What's a *paesanu* doing there?"

"Ponzi goes where the opportunity is. They're mining coal down there. Lots of it. But it's a backwards place. No lights or running water. Ponzi wants to change that."

"Interesting." Bartu refilled his own glass.

Pappa continued. "He needs my help because I know how to run a mining operation."

I waited for him to mention the mine explosions. All those dead *carusi* boys. He didn't.

"What'll we be doing?" Bartu asked.

"One of the bigwigs—U.S. Steel—has taken over the mines. Big operation. Lots of workers. We're going to bring water and electricity to the town."

This time, Pappa filled his own glass. He took a long swallow before continuing. Liquid courage—that's what Stella called it.

"It'll be expensive. But the beauty of Ponzi's plan is that he's going to have the townspeople help finance it. He's setting up a company— Blocton Power and Light. The townspeople can buy stock in it. They'll have better living conditions and a chance to make a sure-fire invest-ment. It can't go wrong."

Despite the warmth in the crowded kitchen, a chill ran down my spine. How many times had Pappa uttered those words before?

"So we'll be stock brokers?"

Pappa nodded.

"I know a lot about that." Bartu slapped his leg. "Hey! I can ask around. See who wants to help sell."

Pappa put out a steadying hand. "Not yet, my boy. For now, Carlo wants to keep it small. Fewer people means more profit."

"But can we invest? You and I?" Bartu asked.

"Of course! We'll work on commission—ten percent of the stocks we sell. And we can buy stock, too. At a reduced rate."

"Excellent." Bartu glanced in my direction, his mouth twisted into a cruel smile. He was gloating.

I stood to clear the table.

"Mimi will help, too," Pappa said.

I felt a rush of gratitude and immediately hated myself for it.

"You know how to make an engraving, right?" Pappa asked. "That blacksmith showed you. Back in Partanna."

Before I could answer, Bartu blurted out that I'd lost the burins.

"That's all right. We can get replacements." Pappa turned to me. "You could help us make the stock certificates. They're like dollar bills."

"Is that really a good idea?" Bartu asked. "We're asking people to invest. We can't use handmade certificates. They should be done professionally. By someone who knows how."

Vafanculu, Bartu. Stella told me the feds referred to me as "The Counterfeiter." They couldn't tell my bills from the ones that rolled off their own presses.

Before I could speak, though, Pappa said, "Mimi can do this." He drew a rectangle in the air. "Blocton Power and Light in the middle. Then words like *this is to certify that*—and *transferable,* and *duly enforced.* A logo—maybe of the coke ovens—they're shaped like beehives. And a border all around. Maybe with these white lilies that grow only in this town." Pappa made a squiggly motion like he was drawing. He and Ponzi had given this some thought.

We stayed at Bartu and Caterina's long past dessert. When Pappa finally rose to go, Sebu was nestled in my lap, dozing. I placed him gently on the daybed and turned toward Caterina. Her arms were wrapped tightly around her chest. I kissed her cheek. A kind of dread—like a premonition —swept over me.

I squeezed her arm. "I'll see you tomorrow." She'd feel better when Bartu left.

But Bartu was stretched out on his chair, coat off, tie loosened. He held an empty liqueur glass loosely in his hand. He wasn't going anywhere. The midwife had given Caterina that douching syringe. I wanted to run into the bedroom and make sure it was still there, wrapped in its burlap bag. I didn't have a chance.

Before Pappa closed the door behind him, I heard him tell Bartu that he'd stop by the barbershop the next morning. "I'm sure I'll have heard from Ponzi by then." His voice echoed in the stairwell.

When we got home, I tried to tell Pappa about Bartu—how he'd turned his back on me and Mamma, and abandoned Caterina and Sebu.

Pappa just waved his hand in the air. "A man does what he has to do."

I stammered that he'd left us to die.

"But you didn't die." Pappa looked at me suspiciously. "You survived. How'd you do that, again?"

I reminded myself. I had an answer.

"I did some drawings. Like the pomegranate for Zio."

"That must have been a lot of drawings. Even for a place like this." He motioned around the room, then asked what kind of drawings I'd been doing.

Pappa looked at me like he knew I was lying. "You need to be careful, Mimi. There are some dangerous people out there."

But it was Pappa who'd placed us in danger—trusting Zio and Clutch. And now, probably this Ponzi.

Pappa struck a match against the bottom of his shoe. The sparks blazed white before drifting to the floor, near where I kept the bills. I shuddered, thinking about them in neat piles. Perfect fuel for a fire. Tomorrow, I'd buy a strong box or two, or three, and tuck the bills inside.

The next Sunday, there was no family dinner. I don't remember why we didn't go to Caterina's, only that when Mamma got home from church, she told me to set the table. I asked if Caterina was coming. Maybe with Pappa home, the family dinner would shift back here—but she snarled that it would only be the three of us. I'd found the shell of a cicada still clinging to a tree. I put it on the windowsill. When I looked for it later, the wind had blown it away.

I stopped by Caterina's the next day. The building was quiet as a tomb. The landlady was mopping the hallway, sloshing dirty water over the sticky floor.

"Goin' up ta see yer sissy?" Her accent was like Belle's, though her S's were sloppy. When I looked at her, I saw that she was toothless.

"The fightin's been brutal up t'ere," she continued. "All hours o' the day. Not just yer sissy. But th' boyo, too." Her words dangled before me, like a worm writhing on a fishhook.

I couldn't help but take the bait. "What do you mean?"

"The husband. He's back. The little man, he tries to protect his mam." She shook her head. "A real shame."

I felt a spike of adrenaline. Sebu was a little boy. No match for Bartu. I ran up the stairs.

"Tell them to keep it down," the landlady yelled after me. "This is a proper building. We don' wan' no trouble with the law."

I ran upstairs and knocked on Caterina's door. No answer. I knocked harder. My mind had begun to go dark places—Caterina, sprawled across the bed. Sebu on the floor next to her—when I heard the shuffle of footsteps. They stopped at the door.

"It's Mimi."

No answer. I tried to stay calm and knocked again. "Caterina, let me in." Another set of footsteps—quicker, lighter—Sebu's.

"It's Zia," the little boy whispered loudly. "Mommy. Open the door—."

From the other side of the door, Caterina sighed. The chain rattled and the door swung open. My sister stood there, her hair matted, her right eye swollen shut, the delicate skin around it a deep plum color. I followed her inside, trying to ignore the buzzing that had started in my ears. I pulled up the window shade in the kitchen. When I turned back, Caterina was slumped in her chair. Sebu was beside her.

The sweat trickled down my back. It was too hot for espresso, but I made it anyway. By the time I placed the cup before her, the buzzing in my ears had quieted.

"We missed you at dinner yesterday," I said.

Caterina stared vacantly at the tabletop.

I turned toward Sebu. "Did you have macaroni?" I asked. Since Pappa had returned from prison, he'd been using the American words for things, like macaroni. When Sebu didn't respond, I repeated, this time asking if they'd had pasta.

Sebu shook his head no.

"What did you eat?" I asked.

No response.

"Answer me, Sebu." My voice was sharp. "What did you eat?"

The boy covered his face.

I went to the icebox. Empty, but for a past-gone head of garlic and some dried-out carrots. The last time I brought groceries was two weeks ago. I didn't want to think about how long it had been since they'd eaten.

I closed the icebox door. "I need to go to the market." I tried to keep my voice light. "Let's all go together."

Caterina turned away, wiping her tears from that poor, bruised cheek. "The fresh air will do you good."

She covered her face with her hands. "Just go. Leave me in peace."

I took Sebu's hand. When he hesitated, I gently tugged him forward. "It'll be all right. We'll bring Mommy something good to eat."

I bought only what I could carry in a string bag. A loaf of bread. A bit of cheese. Some eggs. On the way home, we stopped at an ice-cream wagon. As the hokey-pokey man scooped vanilla ice cream into a wafer cone, Sebu's mouth opened and closed, like a baby bird's. I couldn't help but smile.

I pointed to a park bench. "Let's sit over here." We sat in silence, all of Sebu's attention on his cone. When he was done, I wiped his sticky hands with my handkerchief. I started to stand but Sebu pulled me down.

"I don't want to go home. Daddy's mean to us." His voice dropped to a whisper.

I said something inane—about how Bartu didn't mean it. He worked hard and sometimes he was tired. Sebu narrowed his eyes. He didn't believe me. Why should he? Bartu had given his mother a black eye.

"I'm sorry." I put my arms around his shoulders, drawing him near.

"Don't leave us." His eyes were dark as coal.

I promised I wouldn't. A lie. As soon as I could finish the work for Ponzi and get my parents settled—in Westchester or wherever they wanted to go—I'd probably be gone.

I smoothed his hair. "Shall we bring some ice cream to your Mommy? And maybe another cone for you?"

When we returned to the apartment, Caterina was curled up on the edge of the bed.

I took the cup of ice cream from my bag and tried to find a place for it on the cluttered bedside table. I cleared off Bartu's girlie magazines and some empty cigarette cartons, looking—though I'm not sure I realized it at the time—for that douching syringe. That's when I saw the white powder, fine as sugar. Next to it, a straw, the kind you'd get at a soda fountain. I touched my finger to the powder, then put it on my tongue. My eyes watered from the bitterness.

Caterina bolted upright. "That's mine!" she screamed, lunging for the straw. I knew this Caterina. The agitation. The despondency. She was using again. And Bartu was supplying whatever she was taking. She needed to get away from him. The sooner, the better. I'd make a pot of strong coffee. We'd try to figure out what to do.

I started to go to the kitchen. That's when I saw it: the rumpled bedspread, the stained sheets, and Bartu's discarded boxers, inside out on the floor. Bartu and Caterina were having sex. I turned to the dresser and pulled open the drawers, rummaging inside for that syringe. It wasn't there. A chill went through me, remembering those scabs on Caterina's arms and legs. Her plucked-out eyelashes. Her emaciated body. The midwife had been clear. Another pregnancy could kill Caterina.

I could ask Stella for the midwife's address. But we'd decided not to see each other, at least until Pappa was fully occupied with whatever he was planning. Hopefully, Caterina was using the syringe and had just tucked it away for safekeeping.

Ponzi's telegram came as the leaves started changing from green to gold. As Pappa read the letter, his expression changed, too, from excitement to resignation. I asked him what was wrong. He brushed me away. Later, though, when he went to Western Union to reply, I read the telegram he'd left on the table.

WORKING AS TOWN NURSE STOP CONTINUE
PREPS FOR STOCK CERTIFICATES STOP WILL SEND
WORD ASAP

Ponzi seemed to be saying Pappa should continue on without him. But why was he working as a nurse? How long would ASAP be? When Pappa finally returned, I heard him fumbling with his keys. I opened the door for him. He went straight to the wine decanter and filled a water glass to the top.

He lifted the glass. "A toast to Carlo." The red wine sloshed over the side. Pappa was drunk. Pappa gulped down his wine. "Carlo's ingenious: offering to work as a nurse," he said, waving the telegram in the air. "It looks generous. Helping someone in need. But he only does it to help himself. He's cunning. Resourceful. Like Machiavelli."

I tried to remember who Machiavelli was. "He does sound smart." I wanted to keep Pappa talking. "How does working as a nurse help him?"

Pappa poured another glass of wine. "The town needs a nurse. Backwoods places like that always do. As the nurse, he'll gain the people's trust. That'll go far when it comes time to get people to buy the stock."

I asked why he needed their trust.

"He's asking them to give him money to build something that doesn't exist yet. He needs them to believe in him."

But who would buy something, sight unseen?

"We need to get going on the stock certificate." Pappa went into the bedroom and returned with a coin. But this wasn't his lucky coin. This one was brass-colored, not silver. At its center was a beehive, instead of that queen. "From Blocton," he explained.

"They have their own money?" I asked, confused because Stella had told me the U.S. wasn't like Italy, where every province made their own coins and bills.

"Only for the company store. Look, this is what Ponzi and I want on the stock certificate." He pointed to the beehive. "With calaba lilies all around."

"What do those look like?" I thought of the acanthus leaves on the five-dollar bills.

"Fancy. Cup-shaped like a crown. With white petals. Like the narcissus back home."

Narcissus. The plant Persephone was picking when Hades took her to the Underworld.

Pappa must have sensed my hesitation. "Don't worry about it, Mimi. If you get it wrong, you can fix it. Carlo is very patient."

CHAPTER 47

MY STRING BAG IN HAND, I stepped out onto the sidewalk. Small eddies of leaves circled around each other, the rustling sound lost to the honking of car horns and the pounding of jackhammers. I turned toward the market.

It was another day, like so many since Pappa had returned. I'd dragged myself from bed, pulling on my clothes. There'd been no reason to hurry—there was no ferry to catch, no new batch of bills. I'd finished crafting Ponzi's stock certificate—there'd been no real challenge to the lily and the beehive.

"Keep it simple," Pappa said. So I had.

Pappa had sent the certificate to Ponzi more than a month ago. Carlo still hadn't responded. Pappa told us it was the war in Europe. But it seemed like just an excuse for why things had gone wrong this time.

I turned down 110th. People had gathered outside the rope factory. Some held placards calling for an eight-hour day or a 5-cent hourly raise. Every day, it seemed there was another group of disgruntled workers— the button makers, the macaroni workers, even the people who sorted donated clothes for the needy. Near the river, the crowds finally thinned out. I unrolled my string bags and made for the green grocer's cart.

I was filling a bag with greens when I heard her familiar voice.

"Hello, Mimi."

I looked up. Stella stood there, hands on her hips. We hadn't seen each other in more than four months. I had an almost overwhelming urge to rush to her.

"I've been hoping to run into you," Stella said.

"Me, too."

"How are things going?" she asked.

I told her that Pappa was working on something new. "Down south," I added. "In Alabama."

"What is it?" she asked.

"It's legitimate," I said, too quickly. "He's helping a friend sell stock."

Stella snorted. "Sure. And what does he have you doing?"

I hesitated.

"Come on, Mimi. I know you're involved."

"Not really involved. I just helped with a drawing for the stock certificates."

"Always the dutiful daughter."

"It's just a few more months."

Stella shook her head. "When will you learn, Mimi? Your father's using you. You need to get away from here."

I mumbled that it wasn't that easy.

"Just tell him no. I swear, Mimi. You make everything more complicated than it has to be."

But it was complicated. Not just because of Pappa. There were those vials on Caterina's bed stand. That missing syringe.

I told Stella I needed a favor.

Stella nodded.

"Maybe I shouldn't worry," I began. "Bartu has a *puttana*. He's not interested in my sister."

"Ask me, Mimi."

My words came out in a rush. "I went to look for that thing the midwife gave Caterina."

"The douching syringe?"

"Yes. It wasn't there."

"She lost it?"

"I'm not even sure she needs it. Bartu spends most nights with his *puttana*."

"That doesn't matter. She needs that syringe."

"Can she get another?"

"The pharmacy on Third sells them. But Caterina will need Bartu's permission."

"His permission?"

"I know. Ridiculous."

"What about the midwife?" I asked. "Would she help?"

"Signora Brasi?"

I nodded, though I hadn't remembered her name.

"Maybe. If you give her enough money."

"How much?" I asked.

"Her decision. If you want her help, you pay."

I nodded, already thinking about how I'd have to wait until Pappa was asleep to pry off that floorboard.

Stella grunted. "It's your money. You earned it. But I don't know why you'd waste it like that."

"It's not a waste."

"Caterina is weak. She'll never get out from under Bartu's thumb."

I looked around. People were hurrying past, seeming to pay no attention to me and Stella.

"She shouldn't get pregnant again," I whispered. "You know this."

"She has a husband. A mother. How is this your responsibility, Mimi?"

Sebu's fingers around mine. The sweet smell of his sweat. The way he stuck out his tongue when he was concentrating. If Caterina got pregnant again, he'd be old enough to remember it. Who knew how deep his scars would be?

"Mimi, your sister needs to take care of herself."

I nodded, though Nonna's long-ago words came to me again. The Madonna had saved me from the consumption so I could help her and her children.

"I just need to do this one thing for her."

She scoffed. "And you're the only one who can help?"

The jagged cuts on Caterina's hands and feet. Her glassy eyes. That white powder everywhere. Mamma and Bartu hadn't cared, as long as Caterina did what was expected of her.

"Yes. I'm the only one."

"Saint Mimi." Stella raised her arm above her head, like she was holding a sword.

"That's not fair."

Her arm dropped to her side. "I'll tell you what's not fair. Every day, it gets more dangerous here. We should take our money and go. But you refuse to leave your family." She leaned in close, the smell of anisette making my head spin. If we'd been at the farmhouse, I would have put my arms around her. Held her until we both trembled from pleasure. On this park bench, I could only squeeze her hand.

"As soon as my sister's settled. Then I can leave with a clear conscience. Go anywhere you want—Florida. California. I won't ever need to come back here."

Stella drew back her hand. She laughed, softly. "You'll never leave."

"You're wrong. You'll see. Just tell me where to find the midwife."

A few minutes later, I started back home with the folded paper in my pocket. I'd memorized the address—269 Second Avenue, near 117th Street. If I lost it, I suspected Stella wouldn't give it to me again.

The next day, I set out to find the midwife. I walked along Second Avenue, the elevated tracks towering overhead. A shadowy underworld, where people scuttled along the sidewalks like rats. I looked up. Ah. There were the Moorish stars and crosses that I'd drawn that first day. From far enough away, it was beautiful. Up close, though, it was impossible not to see the way that cold steel metal cut the azure sky. Or how the screeching of metal on metal obliterated all other sounds. Sooty smoke blew through the corridor—then abruptly shifted direction—a maelstrom created as north- and south-bound trains passed each other.

Number 267 Second Avenue, then 271. Where 269 should have

been, there was an alleyway. It was dark. It took every ounce of courage not to run away. But Caterina needed that syringe. I stepped into the alley. It was so narrow I could reach out and touch the buildings on both sides at once.

As I went deeper, it got darker. I had to keep one hand on the brick to keep moving forward. Ahead was a sliver of light. The air was sour, sulphury. I forced myself to keep going. Ahead, the light was coming through the cracks in the door frame. When I got close enough, I felt the sides of the frame like I was a blind person. 269. I rapped on the door. No answer. I rapped again, harder this time. Still no answer. As I raised my hand to knock again, the door opened a crack.

"You're trespassing," Signora's voice was sharp as a knife. "What do you want?"

"My sister is Caterina Amoruso. You helped her."

She said nothing.

"Stella Frauto gave me your address."

She closed her eyes like she needed all her concentration to decide what to do next.

"I need your help," I said. "I have money."

Signora opened the door wider and pulled me inside. After the darkness of the alley, the light hurt my eyes.

"What do you want?"

"You helped my sister have her baby. He's four." There was the scurry of movement in the corner. I tried to focus on her face—ruddy, with tiny red lines crisscrossing the surface. Cook would have said she'd liked the drink.

"I help lots of people."

"You told my sister that she shouldn't have another baby. You gave her a syringe to keep her from getting pregnant."

She folded her arms over her substantial bosom.

"She almost died," I added.

Signora shrugged, as if this were unremarkable.

"She needs another syringe."

"What happened to the one I gave her?"

"I don't know."

"Did she send you?" she asked, raising an eyebrow.

"Yes," I answered. Too hastily, I could tell, by the way she sneered.

"You don't need to make up a whole story." She glanced at my naked ring finger. "I don't care if you're unmarried. I help single girls all the time."

"It's for my sister," I repeated.

"Oh, sure. The same sister who almost died having her last brat. But she somehow misplaced the only thing that could keep her safe?" She smiled at the ridiculousness of what I was saying.

"I can pay."

"How much?"

"Five dollars?"

"I'm no do-gooder, like that Sanger woman. I'm sure as hell not risking my neck for five dollars."

"So how much?" I asked.

"Birth control for an unmarried woman? That'll cost you fifty dollars."

The same thing in a drug store was probably ten cents. But I couldn't just walk into a store and buy one.

"I'll pay."

"You must have a wealthy boyfriend." She looked at me askance. "Not exactly attractive, are you? Your talents must lay elsewhere."

I was an artist. Wealthier than she'd ever be. I had the sudden urge to hurl it in her pig-face—this woman, who fed off the pain of other women. But Stella would say it wasn't prudent.

"You're right," I said. "It's for me."

She nodded, satisfied. "Come by on Friday. And bring your money."

It was raining when I stepped outside. I pulled my shawl tightly around myself and made my way back to the tenement.

I'd just walked in the door when I heard Pappa's voice.

"Bartu? Is that you?"

Since when did Bartu come and go from our apartment?

"It's me, Pappa."

I made my way down the hall into the kitchen. A haze of smoke hung in the air, the ashtray on the table, overflowing.

"I sent word to Bartu. I thought you were him."

Obviously.

"Why do you need Bartu?"

"I've heard from Ponzi." Pappa placed his hand on the cream-colored Western Union telegram. "I have a proposal for Bartu. An excellent opportunity."

By the heap of ash, Pappa had been chain smoking. He only did that when he was nervous.

I opened the tap and filled the espresso pot. I knew Pappa. The longer I lingered in the kitchen, the more likely it was that he would tell me what was going on. I poured the oily black beans into the grinder, then turned the handle. Round and round as each bean was caught in the blades. I scooped the ground coffee into the top of the espresso pot and set it on the stove.

"Be careful," Pappa said, ominously.

For a moment, I thought he'd found out about the midwife. Or what I'd been doing with Stella. I took a few breaths, the steady shush of the flame calming me.

I was trying to figure out how to respond when Pappa pointed to my cuffs. "Your sleeves. Be careful of the flame. Stoves can be dangerous." Pappa held up the telegram. "Ponzi sent word that someone he knows down South had an accident while she was cooking. Her clothes caught fire." Pappa grimaced. "Terrible. She would have died from it."

Pappa put the telegram on the table between him. "But Ponzi's offered to have an operation for her. A skin graft. His healthy skin will be sewn onto her burns. The doctors think she'll recover."

I shuddered. Ponzi's skin flayed from his body and sewn onto hers. Ghoulish. And painful, I thought, feeling for my own scar. "Is it dangerous?" I asked.

"It's not much skin. He's young. Healthy. The doctors say he'll bounce right back."

The espresso pot was boiling. I lowered the flame, then poured the black liquid into two demitasse cups.

"So everything's good with the stocks?" I was eager to get the conversation back on track.

"Oh, yes. And it'll be even better after the skin graft."

What did a skin graft have to do with selling stocks? I guess Pappa saw my confusion.

"Stocks are a confidence game. If people trust you, they'll invest. Nothing builds trust like a big sacrifice. Like him working as a nurse. Or this: going under the knife for someone he hardly knows. He's a smooth operator, that Ponzi. The townspeople will be falling all over themselves to invest. We'll need a wheelbarrow to carry all the money!"

So Ponzi's sacrifice came from greed, not altruism. As the old Sicilians say, *dogs bark and oxen graze.* This was who Ponzi was.

"Why do you need Bartu?" I tried to keep my voice light.

"In case not all the stocks sell. Ponzi says it's good to have a back-up plan."

Pappa pulled on his jacket. "I'll stop by the barber shop. I need a trim, anyway."

I could have stopped Pappa then and there. Explained that the longer he dangled those stocks in front of Bartu, the more danger Caterina was in. Offered to buy every stock Ponzi had, to keep my brother-in-law away. Things might have been different if I had.

CHAPTER 48

I LEFT THE TENEMENT THAT FRIDAY, my pockets stuffed with cash. I walked quickly to Signora Brasi's house, not hesitating this time at the alleyway. Soon, my sister would have that syringe. Even if Bartu forced himself on her—and from the way she winced when his hand came near, I suspected he was—at least she wouldn't become pregnant.

I rapped on Signora's door. When there was no answer, I knocked more loudly. The last time, Signora hadn't opened her door until after I'd knocked three times. So I banged on the door a again.

Perhaps she'd gone to the market, though she'd instructed me to come first thing in the morning. I looked at my watch. Half past eight. Could she still be sleeping? I rapped again. Still, no response. I leaned against the alleyway wall, feeling the cold seeping through the stones. At ten, I decided to wait until eleven; at eleven, I resolved to stay until noon. At one, my stomach was growling and I remembered I hadn't eaten breakfast. I knocked one last time. Then I turned and left.

I returned later that afternoon, and then again on Saturday and Sunday, my pockets still stuffed with bills. Each day, more flyers littered her alleyway. Leaves piled up against her door. On Monday, desperate for help, I went to Stella's. When I told her Signora was gone, I thought she'd tell me I had to go back.

Instead, she said Signora had been arrested. "Be glad you weren't there. You would have been arrested, too."

"When will she be released?"

Stella shrugged.

"But Caterina needs that syringe."

"There's nothing you can do. Anyway, didn't you say Bartu was still seeing his *puttana*?" But hadn't she told me that *puttana* or no *puttana*, my sister had to protect herself?

"How's your father?" Stella asked, abruptly. "Did he make his million dollars yet?"

I tried to ignore the dig. "Not yet. He's looking for investors." Investors. It even sounded legitimate.

"Only a moron would give Antonino money. But you know what they say," Stella continued. "There's a fool born every minute. Just don't be that fool, okay? Any hint that you have money and your Pappa will sweet talk you into giving him every last cent."

Did she really think I was that stupid? No. If I gave Pappa the money, it would be my choice.

"We should talk about what's next," Stella said. "Can you come to the farmhouse soon?"

"Pappa is going to Blocton next week. I can come then."

"Why wait until next week?"

"He wants to be here for All Souls' Day. He hasn't been to Nonna's grave yet. He wants to plant chrysanthemums. It's tradition."

Stella laughed. "I'm sure the Lucanis will appreciate that."

"We'll have our own plot soon." Why was I defending Pappa?

"You'll have to move the old lady."

I shrugged, pretending that the thought didn't make my stomach turn.

"You'll be together. One big happy family."

I could have reminded her—baby Nino lay in the cemetery at *Binvinutu*. When the time came, Caterina would be buried in the Amoruso family plot. I tried to change the conversation. "Have you decided where we'll go? You know, when we leave?"

"Are we leaving?"

I took Stella's hands. They were coarse, unlovely. I brought them to my lips. "Yes," I whispered.

She turned toward me. "We'll drive west." Now her voice was sure. "There's a place in California where women run their own sardine-packing businesses. No one bothers them. Monterey, it's called. If we go by car, we can bring the Pearl." In my mind, I could see the printer, carefully packed in padded blankets, safe in the back seat.

I asked if we'd dig up the copper plates from under the cattails.

"I was thinking we could go legitimate. The Monterey businesses are shipping more and more of their sardines back east. We could help them with their advertising. You know, pamphlets and catalogs. That sort of thing."

That had been my alibi—something to throw Pappa and Bartu off track. But I was an artist. I was meant for more than pamphlets and catalogs.

She must have sensed how I felt. "We could live a good life out there," she continued. "Quiet. Respectable. We could be happy."

I nodded.

"Good," she said. "When can you leave?"

"First I need to find a house and settle my family in without Pappa finding out about the money."

"That sounds challenging."

I shrugged. There was no other way.

"Well, make it soon." Stella gestured outside. "It's crazy out there. Micks killing Micks. Paesani killing Paesani. And the Napolitani, like rats, feasting on the corpses."

On the way home from Stella's, I picked up *The Herald* and turned to the real estate section. Because they weren't allowed to advertise "No Italians Allowed," they wrote that the properties for sale were in "First Class American Neighborhoods," or on the "American Side of Town," and then proceeded to turn down families like mine. I'd get around the bullshit by giving my name as Mimi *English*—it was the translation for Inglese, anyway, and offer over asking price. That would be enough to secure a place for my family.

When I'd circled five listings—in places like Dobbs Ferry and Mamaroneck—I tucked the paper into my bag, next to the stack of bills. Had it only been this morning when I'd been to the midwife's house? Never mind. Soon my sister would be far from Bartu. When Pappa left for Blocton, I'd start looking at the places I'd circled. Mamma would be excited. When Pappa returned, she'd already be packed. Caterina, too, if I could convince her. I just had to wait until the Day of the Dead, four days away.

On that morning, I awoke feeling uneasy. I rose from bed and dressed quickly. One sweater. Two. Nonna's grave was on a hill. It would be windy. I went to the kitchen, expecting to see Pappa smoking his cigar and reading the morning paper. Instead, his head was in his hands. He was weeping.

"I should have been here," he cried. "When Matri died. She was alone."

I put my hand on his chair. "No, Pappa. We were with her. Me and Mamma."

He shook his head. That didn't matter. He wasn't there.

"Nonna was comfortable," I added. No need to mention the old woman's confusion, or how she'd cried out for Curro.

"It was my fault," Pappa cried. "All of it."

"She died of old age. It wasn't anyone's fault."

Pappa slammed his fists on the table. "No! If it wasn't for me, she would have had a good life as the wife of a nobleman. Instead, she was forced into that nunnery."

I could have reminded Pappa: Nonna had chosen the nunnery over an arranged marriage.

"She was just a girl." Pappa's voice broke. "Made to put her baby in that terrible wheel."

But Pappa had suffered, too. Forced to live with the shame of being Camastrino—a bastard with no father to claim him. Maybe he was thinking this, too. He put his head in his hands and began to sob.

I should have felt sorry for him. But that had all happened a long time ago.

I offered to go to the bakery for the *martorana*, the traditional marzipan fruit for Day of the Dead. By the time I returned, a rainbow of strawberries, oranges, lemons, pears, figs and pomegranates in the white bakery box, Pappa was himself again. We set out for the cemetery. Caterina and Sebu would meet us there.

After a two-hour train ride, most of it spent clasping a ceiling strap and swaying forward and back, we arrived at Calvary Cemetery. We stopped at the small stone building with an *OFFICE* sign over its entrance. Pappa shut off the car. "I need to see the caretaker." Pappa got out.

I'd already told him I knew where the Lucanis' marker was. G section, in one of the new areas. Mamma followed Pappa. Should I go, too?—or wait for Caterina? I imagined her, pulling Sebu through the maze of statues and gravestones, searching for us, like Demeter had once searched for her daughter, Persephone

Pappa held open the door. "Come, Mimi."

I went in. Mamma was at a counter where a white-haired clerk stood, writing on a paper.

Mamma said something about the new chapel. "According to the Ladies, it's the best section."

The clerk reached down and pulled out a large map.

"You're buying a plot?" I asked. But Pappa had no money. And a cemetery plot wasn't something you could buy on credit, like groceries or a motor car.

"Of course," Pappa said, like it was ridiculous to ask. "We're Americans. We should have our own plot. Inglese." He drew a rectangle in the air, not unlike the one he'd made when he first described the stock certificates.

But only Sebu was American. Before the war in Europe had started, Pappa talked about becoming a citizen. Now, though, citizens could be drafted. As if the army would want someone his age.

The clerk spread out the map.

"Our available plots are there." He gestured toward the edge of the map.

"We need one near the chapel," Mamma demanded.

The clerk shook his head. "That's here. But anything around it is reserved for our Holy Orders."

Pappa leaned in close. "Surely we can figure something out." There was something vaguely threatening about Pappa's tone that surprised me.

A car horn blared.

Pappa looked out the window.

"It's Bartu!"

My stomach dropped.

Pappa hooked his thumbs into his suspenders and smiled. "I knew he'd come."

After a moment, my brother-in-law burst into the office.

"I got your message." He slapped Pappa on the back. "I'm all in."

Pappa smiled. "Good, good. Let's talk about it afterwards. Sebu is with you?" Pappa craned his neck to look out the window.

"I thought we'd talk now. I have places to be."

If Pappa thought it disrespectful, he took no heed. "Of course! Let's go outside." Before he opened the door to leave, Pappa turned toward the clerk. "I'll be in touch." He laughed, wryly. "Because sooner or later, we'll need you. Hopefully, later!"

As I left, I made sure to touch the metal doorknob, though I didn't quite believe that touching iron would ward off the bad luck Pappa's words had summoned.

Once outside, Bartu asked why Pappa had called for him.

"*Aspittu*, Bartu. Where is my grandson? Is he in the motorcar?" Pappa started toward Bartu's automobile. "Mimi, bring the *martorana*."

I took the white box from my satchel and handed it to Pappa. He slipped his fingers under the string and made for the car. I followed.

When Pappa got to Bartu's car, he leaned in the window. "Sebu! Let me see you!"

The boy's face appeared. He looked miserable. Caterina, too, her eyes, staring into the distance.

"I have something for you." Pappa handed Sebu the bakery box. "It's candy. From your Bisnonna." A terrifying idea for the six-year-old—that his dead great-grandmother had somehow brought these fruit.

"Come." Pappa opened the door and Sebu tumbled out. Pappa crouched down. He pulled the boy to his knee. Pappa untied the string and took out a pomegranate. I shuddered. The food of the dead. If I'd been closer, I would have grabbed the *martorana* from the boy's hand and eaten it myself, to keep the stain of death from his lips. But the boy was already nibbling it, the aubergine dye staining his lips.

Bartu caught up. "What's your big news, Nino?"

Pappa stood. He put his arm around Bartu's shoulders. "I've heard from Carlo."

"Ponzi? What did he say?" Bartu asked excitedly.

"He's given us the opportunity to find investors up here. For the power company."

"The one down south?"

Pappa nodded. "The company just got a contract with one of the big steel companies. That means more mining. More workers. More need for electricity and water."

Bartu was speechless. A first.

Pappa continued. "It's a once-in-a-lifetime chance. Carlo says so."

Bartu raised his hand. "But wait a minute. Wasn't Ponzi going to find his own investors? If it's such a great opportunity, why does he need us?"

"A good question, my boy." Pappa said, smiling. "Remember I told you how Carlo gave his skin to that nurse? The one with the burns?"

"Yeah. Stupid, if you ask me."

"Well, Carlo's a good man. The woman would have died without him. Three operations. It's taken a lot out of him, though. He can't be running around, looking for investors. Not now, anyway."

"I don't know, Nino. Maybe the locals decided the stocks weren't such a good idea, and he's pawning the certificates off on us."

Pappa pressed on. "Ask your Wall Street clients. They'll be falling over themselves to invest. It pays out dividends—you make money just by holding the stock. As the stock increases in value—and it will, because every one of those workers will need water and electricity—you'll make more money."

Bartu shrugged. "I'll ask, but these are sophisticated men. They may not care about some small-town power company out in the sticks."

Pappa smiled. "I think you'll be surprised."

"I hope you're right."

Pappa squeezed Bartu's shoulder. "Here's the best part. To repay our trust, Ponzi's offering a fifty percent bonus. For every stock you sell, you'll earn half a share for yourself. Sell ten stocks and you earn five stocks. Sell a thousand and you make five hundred. It's a no-lose proposition. With your connections, you're the perfect man to do it."

Bartu stood up straighter. Ah, flattery. Pappa knew just how to hook a person. Pappa pulled Bartu closer. They were standing head to head.

"I want you to do this," Pappa said. "To be successful. Independent. To not be beholden to anyone else."

He'd said the same thing to me when I started lessons with Monsieur Laurent. I desperately wanted to tell him: I'd been successful. Me. Without Monsieur Laurent or Zio or Clutch. But I'd promised Stella I'd stay quiet.

I thought of that sturdy beehive oven and the calaba lilies, their faces to the sun. Maybe Ponzi would pay me for the certificates in stocks, like he'd offered to do with Pappa and Bartu. According to Stella, the stock market was nothing but a numbers racket, rigged to benefit the wealthy. That was me. I'd make enough money to fill the space under every floorboard in the apartment.

There was enough time for that. But first, Bartu had to sell the stocks. I watched him climb back into his car. He slid his hand up the inside of my sister's thigh. She shrank back in her seat. I felt guilty, like I'd been a pimp. Because for Carlo's plan to succeed, we needed Bartu. By the time I emerged from the subway a few hours later, I'd resolved to keep going back to Signora Brasi until I got my sister another syringe. With Bartu back in Caterina's bed, I had to make sure she didn't become pregnant.

CHAPTER 49

My feet were so cold it felt like someone was sticking needles in them. I stepped into the frozen footprint—my footprint—evidence of the many times I'd trod the midwife's alleyway. The first few weeks, I'd cleared the snow from the path. When Stella told me that people would be suspicious if they saw the shoveled walkway, I let it pile up, placing my feet into the same icy prints I'd made before. Through months of freezing and melting, the frozen footprints had become so hard that it hurt to step into them. Stella kept saying the midwife would be released soon. I didn't want to miss her.

Every day, I pried off that floorboard and took out the fifty dollars; at night, I returned the money to its hiding place. I'd done it so many times that the nail hole had widened so that even tapping down the nail with my shoe heel didn't secure it. I'd moved the table over slightly so the leg rested on the raised nail and no one could see.

Now I touched the folded bills in my pocket. Using both fists, I hammered on Signora's door. Again, no answer. I turned and headed for the park.

Later, as we sat on the bench, Stella told me to just keep checking. "The cops can't keep her forever."

"It's been six months," I said. "Why is she still in jail?"

"The cops are trying to make an example of her."

"Why?"

"To show you'll go to jail if you help women who don't want to have babies."

"You mean with the syringe?" I asked. "Why would they care about that?"

Stella shrugged. "Who knows why the Americans do what they do? Anyway, Signora will be back. There are too many desperate women—and too much money to be made—for her to walk away. When she does, though, be careful. The cops'll be on the lookout for her customers."

"Why?"

"Because they're breaking the law, too." Stella stretched out her arms, like a cat. "It used to be that the cops would only be after the worst of the worst—back-alley butchers who would tear a fully-grown baby from its mother and leave them both for dead. But these reformers." Stella shook her head. "They're after everyone."

All at once, I understood. Signora Brasi didn't just keep women from getting pregnant. She was an abortionist. Monsignor had railed against abortion, saying it was a mortal sin. Women who succumbed to it—and there were many, according to him—were damned to hell.

"Is it safe?" I asked.

"That depends. Early enough, and it's like a heavy period. Too late and it can kill you."

"Why would someone risk that?"

"A woman will do anything if she's desperate enough. You understand this, verù?"

I nodded. Stella took my hands in hers. "Just be careful. It would be ridiculous for you to go to jail for buying a damn syringe."

Pappa had been waiting for me at home. As I walked into the kitchen, I saw it at once: The table had been moved.

"Where have you been?" he demanded.

My stomach clenched. "We needed some things at the market." I held up the string bag. The garlic stalk poked through.

Pappa nodded but his eyes were narrowed. Suspicious. I stole a glance at the table. The table no longer rested on the popped nail. Even from where I stood, I could see the raised edge of the floorboard.

"You come and go like a man." Pappa was angry. "I trust you. But I wonder—where do you really spend your days?"

My heart was racing but I forced myself to empty the string bag slowly. Only when I'd severed the stalk of the garlic and put its head into the basket did I turn to Pappa. "You seem tired. Is everything all right?"

Pappa snorted. "Tell me. Was there ever a time you were thinking about what would be best for this family?"

I felt like I'd been struck. Pappa had never talked to me like that.

"Pappa—."

"When were you going to tell me?"

"Tell you what?" But I already knew. He'd found the bills.

"Really, Mimi. One end of the floorboard was sticking out. I would have found it even if I wasn't looking for it."

Had he been looking for it? My mind raced. Only Stella knew about the money. She'd never tell.

"You kept it from me." Pappa's voice was steely. "After everything I gave you. The fancy tutors. The expensive paint and canvases. The snooty art shows in Palermo. People laughed at me for thinking you'd ever be a real artist. Still, I supported you. And you repay me with this— deception. Lying about where you've been going. And who you're with. Running around with that Stella Frauto woman. Doing whatever it is you do together." He looked at me in a way that left no doubt that he knew what Stella was. What we were. "Bartu says I shouldn't blame you. Frauto is cunning. She tricked you into making those bills."

"No one tricked me," I said quietly, thinking of Persephone and those seeds.

"All that money. Thousands of dollars" He pointed toward the floorboard.

Twenty thousand dollars, to be exact.

When he looked at me, his eyes were cold. "No woman makes that much money unless she's bringing disgrace to her family."

I almost laughed out loud. Pappa thought I was a prostitute.

He balled his hands into fists. "You should have been helping your Nonna," he said. "Your sister."

"I did help them. I used the money to pay the rent. To buy food."

"You're lying!" Pappa shouted. "Vito paid for all that. Bartu told me."

I tried to stay calm. "No, Pappa, If Zio sent money, we never saw it. Bartu left us on our own."

"Bartu took care of you. Why would he lie?"

"Maybe because he was keeping Zio's money for himself?"

Pappa's eyes bored into mine. "Or maybe you were jealous of your sister. Of what she had—a husband. A child. You tried to drive Bartu away so Caterina would be alone. Like you."

The floor beneath me felt like it was moving. I sputtered something about how it wasn't true. I loved my sister and nephew. More than anything, I wanted them to be happy.

"You're a selfish girl," Pappa snarled. "That's why you'll always be alone."

But I wasn't alone. I had Stella.

There was a knock on the door.

"It's me. Bartu."

Pappa went to the door and opened it.

Bartu smirked when he saw me, then strode into the room like he lived there. "You've told her?"

Pappa nodded.

"Kudos to you, sister dear, for keeping it a secret all this time." Bartu tipped his hat. "The five-dollar bills. And Stella. I didn't see that coming. The old hag and the invalid. A love story." He snorted, like it was a great joke. But only he was laughing.

Pappa looked nauseous. Like the thought of it—of me—made him sick. That familiar shroud of shame fell like a heavy cloak around my shoulders.

"Don't get me wrong," Bartu continued. "You did a good job. Everyone kept going on about what a good counterfeiter you were. I didn't believe it. I mean, a woman? But when your father showed me all that money you made, I knew it was true."

I imagined Pappa on his hands and knees, prying off that loosened floorboard. Pulling out the stacks of bills, one after another.

Pappa turned to me. "You knew we needed the money. To invest in Ponzi's thing. But you would have let Bartu and me go door-to-door, like beggars."

"And the prison fine," Bartu added. "You must have had the money for that, too."

The color drained from Pappa's face. "Is that true?" he whispered. "You had the money even then?"

I didn't respond. It wouldn't do any good.

"You let me rot in prison. With all those—animals. Every day, wondering if that would be the day Clutch got to me. Especially after his son was killed. Carlo said Clutch blamed me—if he hadn't been sent to prison, his son would still be alive."

But I'd heard something different. "It was revenge," I said, repeating what Stella had told me. "His son killed another man."

"Shut up!" Pappa drew back his fist. I braced for the impact. When the blow didn't come, I opened my eyes.

"What happened to you, Mimi? I don't know you anymore."

Bartu was tsk-tsking in the corner. "If I hadn't told your father about that money, you wouldn't have offered it, would you have, Mimi? You would have left your father twisting in the wind—no investors for the power plant. Vito, breathing down his neck, demanding to be paid. You would have continued your whoring with Stella Frauto. You abandoned him. Your Mamma. All of us."

Abandoned—the way Pappa had been left in the wheel. By Pappa's stricken expression, I could see that Bartu had gotten the reaction he wanted.

The words spilled out before I could stop them. "If anyone's abandoned the family, it's you, Bartu! Leaving Caterina and Sebu for some *puttana.*"

Pappa leapt to his feet. "Enough! I don't want to hear anything else. Mimi, you're my daughter. That money is mine."

"No, Pappa! It's for a house in Westchester. For Sebu and Caterina. And you and Mamma. To get out of the city. Away from all of this."

"This is our home."

Didn't he see the black mold on the ceiling? The cracks in the walls? The mouse holes in the corners? "Anyway. I've already invested the money."

There was a loud buzzing in my ears. The money it had taken me nearly three years to save—Pappa couldn't possibly mean that it was all gone.

But that's exactly what he meant. "I sent it to Ponzi. For the power plant. We just got it to him in time. Other people had begun making inquiries. From Atlanta. Baltimore. Boston. We beat them out."

Bartu piped in. "They knew it was a good investment, too."

"Ponzi's smart. We're lucky to know him."

Pappa had once talked about Zio Vito this way. Clutch, too, I remembered with a shudder.

"If I decide to move this family to Westchester," Pappa continued, "and that's a big if, by the way, I'll use some of the Blocton money to buy a house. By then, I'll have earned so much on that investment that we'll be able to buy up a whole town up there. Until then, we're staying here."

Pappa dismissed me then, telling me to go into the bedroom until Mamma got home from her Rosary Society meeting. I listened to the two men for a while—Pappa pontificating about the brilliance of Carlo Ponzi, Bartu congratulating Pappa for his good judgment—until I'd had enough. I laid down on the floor of my parents' bedroom and covered my ears with my hands.

CHAPTER 50

THE VESTIBULE IN CATERINA'S building smelled like rotten eggs. Still, it felt good to be inside. A winter storm was brewing—gray clouds loomed overhead, heavy with snow. I wrapped my shawl more tightly around my chest and started up the stairs.

Pappa trudged behind me. He hadn't let me out of his sight since he'd found the money. I hadn't seen Stella in months.

I paused at the second-floor landing, my chest tight. Pappa hit the back of my legs with his walking stick. I kept moving.

The hallway was lined with sacks of garbage. The cold weather encouraged people to relax their vigilance about vermin. The sour smell was the least of it. A flash of movement—roaches—on the walls and stairs. I kept my eyes down and continued to the fourth floor.

Finally, I stood in front of my sister's apartment. Bartu opened the door.

I'd been there two days ago, but the sink was already full of dishes and mounds of clothes—dirty or clean, I couldn't tell—laid on the floor. Bartu sat at the table. He was in his shirtsleeves, despite the cold. Though it was only half past ten, he pushed the half-empty bottle toward Pappa.

Whiskey. He must have picked up that habit from his Irish *puttana*.

"Go," Pappa ordered, pointing to the bedroom. "Check on your sister."

Filled with dread, I started down the hallway. The last time, I'd found Caterina and Sebu sprawled on the bed, side-by-side, the rise and fall of their chests nearly imperceptible. This time, Caterina lay across

the bed, her nightgown pulled up to her thighs. A leather strap—like the
kind Pappa had for shaving—lay across the footboard. Sebu was huddled in the corner. He was shivering. I took my shawl off and wrapped
it around his small body. He edged closer.

"Why are you on the floor?" I whispered.

Wide-eyed, Sebu whispered that his father had told him to stay
there. I tried not to think about what that boy had seen—his mother
catatonic while his father pumped away on top of her.

I went to my sister. "Come on, Caterina." I pulled her up by her
armpits and was about to slip her nightgown over her head when I
saw the oozing, jagged cuts on the insides of her thighs. Red. Swollen.
"What have you done to yourself?"

She turned toward the wall.

I tried to ease her back. "Those look infected. Let me help you." I
opened the drawer, looking for something to clean the cuts with. Inside,
more empty vials and used syringes. Along with Nonna's crucifix—the
one with the metal edges.

"Leave me the fuck alone!" Caterina flailed her arms, catching me
on my bad side. I doubled over in pain.

Sebu cried out like it was he who'd been struck. "Zia!" He fell onto
the floor next to me and started to sob.

I took his hand. "It's all right."

But as I turned to look at my sister, sitting upright in bed, her hair
matted, her arms and neck covered with scratches, I knew it wasn't all
right. Not at all.

Bartu was alone in the kitchen. I asked where Pappa was.

"Gone to Western Union. I'm your babysitter." He pushed back his
chair and splayed his legs. There was something obscene in his gesture
that made my stomach turn.

"Did he hear from Ponzi?" I asked. Every day, Pappa went to
Western Union, waiting for some word about his investment.

"That piece of shit with eyes. It's been two months since Antonino
sent him that money. And still, no word."

"Did Ponzi sign for the money when he got it?" I tried to imagine twenty thousand dollars, flying away like a canary from a magician's hat. Bartu shrugged. "I told Antonino. He should have taken the money down there. Given it to Ponzi, face-to-face. But Antonino had to stay here. With you."

I tried to ignore the implication that it was somehow my fault that Pappa had lost everything. Instead, I asked the question that had been kicking around my brain for weeks. "How did you know about the money?"

He smirked. "People talk, Sister Dear."

"Who? The Camorra?"

He shook his head.

"Then who? Your clients?"

"Nah. It was a little birdie." Bartu was enjoying this. I waited. Finally, he continued. "I have a good friend who told me that you were making bills and that they were pretty good. Her people were using them. In Brooklyn."

Belle Hannity. That had to be the connection.

"Your *puttana*?" I spat out. "Is that who told you?"

"I take offense at your words. Margaret is a lady. Her people in Leister were nobility. Before the British took it all."

I repeated my question. But I already knew. Wittingly or not, Belle had told Margaret Kelly.

"Don't look at me like that, Mimi. Anyway, it was Antonino's decision to invest everything in Ponzi's plan. I told him to diversify. He wouldn't listen."

Pappa never listened. Another "sure-fire investment" that he put everything we owned—that I owned—into.

"You shouldn't have told him about my money."

Bartu laughed. "*Your* money?"

"Yes. Mine. I earned it. You had no right to tell him."

"No right?" Bartu stood. "Antonino left me in charge when he went to prison. I knew something was going on with Stella. But you wouldn't let me in. If you had, I might have been able to make a deal with the Camorra. We would all be better off."

"I didn't want to let you in. I didn't trust you. I still don't."

Bartu laughed. "What do I care if you trust me? You're a woman. You need to get into line."

I ran to the door. I had to get away. See Stella. Figure out what to do. Bartu bounded after me. He locked the door then put his hand over the deadbolt.

"You're not going anywhere," he snarled.

I tried to shove him away.

"You're an invalid. You really think you're going to push your way out of here?"

My hand still on the doorknob, I pulled.

Bartu laughed. "You're not going out. You're not well enough."

"I haven't been sick in years."

Bartu shook his head. "It could happen at any time. Especially with you running around with people like Stella. But there's a place in the mountains. I was telling Antonino about it. A Sanitarium up north, near Canada. Fresh air. Lots of trees. You'll be safe there."

I'd be damned if I was going to let them send me away. I closed my hand tightly around the knob and pulled with all my might. I couldn't budge it. Tears of frustration filled my eyes. I blinked them away. Finally, Bartu took his hand off the door and I fled, the sound of his laughter in my ears.

CHAPTER 51

PRESSING CHARCOAL TO PAPER, I began to sketch, grateful for the simplicity of the composition. Rectangles for the backyards behind our tenement, a shanty town of lean-tos with scraps of wood littering the ground. More rectangles for the tenements, with windows streaked with dirt. Clotheslines crisscrossed the yards, dingy shirts and sheets flapping in the April breeze. A study in geometry—all lines and angles. Not difficult. But it required focus, an escape from the mind-numbing sameness of each day.

Pappa came into the kitchen, holding his satchel. My first thought was that he was sending me away. But when he opened the satchel to slip a notepad inside, I saw it was filled with his clothes.

"Are you going somewhere?" I asked.

"Alabama." He snapped shut the satchel. "Something must have happened to Signore Ponzi."

Pappa must have sent a hundred telegrams, but Ponzi hadn't answered one. Surely, Pappa had been swindled. But as usual, Pappa couldn't see it. I wasn't complaining: if Pappa went to Alabama, I could finally see Stella and figure out a way to make more money so I could get away. Pappa may have my bills, but the burins were still tucked in safely below the floorboard near the window, every nail hammered flat.

From my daybed, I watched Pappa as he slipped his lucky coin into his vest pocket. Even in the dim light of dawn, I could see how nervous he was, rubbing his neck and raking his fingers through his hair. Then he picked up his satchel and left.

I dressed quickly and went into my parents' bedroom. Mamma's eyes were closed. I whispered I was going to Caterina's. Mamma's eyelids fluttered open.

"Pappa said I could go," I continued. A lie, but Mamma didn't seem to care. She stumbled to the dresser and picked up a small box. She gave it to me. "This is for Caterina. From Father Marino. It's a rosary pin."

Why would he do that? Caterina hadn't been at Mass in months.

Mamma sensed my hesitation. "He visited her last week. They prayed together. She was upset. If you visited her more often, you'd know."

But I wasn't allowed to go to Caterina's unless Pappa was there, too. Even then, she was in a stupor. Drugged with whatever Bartu had given her.

"Is she all right?" I asked.

Mamma sighed, then pointed to the dresser. "Just take the pin."

The rosary medal was about the size of a brooch. On the top, a tin piece, embossed with *ROSARY SOCIETY*, joined to a small medallion with a Marian blue ribbon. I picked it up, the medallion dangling. Around its edges, the words, *Queen of the Most Holy Pray for Us,* with a silhouette of the Madonna. Pappa had a medal like that on the army uniform he'd left hanging in the closet at *Binvinutu*. I slipped the rosary pin into my pocket and headed out.

I told myself the stop at Caterina's wouldn't take long. There would still be plenty of time to get to Stella's. But as I neared my sister's apartment building, my pace slowed. I could keep going. Tell Mamma I'd forgotten to give Caterina the pin. Or that Caterina hadn't been in. If I'd done that, maybe everything would have been different. But I turned down her street. A moment later, I was at her door.

Sebu opened the door, his eyes wide with fear. "Mommy's sick." The boy put his thumb in his mouth—something I hadn't seen him do since he was a toddler.

Caterina was in bed. I pulled open the damask curtains. Late morning light flooded the room.

She pulled the sheet over her head. When I tried to tug it down, she kicked me away. I didn't need this. But Sebu. How could I leave him here with her?

I pulled off my shawl. "Mamma sent you something from Father Marino. Why don't you come to the kitchen and I'll give it to you? Come on, Caterina." Again, I tried to ease down the sheet.

She screamed, "Get the fuck out of here!" her arms, flailing.

Behind me, I heard whimpering. Sebu was standing in the doorway. Watching.

I went to him. Crouching down, I took his small hands in mine. "Sebu, why don't you go into the kitchen and get out your drawing pencils? I'll be there in a minute." Reluctantly, he turned away. I went back to my sister.

"You need to get up. It's almost noon." I slid the sheet off her head. "Father Marino sent you a medal," I repeated. "He thought you might like to pray."

She glared at me. Her eyes were cold. "Why would I do that?"

I shrugged. "I guess he thought praying would help."

"Yeah, like you really believe that."

I could have dropped it. Talked about something inane, like the heat wave we were having, or the high price of ice. Instead, I took it from my pocket and slid it across the bedside table, trying not to notice the mostly empty bottle of Bayer's Heroin.

She slid the medal from the tabletop. My devout sister. She'd bring the medal to her breast. Ask the Madonna for forgiveness. Guidance.

Instead, she picked it up and hurled it at me. "Fuck Marino!" she raged. "Fuck the Madonna! And fuck you!" The medal hit the wall behind me and clattered to the floor.

I looked back at her. Her covers were off. She was naked. There were angry red patches, shiny and wet, on her breasts; and two bruises— one yellowish-blue, the other, purple, on her ribs. The most shocking of all—there was a swelling just below her belly button. I stared as I struggled to take it in.

"You're pregnant."

She blinked back at me, like a cornered animal.

"And you're hurt." I approached her carefully, as I would an injured animal. "Who hurt you?"

I wanted her to say it was Bartu. Then I could tell Pappa and he'd have to take Caterina and Sebu in. With them safe, I could get away. Disappear into the crowds at the market or slip away when everyone had gone to sleep.

I asked again. "Who hurt you?"

Caterina opened the nightstand drawer and took out Nonna's beads. "Leave me the fuck alone!"

Before I could register what she was doing, she scraped the metal edge of the crucifix across her forearm. A bright red streak appeared.

Her lower lip trembled. Her tears came. Slowly at first, then a torrent.

Pushing aside my revulsion for her mutilated, naked body, I put my arms around her. She was a little girl, then—heartbroken about some wren who'd fallen from its nest, or the mouse in Cook's trap. Sebu started crying. I held out a hand to him and he came to his mother's bedside. We stayed there for a long time, like that photograph of the survivors of the *S.S. Lusitania*, huddled in their lifeboats. They finally stopped crying.

When Caterina spoke again, her voice was clear. Strong. "I won't do it. I won't have his bastard."

For a moment, it didn't register.

"I've been trying to get rid of it," she said. "Sticking things in there."

Horrified, I managed to ask what kinds of things.

Her eyes went to the darning needles in the basket on the floor.

"No, Caterina. You can't. You could die!"

"I don't care."

"You don't mean that."

"I do."

"Think of Sebu."

"If you don't help me, I'll take the gas. Me and Sebu."

I shuddered, thinking how easy it would be. Just turn on the gas jet and fall asleep to its gentle shush. Side by side, drifting off to endless slumber. I told her things would be better when the baby came. "Remember? That's how it was with Sebu." Not true. Caterina hadn't started feeling better until Bartu went back to his *puttana*. That wouldn't happen this time, with him working with Pappa.

Maybe she could come with Stella and me when we went West. But I knew Stella would say it was too complicated. Bringing along a mother and two children, one of them, a baby.

"I'm going to that midwife. There are things she can do to stop a baby from coming." Caterina said this as matter-of-factly as if she were going to the market to buy a dozen eggs.

I asked Caterina if she had any money.

"Bartu gives me only enough money for groceries."

I thought of those plates again—the ones buried under the cattails. I could make the bills my sister needed, but it would take time. Judging by the swell of her belly, that was a luxury she didn't have.

"Your rosary beads." I motioned to the strand of pink pearls dangling from her hand. "I can pawn them."

I expected her to say no. From the moment Nonna had laid those on her lap—a family heirloom going back generations—Caterina had kept those beads in a silk bag, rarely taking them out. She handed them to me.

The next morning, I rose early to go to the pawnshop. Two copper pots, their bottoms burnished from use, hung in the window. A lace tablecloth lay over an armchair; next to it, a man's camel hair coat. People would jettison all kinds of treasures to keep themselves afloat.

I pushed open the door. The chime jingled. A man in an apron was tinkering with a mantel clock. He didn't even look up. After I'd waited a few moments, I cleared my throat.

When he still ignored me, I pulled the beads from my pocket. "Can you help me?" I asked.

That got his attention. He stood, wiped his hands on his apron, and came to me.

"South Sea pearls," I said. "Very rare." I sounded like a hawker on Canal Street.

He rubbed his thumbs and forefingers together.

I continued. "It's from the 1700s. Very valuable. It belonged to my great-great-great grandmother. She was a duchess."

The pawnbroker held out his hands. I hesitated for a moment, then reminded myself: this would keep my sister alive. What good was the past if there was no future? He offered sixty dollars. I didn't have the time to haggle or find another pawn shop. He handed me the cash—in ones and fives. I made sure they were real, then pocketed them.

The moment Signora Brasi told me her fee—two hundred fifty dollars—I was sorry I hadn't gotten more.

I lied and told Signora I had it.

"You better," she said. "I don't take charity cases. And remember. Your sister. Alone. No husband, or boyfriend, or whatever."

Once outside, I turned toward Stella's. One more run of bills. Then we could leave.

Stella opened the door a crack. When I told her Pappa had stolen my money, she pulled me inside and deadbolted the door.

"It's not safe," she whispered, though no one could hear us. "We should leave today. With just the clothes on our backs."

I wanted to say yes. I couldn't. "Caterina's in a bad way."

Stella shook her head.

"It's not like that," I said. "I'm going to leave. As soon as she's better."

"What's wrong with her?"

"She's pregnant."

She gave a mirthless laugh.

"She wants to have an abortion," I blurted out. "I pawned her rosary beads. But Signora wants more."

"How much more?"

"Two hundred and fifty dollars. I have fifty."

"So you still need two hundred."

I nodded.

"Maybe more," Stella added, "if Signora decides your sister's too far along."

"One more run of bills. That's all it'll take. And Pappa's away until next week."

"So you figure you'll just pop over to Hackensack and print out a few more hundred dollar bills?"

I nodded, though I heard how ridiculous it sounded.

Somewhere, a door slammed. Stella looked like she was going to jump out of her skin.

I put my hand on her arm. "What's wrong?"

"I guess you haven't heard about Ciro Morello."

My stomach clenched. Ciro. With his thick brow and hulking body. "What about him?"

"Word is that Clutch has figured out how to run things from prison."

I thought of those rats, their tiny tongues laid out beside them. Lined up like Pappa's dead *carusi* boys.

Stella continued. "Clutch has ordered Ciro to take revenge on the people who've betrayed them." When I didn't respond, Stella said that Clutch would never forgive Pappa for testifying against him. "Antonino should have kept his mouth closed and served his time for the telegrams."

"It was twenty years," I said. "He never would have survived."

Stella shrugged. "Better dead in your jail cell then gunned down on the street. Clutch blames your father for Calogero's death. He's a marked man."

I felt like I'd been punched in the gut.

"And it's not just your Pappa the Morellos are after," Stella said. "It's us, too."

I turned to her, her words not registering.

"The counterfeiting operation. They think we stole it from them."

"But I made the engraving plates. You got the Pearl and the supplies. How was it theirs?"

316 • SUZANNE UTTARO SAMUELS

Stella shrugged. "I'm just laying out our situation."

"Situation?"

"The Morellos think that if we were giving them the bills, they would have had more firepower. More protection. Nicolò wouldn't have been killed. Calogero, either."

"Nicolò and Calogero were bad men. It had nothing to do with us."

Stella laughed. "It's so simple for you, isn't it, Mimi? Someone does something bad and they're punished for it. But Nico and Calogero were killed because the other gangs saw the opportunity to take the Morellos out once and for all. To get control of their protection rackets. The lotteries. The girls."

I swallowed, hard. "So what are we going to do?"

"Well, I'm certainly not going to cruise over to Jersey to make more bills."

"What will you do?"

"I'm leaving. As soon as I can arrange things with the Coloreds. They'll hang onto some of my money—I don't need to travel cross country with twenty thousand dollars in my satchel. Once I'm settled, they'll wire it to me. Small batches, so it doesn't attract attention."

"Do you trust them?" I thought of my cubby under the floorboards, its top pried off and laid across the top. Pappa's valise, stuffed with my bills.

She shrugged. "Maybe. They're outsiders even among the outsiders. And I'm paying them well."

"When do you leave?"

"On Tuesday morning. There's a train to Chicago. Then on to Los Angeles." She took my hand. "Please, Mimi. Save yourself."

"I want to. More than anything. But I have to help my sister first. Or she'll hurt herself. And the boy."

Stella exhaled hard. She reached under the sink and brought out a pot. Then she reached inside and took out a wad of twenty-dollar bills. From the color, I knew they were real. She handed me the money. "There's enough here to pay Signora and buy yourself a ticket. Please. Come with me. Remember. Tuesday morning."

I walked back to the tenement, the bulge of bills tugging on my skirt pocket. I'd always planned to leave. Now, the thought terrified me. I wouldn't be here to see Sebu grow to be a man. Or my sister, silver streaks in her hair, become a Nonna. My parents would die; I wouldn't be here to bury them. The small voice whispered about family obligation and loyalty. But those were things none of us could afford. A bomb lobbed into our kitchen window while I was sitting with Mamma at the table. A flurry of indiscriminate gunfire as we walked home from the market, Sebu's hand tucked into mine. It would be bad enough if Pappa were here. If I stayed, we'd all be dead.

I unlocked our apartment door. Mamma was out, so I went to my daybed. I pulled it away from the wall and went down on my hands and knees, feeling for the nail heads. By the time I'd pried them all away, my nails were torn and bleeding. I pulled up the board. Underneath were my burins, safely tucked into their mahogany box. I ran my fingers over the gold embossed lettering— *MCI*—my initials. I peeled off three hundred dollars from what Stella had given me, then tucked the remaining money—ones and fives, mostly—into the box. I lowered the box into the floor, then hammered the floorboards into place. When I was done, I slid my daybed back against the wall.

The next morning, I went to Signora Brasi. I gave her the money. She told me Caterina should come on Friday.

She wagged her finger at me. "Only her. I don't need no witnesses."

But I was already a witness. I'd seen the dark stains on Signora's oak table. Brown-black, like the splatter of paint. I'd seen the knife drying on the windowsill. The curved rod with the hook.

I'd given Signora the money knowing what she'd do.

CHAPTER 52

CATERINA WAS LEANING AGAINST the stoop railing when I got to her apartment building, her belly round and large. She claimed she was only three months along. She looked closer to five or six. Signora Brasi had been clear—she didn't do this after quickening. "Too complicated," she told me. I felt in my pocket for the extra hundred dollars I'd taken, just in case.

My sister walked in my direction, seven-year-old Sebu struggling to keep up. "Just give me the address," she hissed, when she reached me.

I took Sebu's hand. "Her place is hidden down an alleyway. I'll walk you there."

When we got there, Caterina paused at the entry to the alley. Maybe she was thinking of Saint Agata or the Madonna, someone who'd been tested but remained steadfast. Or maybe she was thinking of Bartu's cruel eyes and the strap he kept by the bed. Whatever it was, it seemed to give her strength. She strode down the narrow passage, cellophane wrappers and leaves catching on the hem of her skirt. She rapped on Signora's door. A moment later, the door opened.

Signora grabbed Caterina's sleeve and pulled her inside. Before she could slam the door shut, I put my hand in the door jam. "Here," I said, reaching for the extra hundred-dollar bill tucked into the lining of my satchel. Signora smiled, a gap-toothed grin that sent shivers down my spine. The door closed.

Still holding Sebu's hand, I stepped out of the alleyway. The sunlight made my eyes water. I thought of Persephone—of the pain that attended each leaving—from the Underworld, where she reigned; from Earth, where flowers bloomed and crops yielded fruit.

Overhead, the El roared past. Sebu trembled.

We found ourselves at a nearby park. Green on the edges. At its center, an immense, cast-iron structure. *A FIRE TOWER*, the plaque read.

"What is it?" Sebu asked.

How to explain to the boy that in a city like New York, the same fire that warmed us cooked our food and boiled our water could be dangerous?

"It's a place where firemen can look out over the city," I explained. "If they see smoke, they can send the fire engine to put it out."

"Smoke?"

"From small fires," I assured. "The firemen stop them before anything bad happens." Another lie. Every day, it seemed, there was another story about a factory or tenement reduced to ashes.

We sat. Sebu was so close that he might as well have been on my lap. He was so much like Caterina. I told myself I shouldn't be annoyed.

"Zia," he whispered. "Is my Mommy all right?"

"Yes. Of course," I said, too quickly.

"But that lady—." He'd hidden behind my skirts when Signora came to the door.

"Your mommy hasn't been feeling well. That lady's going to help her get better."

I focused on this—Caterina would be well—and tried not to think of Signora's terrible tools. "Shall we sketch the tower?"

He nodded. I took a piece of paper from my satchel.

"First the sides—they're just metal rods, so we can sketch like this." I made a few long strokes with my pencil.

Sebu pointed to the tower. "And the steps—."

"They kind of crisscross, right?"

He nodded. Together, we added the metal staircases—one, two, three—reaching toward the lookout. There was a beauty in its symmetry. It reminded me of the drawing I'd done of the Brooklyn Bridge, so long ago.

"And the bell, Zia Mimi. Here, in the middle."

I smiled. "Yes, that's the most important. From there, the firemen can sound the alarm that sends the truck. You draw that." I gave him the pencil. He hesitated a moment. "Go ahead."

"But what if it isn't right?"

How many times had I had the same worries? "Just draw what you see."

He bit his bottom lip. "But what if it's wrong?"

I thought of my engraving of the five-dollar bill. A perfect replica. No margin for creativity. This wasn't anything like this. "It's your picture, Sebu. It can't be wrong."

With each pencil stroke, he breathed more easily. It had been like that for me, too. Drawn into a world of my own creation, I lost all sense of time and place. When it was time to leave, he'd finished the tower and the large oak beside it.

I tucked it into my bag. "We'll show it to your Mommy."

He was quiet for a moment. Then he turned to me. "I don't want to go home."

"Things will be better," I said, wanting to believe.

Signora was leaning against the building when we arrived. Her face was shiny with sweat. There were stains under her arms.

"You lied," she said. "Your sister was much further along."

I thought she'd say that she sent Caterina home. Or that she needed more money before proceeding. Instead, she opened the door and gestured that I should follow. Sebu trailed behind.

The moment I stepped inside, I smelled it. That metallic, slightly-sweet smell of blood. In the kitchen, Caterina was laid out on the table. I'd never seen her so pale.

"I gave her some medicine to help with the pain," Signora said.

I waited for her to assure me that my sister would be all right. A day or two, and she'd be back on her feet. Instead, she repeated that I'd lied about my sister's condition.

I started to say that I was just repeating what Caterina had told me. But I wanted to get her and Sebu out of here.

"You'll need a cab." Signora shoved Caterina's shawl at me. "Go to Second Avenue. I don't want anyone to see you leaving here."

"That's almost a block away."

Ignoring me, Signora pulled up my sister by her arms. Caterina's head lolled back. Her eyes were half-open, but she didn't respond. I asked Signora what was wrong with her.

"I couldn't have her in here screaming," she said. "I gave her morphine."

I reached into my pocket. I had no money for the fare. Signora must have seen, too.

"Here." She motioned that I should hold up Caterina. "I'll give you the fare." She reached for a cigar box on top of her icebox and took out a one-dollar bill. She handed it to me.

"I'll pay you back."

"Just go."

Sebu and I managed to drag Caterina to Second Avenue. At the corner, we propped her against the gas lamp. I stepped into the street and tried to wave down a cab. No one stopped, until I took the dollar bill from my pocket and held it up. A ridiculous price to pay for a nickel ride. But it worked. A cabbie slowed, then stopped. Sebu and I wrestled Caterina inside.

I ignored the nosy cabbie's questions about Caterina, and spent the ride holding her head so it wouldn't bang against the back window. After an impossibly long time, the driver pulled in front of Caterina's apartment building. Sebu and I struggled to get her out of the cab. For a moment, I wondered if we should just go to the hospital. But surely, Signora would have told us if that was necessary. We nearly lost our footing on the hallway stairs. I had a vision of the three of us landing in a heap at the bottom. I thanked the Madonna when we finally got her to the apartment.

After we'd helped her into bed—her arms and legs like a ragdoll's—I saw that Sebu's cheeks were wet. He was just a boy. I should tell him everything would be fine. But I couldn't.

I made some tea for my sister, but when I held the cup to her lips, it just dribbled down her chin. She began thrashing at the air, screaming at me to get off her. I didn't want to think about what would happen when the morphine wore off. I rummaged in the bed table drawer, but there were only empty vials.

"We need to find your Daddy," I told Sebu. I lightly tied my sister's wrists and ankles to the bedposts so she wouldn't fall from the bed. Then I took Sebu and we headed for Stella's.

Even before Stella could open the door all the way, I blurted out that Caterina was sick and that I needed to find Bartu.

Stella took her shawl off the hook and wrapped it around her shoulders. "I'll go to Margaret's. If he's not there, she'll know where to look. In the meantime, go home. You look exhausted. I'll let you know when I find him." She reached out and brushed a lock of hair from my face. I started to crumble, then remembered I needed to be strong. I took Sebu's hand. Together, we started back toward my apartment.

CHAPTER 53

ONLY BAD NEWS COMES AT NIGHT. That's what Nonna always said.

At first, I thought I was dreaming. But the buzzer was too loud. Too insistent. I pried Sebu's fingers from my arm and got up.

"Let me in!" Bartu's voice. Panicked. "I need help!" I ran to the front door and threw it open. I didn't have time to ask what had happened.

"It's Caterina," Bartu cried. "The pain—." His voice broke.

Mamma appeared from the bedroom, yawning. "It's just her monthlies. I suffered like that. Wait. I'll get the hot water bottle."

"No!" Bartu cried. "Something's wrong."

When I saw how distraught he was, I felt a pang of guilt. I'd been telling myself he was a bad man—that my sister would be better off without him.

"I need help," he repeated, his eyes ghoulish in the lamplight. "Please." I don't think I'd ever heard Bartu use that word. It was that, more than what he said about my sister, that made me act.

Before I left, I went to the daybed and crouched beside Sebu. His arms were at his sides, like one of those lead toy soldiers in the window of Woolworth's. "I'll be back soon," I promised. I kissed the top of his head.

I heard my sister as soon as we walked into the apartment vestibule. A high-pitched keening that reminded me of when Pappa's favorite mare broke her foreleg. I'd almost been relieved when Pappa put a bullet between her velvety ears.

The bedroom door was ajar, light seeping along the frame. Beyond it, my sister was waiting. I wanted to run away. But I could hear Nanna's voice, reminding me that Caterina was my responsibility.

Caterina was kneeling on her bed, clutching her sheets. Her brow was hot. She was breathing too fast—panting, really—and her skin was bluish and mottled.

I called Bartu. "Bring me a pot of water and a rag." There was the squeak of the faucet and the running of water. I turned to Caterina. "You have a fever. We have to bring it down." Bartu put the pot and rag on the floor. I began to sponge off Caterina's face and neck. Gingerly, I pulled down the covers. There, on the front of her nightgown, was a swath of crimson. As I was puzzling out that it was blood—her blood—she began to writhe from side to side. That's when I saw it. A pool of yellow-tinged pus beneath her.

From the doorway, Bartu asked what was wrong with her.

The midwife made us swear we would tell no one. "I don't know," I lied.

Suddenly, Caterina cried out again.

I frantically searched the top of her bed table. When I could find nothing—no vials, or pills, or powder—I started dumping out the dresser drawers, spilling their contents onto the floor. When I could still find nothing, I turned to Bartu. "She needs morphine. Where is it?"

He shook his head.

"All those drugs you gave her. To keep her quiet. Where are they?"

He turned his palms up. Empty.

I don't know what came over me. Suddenly I was hitting him—his face, his arms, his chest. Because here he stood, the smell of Margaret Kelly's cheap perfume on his jacket, while my sister lay here bleeding.

Caterina bolted up. "Help me, goddamn you!" She was thrashing around, her eyes wild.

Bartu turned toward the door. "I'll get some medicine." Though I'd just been furious with him—and still was, to tell the truth—and though Caterina needed the morphine, I didn't want him to go. I guess he saw it, too.

"I'll be back soon," he promised, before the door closed behind him.

I'd almost wished Pappa was here with us and not in Alabama, or wherever he was.

As the minutes and hours passed, I told myself Bartu hadn't abandoned us. He'd gone to find medicine that would take away Caterina's pain. In the morning, I'd get Signora. I'd offer her so much money she couldn't say no. She'd know what to do. Caterina would get better.

Near morning, Caterina quieted. When I touched her forehead, she was cool. I tried to look past her strange breathing—a few fast breaths followed by nothing—and her clammy skin. The prayer came to me. *Hail Mary, full of grace, the Lord is with thee.* The words were like marbles in my mouth. I got down on my knees beside the bed. *Blessed art thou among women. And blessed is the fruit of thy womb, Jesus.* I dug my nails into my palms. The fruit of my sister's womb—her unborn baby—torn from her by the abortionist. *Holy Mary, Mother of God, pray for us sinners, now and at the hour of our death.*

Please, Madonna. Let my sister live. I'd stay in New York. Give up Stella. Stop wanting to make art. When Caterina's breathing grew more erratic, I offered up my life in place of hers.

After an impossibly long time, I heard Bartu's key in the lock. He went on his knees beside Caterina and plunged a syringe into her arm.

Caterina's breathing slowed. I told myself she'd sleep. When she woke, she'd feel better. Then I saw it. A new blood splatter, seeping through the sheet that covered her. Deep red at the center, wet and viscous. Smeared at the edges. Like that engraving of the cloud nebula Stella had shown me in the newspaper. Spiraling through the universe, spinning off bits of stardust. I eased down the sheet. The smell was overpowering. The room began to spin. I grasped the bedrail so I wouldn't pass out.

I don't know why, but I thought of Dr. Florio in his crisp, white coat. It must have been hard to keep that clean, with all the cutting and suctioning he did.

Dr. Florio, with his satchel full of bandages and antibiotics.

"We need to get Caterina to a doctor."

Bartu stared at me open-mouthed, like I was speaking a foreign language. Then he seemed to understand. "There's a hospital on 125th. Near the park."

In one motion, Bartu swept Caterina from the bed. I tried to tuck in the blanket around her so that people couldn't see. It suddenly seemed very important that my sister have her dignity. But it did little use. The blood seeped down Bartu's pants and onto the floor, leaving a trail down the steps and into the vestibule. He was running and I was trying to keep up, wheezing in the humid morning air. As Caterina's blood fell onto the sidewalk, it splattered, like paint on a new canvas. A grisly trail, block after block, ending finally at the doors of the hospital, where she was wheeled away on a gurney, the emergency room doors swinging closed behind her.

CHAPTER 54

HERE'S WHAT I REMEMBER: Pappa showing up at the hospital waiting room, travel satchel still in hand. The relief as he sat down next to me. Then the shame, as he came to understand what had happened. Walking out of the hospital late that afternoon, the song of crickets filling the air. Pappa hurrying ahead, as if he didn't want me to follow—as if he wanted nothing to do with me at all. People rushing by, laughing, talking, oblivious to what had happened. The world spinning on its axis, as if nothing had changed.

Caterina was twenty-four; I was thirty-two. I'd been the first one to hold her when she was born. I'd helped her learn to embroider. We'd knelt beside Rosalia's grave together. I'd been with her when she became a bride. A mother. I should have a million memories of her. But walking back to the apartment, all I could think of were those last, terrible hours. How the orderly had finally ushered us from the waiting room, through those swinging doors. How I tried not to gawk at the man holding a blood-soaked rag where his hand should have been, or the old woman, tied to her bed frame and babbling incoherently.

And how I—not Pappa or Bartu—was led through another, smaller door at the back of the ward. My sister lying there, her filthy nightgown hitched up to her thighs. I wanted to tug it down and wipe away the brownish drool trickling from the corner of her mouth. But someone was holding me back.

I turned and saw a badge. A gun. A cop started asking who'd done this to Caterina. But I'd promised Signora that I'd tell no one.

He threatened that if I didn't tell, the doctors wouldn't treat Caterina. I was harboring a criminal. I'd go to jail. What would happen to Sebu? I guess I already knew my sister wouldn't be there.

Caterina cried out, her eyes wide. She was panting. Starving for air. Long ago, I'd known that terror. Dr. Florio saved me with his knife. Please, I prayed, let someone save my sister.

"Just two names," a second cop demanded. "The woman who did this—." How did they know it was a woman? "—and whoever told you about her. Two people—." He held up two fingers "And we can help your sister."

Caterina's breath was ragged. Her lips were blue. I should have known it was hopeless. But how could I do nothing, when she might still survive? Or at least not die in pain, the small voice inside whispered.

Two names. Signora Brasi was easy. But Stella—how could I betray her?

"Ever been in jail?" one cop asked. "Too hot in the summer; too cold in the winter. Not the place for someone like you." He touched his chest, leaving no doubt about what he meant.

"Your father says there's a boy," the other one offered. "If something happens, he'll go live with his father, I guess. Shame, though. Your father says the two of you are close." Sebu, living with Bartu and Margaret. What if they didn't want him? Storybooks are filled with motherless children left to fend for themselves.

"Just two names," the other cop reminded. "Don't you want them to pay for what they've done?"

My sister began to thrash around, her tongue lolling from her mouth. An animal in pain.

"What do you owe them, really?" one of the men may have asked.

I didn't owe Signora anything. But Stella had loved me. Believed in me. More than anyone ever had.

Pappa appeared beside me. "Please. Mimi—."

"Help us take care of your sister." The cop held out the pen. "Two names and we'll give her the medicine to stop the pain."

I reminded myself. Stella was leaving New York on Tuesday. That was, what—two or three days from now? By the time the police discovered where she lived, she'd probably be gone. And the police would have Signora. That's who they really wanted.

I scratched the names on the cop's pad of paper. Soon after, a nurse appeared, holding a metal device that looked like a spoon strainer, though it was lined with gauze. She poured a bottle of something sweet-smelling on the gauze. It reminded me of the kind of solvent I'd use to clean paint brushes or wipe down a copper plate. When the nurse placed it over Caterina's nose and mouth, my sister tried to push her away. But a moment later, Caterina's hands fell to her side and she was still.

The nurse stepped away. I rushed to my sister. I pressed my fingers against her wrist, the way I'd seen Dr. Florio do. Her heartbeat was weak, like a piece of thread pulled slowly through muslin.

I had to have known her time was near. I'd been there with Nonna and baby Nino. I'd seen the dusty blue cast of their lips and fingertips. I'd heard that terrible rattling in their chests. But all I could think of was that yesterday, she'd been so desperate to live that she'd accepted eternal damnation. She couldn't be here now, her breathing shallow, her skin the color of a thundercloud.

Her eyelids fluttered open.

"Take care of my boy," she whispered.

"Please," I cried. "Don't go." Hadn't I uttered the same words at Rosalia's graveside? I was squeezing Caterina's hands hard, but she didn't seem to feel it.

My sister looked at me for a moment, like she was deciding. Then her whole face relaxed. And though her eyes were still on mine, she was seeing something far away.

CHAPTER 55

IF I HAD OILS AND A CANVAS, maybe I could paint that image and I'd have peace. Her chestnut hair, matted and dark with sweat. Her belly, still round—how could she still look pregnant?—under that bloody sheet.

Others, too.

The gravediggers, leaning on their spades as they waited to lower Caterina's casket into that gaping wound in the earth. That first winter. My sister, shivering beneath the snow. Pappa's flushed cheeks, his bulging neck veins, as he screamed that I'd made an orphan of Sebu.

And Rosalia, in her grave on cemetery hill at *Binvinutu*. Lying amidst all those strangers, past and future, who'd made claim to the estate.

I only needed a few colors to paint those images. White. Red. Black. Even a beginner had those paints in their box.

CHAPTER 56

WHEN PAPPA RETURNED from his morning walk, he didn't kiss the top of Mamma's head, like he usually did. Instead, he slapped the folded newspaper on the table. He pointed at a news story at the bottom of the page.

"That bitch is finally going to jail."

I felt a jolt of terror, then remembered that Stella had gotten out, and the police had no idea where she'd gone.

Pappa pointed to the newspaper. "Fifteen to twenty years. We won't see Signora Brasi again."

Mamma gave a look of disgust. "She should have been shot for what she did. Making an orphan of a little boy."

Sebu froze, farina dripping from his spoon. He wasn't an orphan. Bartu was still alive. But he was living downtown with his *puttana*. I thought of them sitting at the pew in front of us at Midnight Mass. His arm around her shoulder. Her new gold wedding ring glinting in the dim light. Bartu hadn't come around since Caterina's funeral repast, when Sebu had found his lighter and set fire to the edge of his overcoat. I still shuddered, thinking about what might have happened had I not gone into the bedroom to check on him.

Pappa motioned for me to pour him some espresso. I'd once been his daughter. Now I was his servant.

He touched the newspaper. "Death's too good for her. She should suffer for what she did."

"She'll get her punishment in hell." Maybe it was Caterina's death, or the new church Mamma had started to attend, but these days, Mamma only came to life when she was talking about eternal damnation.

The fires of hell. That's where I was headed. Mamma said it at least once a day. I didn't care. Knowing what I'd done to my sister—that was worse than any cosmic punishment God or the Devil could devise. I'd almost hoped they would send me to jail for my part. At least then I wouldn't have to bear my parents' anger or Sebu's gut-wrenching sadness.

Pappa, long accustomed to others' judgments, conferred the most terrible penalty. I was to live there with no pencils or paper, no art of any kind, and care for Sebu. It was my job to hold the boy at night when the terrible dreams returned, and in the morning, when he woke, remembering again that Caterina was gone. To experience, day after day, his pain. There was no worse punishment. But I accepted it. I owed it to my sister, buried in that pine box. Cut from breasts to privates, her organs taken out and reassembled, like some freakish doll.

Mamma pulled the paper to herself. "Does it say anything about that Stella Frauto woman?"

Pappa shook his head. "But she can't hide forever. And when the cops find her, they'll lock her up and throw away the key." Pappa pantomimed turning a key and tossing it over his shoulder. Then he looked to me, maybe to see my reaction.

But I wasn't the same girl Nonna long ago said held her heart in her hand. In the year since Caterina had died, I'd learned to hide my feelings. It was better this way. I mean, what could I say? Pappa hated Stella. I think it was because she dared to have a life of her own and didn't settle for other people's crumbs. Or maybe because she'd tricked me into believing I could have a life, too. She'd taken advantage of me, those copper plates no less compelling than Hades' pomegranate seeds. But I'd chosen, that small voice inside whispered. It wouldn't do any good to tell Pappa that.

I turned to Sebu. "Are you ready for school?"

He slid out of his chair, then put his book bag over his shoulder.

Mamma asked if he had his prayer book. He nodded.

"Don't forget, you have catechism class afterwards." First Holy Communion. Mamma would insist on new clothes for all of us. Now, appearances mattered more to her than ever before.

Pappa patted Sebu's head. "Work hard at school, Sebu. Make us proud. And you," Pappa said, not bothering to even look at me, "come home as soon as you drop him off."

After leaving Sebu at school, I walked back along streets thronged with morning shoppers. Women, empty market baskets and string bags slung over their arms; men, walking purposefully to the subway or the bus. Assuming that today would be just like yesterday and the countless days before. Not yet seeing that one day, everything would change and their old lives would be unrecognizable. I'd once been like that, thinking I had all the time in the world to paint my one big masterpiece, or to draw that mountain lake. Now I knew differently.

Back home, the apartment was empty. I touched the radiator. Cold. When I was home alone, which was often, Pappa didn't waste the coal. Maybe he hoped the consumption would finally take me. Or maybe I was like a servant—a fieldworker or maid—out of mind once the work was done.

I straightened the blankets on the daybed, the warmth of Sebu's body long since dissipated. I tried not to think about the way he nestled into my neck. Or how, half-asleep, he called me Mommy. Those were pleasures I didn't deserve. I pulled the bed away from the wall. I got down on my knees and tapped the floor gently. First hollow; then solid, over the place I'd hidden the satchel with the burins and Stella's money. I thought again, as I had a hundred times, that I should surrender it to Pappa. Because as long as I had those things, I could still think of California and Stella. A few times, I'd even gotten a knife from the kitchen drawer and started to pry off the nails. But something kept me from doing it. So the satchel stayed in its place. Entombed.

I didn't allow myself to consider the alternative—taking the money and the burins and leaving for good. I was responsible for Sebu. And the boy needed a man, even if it was Pappa, to help raise him. Pappa had had Zio's father to look out for him at that awful orphanage, to show him how to break a stallion and hunt for rabbits. Probably because of him, Pappa had been saved from the sulfur mines, a fate that few orphan boys escaped. If I took Sebu away, who would protect him and teach him what a man should be?

So I couldn't take Sebu, but I couldn't leave, either.

CHAPTER 57

"HAVE YOU EVER SEEN BABE RUTH?" Sebu asked Pappa. It was a frigid April morning. Winter still hadn't loosened its grip on the city. I had a cold I couldn't seem to shake. I wrapped my shawl more tightly around myself. Pappa hadn't mentioned the sanitarium since Caterina had died. But if I relapsed, he'd never risk Sebu's health. He'd send me north without a second thought. In that far-away sanitarium, what could I do for the boy?

Pappa stirred a sugar cube into his coffee, the spoon clinking against the side of the cup. He smiled slyly. "Babe Ruth? Sure. He's a big man. Strong. Not fat." To Pappa, fat meant undisciplined, lazy.

Sebu started fussing with the cuff of his sweater. I'd already darned one spot where he'd pulled the yarn loose. Pappa pushed his hand away. "Since when are you interested in baseball?"

Sebu shrugged. "The boys at school talk about it all the time."

Pappa shook his head. "It's a stupid game. Men in little-boy knickers. Trying to hit a small ball with a stick of wood." He pulled out his ledger and opened it. As usual, it was covered with columns of numbers.

"They call me a greaser." Sebu spoke so quietly I could hardly hear him.

Pappa responded that people are cruel. Another life lesson.

"They say I'm not American."

"Then they're stupid, too. You were born here. You can't get more American than that." Pappa's eyes narrowed. "Who are these boys? Maybe I should talk to your principal. This is a public school.

Everybody's welcome. Jews. Coloreds. Sicilians."

The boy's fingers found his cuff again. "It's the Sicilian boys who say it."

Pappa waved his hand dismissively. "They're jealous, that's all. While their ancestors were digging in the fields, yours were learning Latin."

Sebu looked away. What did it matter what some long-dead family members had done, when the boy felt so alone? Maybe Pappa saw it, too. He pulled the ledger closer to him.

"How are you with numbers?" Pappa asked.

Sebu shrugged, but we all knew he was gifted. The principal wanted Sebu to skip two grades in the fall.

"Look at this." Pappa pointed to the columns of numbers, then began to describe how he'd been figuring out the exchange rate for trucks sold to the French government.

"This is important work," he told Sebu. "They'll use these trucks to get the Krauts out of France once and for all. Look. Here's the price of the truck—fifteen hundred dollars in US dollars, and the exchange rate: five and a half francs to a dollar. So if the Frenchies buy one truck, how much do they have to pay in francs?"

Sebu closed his eyes, concentrating. After a moment, he gave the answer. "Eight thousand two hundred and fifty francs."

I'd seen him do this before at the grocers—adding up our bill without a pencil or paper. Still, when he came up with the correct answer, my chest expanded with pride.

Pappa's eyes got wide. "You did that in your head?"

The boy nodded, but cautiously, like maybe he'd done something wrong.

Pappa smiled. "That's impressive." The boy relaxed. "Soon you'll be working with me."

I felt a jolt of terror but told myself that Pappa couldn't possibly mean to involve the 8-year-old boy in his business, whatever it was. But he'd involved me. The engravings. The pomegranate logo. The earthquake telegrams. After I dropped Sebu at school, I headed toward the market. The air smelled musty—the scent of new life in spring—no less powerful than the smell of decay and death in autumn. I'd stopped at the greengrocers for some pussywillows when I heard two women talking.

"I tell you. It's not safe anywhere. That woman and her daughter. Gunned down in broad daylight."

"Did you see that picture in the newspaper? That little girl's shoe laying in the gutter?"

"Used to be, gangsters didn't go after each other's families. I guess that's changed."

Stella's words: Ciro Morello would make Pappa pay for his betrayal. I'd never considered that Sebu could be part of that payment.

I don't remember putting down the pussywillows or leaving the market. By the time I got home, I was out of breath and drenched in sweat.

When Pappa returned, I was waiting for him. I took his notepad and papers as he slipped out of his overcoat.

"Pappa," I started, "I overheard some women at the market today. They were talking about a woman and a little girl." I paused, trying to collect my thoughts.

"Yes?"

"Men with guns came. They shot them."

"It happens all the time. Innocent people caught in the crossfire. It can't be helped."

"It sounded intentional. Like the men meant to shoot them."

Pappa exhaled, annoyed. "I'm sure you heard it wrong. Why would anyone shoot a little girl?"

I had no answer. He was right. There was no reason anyone would kill a child. And wouldn't Stella have told me if Clutch and his brothers intended to kill Sebu?

Pappa asked, "Where's the morning mail?"

I handed him the mail-order circular. The ice man's bill. And a letter postmarked Massachusetts with no return address.

Pappa leafed through the post until he got to the letter.

"It's from Carlo," he said, excitedly. "I recognize his writing." He opened the envelope and began to smile.

"This is why we haven't heard from him! He's been on his honeymoon. That Carlo! He's a man who loves to be in love." As if Carlo hadn't stolen twenty thousand dollars from us.

"Where's your mother?" he asked.

"At noon Mass. She'll be home soon."

Pappa rubbed his hands together. "Good. Next Sunday we're going to have company. Carlo and his wife. It has to be perfect. Like in Partanna." But this apartment, with its mice scat in the corners and cockroaches skittering inside the walls, wasn't *Binvinutu*.

He met Mamma at the door. "We've had good news."

Mamma stepped back, the movement almost imperceptible.

He held up the telegram. "I've heard from Carlo."

"What does he want?"

"I know what you're thinking, Maria. But he's trying to make things up to me."

Mamma shrugged off her wet coat. "He stole your money."

My money. I thought.

Pappa took her coat. "I told you. It wasn't Ponzi's fault. It was an investment. And investments don't always work out. Anyway, he has a proposal."

Mamma raised an eyebrow. "What do you mean?"

"Something he wants my help with."

"Don't you already have a job?"

"What? You mean the exchange rates?" Pappa waved his hand in the air. "There's no challenge in it. I cut my teeth on that work, helping Vito's father figure out pasturage fees. No. I mean real work. Something new."

Mamma rolled her eyes. "What is it?"

"He didn't say in the telegram. But I'm sure it's good." Pappa smiled.

I lay awake most of the night, thinking not of that telegram, but of the little girl's shooting. By the time the anemic light from the air shaft had made its way across the linoleum, I'd almost convinced myself it was the mother's fault. She should have been more vigilant. Called for help when she saw those men coming. Ducked into a store. Told her girl to run. And if it came to it— if there was no other way—she should have used her own body as a shield.

I looked at Sebu, lying next to me. Just eight and he almost reached my shoulder. He'd be bigger than me soon. How would I keep him safe then?

CHAPTER 58

I'D NEVER MET SIGNORE PONZI, but I knew him by his confident step on the stairs, and the tapping of his walking stick on the landing.

He bowed first to Mamma, then to me. I took him at a glance: the impeccable morning coat and the straw hat pulled jauntily to the side. *Bella figura.* This was a man who cared about how he looked. His wife was pretty in a Gibson Girl kind of way, her hair tucked into a soft bouffant, her waist cinched tightly. But when Ponzi began to talk, he seemed to swallow up all the air in the room. His voice was loud. Animated. When he wanted to make a point—which was often—he tapped his stick, its large ruby topper glinting in the light.

"With America finally in the War," he said. "It'll soon be over. Germany's on its last leg."

Pappa nodded. We'd all been following the news. It was impossible not to. Overnight, posters had appeared on every street corner and subway kiosk, calling for men to enlist. Every day, newspapers screamed about another assault on the Hindenburg Line, or a U-boat being captured—hauled out of the water like some bloated metal fish.

"When it's done, people will want to get back to normal," Ponzi continued. "There's a lot of pent-up demand for goods from Europe. Wool from Britain. Perfume from France. Butter from Norway. And you, my dear Maria. What have you been missing?"

Mamma smiled shyly. "Swiss lace?" she offered.

"Of course. Ladies like you and my Rose should be dressed in the finest clothing." He ran his hand over the ruby topper, then turned to me. "And Mimi. Our artist. I was very impressed with those drawings you made for the coal stocks."

I waited for him to apologize for losing all our money. Instead, he just smiled, his toothy smile like a jackal's.

Mamma nudged me.

"Thank you, Signore Ponzi," I said.

Ponzi continued. "So Signorina. What have you been doing without?"

My freedom, I thought, but didn't say. The chance to draw, and paint, and dream.

"Burin bits? A whetstone? Chamois cloth?"

Later, I'd marvel that he knew about these things. Now, I just told him I wasn't an artist anymore.

Ponzi laughed. "Not an artist! That would be like me trying to stop being a businessman. No, Mimi—may I call you Mimi? I'd wager that being an artist is what you are most."

If Pappa wasn't there, maybe I'd have agreed. But I sat there, saying nothing.

Ponzi asked if he'd offended me. Pappa answered that my health was fragile. Touching his chest, he added that I needed to limit my activities.

"She seems healthy," Ponzi said. But the chair leg squeaked on the wood floor as Rose eased back a few inches.

Pappa explained. "It's tuberculosis. She can relapse at any time. Rest is the most important thing."

I thought about what Stella had said about how my family used the consumption to keep me in my place.

Ponzi's head tilted. "I didn't know that. I'm sorry."

Pappa shrugged. "Anyway, she's busy with the boy. My younger daughter's son."

Ponzi looked confused. "There's a boy?"

I was surprised. Could it be that Pappa hadn't told Ponzi about Sebu?

"My grandson," Pappa said. "His mother died."

Ponzi shook his head like he didn't understand. Quietly, he stood and walked to Mamma's chair. He took her hand. "You've lost your child?"

Mamma nodded.

Ponzi pressed her hand to his lips. "I'm sorry. I know this is difficult. I too have recently suffered a terrible loss." His voice broke. "My sainted mother." Ponzi pulled out a perfectly pressed handkerchief and wiped his eyes. "The angels sang in heaven when my mother passed. I'm sure it was the same with your daughter."

Mamma began to sob. Maybe she was remembering how Monsignor had refused Caterina a Catholic burial. She'd died in a state of mortal sin, unrepentant. There would be no heaven. No angels. Only the fires of hell. Monsignor had been clear about this.

Ponzi patted Mamma's hand. "One foot in front of the other, Signora. We have to go on."

Mamma continued to cry. Finally, Pappa cleared his throat, impatient.

Ponzi took the hint. "All this pain. This suffering. And those dead soldiers. The ones who return, missing limbs. Their faces burned, sometimes beyond recognition. People have had enough. They want to live again. Enjoy the things they enjoyed before the war. We can help them with that."

We. The word hung in the air.

Ponzi leaned back in his chair and clasped his hands behind his head. "'Doing well by doing good.' That's what we're after. I only hope that people can be half as happy as I am." He put his arm around his wife. "My Rose. My American beauty."

Rose blushed deeply. It was hokey. All of it. Still I felt an ember of jealousy, burning in my belly.

Pappa smiled a tight-lipped smile. "How can I help?"

Ponzi leaned forward and put his hand on Pappa's knee. "My *paisano.* I've been going up and down the East Coast, offering this special opportunity to people I trust."

I needed to use the water closet. But I didn't want to miss this. I crossed my legs and tried to focus on the conversation.

Ponzi continued. "I'm going to put all the export companies in one catalog. I'm calling it the Traders Guide. I'll distribute it to businesses all over the country. Companies with goods to sell will pay for advertisements. I've set a goal for myself—it's always good to have goals, right?"

Pappa smiled too broadly. "Yes, of course."

"I want to make a big splash. One hundred thousand advertisers for the first publication. Then double that number every six months. It'll be the biggest trade catalog in the world."

Pappa clapped his hands together. "That's brilliant, Carlo. As usual, you've come up with something no one else has thought of."

It was the kind of insipid compliment Pappa was always giving Zio Vito.

"What I do, I do for the people I love." Ponzi put his hand on Rose's.

Pappa smiled. "What other reason is there?"

If I stayed there another moment, I'd scream. I stood and excused myself. When I returned from the water closet, Ponzi was writing in a notebook with a bright red cover.

"In terms of exports, we're looking for American companies that sell things that are in demand in Europe. Radios. Cotton. Electric ice boxes." He ticked off these items in his notebook. "Know anyone who makes any of these?"

Pappa appeared to think about this but I could have told Ponzi. Pappa might be good for doing calculations. But as far as I know, he never left our neighborhood. If anyone made these things—electric ice boxes?—they were downtown, not here. After a few tense minutes, Pappa said he'd ask around.

Ponzi smiled. "Don't stress yourself, my friend. I think I know someone back in Alabama. I already have someone in Boston for the radios. I just wanted to let you in on the ground level." Ponzi was quiet for a moment. Then he put his hand on his forehead, like he'd just remembered something. "What about your son? Maybe he could help find people. Doesn't he work on Wall Street?"

His son? I waited for Pappa to correct Ponzi. Bartu was his son-in-law, and he was married to another woman now. He worked in a barbershop, not on Wall Street. But Pappa promised that he'd ask Bartu when he saw him. He didn't tell Ponzi that it had been months since Bartu had been to see Sebu. Or that Bartu's new wife was pregnant.

"Good. Good." Ponzi crossed one foot over the other. "That'll be a help. But the real reason I came to see you was to talk about imports. That was your biz, right? When you first came here?"

I thought Pappa would talk about his grocery. How it had been the largest one in the neighborhood. He just nodded.

Ponzi continued. "You still have contacts in Sicily? Olive oil. Almonds. Silk. These are the big imports. When we were in Atlanta, you told me you knew Vito Cascioferro. He was a bigwig in the import/export business a few years ago. Didn't you say you were boys together?"

"That was a long time ago."

"When men are boys together, they can never be completely out of each other's lives. You should reach out to him. Ask if he wants to be included in the Trade Journal."

All those unanswered letters and telegrams to Zio—if there'd been a bond, it had been severed when Pappa went to prison. I guess it was to be expected. All those money-grams we'd sent to his factory. A tidal wave of fake five-dollar bills returned to him. I still wondered if all that attention had gotten Zio in trouble.

Ponzi pressed Pappa. "What do you say, Nino? It could be good for you. And I'm sure Signore Cascioferro would appreciate it."

At that moment, I understood what so many would learn about Ponzi in the next few years. He could make even the impossible seem inevitable. He could ask you to cut off your nose to spite your face and you'd go running to get the knife. I wasn't really surprised when Pappa agreed to post the letter.

Ponzi grasped Pappa's hands. "Thank you, my friend. I knew I could rely on you." Ponzi rose. Pappa followed. They shook hands one last time. Then Ponzi and his wife were gone.

"That Ponzi!" Mamma said, just as the door was closing behind our guests. "You didn't tell me how charming he is. And smart. Descended from nobility, like us." She tilted up her chin. "That wife, though. Quiet as a church mouse. How can a man like that be satisfied with such a little nothing?"

Pappa went to the drawer where he kept his stationery and took out a sheet.

"I'll write to Vito. Offer him the opportunity to be in Ponzi's directory. In exchange, maybe he can help with Clutch and Ciro."

My stomach dropped. That mother and her little girl. I couldn't get them out of my mind.

Mamma told him he was wasting his time. "He'll ignore you. Like always."

This time, when Pappa glared at Mamma, she didn't back down, as she usually did. He finally broke eye contact and set his pen to paper.

It must have been a brief note, judging by how quickly Pappa wrote it. When he was done, he sealed it in an envelope and addressed it to Zio. He put it on the coat stand near the door. After he'd gone for his afternoon walk, I took it from the stand.

Signore Vito Cascioferro, the first address line read. But it wasn't addressed to his Palermo factory—I knew that address by heart because of the earthquake telegrams. Instead, Pappa was sending it to Zio's home in Bisacquino. Strange. When Zio wasn't meeting Pappa or his other associates at their homes throughout the countryside, he was in his Palermo office. I'd never known him to do business at his home. I had a sick feeling in my stomach. There was something Pappa wasn't telling us about Zio. And I had a sinking suspicion it would bear on the kind of protection Zio could offer from Clutch and his brother.

That summer, we waited.

We waited for the rain to stop; the war to end, and the troops to return. We waited for the lingering sickness the newspapers called the Spanish flu to finally disappear. But most of all, we waited to hear from Zio Vito. We tightrope-walked through each day, at any moment expecting Ciro Morello to show up and demand his revenge. Every move—a trip to the grocer, a walk in the park—felt like it was fraught with danger.

It couldn't go on.

But it did.

Sebu felt it, too. He slept fitfully, tossing and turning, and sometimes calling out for Caterina. Most mornings, I found him curled up on the floor next to our daybed. The rain and cold were even more disorienting. The sunlight should be blinding; the heat, oppressive.

In October, people began to die. The newspapers assured the Spanish flu was confined to transports of soldiers returning from Europe. That while it was gaining—even more widespread as the month progressed—it wasn't severe. But I watched out the window as an elderly widow in the first-floor apartment was carried out on a stretcher. Then the three-year old daughter of our superintendent, Mr. Cranch. He took to the drink after that, the smoky smell from his home-made still filling the hallway. Finally, our next-door neighbor, Max Sugarman, the youngest of the Sugarman boys. His army uniform hung on the front door of the apartment, a black crepe ribbon on the hanger. He'd been waiting to ship out to France. Death found him here instead.

The schools were open. But by the end of the month, Pappa had decided Sebu would stay home. I was relieved. Not so much for me—if the consumption returned now, so be it—but for Sebu. Determined not to let Sebu fall behind, Pappa brought home a paper bag filled with pencils and paper. Every morning, he'd fill several pages with equations to be answered. When I asked about other subjects, like reading and penmanship, Pappa brushed aside my concerns. "Mathematics. That's all the boy needs."

But that wasn't true.

One morning, I found Sebu doodling on his math pages. He tried to hide the paper when he saw me looking.

"Nonno will be angry," he whispered. I was surprised at first. I'd thought the boy was too young to know what Pappa was doing when he threw away my sketch pads and pencils the afternoon we returned from burying Caterina. But the apartment was too small to have secrets.

I moved his hands away from the sketch. There, on the edges of that paper, filled from left to right with addition, subtraction, multiplication and division problems, Sebu had drawn great flourishes and curlicues. They reminded me of van Gogh's *Starry Night*. I sat down next to the boy and pulled out a fresh piece of paper from Pappa's ledger. I slid it toward him.

Sebu put pencil to paper and began to draw, not stopping for lunch or tea or even to sharpen his pencil. Now, he seemed to draw without thinking of whether it was good or correct, or whether people would like it. I'd once been like that—before the talk of the Academy, or Zio's logo, or the five-dollar bill. Art for its own sake—to convey what you couldn't say otherwise—I'd lost sight of that a long time ago.

While the outside world continued to spin out of control that October and November, I stayed at that table with Sebu, watching as he drew. Every morning and night, Pappa returned from the vestibule with no postcard or letter from Zio about Ponzi's catalog. He'd pour himself another glass of grappa and down it quickly. Then he'd retire to the bedroom until it was time to eat whatever meager fare I'd managed to put together. Mamma's world grew smaller, too. Having expended her rage at Zio for abandoning us, she began to spend her days staring out the window and trying not to notice when Pappa slipped another goblet or piece of silverware in his bag to bring to the pawnbroker.

One early December morning, Pappa announced that he had an appointment. Before the door slammed behind him, he reminded me to check the mail.

I asked Mamma where he was going. She just turned up her nose at me. "You heard your father. Check the mail."

"Does he still think Zio might respond?" I asked.

She turned on me so swiftly that Sebu reflexively raised his hands over his head. It had been two years, but whatever he'd seen between Caterina and Bartu stayed with him.

"How is that your business?" Mamma asked.

I shrugged. "I'm just asking."

"It's your fault Vito isn't replying. He blames your father for your shenanigans with that Stella Frauto woman."

"Shenanigans?"

"The five-dollar bills," Mamma hissed. "Why couldn't you just stay in your place? That was Vito's business. Not yours."

That was true. The shitty lime-green bills were Zio's. But the ones I'd made in the farmhouse—the ones in the perfect shade of jade-green, the president and Pilgrims exact copies of the real bill—were mine and Stella's.

"If not for you, we'd be on our way home." Mamma's expression was cold.

"Home? You mean to *Binvinutu*?"

"Palermo," she corrected. "We have people there who'd help."

Fair weather friends who suddenly appeared when Pappa got *Binvinutu* and disappeared just as quickly when he ran into trouble.

"What would Pappa do there?"

"He'd work with Vito again. Signore Cascioferro—Vito's father— told your Pappa that there'd always be a place for him."

"What about the rest of us?" I asked, wondering if there'd be work for me, too.

"What? You mean Sebu? There would be work for him, too. Especially if he has the Inglese name."

I'd been hoping Pappa would forget about changing the boy's name. Sebu'd had enough turmoil in the last few years.

"Do you forget, Mamma?" I asked. "All the young men in Partanna—all angling for a way to get out? There's no work there. No opportunity. That's why so many of them come to America."

Mamma tilted up her nose. "At least there, he'd be someone. Not a street sweeper or ditch digger, like here."

I was suddenly furious. "Who would he be, Mamma? The grandson of the Baron Inglese? It won't matter if he changes his name. No one cares about the Ingleses. Not anymore."

Mamma looked at me, her eyes wide. "Would you rather be Camastrino? Daughter of a bastard—a bastard herself? I can't believe you're this ungrateful. After everything Nonna sacrificed so we'd have this name. And Zio's father. And Zio. All of them made sure you and your sisters would want for nothing."

I wanted to scream at her. My sisters were dead. I was a consumptive. And all I really wanted was to be an artist. The very thing she and Pappa were denying me.

"Now we're alone." Mamma's voice cracked. "With no one to look out for us." We'd been alone a long time, though she refused to see it.

Lying in my bed that night, I thought about what Mamma said about us being alone. That might have been a good thing. Zio gone. Ponzi, too. Pappa forced to stand on his own feet, finally. Except that Pappa was a weak man. And as much as I wanted that to change, I didn't see it happening. Tomorrow, I'd talk with him about letting me get a job. I'd work for a newspaper, doing the photo engravings they used to print papers. Or make logos, like the pomegranate I'd done for Zio. Maybe we'd get away from New York City and start again somewhere else. Chart our own course, if only for Sebu's sake.

CHAPTER 59

But Pappa wasn't interested in leaving.

"New York's at the center of things," he said, one frigid morning just after the New Year. "It makes no sense to leave."

Our coal bin was nearly empty. No matter how much we conserved, we couldn't afford another delivery. Thankfully, Sebu was back in school, where the radiators hissed and pinged—the heat a safeguard against another wave of influenza. Though little good that would do if he spent the rest of his hours huddled under blankets in this apartment.

Pappa seemed to read my mind. "Don't worry, Mimi. Things are changing here. There are new opportunities. You'll see."

Pappa hadn't delivered Zio's business, but maybe Ponzi would have something for him anyway. "Will you be working on the Trade Journal?"

"No. I haven't heard from Ponzi. I guess it didn't work out." Pappa struck a match and lit his cigar. After he'd blown some rings, he leaned back in his chair. "That journal was too ambitious. A hundred thousand subscribers in the first six months." He laughed. "Ponzi always did dream big. It's harder to do that when you have a family."

That had never stopped Pappa.

"What's the new opportunity?" I asked.

"Patience, Mimi." Pappa smiled. I felt the warmth spread through me, then hated myself for how grateful I was for his crumbs of affection.

"Is it Bartu?" I muttered, afraid that saying his name too loudly would conjure him.

"No. But I heard his wife had her baby. A girl." Pappa pressed his hand to his mouth, as if trying to suppress a smile. "Oh, well. The woman is young. There's time for her to have a son."

I felt a surge of anger. I went to the dish drain to start drying the breakfast dishes but turned back. "What about Sebu?"

"A man wants many sons. Anyway, with Sebu living with us, it's just a matter of time before he becomes Inglese."

"Bartu will never allow Sebu to change his name."

"Boys become men. They make their own choices."

I bit the inside of my lip to keep myself from saying the obvious: Pappa was an old man. Yet he still did other men's bidding.

I needed to steer the conversation away from Bartu. "So what's the opportunity?" I asked again.

Pappa laughed. "You're like a dog with a bone, Mimi. Always have been." It didn't sound like a criticism so for the second time that morning, a wave of gratitude swept over me.

Pappa blew a smoke ring. Then another. "Remember when you thought these rings rose all the way up to heaven? And that angels floated on them?" Pappa smiled sadly.

Angels. Maybe he was thinking of Caterina. Or Nonna. They'd made mistakes. But if God was a fair judge, surely they'd reach heaven. I waited for his thoughts to turn back to whatever opportunity he was hinting at.

"I've finally found a job that matches my talents," he said, finally.

I nodded, waiting for him to continue.

"The currency calculations are good. But I need something more challenging. And lucrative."

He blew another smoke ring.

"I'm going to be working for some men who run the lottery."

I nodded. I'd seen the boys hanging around the bocce ball court, jotting numbers into small yellow notebooks. Stella told me they were runners. The whole thing was rigged, but the cops didn't care as long as it stayed in Harlem.

"I calculate the payouts on bets," Pappa said. "That's how much the bookie needs to pay if a bet wins and how much he needs to collect if it loses."

"Is Ciro involved?" I blurted out. The Morellos were never far from my mind.

Pappa snorted. "He's busy with his artichokes. No. The guy who runs this operation is smooth. Cultured. Toto D'Aquila. He's from Palermo." As if that explained everything.

I couldn't help myself. I asked if he knew Zio.

Pappa stabbed out his cigar. Ignoring my question, he said that he and Toto understood each other. This time, things would work out. His words seemed measured, but his voice had gone up an octave.

For the next few months things went well. Pappa came home each night, a spring in his step, his wallet stuffed with bills. One afternoon, as Sebu and I sat drawing at the kitchen table, we heard Pappa's key in the lock. I quickly covered our drawings with yesterday's newspapers. Then I stood and waited for Pappa to come into the kitchen.

He went to the coffee can where he kept his extra cash and pulled out some bills. After he'd slipped them into his vest pocket, he came to the table. Too late, I saw the corner of Sebu's picture, poking out from underneath the newspaper.

Pappa extracted the paper. "What's this?"

The boy's cheeks turned pink.

Pappa brought the paper closer. "Oh. I see. It's a plane. Is it the one that flew across the ocean last year?"

Sebu nodded.

"Hmm. It looks like a boat with wings. And I like how it's bobbing up and down in the water."

Sebu had an artist's eye—intuitively picking up the scale of the plane and the fluid line between the hull and the wave crests.

"It's a seaplane."

"And it flew all the way to Britain." Pappa smiled. "Amazing, isn't it? A boat that becomes a plane, and then a boat again. Neither fish nor fowl, as Shakespeare would say."

As Pappa studied the drawing, I thought how much he and I were like that seaplane. He, abandoned to the orphan's wheel with a silver coin tucked into his blanket. I, an artist whose biggest accomplishment was making counterfeit bills.

Pappa looked at me. "You were drawing, too."

I held my breath as Pappa swept the newspapers from the table, uncovering my drawings. I'd been doing small sketches of the shadow cast on the water by the seaplane's wing, and the roundness of the plane's nose. I'd just begun to sketch the turn of the rudder—perpendicular lines extending from the back of the vessel.

I steeled myself for his anger.

He passed the paper back to me. "This looks so real. But you need better paper. Graphite pencils. I'll get some for you. For both of you."

My jaw dropped open. Before I could figure out how to respond, Sebu thanked him.

"You're welcome, my boy." Pappa tousled Sebu's hair. "It's good to have a skill like this. You never know when it'll come in handy."

I should have been relieved. But there was something about Pappa's words—that my art, or worse, Sebu's, might be useful—that made my blood run cold. I told myself Pappa was just making conversation. Bookmaking was about numbers. He didn't need sketches of seaplanes or oceans. But when he'd arranged for me to go to Monsieur Laurent's *atelier* so long ago, who would have guessed I'd use those skills to make logographs for Zio? Or later, when we were aflush with Zio's crummy bills, that I'd be writing bogus telegrams? Or then, having grown accustomed to breaking the law, that I'd willingly (and happily) travel out to Stella's farmhouse to make my five-dollar bills?

It was impossible to predict where one step would lead. But sitting there at that table, I knew I'd never be free of Pappa's hold as long as I stayed here. And with Sebu depending on me, and no means of leaving New York, here I'd stay.

I was still thinking about the twists and turns my life had taken when I retrieved the mail a few weeks later and found a letter addressed to me, in a hand I knew better almost as well as my own. Stella. Quickly, because it was morning and people were hurrying in and out of the building, I slipped the envelope in my skirt pocket. As usual, Pappa was at the bookmaker's. I made myself wait until Mamma left for Mass. My heart pounding in my ears, I sat on the daybed and opened it.

Inside was a postcard. No letter or instructions. Only a photograph of a room with women seated at long tables. Their hands were busy, but they turned to look at the photographer as he snapped his picture. Smiling. Content. I turned over the postcard. Monterey Canning Company, Monterey, California, the back read. Relief washed over me. Stella was safe. Living somewhere in California.

Without thinking about it, I crawled under the table. I pried open the floorboard and pulled out the money Stella had given me for a ticket. More than fifty dollars in ones and fives, tucked into my burin box. I wanted to put the postcard in, too. But it would be too risky. I tucked it back into my pocket. I'd dispose of it later.

The next morning, after I dropped Sebu at school, my feet found their way to the subway steps. I hadn't planned it but I started down. The newly tiled walls were glossy white. Unmarred. There was one long staircase—as high as our tenement—then another. Still, down I went. Under the city streets, into the underworld. I reached the ticket booth.

I asked the clerk how to get to Grand Central Station. He signaled toward a map on the wall. The Lexington Avenue line bisected Manhattan, running north to 125th and south to Bowling Green. Grand Central Depot was marked with a square. I counted the stops—there were seven stations between here and there. I took a nickel from my pocket—Pappa wouldn't miss it from the coffee can where he kept money for food shopping—and returned to the ticket counter.

The clerk passed me the ticket. "That's the southbound train. The next one will be along in a few minutes."

I thanked him and followed the other riders toward the platform. There I stood, waiting. It was cooler deep under the city streets. Though every once in a while, a hot blast would gust through the tunnel, reminding me of the sirocco winds in Sicily. I tried not to think of all that weight above me. If it collapsed, like Pappa's mine, there'd be no surviving. Still, people milled around as if there weren't tons of dirt and pavement and people above us. Finally, I saw the headlight of the train in the tunnel. Wheels screeching, it ground to a stop. I got on. Found a spot on a wicker bench near the window and then started counting down the stations.

The Grand Central station was well-marked. I walked up one flight of stairs and entered an immense room with a soaring, barrel ceiling. It was so bright, especially after being underground. My eyes adjusted. The ceiling was painted cerulean—a perfect greenish blue. There was an overlay of delicate zodiacs and thousands of stars, some of them lit up. It was one of the most beautiful things I'd ever seen.

There was a sound, like the clacking of pebbles on the beach as the waves retreated. I looked over. A huge board with *DEPARTURES* across the top, city names disappearing and reappearing as trains came and went. I looked for Monterey. It wasn't there.

"Can I help you, miss?" A tall man with white hair and a handlebar mustache stood before me. "I'm a White Cap." He touched the brim of his hat. "I can answer any questions you may have."

I pointed at the board. "I'm looking for Monterey."

"Yes, of course." He pulled out a card and consulted it. "You board the 20th Century Limited to Chicago. You transfer there to the Overland Limited and take that to San Francisco. From San Francisco, you take a local train, the Del Monte, to Monterey."

Stella had mentioned Chicago and something about California.

"It's so complicated," I said, aloud.

The porter lowered the card. He smiled kindly. "You just have to remember the Twentieth Century and the Overland. You buy your Del Monte ticket in San Francisco, so you don't have to think about that now."

I nodded. Two trains. I could remember that.

"It departs at 7:40 a.m. You can buy your ticket at the window." He pointed to a row of arched windows." And because I must have looked like I needed to know, he offered that the tickets were twenty-four dollars—or thirty-seven if I wanted a Pullman car.

Twenty-four dollars per ticket. I'd have enough money for both Sebu and me. I knew it was ridiculous. I couldn't take the boy. But there was Caterina's face, gray, twisted in pain. Asking me to take care of Sebu. And there was the apartment—no money for coal or food. Pappa chasing after another sure thing. Praising Sebu for his numbers or his sketches, assessing how to make best use of him.

As I walked back to the subway, I passed a metal trash can and pulled out the postcard. My only link to Stella. How could I part with it? I touched its surface and felt Stella's smooth skin; its corners brought back the angle of her elbows, the bend of her knees. I held it to my nose, imagining I was breathing in Stella's musky smell.

I looked at the women on the front of the card. Stella said it was different out there. Women could make their own decisions. This could be my life. Our life.

What harm would it do to keep the postcard just a little while longer? I started to put it back in my pocket, then stopped myself. As long as I had this postcard, with its image of Cannery Row, Stella was exposed. Tears in my eyes, I ripped it in half, then quarters and eighths. By the time I'd reached the subway stairs, the card was gone. All the way back, I repeated the names of the trains—the 20th Century. The Overland. When the time came, I'd know what to do.

CHAPTER 60

I STEPPED OUT ONTO THE PAVEMENT, strewn with crimson leaves. That color. Blood-red tinged with purple; their edges, amber.

I turned onto Lexington, toward Sebu's school. The sidewalks were bustling. The line outside the pharmacy stretched around the corner. As I passed, I heard people talking about Prohibition. They'd stock up on liquor now. It would be illegal soon. And expensive. Pappa liked to say that people always find a way to satisfy their vices. The do-gooders might have thought they'd accomplished something by banning alcohol, but in New York City, the law was usually beside the point.

Back at home, Sebu pulled out his homework. I started dinner. Mamma was reading the *Ladies Home Journal*, its lead story about the Spring fashions. I glanced over at the floorboard. Nestled underneath, alongside the satchel with my burins and Stella's money, was a sketch I'd done the last time I'd visited Caterina's grave. The limestone angel, standing sentry atop her headstone. The sweep of her arms, open in embrace; her eyes, soft; her smile, gentle. The sculptor had gotten her expression just right—a mix of pathos and welcome. Intended as much for the mourners as for the dead. Once I left New York City, I might never see it again. At least I'd have this drawing.

Pappa came in. He wrestled out of his coat and fell into his chair. His brow was knitted and he was clenching his jaw. I had a sinking feeling in my stomach. Pappa was in trouble. Again. I reminded myself that

Pappa's trouble was his own. This time, I almost believed it.

Pappa motioned to a chair. "Sit. I need to talk to you."

I forced myself to breathe in and out. Slowly.

"I've just come from Toto's."

Of course, he did. He went there every day. I nodded.

Pappa shook his head. "This alcohol thing. Toto thinks it's going to be trouble."

Honestly, I thought this was the kind of thing that Toto would find a way to take advantage of.

Pappa continued. "Ciro and his gang are jealous of Toto. They want to buy up all the alcohol so that when it becomes illegal, they can sell it at a huge profit. With all that money, they'll be able to push Toto out."

I nodded. What did this have to do with me?

"Toto's asked a favor."

My stomach lurched. "What kind of favor?"

"He's heard about your engraving work. He wants you to make some bills. With enough money, Toto can play the game, too, by buying up every bottle of alcohol he and his guys can get their hands on."

I blurted out that I didn't have the burins anymore, being sure not to glance at that spot under the daybed. "He'd need a printing press," I continued. "And special paper."

"Toto can get whatever you need."

I couldn't speak.

Pappa took my silence as assent. "It's an honor to help a great man like Toto."

I thought for a moment. Only a few people knew about the five-dollar bills. How had Toto found out? Of course. Pappa had told him. He was going to lease me out, like I was a peasant at harvest time.

But it wasn't just me anymore. Soon Sebu would be trapped here, too. And the cycle, begun so long ago, between Pappa and Zio—or maybe Zio's father—would continue.

I'm not sure who decided it, but soon after, I was told I should start on the twenty-dollar bill. I guess it was a sign of how desperate Toto was that the decision was made to start with a bill that big. It seemed that every day, Pappa returned with more dire news. Ciro had teamed up with the Napolitani to take over Toto's lotteries. They'd also managed to get control of the Brooklyn vegetable markets. Then the worst news of all: Clutch Morello was being released from prison.

When Pappa told Mamma, she was frantic.

"You told me it would be at least another ten years. Ten years!" she pounded Pappa on the chest. "They can't release him now!"

I don't know why Mamma thought things would be different in another ten years. But now, Pappa made his usual assurances. He had a plan. Whatever trouble there was would pass. Everything would be fine.

Lies, all of it. Things would never be fine. Mamma knew it, too. She was inconsolable.

"Get back to work," Pappa told me. "We need that money."

I got my pad and opened to the sketch I'd been working on. On the front, a man named *Cleveland*; on the back, a steamship, a tugboat, a train, and an automobile. I guess it made sense. In America, people were always on their way to someplace else. Like Grand Central Station. The hum in the air, the sound of footsteps hurrying across the Great Hall. I'd be there soon. I just needed to make enough money for Toto. Even as I thought it, I know how stupid it sounded. If things were as bad as Pappa said, there'd never be enough.

I turned back to the twenty-dollar bill and tried to focus. This bill should have been easier than the five-dollar note. Cleveland was facing right, not forward, so the eyes were easier than the other president's. The images on the back were just machines. There were no expressions of despair or hope, like there had been with those Pilgrims. As I got further along in the sketch, though, I noticed some things. First, there was a tiny biplane nearly hidden in the steam from the locomotive. I studied the bill again, wanting to make sure I wasn't missing anything else. The next thing I noticed was how much empty space there was. The pilgrims had been positioned at the center of the five-dollar bill. Here, though, the center was blank—a huge space devoid of anything—with the vehicles on either side.

At first, I thought the government was intentionally leaving it blank for whatever newfangled invention would come next. But then I remembered one of Monsieur Laurent's lessons: A busy canvas leaves more room for error because the viewer isn't sure where to look. But a blank space focuses the viewer's attention on the composition. With the Pilgrims, there was so much going on—the man at the helm, pointing toward shore; the sailors, frantically paddling their oars; the waves, threatening to capsize the small boat; and the woman comforting her squalling child—that it would have been harder to notice mistakes.

With the twenty-dollar bill, though, that blank space made it easier to see what I'd gotten wrong—not only the details on each vehicle, but their scale and relationship to each other.

I worked on the sketch the rest of the day. As the light was fading, Pappa returned from wherever he'd been. He came to where I was sitting.

"Are you done yet?" he asked.

I explained that I thought I needed to rework the plane.

"It's fine, Mimi," Pappa said, impatiently.

"It's not in scale. See?" I pointed first to the airplane on the real bill, then to my sketch.

Pappa put his hand up to stop me. "Enough, Mimi." He reached into his bag and took out something wrapped in a handkerchief. When he unwrapped it, I saw it was a burin. Not fine or expertly crafted, like the ones Zio had made for me. No. This burin was rough hewn—the handle, much too thick for me; the blade, dull, like it needed sharpening. I thought of my burins, secreted under the floorboard.

"Toto sent these, too." Pappa pulled out two sheets of copper. The surface was gleaming, but when I picked one up, it was so thin that I wondered how I'd keep the burin from poking through.

Pappa sneered. "What's wrong?"

"Nothing."

"Something not up to your exacting standards?"

I shook my head.

"Good. Because no one wants to hear it. Just do your job, Mimi."

My job? I wanted to scream at Pappa: How had this gotten to be my job?

"Toto appreciates what you're doing."

When I didn't respond, Pappa got angry. "Did you hear me, Mimi? He's a good friend to have. He's powerful."

I should just have stayed quiet. "What about Clutch?" I blurted out. "What happens when he comes back?"

"Toto will be ready for him. And what you're doing is helping. Toto's going to be indebted to you. You'll be able to write your own ticket."

"Will I be able to stop?" I asked quietly.

"Stop? You're an artist. You don't want to stop."

Had that ever been true? Maybe when I'd been a girl sketching whatever moved me—the swaying wheat fields, the face of a daisy, Wolfie's coarse, wooly coat. When my art was mine. Not just something to please Zio or pay the rent or help Pappa with his latest scheme.

That had been a long time ago.

By the time I finished the engraving—a painstaking process that left me so frustrated that twice, I'd flung the burin at the wall—I'd made a decision. I'd make Toto's bills. As many as I could before Sebu's communion in the spring. Then I'd leave for California. I told myself that whatever debt I owed Pappa or my family would be discharged by then. But that gnawing feeling in my belly told me there'd never be enough penance to absolve me of what I'd done to my sister.

My sister. How could I take Sebu, not knowing what lay ahead? It had been months since Stella sent that postcard. She might have left Monterey or even been chased out. No. He had to stay here.

Once I'd decided to go without him, though, I found myself overcome with grief. I'd watch him reading or praying or sleeping, and the darkness I'd felt when I lost Rosalia and Caterina would return again. Like bitter seeds propagated on a fertile field, an unimaginable emptiness took root, threatening to destroy everything.

CHAPTER 61

SEBU KNELT AT THE DAYBED, hands clasped and head bowed. The priest instructed that First Communicants should prepare for penance. Next Saturday, they'd give their First Confessions.

The boy's eyes were squeezed shut. He was mouthing that rote prayer: *Forgive me Father, for I have sinned.* Ridiculous. He was only nine years old. What sins could he have committed?

I looked down at my fingernails, stained green from the ink. No number of *Hail Marys* could save me.

Sebu knelt for a long time, his mouth not moving. Finally, I asked if he was done practicing. When he didn't answer, I asked if something was wrong.

He shook his head. "I can't talk about it."

Why not?"

"Father Marino says it's between me and God. No one else." No one else but the priest, that is.

I tried to keep my voice even. "Whatever you've done, God will forgive you."

Tears streamed down his cheeks. "No. I've been—bad."

What could he have done? Fibbed about brushing his teeth? Talked back to me or Mamma? Swiped a caramel from Pappa's candy dish? That was nothing compared with infecting one of your sisters with tuberculosis and arranging for another's abortion.

Sebu collapsed against the dresser. Hugging his knees to his chest, he began to sob. "Mommy's dead," he cried.

I rubbed his back. "Yes. I'm sure you miss her."

"No," he said, his voice shaky. "It's my fault."

"Your fault? How could it be your fault?"

"I didn't want to live with her. She was sad all the time. I asked God to let me stay with you."

"That didn't make your Mommy die."

There was no comforting him. If I wasn't a coward, I would have told him the truth: It was I who'd killed his mother.

"If I tell Father," Sebu continued, "he'll know I'm bad."

"No, he won't." Father Marino knew how Caterina died. But what if he told Sebu I'd been involved? I didn't think I could bear to see the look of betrayal in the boy's eyes.

"God knows," I continued. "If you pray about it, you don't need to tell Father. God will forgive you."

He brightened. "Really?"

I nodded. Another lie. But what did it matter now? There'd be no redemption for me. No path back.

The following Saturday, Mamma and I took Sebu to Our Lady of Mt. Carmel for Confession. As we walked into the church to the smell of incense, the soaring ceiling, the yellow-gold marble statue of the Madonna welcoming all to worship, I felt like Nonna was there. It gave me courage. Sebu joined his class in the front. Father Marino was there. Talking gently, sometimes laughing. The children sat in stony-faced silence.

Mamma knelt. She took out her rosary beads and began to pray. I slipped onto the kneeler beside her.

The entrance door swung open. The hum of traffic and occasional blaring of a car horn shattered the stillness. Two women walked in, their heels clacking on the marble. They settled in a few rows ahead of us and sat down hard on the pew.

"All those people!" one whispered, unwinding the scarf from her neck. "The crowd must have been five or six deep. All there to see him."

The other shrugged off her coat. "Out of respect. And all those cops. Did you hear them applaud when he got out of the car?"

"He's been gone for ten years."

"It doesn't matter. He's back now."

Someone *ssshed* them. The women got quiet after that, though I still heard the occasional snippet. About the man's murdered son. His dead brother. How he was framed and wrongfully imprisoned. They were talking about Clutch Morello. He was back in New York.

The next morning, I watched Sebu make his way up the aisle, his clothing, stark white, his hands steepled in prayer, and his hair slicked back with Pappa's pomade. He moved slowly, like the priest had directed at the rehearsal. But, he'd been struggling. He'd had a sick stomach since last night. In the hush of the night, he'd whispered that he didn't want to go through with the ceremony, even though he'd been preparing for almost a year.

I understood his struggle. I'd finished what I told myself was my last run of bills yesterday, quietly taking the engraving plate from the hand-crank press and wiping it free of ink, then wrapping it in a cloth and laying it on top. I'd tightened the cap on the ink I'd mixed, placing the formula [7 percent red, 59 percent green, 33 percent blue], next to the unopened bottles. Whoever Toto replaced me with would have everything they needed to continue production. There was a kind of solace in that, a salve for the unexpected ruefulness I'd begun to feel about giving up the bills.

The altar was bedecked with white flowers. Sebu took his place in the front pew with the others. The first strains of *Ave Maria* rang out from the organ loft, and I was back at the chapel at *Binvinutu*. I let the music wash over me, my heart swelling as the organist reached the bridge. So much had changed since I'd stood in that old chapel. But this music remained. I'd been telling myself I wouldn't miss New York. The last few days were like my final ones at *Binvinutu*: I'd spent them studying the trees and the buildings, breathing in those familiar smells, listening to those sounds. Committing all of it to memory.

Father Marino led the children in the *Our Father*. When he spoke of the children's preparation—a year of Catechism leading to their first soul-baring confessions and now this rite—Sebu glanced back at me. More than anything, I wanted to take away his guilt about Caterina's death. But he wouldn't stop blaming himself.

The children stood and lined up for Communion. I watched Sebu go to Father Marino. The priest held up the morsel of consecrated bread. "Body of Christ," he said. Sebu answered with *Amen*, as he'd been instructed. He opened his mouth, like he had when he was a baby. But he'd soon be a man. He wouldn't need me anymore.

After the ceremony, we lined up for a family photograph. There was something about it that felt so exposed—Mamma and Pappa on either side of Sebu, me at the end, next to Mamma—lined up in front of the church doors. But Pappa had insisted. After the photographer snapped the picture, Mamma went to talk to a few of the Rosary Ladies, leaving Pappa, Sebu and me near the wrought iron fence leading to the street. I was distracted, obsessing again about when I should leave, when I felt someone near.

I turned to find Clutch Morello, thinner and his hair whiter, smiling at me. He put his monstrous claw hand on Pappa's shoulder. "My old friend. How are you, Nino?"

Pappa turned toward Clutch, partially shielding Sebu. "It's good to see you, Clutch. When did you get home?" As if this was a pleasant surprise.

Clutch laughed. He moved his claw closer to Pappa's neck. "Believe this guy?" he said to Ciro, standing behind him. "Always a gentleman." He drew out the last word, punctuating each syllable. He was squeezing Pappa's neck so hard that I could see the tears in Pappa's eyes. I steadied myself by grasping the iron fence post. Surely, Clutch wouldn't hurt Pappa here, in the church courtyard.

He leaned in even closer. "Missed you in Atlanta. I wish I had your cushy assignment. Stonecutter's Room. Heard you made some friends there. How's that thing with Ponzi working out for you?" Clutch laughed. "And Vito Cascioferro. I'll bet you haven't heard much from him lately."

A chill ran down my spine. Clutch knew about Zio Vito's silence. Clutch continued. "I guess Vito's moved on. He does that. Decides someone else would make a more valuable friend. No real loyalty to anyone. Except himself. I should know. He threw me aside like that." His eyes were cold. Reptilian. "You probably remember. With the import business. I'd been working here for years, then all of sudden, he puts you in. Well, that didn't last. Now you're out, and I'm in charge. Imagine that."

Clutch and Ciro laughed. Clutch released Pappa and turned to me. "Signorina Mimi. It's good to see you looking so well." He smiled, his gold eye teeth glinting. "I hear you've been busy with your art. Tell me, what do you hear from Stella?"

I mumbled something about how I hadn't seen Stella since the earthquake telegrams. Clutch laughed. "You're a terrible liar, Mimi."

My hair was hanging loosely at my shoulders. He picked up a lock. "I always had faith in you. Even when others thought you didn't have the talent to do the bills." He looked at Pappa, leaving no doubt about who hadn't believed in me. Black spots were floating before me. I counted to ten and then again.

"I always thought we could work together, you and me," Clutch continued. "What a terrible thing to let all your talent go to waste."

Now Clutch turned to Sebu. The boy was holding onto me. He was trembling.

"Who do we have here?" Clutch asked, grabbing at Sebu's arm but not catching him. "You must be Caterina's boy."

"This is Sebastianu Amoruso," Pappa said quietly.

"A handsome boy," Clutch continued. "He looks like his mother. She was a beauty. I always thought she and Nicolò would make a good match. We could have been a family. That would have been nice." A small crowd of admirers was forming around Clutch.

"Oh, well." Clutch sighed dramatically. "Water under the bridge, as they say. This boy is a blessing. Another bud on the Inglese tree. Because what do we have, if we don't have family? Right, Nino?" The corners of Clutch's mouth twisted grotesquely.

Pappa gave a half-nod. I think we all knew where this was going.

"My poor brother, Nicolò. Gunned down on the sidewalk outside my mother's house. A terrible thing."

Pappa agreed. It was terrible.

"And before that, my Calogero." Clutch's claw hand went to his chest. "Twelve years old. The warden told me it was an accident. That he'd stepped out into traffic. But I know the truth. My wife still cries herself to sleep at night. Our only boy. And her, too old to have another."

I almost felt sorry for Clutch. To be so far away and unable to protect his family. Then he put his claw on Sebu's head. "You must take care not to get into any accidents, Sebastianu. You're your Nonno's only heir. The Inglese line dies with you." Clutch looked at me. "Generations of nobles and it all comes down to one child."

Mamma had planned a nice meal. But when we got home, no one was thinking about food.

"Somehow, he knew Sebu was receiving Communion," Mamma said, shaking her head.

It was in the church missal. Mamma should know that. Since we'd arrived in America, she had a habit of studying the missal for church news and any hint of gossip.

I turned to Pappa. "We should leave New York. All of us."

"Nonsense," Pappa said. "I can't abandon Toto."

"Why not?"

"We're partners. I can't leave him in the lurch."

Always, this misplaced sense of loyalty. With Zio. With Ponzi. Now, with Toto.

"But Pappa. It's dangerous."

"Clutch is all talk. No action."

That's not what I remembered. The bombings. The explosions. The hands or feet of victims returned to their families in little boxes.

Later that night, I took a bath. I lay there, the water growing cool, as all around our neighbors laughed, fought, and made love. I ran my fingers along my side, feeling for those old scars. Then I pulled up the stopper and stood, listening as the water gurgled down the drain. Tomorrow, I'd try to change Pappa's mind. I'd tell him about Monterey. The piers. The wide ocean.

There was still time.

CHAPTER 62

I LAY THERE IN THE DARK, listening to Sebu's breathing, slow and regular. Worn out from days of worrying about his Communion, he was fast asleep before I even returned from my bath. I was grateful for the quiet. The chance to plan out exactly what I'd say to Pappa—how I'd convince him we had to go. I'd remind him of Clutch's terrible claw, laid atop Sebu's head. His cruel smile. His threats. I must have come up with ten or twenty ways to phrase it—sometimes oblique, sometimes direct. Every time, the same message. Which was that if we stayed in New York City, we'd die.

Stashed in the burin box beneath my daybed was enough money for two tickets. Surely, Pappa had enough for two more. We could pack our bags and disappear, like Stella had. By the time I finally drifted off, I'd almost convinced myself that Pappa would agree. But it was there, just on the edge of consciousness: my realization that he'd never leave New York City. People might call him a rat. A traitor. A liar. But here, people knew him. He wasn't a nobody, like he had been when he was Camastrino, living above his father-in-law's butcher shop. And like he'd be again, if he went to California.

I'd been sleeping the dreamless sleep of one who needs to forget when I startled awake. My chest was tight. I couldn't take a deep breath. A haze floated through the air. I rubbed my eyes, trying to clear my vision. The haze remained. The air smelled chemical—like an empty pot left on an open flame. Sebu slumbered on. I slipped from the daybed, telling myself it was Mr. Cranch's gin still—the stench of yeast and potatoes left to ferment. It ran all hours of the night. In the morning, men in suits carried it away in small wooden barrels. With Prohibition in effect, that drunkard must be getting rich.

I tried to go back to sleep but couldn't. I listened for some sound from my parents' room. It was closer to the hallway, so if the smell was from Mr. Cranch's still, it would be worse in there. I heard only a whispering, like wind through the trees. I turned onto my belly. The smell must be coming from outside the building. Maybe from one of those factories on the East River that belched smoke into the sky. Or a fire in a trash can on Lexington. A still-lit cigar tossed onto some discarded newspapers. Contained in the can, it would burn itself out quickly. I pulled the sheet over me. The smell would soon be gone.

But it wasn't.

I opened my eyes. The haze was now lingering atop the kitchen table and sink. I sat up in the daybed, some animal fear driving me now. I reached over to Sebu, curled up next to me. I placed my hand on his brow. He felt sweaty. That old fear returned: that I'd somehow passed the consumption to him. I put my hand on my own forehead. It, too, was beaded with sweat. Could we both be sick? When I threw off the covers, though, it was sweltering. Maybe Pappa had put the heat on before he turned in? But it was May. The heat hadn't been on since winter.

I rose from the bed. The heat made me dizzy, like I'd been spun around and left to steady myself. I found my skirt and shawl on the chair and pulled them on. I'd just go out to the hallway. Maybe someone out there knew what was going on. Before I started to the door, I reached under the bed and felt for those familiar nails. Without thinking, I pried off the floorboards and took out the satchel with my burins and money. When I stood, the haze was thicker. More like smoke. It unfurled into tendrils as it rose toward the ceiling.

I wrapped the straps of the satchel around me, like a suffragette's sash. The burins knocked against my chest as I walked toward the front door. There was a strange flickering under the door. Like candles blazing in a darkened room. I put my hand on the glass doorknob, then drew it back instantly. I tucked my burned hand into my sweater, my palm throbbing. The murmuring was louder—a muttering, not a whisper. The smell had changed, too—the faint chemical odor giving way to something acrid. It was getting harder to breathe. I drew the ends of the shawl close, covering my mouth.

I thought I heard Pappa but the sound was too far away to be in the next room. Was I dreaming? I touched the blistering skin on my palm, the searing pain proof that I was awake.

Sebu was coughing. I returned to the daybed. The smoke was thick, like the fog that sometimes blanketed the East River. As I watched, it rose, swallowing the tops of the cupboards and the checkered curtains I'd hung when we first moved in. I dropped to my knees and pulled Sebu from the bed. That flickering light from the hallway was so bright I could see him clearly now—his eyes, wide from confusion or fear; his chest rising and falling as he strained to breathe; his hands, reaching toward me, clawing at my arms in desperation, like he was drowning. He knew, even if I couldn't face it yet, that we had to get out of there.

My parents. If I didn't warn them, they might rush into that hallway and be consumed by the fire. I took Pappa's overcoat from the wall rack. I wrapped the coat fabric around my hand and returned to Mamma and Pappa's door. It was swollen, like on a humid day. I couldn't budge it. Sebu seemed to understand. He threw himself against the door. Finally, it gave way. The first thing I thought when I saw inside my parents' room was that I was standing at the gates of Hell. Flames lapped at the walls. Embers drifted down onto the sheets and blankets, like the winged seeds of maples in the fall. The bed seemed empty, dresser drawers pulled out and left hanging from their frames.

Sebu pulled me away from the room. He was trying to push me to the floor and mouthing something that looked like *get low*. They'd had fire drills at school. I thought it was cruel to make a child imagine that kind of inferno.

On our hands and knees, we made our way back to the kitchen. Sebu pulled on his pants and sweater. We slipped our feet into our boots. The daybed was engulfed. The cupboards, too, paint peeling off in long strips. I was dizzy and so tired. But I had to get Sebu out of here.

I turned toward the small kitchen window. It was barely wide enough for either of us to fit through. The windowpanes looked like they were melting. It made such a pretty pattern, like rivulets moving toward the stream. I wished I could sketch it. But Sebu jerked my arm. He pointed at the ceiling. A terrible storm cloud was gathering there. An immense, ominous thing. Sebu grabbed my arm. When I turned to him, I saw that same, inexpressible horror I'd seen on Caterina's face on the night of her death. That memory brought me back to myself. Our only escape was through that window to the sidewalk three flights below.

I tried to pull open the window. When it didn't budge, I picked up a dining room chair and hurled it at the glass. A crack appeared but the window held. Sebu and I picked up another chair. Together, we threw it at the window. The frame splintered into jagged pieces. A great whoosh of air rushed in. The flames roared and then jumped to the frame where the window had been. I went back to the hallway and grabbed Pappa's overcoat. I slipped it on. Then I took Pappa's pea coat and started back toward Sebu. I could hardly see.

Dr. Florio's words came to me from across the years. Sip the air; exhale slowly. Concentrating on that, I wrapped the peacoat around Sebu's shoulders. The curtains held for a moment—red-hot cinders—before fading to nothingness. Pappa's coats would burn, too. But they'd give us a minute or two to get out. It would have to be enough.

My arm around Sebu, we returned to the window. Just beyond the alley, lights flickered red and white. Firemen were running toward our building. Some were hefting enormous hoses. They'd be here soon. Maybe we should crawl under the table and wait. But embers were falling from the ceiling now. Floating down like snowflakes, flitting this way and that, setting fire to whatever they landed on. They seemed to seek out places where they could do the most destruction, landing on the newspapers near Pappa's chair and the pile of handkerchiefs waiting to be ironed.

Then the unmistakable smell of hair burning. Panicked, I touched Sebu's head. But his hair wasn't aflame. Mine was. We were running out of time. It took all my strength, but I hefted Sebu onto the windowsill, the straps of the burin satchel nearly getting tangled up in the fabric of the pea coat. He fought to get down, scratching and kicking. Flames licked at his coat. I stepped forward, the greedy tongues of fire moving closer. Sebu fought harder, desperate to get off the sill. Only nine years old and he was so strong. He and I were frozen in place, like those tiny figures in a snow globe, standing still while flurries swirled around them. Maybe this was a dream. But the flakes that fell on Sebu and me—flaming embers and bits of char—those were real.

The courtyard below was a mass of confusion. The hose jumped to life like a giant viper. Soon, the firemen were spraying water onto the building. But the spray didn't seem to reach any higher than the second floor. Some other firemen were preparing round disks of some sort. Nets, maybe. One was looking up toward us, shielding his eyes from the flame like he was looking at the sun. Sebu could jump into one of those nets. I just had to get the men's attention.

On the verge of passing out, still, I held Sebu there. I waited as long as I could, hoping the firemen had seen the boy and positioned the net beneath him. I tried not to think about all those girls at the shirtwaist factory fire a few years ago. They'd jumped from the ninth floor and broken through the nets to their deaths.

When the fire caught hold of Pappa's peacoat and I could wait no longer, I stepped away from Sebu and pushed him from the window. The last thing I saw was him reaching for me and finding only air, then his panicked face as he realized he was falling.

Something crashed to the floor behind me. I turned, but all I could see was billowing smoke. I placed my hand on top of the shawl, trying to keep the smoke out of my face and mouth. But it was no use. The fire was devouring everything—the walls, the ceilings, the very air. Darkness was closing in. I'd never felt so exhausted. I eased onto the floor. I'd just rest for a little while. Sebu was safe. Surely, the fireman had caught him. The smoke cloud descended to the wall. I ducked down further, my legs tucked under me, my arms over my head.

I thought of Clutch's face, twisted with hate. Surely, he'd leave the boy alone if Pappa and I were gone. But how could I leave Sebu an orphan? I'd promised Caterina I'd protect him. And Nonna's long-ago words: the Madonna had saved me from the consumption so I could care for my sister and her children. Caterina was gone. But Sebu was here. Down there on the street somewhere. Alone. Afraid. Maybe hurt. I had to get to him.

On my hands and knees, I crawled to the window. I held my breath and inched onto the sill. I gulped in the cold night air, as much as my lungs could hold. *Please Madonna,* I prayed, *let him be all right.* My mind clear, I looked down. Smoke poured from the building, obscuring the street below.

I didn't jump as much as ease myself out the window. It took a long time to fall, but it felt strangely peaceful, my burins held fast to my chest, my unbound hair skimming the breeze. The only sound, the flapping of Pappa's overcoat. When I finally hit the net, it was like falling backwards onto a hard floor. For a moment, there was nothing. Then the sound came up around me. Sirens. Screaming. The roar of the fire. I tried to focus. I'd lost someone or something. I couldn't remember who.

I don't know how long I was out. I woke up coughing, my chest heavy, my throat burning. I was propped against the streetlamp across from our building like a marionette waiting for the puppet master. With a start, I remembered Sebu. I tried to get up all at once but fell back on the ground. Slowly, I raised myself to one knee, then the other, and stood, as tentatively as a toddler, my arms grasping the lamp post. That's when I saw him. Sebu. Running toward me, his arms outstretched.

"Mommy!" he cried, forgetting himself. But I didn't care. He was in my arms. We were crying.

I pulled back. "Are you all right?"

He nodded. We embraced again.

"Oh, Madonna," I murmured. "Thank you."

When I finally let go, it was because Sebu had released me.

"Nonno. Nonna."

The building was engulfed in flames. How could I tell him that they were gone?

He pointed at the tenement. "They're over there."

Pappa was on a stretcher. Two orderlies were holding him down. They were wrapping his chest and arms with some kind of bandage. Mamma was next to him, her face buried in her hands. I took Sebu's hand and we started toward them. That's when I saw the two cops, standing next to Pappa's stretcher. They seemed to be waiting for something. Another cop was talking with someone who looked like Mr. Cranch. The still. Maybe that had caught fire. Surely they'd arrest Cranch and send him to jail. But then the officer closed his notepad and went to stand by Pappa's stretcher, too. Whatever was going on here, it didn't have anything to do with Mr. Cranch's still.

I thought of those mutilated rats. Clutch's claw hand on Sebu's head. His threats. And I knew. Clutch had done this. I scanned the crowds for any sign of him. Would he and Ciro show up to revel in the misery wrought by their crime? If they did, they were keeping well-hidden. And if they'd seen, they'd know that Pappa was still alive. And that I was, too.

I felt in my satchel for the burin case. Inside was the money Stella had sent. I remembered the route: nine subway stops to Grand Central Station. The Twentieth Century Limited to Chicago. The Overland to San Francisco. There was a train in the morning. Sebu and I would be on it.

I placed my hand on Sebu's head. "We need to go."

In the firelight, his eyes were wide, unblinking. He nodded.

His hand in mine, we started toward the subway station. The train was mostly deserted. That was a good thing. Sebu's pant leg was torn; beneath the fabric, I could see his skin was blistered. My palms were burned, the skin charred. Sections of my hair were singed and hung down in clumps. The few people we saw dropped their gaze. Maybe they knew we were in trouble. And maybe anyone traveling in the middle of the night has had enough trouble. Sebu was quiet. For this, I was grateful. Because I didn't know how to tell him that his Nonno—my Pappa—was a dangerous man. How to explain to the boy that the only future we'd ever have would be far from here, where Pappa couldn't find us.

We exited the subway and walked up the ramp to Grand Central. At the entrance to the station, I let myself look back toward the tunnel. Behind us was Partanna and Harlem. Ahead was California. My hands charred, I grasped the door handle. Like Persephone, making her way above ground to the Earth in the Spring and back down to the Underworld in the Fall, part of me would always be missing. But the past wouldn't hold me back. My life would be my own.

So I turned the handle and walked through that door, into my future.

Enjoy more about

Seeds of the Pomegranate: A Novel

Meet the Author

Check out author appearances

Explore special features

Photo credit: Paige Lamb

ABOUT THE AUTHOR

Suzanne Uttaro Samuels, a legal scholar and former college professor, has long been fascinated by the complexities of family and social life and the ongoing struggle for freedom and equality in the United States. Her books, essays, and short stories explore these themes. Born and raised in Staten Island, she spent much of her life in and around New York City and now lives in a small cottage high in the Adirondack Mountains with her husband, dog, and two cats.

She is currently working on *The Orphans' Wheel*, set in nineteenth-century Sicily during the Wars of Independence and featuring a young Rosina Inglese, the Nonna from *Seeds*.

AUTHOR'S RESEARCH NOTE

The beginnings of this story were shadowy: half-whispered secrets about hidden scars under my grandfather's sleeves and pant legs; Grandpa's remembrances of his great-grandmother, who emigrated to the U.S. as an old woman, and his cryptic comments about the fire that killed his family. Behind his smile and good-natured personality, I sensed there was something darker. More sinister.

Grandpa died when he was 97. By then, I was well into my career as a writer and teacher, with several well-regarded books about law, politics and society in print. I pieced together what I knew. The fire had occurred in East Harlem. My grandfather was eleven years old, which meant the fire happened in 1922. I searched the *New York Times* archive. There were dozens of fatal fires in New York City that year. But then it was there: the fire. October 22, 1922:

*20 DEAD, TRAPPED IN TENEMENT BLAZE ON UPPER
EAST SIDE.*

I found my grandfather's mangled name on the list of those injured. The next day's paper named the more than a dozen people killed in the blaze. Among them Grandpa's two brothers, Tony and Eugene (aged nine and seven), his 85-year-old great-grandmother, Rosa Inglese, and someone I'd never heard of: 30-year-old Mattia Inglese. There was no mention of Grandpa's parents or grandparents.

In the months and years that followed, I tried to figure out who was there and what had happened. At first, the papers claimed that "a

390 • SUZANNE UTTARO SAMUELS

madman" was responsible for setting fire to a baby carriage left under the central stairway. That trail soon ran cold, though, and after the initial reports, there was no further mention of who might be responsible. As for who had been there, the 1920 census revealed Grandpa's grandparents were living in the apartment, too, but they either weren't in the apartment at the time of the fire or had escaped unscathed. Missing too were my grandfather's parents, Caterina and Bartolomeo Amoruso.

Piece by piece, the story took shape. By the time of that fateful fire, my grandfather's mother was dead and his father was married to someone else. Autopsy reports revealed that Mattia's body had been found in the cellar, along with the two little boys. The fire had been so intense that the structure had imploded. Aflame, their bodies had plummeted four floors. Whoever Mattia was, she'd been with those boys.

Grandpa rarely talked about the fire, except to say that he'd been saved after falling or being pushed out a window into the arms of a fireman on the street below. It wasn't a stretch to assume the person who'd placed him on that windowsill was his Aunt Mattia. She'd died without a trace: there were no records, and my aunts and uncles said my grandfather had never spoken of her—this woman who probably saved his life.

At the time, my children were about the same age as my grandfather and his brothers had been on that fateful night. What would it have been like for her, as the flames closed in on Mattia and those little boys? Whoever she'd been, whatever she'd wanted or hoped for, was erased in that fateful moment. But who had Mattia been? As the years passed, I was able to fill in some of the gaps.

First, when she arrived at Ellis Island in 1906, she lied about her age: she said she was twelve when she was really twenty-one. I puzzled over this until a researcher suggested she probably had a chronic disease like tuberculosis that had stunted her growth. She lied to evade scrutiny by the Ellis Island doctors, who would have likely detained or deported her. Altering her birth year solved this problem. The presence of a disease like tuberculosis also helped explain why Mattia had never married, since pregnancy posed a considerable risk for consumptives.

Once Mattia was freed from the constraints of marriage, I was able to consider a different life for her. Noble girls were exposed to art and music. What if she was a talented artist? Her father, Antonino, long shut out of polite society by his bastard birth, might have been convinced to allow his invalid daughter to pursue a career as an artist. When I discovered Antonino served prison time in Sicily and the United States, it wasn't hard to tie Mimi's work to a nefarious enterprise.

So then, the outlines of this story are true: Mimi likely had a wasting disease like tuberculosis. The Inglese family had close ties to the powerful Sicilian mafioso, Vito Cascio Ferro. Antonino served time in the Atlanta Penitentiary at the same time as both Carlo Ponzi, the infamous con artist, and Clutch Morello, the first head of the Five Families in New York City. It wasn't hard to imagine that Clutch and others were tied to that terrible tenement fire since the mafia often used fire as a tool of both intimidation and punishment during this era.

The rest of the story is imagined, proceeding from the historical record and what would have been feasible, given the social and economic constraints of this period. Many Sicilians came to the United States because they believed it was a place of great opportunity, not all of it legitimate. It has taken some time for me to understand that my grandfather's grandfather may have come here to expand the criminal enterprise he had undertaken back in Sicily. Again, I derive this not from diaries or interviews with Antonino, but by considering the larger context for this story.

As in all things, any mistakes I've made here are my own.

ACKNOWLEDGMENTS

I've been working on SEEDS in one form or another since 2008. Over this decade and a half, I've been fortunate to find friends and guides to help me on my way.

At the top of this list is editor and teacher Tim Storm, who encouraged me to go deeper and to place Mimi at the center of the narrative. With each successive draft of these pages, Tim asked probing questions that encouraged me to go further. Whatever SEEDS is, it owes in large part to Tim's insight.

Thanks, too, to Kirsten Bakis, who invited me to think differently, moving beyond the facts of what I knew about Mimi to consider who she might have been had she not died in that tenement fire. When Mimi started whispering to me, Kirsten encouraged me to listen.

My gratitude to all my critique partners through the years, whose generosity and brilliance made this a better story. Thanks, especially to writers Heidi Sjostrom, Anne Keller, and Mary Randlett. My work, and my life, have been enriched by knowing you.

Thank you to my friends at the Women's Fiction Writers Association, especially those in the Histfic Affinity Group, and to my Writing Date buddies, whose daily encouragement helped me stay on track.

Thank you to my dear friend, Stacey Donohue, for reading multiple drafts of the story and for her gentle and thoughtful questions and comments. Thanks to Judy Biener and Mary Gilbert. At the start of SEEDS, Mimi is about the age we were when we first met at Binghamton University. I loved remembering how thrilling it was to make friends with such smart, witty, and thoughtful women, and to see the world again through a slightly larger lens.

As always, I'm grateful for the humor, warmth, and loyalty of my "ride and die" friends, Susan Barbano and Dawn Walter. SEEDS is about friendship, first and foremost, and about how friends help us to fake it 'til we make it. You guys are the best fakers out there! Thank you.

Thanks too, to Deanne Halvorsen, Ann Monroe, and Vicki Case, for your constant encouragement. My deepest gratitude to the Unitarian Society of Ridgewood Intergenerational Women's Group that I've been privileged to be a part of for almost twenty-five years. Together, we've moved through the seasons of life. Special thanks to the archivists and keepers of the Historic Saranac Lake and the Saranac Laboratory Museum, especially Amy Catania, Chessie Monks-Kelly, Emily Banach, and Alex Cranch. When I was struggling to grasp what having tuberculosis was like for Mimi, your library and archives helped bring it to light.

COVID-19 brought new challenges but also allowed me to work closely with my new Adirondacks neighbors, especially Beckie O'Neill and Tracy Thompson. Many thanks, too, to the Adirondack Center for Writing and its Executive Director, Nathalie Thill, for all they do to foster writing and expression in the Adirondacks. Thank you, too, for the warm welcome from the Cabin Fever Book Club, whose friendship, good cheer, and great discussions are much appreciated. Many thanks, too, to my dear friends in Rainbow Lake whose laughter and love warmed many days.

Many thanks to the staff of Denali National Park (AK) for providing a welcoming space for me during my Artist's Residency. Thank you, too, to Brush Creek Foundation for the Arts (WY) for the quiet space to think and work on revisions. Thanks to the Tin House Winter Writers

Conference, the Novel Conference at the Vermont Conference of Fine Arts, and the Pyramid Fall Fest Writers Conference for all the wonderful people I've met through the conferences and workshops you've offered.

Thank you to the people at Sibylline Press, especially editors-extraordinaire Suzy Vitello and Julia Park Tracey and Publisher Vicki DeArmon, Art Director Alicia Feltman, social media wizard Anna Wilhelm, tech genius Sang Kim, and rights expert Anna Termine. Thank you, too, to my wonderful publicist, Louise Crawford, her excellent assistant, Linda Quigley, and web designer (and artist) Ed Valendria, and the rest of Brooklyn Social Media.

Thank you to the Uttaro and Amoruso families for bearing with me through the many iterations of this story, and the many times I asked, "Did you know that ...?" Undertaking this project has been a journey, maybe one you weren't always thrilled to be a part of, even tangentially. But I hope you see this as I do now: ours was a family of strong and resilient people, who did what they had to do to survive.

My love and adoration to my kids. Charlotte Rose and Sebastian Raphael, you've been living with this story for probably as long as you can remember. Thank you for helping me stay grounded. You are the reason this story exists.

Finally, and always, to my husband, Steven. Through late nights and early mornings, you listened as I worked through this story. You supported me, loved me, and believed in me, even when I didn't believe in myself. You are my life. My love. Words cannot convey how grateful I am to you.

STUDY GUIDE QUESTIONS

1. For Mimi, the goddess Persephone is a kind of guide — someone who points the way forward. What do you think Persephone represents to her? How does her relationship with the goddess change over time? Does Mimi see the goddess in herself? What do the seeds of the pomegranate represent to her?

2. Mimi grows up in a society where noblewomen are sequestered, that is, kept isolated from the rest of society. Still, her father Antonino encourages her to become a painter. Why do you think he does this? How might Mimi's life have been different if she'd been treated like other young noblewomen? How about if she'd never left Sicily?

3. For Mimi, art is an outlet for expression and understanding. Why does Matisse's painting, *Joy of Life*, appeal to her? In your own life, what do you draw upon to keep you grounded?

4. The relationships between the women are at the center of this story. How do these relationships change over time? How would Mimi's life have changed if the lives of these women, particularly Caterina and Stella, had been different? Do any of these remind you of relationships in your own life?

5. Fire appears throughout the story: in the wheatfields and sulfur mines of Sicily, and the streets and tenements of New York City. What does this image represent to the characters, especially Mimi? Do these conceptions about fire change throughout the story?

6. Faith takes many forms in this story. Who has "faith?" In whom or what? Which characters gain—or lose—faith in this story? Do any of their experiences with faith resonate with you?

7. Conceptions of sickness and health are at the core of SEEDS. Were you surprised to learn about the state of medical science and the kinds of treatments that were employed to combat physical and mental illnesses in the late 19th and early 20th centuries? How have our ideas about sickness and health changed as our understanding of physical and mental illness have advanced?

8. Like many immigrants, Mimi has a specific idea about what America will be like at the beginning of this story. Does this resonate with what you understand of your own ancestors' experience? How about the experience of those trying to immigrate today? Do you think Mimi's ideas of America change in the course of the story?

9. What do you think happens after the story ends? What becomes of these characters in one year? Five years? Twenty years?

Sibylline Press is proud to publish the brilliant work of women authors over 50. We are a woman-owned publishing company and, like our authors, represent women of a certain age.

ALSO AVAILABLE FROM

Sibylline Press

Other People's Kids: A Novel

By Kim Culbertson

FICTION
392 pages, Trade Paper, $22
ISBN: 9781960573438
Also available as an ebook AND AUDIOBOOK

After a violent incident at her prestigious Bay Area school, English teacher Chelsea Garden returns to her rural hometown seeking refuge and a fresh start. There, she reconnects with a burned-out principal and an old flame, both working at the local high school. *Other People's Kids* follows three educators at different stages of their careers as they navigate second chances, personal crossroads, and the risks of starting over.

Collateral Stardust: Chasing Warren Beatty and Other Foolish Things

By Nikki Nash

MEMOIR
280 pages, Trade Paper, $19
ISBN: 9781960573421
Also available as an ebook AND AUDIOBOOK

Raised in a chaotic, bohemian Hollywood household, teenage Nikki Nash becomes fixated on a bold mission: meet and win over Warren Beatty. With determination and a detailed plan, at eighteen, working in a restaurant near the Beverly Wilshire, her long-shot dream collides with reality. While Warren remains ever present in her life, this is really the story of one woman navigating Hollywood as a producer, comedian, and actor in the eccentric fringes of L.A., brushing up against fame, danger, and dysfunction.

You Could Be Happy Here: A Novel

By Erin Van Rheenen

FICTION
280 pages, Trade Paper, $19
ISBN: 9781960573476
Also available as an ebook and audiobook

When Lucy loses her mother and discovers her real father may be a man from her childhood summers in Costa Rica, she sets out to find him—and herself. But the village she returns to is no longer the paradise she remembers, and her search raises more questions than answers. *You Could be Happy Here* is a story of identity, belonging, and redefining home in a world that no longer fits the past.

The House of Cavanaugh: A Novel

By Polly Dugan

FICTION
248 pages, Trade Paper, $18
ISBN: 9781960573469
Also available as an ebook and audiobook

In 1964, Joan Cavanaugh has a secret affair that leads to the birth of a daughter whose true paternity she takes to the grave. Fifty years later, a Thanksgiving reunion unearths the buried truth, shaking the foundations of two tightly connected families. *The House of Cavanaugh* is a gripping story of hidden pasts, unraveling loyalties, and what it really means to be family.

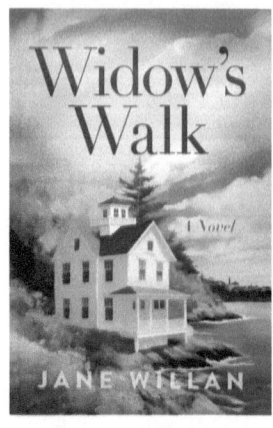

Widow's Walk: A Novel

By Jane Willan

FICTION
336 pages, Trade Paper, $20
ISBN: 9781960573452
Also available as an ebook and audiobook

When new Reverend Miranda McCurdy brings progressive change to a tradition-bound coastal church in Maine, her efforts spark fierce resistance—especially after she challenges the town's beloved Thanksgiving pageant. As the congregation splinters and a woman seeking sanctuary raises the stakes, Miranda must choose between fleeing back to her old life or staying to fight for the community she's slowly come to love. A stray dog and a mysterious stranger may tip the scales in this story of conviction, belonging, and second chances.

Reviving Artemis:
The Making of a Huntress

By Deborah Lee Luskin

MEMOIR
280 pages, Trade Paper, $19
ISBN: 9781960573759
Also available as an ebook and audiobook

At sixty, longtime writer, gardener, and teacher Luskin feels a wild new calling: to leave the safety of her garden and learn to hunt deer. *Reviving Artemis* follows her late-in-life transformation as she confronts fear, embraces the forest, and reclaims a primal connection to nature. Blending humor, vulnerability, and myth, it's the story of a woman choosing to age on her own fierce terms.

For more books from **Sibylline Press**,
please visit our website at **sibyllinepress.com**

www.ingramcontent.com/pod-product-compliance
Lightning Source LLC
Chambersburg PA
CBHW022241020726
47496CB00004B/1011